WASHINGTON DEAD CITY: BOOK III

SEVER

BRIAN PARKER

A PERMUTED PRESS BOOK

ISBN: 978-1-68261-114-2
ISBN (eBook): 978-1-68261-115-9

SEVER
Washington, Dead City Book 3

Cover art by Christian Bentulan

PERMUTED PRESS

Permuted Press
109 International Drive, Suite 300
Franklin, TN 37067
permutedpress.com

Novels by Brian Parker from Permuted Press

Enduring Armageddon

Washington, Dead City
Gnash (Book One)
Rend (Book Two)
Sever (Book Three)

Additional works available by Brian Parker

The Path of Ashes
A Path of Ashes
Fireside
Dark Embers
The Collective Protocol
Origins of the Outbreak
Battle Damage Assessment
Zombie in the Basement
Self-Publishing the Hard Way

But your dead will live, Lord; their bodies will rise—let those who dwell in the dust wake up and shout for joy—your dew is like the dew of the morning; the earth will give birth to her dead. Go, my people, enter your rooms and shut the doors behind you; hide yourselves for a little while until his wrath has passed by.

~ Isaiah 26:19-20 (NIV)

PROLOGUE

15 September, 2256 hrs local
Carroll Park
West Philadelphia, Pennsylvania

The rain splattered against Marcus' window screens and separated into hundreds of tiny droplets before it fell to the old hardwood floor. "Goddamn it, can't I just get a drink and some fresh air in peace?"

"What'd you say?"

"Nothing, dear. I'll get some paper towels and clean up the floors." The old man muttered under his breath as he walked from the study into the kitchen. The worn wooden floors had been in the row home for almost a hundred years and Marcus was sure that they'd seen worse than the little bit of mist that the rain outside had deposited on them.

He was irritated about the water on the floors. The cooler weather was a welcome relief to how hot this summer had been and all that he wanted to do this evening was to drink his bourbon while he assembled his latest scale model. He'd built models for almost forty years; he'd picked up the hobby as a young man in Vietnam. The doctors at that shitty little firebase clinic had given him his very first model—an old sailing ship—as a way to help him deal with the battle fatigue, which is what they used to call PTSD in his day.

It worked. The focus required to place those tiny parts exactly where they needed to go before the glue dried helped him to clear his mind of the horrible sights that he'd seen on a daily basis while his platoon was out on patrol. Young, dumb and full of cum, he'd extended for another tour after only three months in country... *Idiot.* By the time his twenty-three months were up, he'd built eleven models. He'd wrapped his models proudly and carefully to ship back to his parents a couple of weeks before he outprocessed Da Nang, but the box was lost and he never saw them again.

For years after the expiration of his enlistment, he'd suffered what the doctors at the Veterans' Administration called Post-Vietnam Syndrome. It was just another name for the same problem that veterans had experienced for thousands of years. Doctors seemed to like coming up with new phrases to describe the same problem: Shell shock, battle fatigue, PTSD. They were at a loss as to what to do with the outwardly healthy young man who couldn't hold a job and had explosive outbursts of anger for no apparent reason.

Marcus met his wife Alice at the VA clinic in Philadelphia in '77. She was there with her brother who suffered from strange breathing problems after he returned from the jungle in Laos. He'd formed a friendship with old Sam and the man introduced Marcus to his kid sister. They began seeing each other on a regular basis and Alice helped him rekindle his love of model building.

Turns out, the old sawbones in Khe San knew what he'd been talking about. Within a couple of months, Marcus' nerves had calmed enough that he was able to hold down a steady job at the bank as a security guard and his troubling dreams visited him less often. Ever since then, he'd been a true hobbyist, he'd even appeared in the late 80s in a hobby magazine that did a story on him and all the models that he gave away to orphanages when he was done building them.

Marcus had been looking forward to starting a model of an Army Humvee—a High-Mobility Multi-Wheeled Vehicle in military jargon—tonight after his drink. It was going to be the first of four Humvees, which would become the centerpieces in a new diorama that he planned to build for the National Guard armory's main entrance. The scene was going to depict the battalion's firefight at the Sadr City marketplace in 2006 where two of the unit's soldiers lost their lives and a platoon sergeant earned a Silver Star for valor.

"And Marcus?" Alice called after him.

He sighed and answered, "Yes, dear?"

"Make sure that you get the windowsills too."

"Oh, good point," he lied. Of course he was going to wipe off the windowsills, what'd she take him for, a moron?

He unwrapped a handful of paper towels, resisting the urge to slam the roll on the counter. At least he hadn't started with the model yet; he'd just been separating pieces from their frames. He glanced over at Alice where she sat watching one of those television reality shows while she knitted a blanket for his newest granddaughter, Meadow.

Hell of a name, Meadow, he thought. Then again, it only made sense, since his idiot son also had a daughter named Brooke. He and Michael had been on the outs for a while since the kid quit his big-time, high-paying job on Wall Street to be a full-time National Guard soldier in eastern New York.

Marcus had read all about it on the World Wide Web down at the library. They had some special program where people who were in the National Guard could work full-time for the Guard, essentially an active duty Army soldier, but they didn't have to go through all the B.S. hassle that regular soldiers had to endure. He was a proud military supporter, but he thought that his son was throwing away the opportunity to make a lot of money in exchange for a job that he said he loved. That was the problem with kids these days. They wanted to "experience life" and had astronomical credit card limits, so they didn't understand the value of money and what it was like not to have any. Yup, Michael was an idiot who was underwater on his mortgage, had massive credit card debt and struggled to send his two older children to private school, but he loved riding around on those damned tanks.

He walked back to the front of the house where the single window looked out onto the old neighborhood street. Marcus enjoyed gazing out that window at the children playing in the park across the street while he worked on his models. The kids, loud as they were, helped to calm him down and ease the memories that sometimes still haunted him to this day. He pushed the window down firmly into the sill and locked it securely for the night against the rain.

The old Marine's knees popped as he bent down to wipe the tiny puddles of water off of the floor. If he'd continued to look out the window, he would have seen an army of the undead as they advanced steadily northeast under the cover of the storm, intent on making it to the heart of the city before they began their attacks in earnest.

A mostly-bald head appeared in the window right above Marcus and stared down at him for a moment before the creature pulled back a hand and smashed in the old single-pane window that the row house still maintained. Long shards of wet glass rained inside the home and fell upon poor Marcus.

He cowered on his hands and knees while the glass hit him. The wind made a hideous moaning noise as it blew through the broken window above him and something banged against the side of the house.

"What's going on, Marcus? Are you alright?" Alice yelled from the family room.

Marcus didn't know what had happened, but when he looked up, a man grasped frantically at the broken windowpane as he tried to pull himself inside. His feet pounded loudly as they hit the side of the house, attempting to find enough footing to leverage his way in the window that stood a full five feet above the ground outside.

Even at sixty-four years old, Marcus had a few tricks up his sleeve. He shuffled painfully across the floor, the glass cutting into his palms, until he reached the front door and he picked up the commemorative Phillies baseball bat that he kept there. He used the bat to help him to his feet and the combat veteran walked calmly over to the intruder.

"You have one chance to get out of here punk, or I'm gonna bash your brains in and the police won't say a damn thing about it."

The man finally looked up at Marcus and the old man's blood ran cold. He'd seen and done some horrible things in his youth. From the horrors of the war to the hookers of Saigon, his time in the Marines had forever left an indelible mark on his soul, but he'd never been as terrified as he was in that instant when he stared at the thing trying to enter his home.

What he'd thought was an intruder was actually a creature straight from hell. Giant patches of skin and hair were missing causing him to think that the man had a bald head originally. So much of the creature's flesh was missing that even part of its skull shown through dully in the poor lighting of the street lamps. Where the meat still clung to its face in a semblance of its former humanity, the skin sagged away like it had been put through an old-fashioned dough stretching machine and then wrapped back around its head in a grotesque mockery of life.

Marcus could handle the sight of those horrific injuries; he'd seen similar things in Vietnam. His best friend had been on the receiving end of a basket full of grenades when a North Vietnamese sympathizer handed him a bouquet of "flowers" and pulled the pins when they were on liberty in the city of Quang Tri near Khe San. When that much ordinance goes off in such a close proximity it's not a pretty sight.

No, the part that terrified Marcus was the eyes. The creature's eyes were more than dead; they were desiccated—dehydrated and shriveled away to almost nothing. The disgusting, shrunken orbs rotated in the sockets as they followed his movements, like they could still take in images and process them into something that its brain could recognize and that scared the hell out of the old vet.

Marcus knew what he was looking at. He'd seen the news reports, even read stories about these things on the web. It was a zombie. They were supposed to be locked away behind The Wall in Washington, DC. What was it doing here in Philadelphia of all places?

The Marine steeled his resolve and swung with every ounce of strength that he had in his weathered body. The bat connected firmly against the creature's face with a crunch. Bones collapsed inwards as the bat shattered the cheekbones on both sides of where its nose had once been and collapsed its maxilla, which held the zombie's upper teeth in place.

It fell backward to the ground and Marcus caught a sobering glimpse through the vacant window. Zombies filled the entire street from his small patch of grass all the way to the fence around the park. They moved in unison, heading toward downtown.

"Alice, get upstairs. Now!" he ordered.

He moved toward the back of the house where his wife sat trying to collect up her knitting equipment. "Are you crazy, woman?" he asked as he grabbed her arm firmly without being rough.

Alice stared at him like he was a stranger. Hell, maybe he was. Maybe the old Marine that he'd tried to repress for four decades had resurfaced. "Marcus, what is *wrong* with you?"

"Zombies. The zombies got out of Washington and they're here, Alice! We need to go upstairs."

The thudding at the front window returned as the creature with the ruined face reappeared. This time, his wife had a clear view from the family room to the window in Marcus' model-building study and the creatures in the street. She started to scream and the old man's hand covered her mouth like a vice. "Don't, it'll only bring more of them. Let's go," he ordered.

Alice dropped her needles and yarn, running toward the center of their home where the stairs were located. Marcus followed her and shoved her gently in the rear end as she started up the steps. "Call Michael, tell him that he's got to get that National Guard unit of his alerted."

"Shouldn't I call the police?"

He shook his head. "It ain't gonna do any good. Philadelphia is lost. Call Michael first and then we can call the police if it will make you feel any better."

"Where are you going?" she asked in alarm.

"I'm defending my home," he replied and walked into the front room.

The creature continued to try and pull itself up through the window, even though it was clearly too high for it to do so. Marcus wondered fleetingly why it didn't just use the stairs and open the front door. As he got closer, the thing tried pathetically to snap its teeth, but his baseball bat had ruined any chance that it ever had of biting someone again.

"Stay away from my house!" he hissed and smashed the bat down into the top of the creature's head as it stared at him. The bat sunk several inches into its skull and the fight left the creature. He took another swing from the side just to be sure and it collapsed against the windowsill. Gravity took over and pulled the zombie through the window to the ground outside.

Marcus flattened himself against the wall and watched the horde pass by through the broken window. *If this many creatures had made it all the way to Philadelphia, what did the country between here and DC look like?* he wondered. Even more importantly, how did these things avoid being seen and alerting the government?

He hoped that his son would be able to get the word out to all the National Guard units. The police weren't going to be able to stop this; they needed the Army's big guns to put down that many of the things and they needed it fast, otherwise it would be too late.

ONE

19 September, 1418 hrs local
Nash Community College
Rocky Mount, North Carolina

Asher opened the truck door and tossed his backpack across the center console onto the passenger seat. He'd just finished a day of classes at Nash Community College, the small community college in the town where he lived. After this semester, he will have taken enough classes to earn his Associates degree and then he planned to transfer his credits to North Carolina Wesleyan College to seek a Bachelor's of Science degree in Homeland Security.

Homeland Security, what a joke, he mused. If the American public knew what kind of shit lurked behind The Wall, there would be mass hysteria. Last spring, he'd helped the FBI with the recovery of the Charters of Freedom from behind The Wall in the nuclear wasteland once known as the District of Columbia. Now people referred to it as Washington, Dead City because everything in there was dead.

The Wall was a massive brick-and-mortar structure that had stood for almost seven years with the dual purpose of locking the zombies inside and keeping the public from accidental radiation exposure. The unintended consequence of The Wall was that it allowed the nation's organized crime families an almost untraceable alternative to outright murder and provided them with a massive revenue stream as they robbed the abandoned banks and museums.

During the mission to recover the Charters, made up of the US Constitution, the Bill of Rights and the Declaration of Independence, he'd fought against thousands of zombies. They infested the Dead City and Baltimore area. The government told the public that there were only about ten thousand zombies trapped inside, but the truth was closer to a couple million of the fuckers running all over the place. He'd been shocked to learn the truth after a beautiful FBI agent showed up at his house one morning to recruit him for the mission.

He and Allyson Harper had a rocky start due to their strong personalities, but over the course of their train-up for the mission, they grew closer and ended up having a relationship together. Allyson was the perfect woman for him; she was smart, sexy and committed to her career. Unfortunately, that commitment had gotten her killed in early July when she went on the raid of a mob boss' house in New York.

Asher, once known as The Kestrel in the Special Operations community, had taken her death hard. He'd known lots of good men—some of them extremely close friends—who'd died over the course of his thirty-one years in SpecOps. None of them had affected him as much as her death had. They only had a short time together, but those months had given him hope. Hope for the future with a partner who could understand his drive and some of the experiences that he'd been through. He'd even considered the possibility of starting a family with her, something that he'd never really thought about, regardless of the fact that he'd been married twice before. But she was dead and buried in her hometown of Charlottesville, Virginia.

So far, he'd kept his promise to Allyson's mother and called her every week. It was important to both of their healing processes, although he felt like she helped him more than he could ever support her. Asher still held the belief that his insistence that she not go on that final mission to New York was what made her even more determined to go. Mrs. Harper assured him repeatedly that her daughter would have gone regardless of his involvement, but Asher blamed himself anyways. Over the months, they discussed everything under the sun and the last time that he called, they even had an entire conversation without mentioning Allyson. His shrink called it growth.

The engine of Asher's truck roared as he climbed the steep hill that led to his short driveway. Much to his neighbor Rachel's delight, he still ran the hill shirtless every other morning to stay in shape. He saw her working in her flower garden, likely trying to get them to bloom one last time before the fall weather hit, so he tapped the horn a couple of times when he drove by. She turned and waved, dirt falling from her gardening gloves. He waved back and pulled into his driveway.

He'd barely stepped out of his truck when she called over, "Hi, Asher. How was class?"

"Hey, Rachel," he replied as he leaned over and picked up his backpack. "It was okay. I'm just ready to get on with it and actually start taking some classes for my major, you know?"

She'd taken off her gloves and walked across her yard onto his driveway. "Oh, I know what you mean. Jim used to get so frustrated when he had to take all of those prerequisites."

He noticed a pained look on her face. It had been a while since he'd seen Jim, but he'd never said anything to Rachel since it wasn't his any of his business. Instead, he placed the backpack on his shoulder and changed the subject, "How is your husband by the way?"

"Good... He's up in New York for a few weeks. His company is doing a new software release and so all the field reps are up there for training."

"Oh okay," he said. Then since it seemed safe enough, he continued, "No wonder I hadn't seen him in a while."

"Yeah." She sucked in a ragged breath and continued, "He's been up there for a while."

Asher started to ask her if she was alright—she certainly seemed a little off recently—but again, he hadn't survived so long in the Special Operations community by sticking his nose where it didn't belong. "Do you need anything? Maybe some help in the yard?"

She crossed her arms over her flat stomach. "No, I'm okay with the yard. But I have been getting pretty lonely," she stated through lidded eyes. "Maybe you could come over to watch a movie later."

And that's my cue to go inside. "I'm sorry to hear that, Rachel. I'm sure Jim will be home soon though," Asher replied and stepped toward his house. Rachel Robertson had made it evident since the day that he moved in next door that she was willing to engage in a little extramarital action with him. Asher had been a lot of things over his lifetime, but no one had ever mistaken him for an adulterer.

She nodded her head curtly and asked, "Would you like to come over for dinner tonight? I can make a pot roast."

"Sorry, Rachel, but I have plans for tonight," he lied.

"Oh... Are you seeing someone again?"

Out of necessity, he hadn't told his neighbors that Allyson had been in the FBI and was killed in the line of duty last summer. It only would have made them ask questions about how they'd met and that could potentially have led to them figuring out that he was a retired CIA operator. It had been easier to say that they'd broken up and that was why she wasn't around anymore. "No. We have a study session at the library for my Algebra class. We have a test tomorrow."

"Well maybe after you're done studying you could stop by for a glass of wine."

"I'd love to, but I want to get to sleep early for the test. I'm an old man and I need my sleep."

Rachel laughed and placed a hand on his arm. "Old man! You're what, thirty-five maybe forty?" she asked.

"I turned fifty almost two weeks ago," Asher replied, allowing his neighbor's hand to linger on his arm. He didn't intend to let her advances go anywhere, but he was also aware that he walked a fine line with his friend's emotions. There was obviously something going on with her. The body language and looks of sadness that had crossed her face a few times told him more than she would have believed. He just really didn't feel like dealing with her problems while he tried to work through his own emotional roller coaster.

"No you didn't!"

"Yup, sure did. Boomer and I celebrated with an extra-long walk on the nature trail and then we each had an ice cream cone."

She smiled at him and let her hand drop. "Well, you sure don't look it... Okay then, I guess I'll get back to my flowers. Good luck on your test tomorrow!"

"Thank you, Rachel. I'll see you later." Asher took the opportunity to go inside and climbed the stairs up to his house. He inserted the key in his door and turned around. His neighbor still stood on the driveway watching him with a little sad smile on her face. It made her look closer to his age than her actual age of thirty-six. He waved and went inside, where he was immediately attacked.

He fell to the floor playfully while his puppy, Boomer, rolled on top of him. Asher had finally given in to his desire to get a dog after Allyson died. He'd wanted one for a long time, but wasn't sure if he was ready for the type of commitment that an animal would need, but Allyson had taught him that he was capable of love and that somewhere, buried deep inside all those years of death and hatred, there was still a caring man inside. Besides Mrs. Harper's fellowship, Boomer had been a godsend in helping to put his life back together again.

Boomer was a Boxer. She had the typical reddish-brown, or fawn, with a white chest and black around her muzzle. The breeder that he'd purchased her from had already docked her tail when she was only a few days old, otherwise Asher would have left her tail the natural length. Other than potty training, he enjoyed every minute that he got to spend with the dog. She was still too young to go on real runs with him, so they went on walks together through the woods around their home.

"Alright, you crazy little jerk!" he laughed after a moment of wrestling with her on the floor. "Let's see what the damage is today."

It seemed like she made it her mission to chew up something new every day even though she had tons of toys. He'd thought about crate training her, but settled on installing a pet door to the back yard instead. He'd been forced to stay in enclosed spaces during his time on the Teams and with the Agency. As an instructor at the Agency's Survival, Evasion, Resistance and Escape (SERE) course, Asher had submitted a lot of students to the sensory deprivation training. Neither experience made him keen on the idea of putting his dog through that type of existence on a daily basis.

As a result of that decision, his old ratty—but extremely comfortable—furniture was even more abused and he'd learned early that he had to hide every cord in the house carefully or else Boomer thought they were something for her to chew on. It helped him to return to the minimalist type of living that he'd kept for most of his life. Somehow, in the two years since he'd retired from the Agency, he'd developed an appetite for random crap that just sat around the house; stuff that he'd never wanted while he was active. Boomer's incessant puppy-chewing had curbed that desire quickly.

Asher walked through the house; nothing seemed torn up and there weren't any messes on the floor. He reached down and scratched the dog's head behind her ears and said, "That's three days in a row, girl. Are you growing up on me?"

He went back into the living room and sat on the couch where Boomer jumped up and laid her head on his lap. He picked up the remote and turned the television on. "Looks like we have to go find someplace to hang out for a couple of hours tonight," he said to the dog. "Or else Rachel will know that I lied to her about having plans."

Boomer closed her eyes and he flipped through the channels until he came to a documentary about Operation Just Cause, the US invasion of Panama in 1989. After a few minutes, he snorted in derision of all the so-called "experts" and "eyewitnesses to history" who'd allegedly been there and talked about their perceptions of the strategic goals of the operation. *Like a damned private in the Army knew anything about the United States' National and Strategic strategy.* He'd swum ashore from a submarine ten miles off shore three weeks before the Army or Marine Corps troops got there. His team operated completely alone, destroying targets and making it look like mechanical failures or simple accidents so as not to overtly alert the Panamanian Defense Forces that an invasion was imminent. The conventional forces would have easily defeated the banana republic's forces, but the low loss of life—on both sides—was attributed to the efforts of the SEALs who'd made sure that the anti-aircraft batteries and troop transports were unusable to the Panamanians.

After ten minutes of that garbage, he changed the channel again. As he scrolled through the channels, something caught his eye and he went back to the previous channel. It was one of the twenty-four-hour news networks. The reporter talked into the camera and the image behind him showed an aerial view of Independence Hall in Philadelphia. The entire area surrounding the building swarmed with zombies.

*****

19 September, 1527 hrs local
Hoosick Falls Armory
Hoosick Falls, New York

"Alright, let's get these babies loaded so we can go kick some ass!" the company first sergeant shouted at the men in his company. They'd already driven the company's M1A2 Abrams tanks from the motorpool in the back of the old armory and lined them up on the street for transport. It was more than 190 miles from the small town of Hoosick Falls on the eastern New York border down to New York City where they'd been ordered to reposition for defense of the city. That was too far for them to drive under their own power at any type of real speed, so they were being loaded up on semi-trailers for the trip.

The company's tanks were an amazing application of modern military engineering—even if they weren't the newest model that the Active Army used—that had no near competitor in foreign militaries worldwide. They were the perfect piece of offensive gear, designed for fighting in wide, open spaces with lots of maneuver area, but they also made a formidable defensive obstacle under the right conditions. The most perfect condition imaginable for a tanker in a defensive position would be against an unarmed enemy that charged blindly into incoming fire. Fortunately, the zombies terrorizing eastern Pennsylvania, New Jersey and New York did just that.

Mike laughed to himself when he thought about the fact that his unit was moving out to fight against zombies. His company, Charlie Company, 1st Battalion, 101st Cavalry Regiment, part of the 42nd Infantry Division—the Rainbow Division—was headquartered in the small town of Hoosick Falls, New York. The Regiment had inactivated in 2006, but after the nuclear attack on Washington and the zombie outbreak there, they were reactivated as a contingency response force. Captain Michael Miranda had jumped at the opportunity to command the unit, so he quit his job as an investment broker and moved his family from New York City to Hoosick Falls to start a new way of life.

The community was only three miles from the Vermont border and twelve from Massachusetts, so they were almost as far east that a person could go in the state of New York. Since they were so far from everything else, it would take a while to get his men and equipment transported down to the city, where they were expected to defend the approaches and keep the bulk of the state's population as safe as possible until they could be evacuated.

The governor had decided to defend the bridges and tunnels into the city with the state's only National Guard tank battalion. They'd been given a shitty mission, but the tanks would be supported by infantry and the New York City Police Department. They were to hold on as long as possible while the city was evacuated through the air and by sea. Overland travel was considered too risky and all outbound ground traffic from New York was closed off in an effort to keep the roads clear so the trucks hauling tanks from out of town could drive faster toward the disaster area.

Alpha Company and the Battalion Headquarters Company were stationed on Staten Island. Their job was to secure the three bridges leading from New Jersey where the creatures were likely to arrive first. The governor ordered the evacuation of Staten Island northeast to Brooklyn over the Verrazano Bridge, where the Alpha and Headquarters companies would retreat if needed. They would have to make their stand at the Narrows and not let anything past them into the city so the main evacuation could be completed.

The rest of the battalion would secure the remaining bridges and tunnels leading into the city. Delta Company was headquartered in Newburg, only ninety miles to the north of New York, so they were ordered to cross the Hudson and travel the farthest south out of the three outlying companies to the Holland Tunnel. Mike's Charlie Company was the next closest to the city in Hoosick Falls, so they'd be transported to defend the Lincoln Tunnel. Finally, the regiment's Bravo Company was stationed all the way up north in Troy by the state capital, so they were being sent to the most northerly entrance to the city, the George Washington Bridge.

Each company had three platoons, Red, White and Blue. The platoons consisted of four tanks each, plus a headquarters element of two tanks. That gave the companies the capability to lay in interlocking and overlapping fields of fire to cover the entrances to the city with fourteen tanks. They'd been told that if even one of the creatures got past them, it could begin infecting everyone behind their position, so there were infantrymen and police in defensive lines behind them to catch any that made it through.

The idea that zombies were moving steadily north from Washington was absurd. So far, they'd decimated the city where he was born and raised. Philadelphia looked to be a total loss and now it appeared that the numbers of the creatures had swollen to massive proportions. What was even crazier was that the infestation seemed to be coming directly for the city, not deviating too far west from their original course, which is why the governor decided to defend the city at choke points instead of the wide, open areas to the west of the Hudson River. It made Mike think that the horde had set its sights on New York City and would stop at nothing to get to it. *But that's crazy; they're just mindless monsters who travel wherever the moment takes them... Right?*

Some FBI bigwig named Alistair Reston gave a secret briefing to all of the company commanders. Reston had been in charge of the mission to rescue the Constitution last spring, so he'd knew a thing or two about the zombies. He discussed the horde's unwavering groupthink; once they set their minds to do something, they would keep trying it until they either succeeded or failed. Reston used the example of a group in Baltimore that tracked and trapped one of his agents and how they used their bodies to pile on top of one another to get around the fact that they couldn't negotiate a set of stairs individually.

The FBI had given then some valuable pointers about the creatures' capabilities that the soldiers were desperately in need of. First off, the only way to kill the bastards was to shoot them in the head. Second, the damn things *could* swim, but likely wouldn't if there was a bridge or tunnel that they could use. He sent them satellite video clips of the zombies swimming across Baltimore's Inner Harbor as they went after a person who'd become trapped behind The Wall somehow.

The last thing he left them with was to watch out for zombies who looked different than any of the others. There were still some of the original zombies from the Pentagon infestation alive behind The Wall. It was believed that they retained enough brain capacity to think and could plan or react to actions in real time. It was likely that these "Type Ones" as Reston called them were how the zombies were able to escape and then sneak all the way to Philadelphia without being seen. He said that they were relatively easy to spot because of their parchment-like skin and if any of those were seen, they were to expend every effort to kill it. Humanity couldn't afford to let any Type Ones escape. *Point noted.*

Philadelphia. Mike's parents lived there and they'd called him four nights ago, warning him to get his family as far away from the east coast as possible. He'd laughed at his father's early Halloween jokes, but the elder Miranda had quickly made him realize that he was serious. Before Mike called the battalion commander with a threat warning, he booked a flight for his wife and two daughters to Honolulu the next morning. *Better safe than sorry*.

That was the last time that he heard from either of his parents. He'd tried repeatedly over the last several days to reach them as the company prepared for movement southward, but hadn't been able to get through. All the cell phone lines were jammed with people trying to make phone calls and the land lines went directly to an error message. He assumed that the phone lines had gotten severed somehow down south of the city where there was no way to get them fixed.

"Hey, sir. BC's on the phone," the company first sergeant growled from a few feet away. *He must have been inside and made his way down here,* Mike thought. *The grumpy old noncommissioned officer had been outside yelling at the soldiers a few minutes ago, how the hell can that guy be in so many places at once?*

"Thanks, Top," Mike replied and turned away from his spot checks on the vehicles to go inside. He only knew how to be in one place at a time so he'd have to hurry to avoid keeping the battalion commander waiting. He looked up toward the old National Guard Armory as he jogged down the long line of tanks and tracked medical vehicles.

The Hoosick Falls Armory building had been built in the 1880s and was on the National Register of Historic Places. With the exception of the two circular turrets flanking the building, the two-story red brick structure might have been mistaken for a church. Interestingly, the two towers were different from each other. Mike never could figure out why the one to the right of the main entrance was two stories tall and had a conical roof, while the one on the left had three floors with the classic crenelated parapet that so many people identified with medieval castles.

He loved the old-world feel of the building. Generations of former New York National Guardsmen had walked on the original oak staircases and hardwood floors in the offices, including First Lieutenant William Turner, who was posthumously awarded the Congressional Medal of Honor for his actions in World War I. *This will probably be the last time I see the old place,* he thought.

Where the hell did that come from? He'd see his adopted home of Hoosick Falls again, he told himself. The regiment was going to stop the zombies at the bridges and the regular Army was going to sweep in and wipe them out. That was the plan at least. The 10th Mountain Division—a light, truck-mounted organization—from the far northwest part of the state was already assembled in staging areas, just waiting on their opportunity to provide a counterpunch when the zombies stalled against the tanks of the 1st Battalion, 101st Cavalry Regiment.

Mike took the steps two at a time and pulled open the doors. The familiar smells of the timeworn armory hit him in the gut; it had been his home for almost five years as the commander and he would miss it. He'd been extremely lucky to be the commander that long. Most commands only lasted for twenty-four to thirty-six months, but the location of the unit in the middle-of-nowhere eastern New York and lack of armor-qualified officers in the Guard had allowed him to hold on. For the first twenty months, the company didn't even have any lieutenants because the Army wouldn't let anyone get out, sending them directly to duty on The Wall. Everyone thought that things had slowed down, though.

Until three days ago, the majority of Americans didn't even know that zombies still existed in Washington, DC, let alone that there was the potential for them to escape. How fickle the American psyche could be once the network news moved on to a different story. Now that was coming to an end as the entire Eastern Seaboard was in jeopardy of being overwhelmed and tens of millions of people were potentially going to die. Unless the 101st Cavalry could stop the zombies' advance.

He burst into his office and saw the phone sitting off the hook on Specialist Greeley's desk. An unspoken question to the company clerk confirmed that the battalion commander was on that phone when the kid nodded his head and pointed at the receiver.

"This is Captain Miranda," he said into the handset of the old rotary-dial phone that passed for the clerk's office line.

"*Jesus H. Christ, it's about time! What the hell took so long, Michael?*" Lieutenant Colonel Espenshade asked.

"I'm sorry, sir. I was out inspecting my tanks to ensure that they were ready for travel."

"*Hmm... Okay then. At least you were out doing what a good officer should do. Are the lowboys there yet?*" he asked, referencing the heavy-duty semi-trucks which would haul the tanks to the city.

"Not yet," he answered. "We got a call that they were en route about three hours ago, so they should be arriving soon. The cell phone lines are all down, so we can't call the drivers to determine where they are exactly."

The battalion commander's gruff demeanor changed slightly and he asked, "*How are your boys holding up?*"

"We're good, sir. Chaos Company is ready to kick some ass."

"Well, there's going to be a lot of targets for your men, that's for damn sure. Looks like every resident from Philadelphia has been killed and—Shit, I'm sorry, son."

The commander knew that Mike's parents lived in Philadelphia. He'd even met old Marcus at the company activation ceremony before his father found out that Mike had quit his job to be a full-time National Guard soldier and stopped coming around. "It can't be helped, sir," Mike replied stoically. "If we don't do our job, there will be millions of people without parents or children."

"Well, I'm still sorry. I should remember to think before I speak. It looked like the initial zombie horde has swelled to gigantic proportions. Satellite imagery shows them spread out over a ten-mile wide area and they're all moving steadily toward the city."

"I've been thinking about that and about what Mr. Reston said. What if—"

"Remember, you're on an unsecure line, Michael."

The captain grinned despite himself at the stupidity of the Army and the absurdity of his boss' statement. "Sir, it really doesn't matter at this point. The secret about the zombies is out."

"Shit, I guess you're right. Okay, what were you going to say?"

"I think that there *has* to be a Type One with them. Why else would they all be making a beeline for New York? Everything that we've been briefed about the zombies when there isn't a Type One present says that they just follow sounds or go after the nearest shiny object and attack it, but these guys are moving together as a unit toward one objective. Think about it, sir. If we lose New York—and the zombies can grow their numbers by that many people—then this fight may be over before it really even starts. They can simply sweep westward and take over the entire continent."

"You're preaching to the choir, son. That's why Governor McDiarmid is insistent that we stop these fuckers before they can make it into the city."

"Are we actively hunting for the Type One in the crowd?"

"Mike, you wouldn't believe how many armed ISR assets are flying all over New Jersey and Pennsylvania right now looking for that bastard," Lieutenant Colonel Espenshade answered. ISR was the military term for Intelligence, Surveillance and Reconnaissance, which was a fancy way of saying drones and spy planes. *"If he shows his face, they'll get him."*

"Alright. That makes me feel a little better, sir."

"Okay, so besides waiting on transport, you have everything else that you need, right?" the battalion commander asked, getting the conversation back on track.

"I can't think of anything else, sir. We picked up a hell of a lot of ammo for our .50 Cals and 7.62 machine guns, not too much 120-millimeter ammunition though, and we've also got four fuelers that will be traveling with us in the convoy to the city." The 120-millimeter ammunition was the armament used in the tank's main gun. It could punch through just about every type of armor there was, including concrete walls, but there likely wouldn't be much use for it against the zombies, so Mike opted to use that storage space inside the tanks for machine gun ammo.

"Sounds like you're set then. Alright, I'll let you get back to commanding your unit, Mike. Good luck. Give me a call on the radio when you get set in your battle positions."

"Thank you, sir," he replied as the boss hung up the phone.

Mike set the phone down gently on the cradle and glanced at his clerk and asked, "You ready to roll, Greeley?"

"Yes, sir! I'm just sending an email to my mom," the specialist replied.

"Good. I'm looking forward to having you on my tank." He needed a driver because his normal driver had a broken arm and Specialist Greeley was the only soldier in the company who was qualified to drive the M1A2 who wasn't already on a tank.

"Hey, sir," the first sergeant said as he popped his head in the door. "Lowboys are here. Time to mount up."

The commander nodded his head and patted his new driver's shoulder. "Better hit 'Send' before First Sergeant Jenkins rips you a new one for not being down on my tank to load it up."

*****

19 September, 1953 hrs local
Toby's Pizza Palace
Rocky Mount, North Carolina

"Boomer, knock it off!" Asher scolded the puppy. She'd spent the last ten minutes barking every time somebody walked by on the street in front of the outside dining area where they sat. Toby's allowed well-behaved pets on the patio, but Asher didn't want to risk getting kicked out before he got a chance to eat.

He'd spent the day glued to the television watching the events in Philadelphia and Trenton, New Jersey unfold. The news showed that the creatures were everywhere, moving steadily northward toward New York. He'd frozen the image enough times to determine that at least half of the group was newly-turned. Their clothing wasn't tattered and rotting away, but the biggest giveaway were the dark maroon stains that covered them. The blood had dried and worn off of the former Washington residents long ago.

He checked his cell phone constantly to see if anyone tried to call him, but it remained blank. No one from the Agency called Asher Hawke for the firsthand information and experience that he had in dealing with these creatures. What the American people needed now was the Army. All of it.

Eventually, hunger got the better of him and he didn't have anything in his refrigerator or cupboard, so he was forced to go somewhere. Plus, it helped him stick to the story that he'd told Rachel about going to a study group if his truck wasn't sitting in the driveway. He needed time to think about what was happening and what it meant that the zombies were moving toward the city. That was something he couldn't do if he was defending himself against his neighbor's advances.

The one thing that he was certain of was that they had a Type One with them. Those things were focused on one, common effort, so it wasn't accidental or random. One of those smart fuckers was leading the horde toward New York City. The news made a big deal about the evacuation of the city, but no one commented on why they were heading that way. Asher thought he knew.

If they could turn even half of that city and swell their numbers by ten million, then they could split their efforts. Some could continue marching up the coast, moving city to city, while others could move west, some south. They'd spread like an unstoppable cancer once they reached New York. It was a sobering thought and Asher needed the beer that the waitress had brought.

He let his hand dangle over the arm of his chair and scratched Boomer's ears idly while he wrote out a list of supplies on a notebook. The time to bug out was quickly approaching and he wanted everything set, ready to go. After a few quick notes he picked up his beer and took a long swig from the frozen mug. As he swallowed, he contemplated the people on the patio around him.

None of them seemed concerned that there was potentially a mass extinction event happening four hundred miles to the north. They all laughed and drank as if everything was normal; of course, maybe they were trying harder *to appear* normal in order to keep their sanity. Maybe they were miserable at the prospect of death and tried to cope with it in whatever means they could find. Or maybe he'd spent too much time talking with his psychologist and was trying to project his own feelings on those around him.

The waitress stepped across his line of sight and set down the steaming individual pizza that he'd ordered. It smelled heavenly and he had to slip his hand into Boomer's collar in order to keep her off the table. "Need another beer?" the girl asked.

He glanced at his half-empty glass. By the time she brought it back, he'd be ready for one. "Yeah, sure. Same thing, please." The waitress smiled and went back inside to get his drink.

Asher pushed the pizza toward the center of the table and released Boomer's collar. She immediately stood up on her hind legs to try and sneak a bite. He pushed her paws off of his leg and spent a few minutes trying to teach her that it wasn't okay for her to beg at the table. By the time he finally got her to understand that she wasn't allowed up on his lap, the waitress had returned.

"You want me to take this and put it in the fridge?" she asked holding up the glass that she'd brought out.

"No, hold on," Asher replied and downed the rest of his beer. "See, all better!"

The girl smiled again and set the drink down. "Let me know if you need anything else, alright?"

"Sure thing, but this is the last one. I still have to drive home."

She nodded and turned to the next table to see if they needed help. Asher looked down at Boomer and said, "Alright, girl. Are you gonna let me eat in peace?" The dog looked at him and whined. He scratched her ear with one hand and picked up a slice of the pizza with the other.

Back to the problem about the zombies, he thought. It was a given that he should leave the East Coast. He knew that the Army would try their damnedest to stop the spread, but he'd been in combat against these things; what they lacked in brains they made up for with sheer numbers and tenacity. Unless they committed every possible force, maybe even nuking the place, then they weren't going to be able to stop them. *Hindsight being 20/20, maybe I should have supported the plan to go inside The Wall and eliminate the fuckers before they got out.*

He'd almost finished his dinner when a familiar voice interrupted his reverie, "Asher! Hey, Asher!"

He turned and saw his neighbor Rachel and another woman standing outside the fence that surrounded the patio area. "Good evening, Rachel," he called. "How are you?"

He winced when she opened the gate and led her friend inside. He liked his neighbor a lot, but he sure as heck didn't want to have to make another excuse as to why he didn't want to be around her without Jim present.

The two women sat at his table uninvited and Rachel waived her hand to get the attention of the waitress. "Asher, this is my friend Carly."

He reached across the table and gently shook her hand, "Nice to meet you."

"So, how did studying go?" Rachel asked.

"Oh, it was okay. Boring math stuff," he lied again.

"I'm surprised you're done so early. Jim used to be away for hours studying."

"Don't bring up that fucker, Rachel. Just relax and have fun," Carly said.

Asher watched his neighbor's face as she made a conscious effort to smile. "So your study partners didn't want to come out for a drink?"

He laughed a little to give himself a moment to think. "None of them are even twenty-one yet. Besides, I'm way too old to hang out with them," he replied honestly. He *was* too old to go to the study groups that the kids in his classes put together. His only recourse was to work harder on his own and pay attention in class when the instructor talked.

"Good point—Oh, hey," Rachel said to the waitress as she walked up. "I'll have a glass of cabernet."

"I'll have the same," Carly stated from across the table.

"Do you want another one, Asher?"

"No, I have to drive."

"Psh," Rachel said with a wave of her hand. "He'll have another one."

The waitress raised her eyebrow at Asher. "Yeah, okay. One more, then I have to get home." She nodded and headed inside to the bar.

"So what do you think about the zombies escaping and then destroying Philadelphia, Asher?" Carly asked.

"It's... It's a sticky subject. They seem to be headed for New York. If they aren't stopped there, then I think that we'll have a major problem—like the entire continent, not just a few cities."

"You think they're gonna make it to New York?" Rachel asked in shock.

"Oh, shit. I'm sorry," he apologized. "I forgot that Jim is up there."

"Big deal. I hope he gets killed by the zombies," Carly said.

"Carly! Stop. He's still my husband."

"Not once you drop that envelope in the mailbox tomorrow. Then you'll be a single woman again."

Oh shit. Asher tried to remember the last time that he'd seen Jim next door. It had been a *long* time. Hell, it might have been before he went to DC last spring... *Has it really been that long? Have I been that self-absorbed in my own grief?* He picked up his glass and drank the rest of it.

It was uncomfortable and the girls hadn't even had anything to drink. What would happen when one of them got some wine in them? Rachel looked over at him and said, "Jim left me. I'm embarrassed about it and—"

"Fuck that!" Carly said loud enough to make several customers look over. In a quieter voice she said, "That douche was cheating on you, with a bunch of different women."

Rachel held up her hand. "That's enough, Carly. Asher doesn't want to hear about it. Let's just try and have fun, okay?"

Carly's lips were pressed thin as she suppressed an urge to say something else, but the waitress returned with their drinks, saving everyone from further embarrassment. She set the two wine glasses down and placed the beer in front of Asher. "Here you go. Did you want to close out, hon?"

"Yeah, I'll go ahead and take the check," he replied.

"Okay, I'll be right back," the girl said and twirled away to get his bill.

Rachel picked up her glass and raised it. "To new beginnings," she said.

He raised his beer in response and Carly reached across the table. She hit Asher's glass a little harder than was called for and said, "Amen, sister!"

Rachel took a sip and then tipped the glass back, taking a large gulp of her wine. "Do you really think that the entire continent is in danger?"

He looked her in the eyes and replied, "Rachel, we're in a world of shit—excuse me, I'm sorry... This isn't going to end well. If the Army can't stop them and kill every one of those things, then *every person* in North and South America is in danger. If even just one of them escapes, they can just start the chain of infection all over again."

His neighbor stared back at his serious face and took another sip before asking, "Can they stop it?"

He sighed, "I don't know. It's tricky. I've read a lot about the first war with them. They took over the city fairly quickly and somehow they survived the nuclear detonation."

"So we can't even kill them?" Carly asked.

"No, they die—with headshots—but the bomb didn't actually get them. I'm sure the ones who were right there for about a mile around ground zero were incinerated and killed, but the radiation didn't do anything to the ones who weren't."

The waitress reappeared with Asher's check and he handed her his debit card. Rachel ordered another drink and then muttered, "Wow. That went down quick."

"It's okay, I'm driving. You deserve it," Carly said.

She nodded and placed a hand on Asher's arm. "I'm so scared of all this stuff. I mean, what can you do to protect yourself against it?"

"You could always prepare for it. The two most popular ideas in preparing for something like this are to hole up somewhere with a bunch of supplies and let the disaster pass or to run. Staying put seems like you're just waiting for your own inevitable death to me. I think the key is to stay mobile. Have plenty of supplies and keep moving from place to place in order to stay ahead of them."

"Wouldn't that be more dangerous than staying in one place that you can fortify and defend?" Rachel asked as the waitress returned with her drink and Asher's card. "Thanks."

Asher picked up the pen and added a tip to his bill. "I don't know," he replied while he signed. "I think the zombies are a very real threat, but from everything that I've read, if you don't let yourself get trapped, then you should be okay. The biggest problem is going to be the other survivors who need your supplies. You may be able to zombie-proof a building, but there's not much that can keep a determined human being out of someplace, especially if society has collapsed and there's not a police presence to deter them from doing violence."

"Do you really think people would be that petty?" Carly asked. "They'd all be survivors and people tend to join together in times of crisis."

Asher took a small sip from his still mostly-full beer and glared at her. "How much time have you spent in the Third World? Or even closer to home, have you been in a hurricane or tornado disaster area before the government arrived?"

The woman sniffed and leaned back, crossing her arms over her breasts. "I haven't ever been to any of those types of places."

"You're lucky. I've spent a lot of time in shitty little backwaters and human life means absolutely nothing there. If you have something that they want and they have the means to take it from you, then you're done."

Rachel cleared her throat. "So, what were you doing in all those bad places?"

Asher tore his stare away from Carly and smiled at Rachel. "I negotiated natural resource extraction contracts for a little more than thirty years—mostly oil and metals in the worst possible environments that you could imagine. You'd be surprised how far companies will go to further their interests." He'd used that cover the entire time that he was with the CIA. Over the years, Asher had learned quite a lot about the processes after telling the story. If pressed, he could even give a quick down and dirty lesson on how an international company would move into an area, dazzle the locals with promises and small payments, devastate their lands to mine whatever they wanted, then leave the area without cleaning up their mess. It was a terrible practice, but nobody gave a shit when it happened outside of the United States or Western Europe. Plus, most people thought that sounded like an extremely tedious job, so they tended to not ask any questions and his cover held up.

"Wow, that's fascinating," Rachel said. "Do you have a plan? If they can't stop them in New York, I mean?"

"Yeah, I'm gonna bug out. I'm planning to head west to give myself some time to figure out what's happening back east. I've got a little pull-behind camper in storage over at the E-Z Store that I'm gonna pick up tomorrow after my test. I'll get that filled and ready to go in case I have to leave in a hurry. If things turn out okay, then I'll just chalk it up to a good workout."

Rachel drained her glass again and leaned over toward him. "I know how much you like to work out..." her voice trailed off and she circled one fingernail across his forearm.

Asher stood up and Boomer jumped to her feet. "Alright ladies. I've gotta go to bed so I can be ready for my test tomorrow."

"Aww, it was just getting interesting," Carly stated.

"Yeah. Well, school's important, you know. It was nice to meet you, Carly."

"Likewise," she smirked with a glance at her friend.

Rachel stood up a little unsteadily and hugged him. "We should do this again. I loved talking to you."

"Okay, I'd like that," he replied and leaned back.

She planted a kiss on his cheek, "Bye."

"Bye." He waived back at the women and led Boomer out the patio's gate.

Well, that couldn't have gotten more uncomfortable.

*****

19 September, 2337 hrs local
Asher Hawke's Residence
Rocky Mount, North Carolina

Asher took a sip of his beer. He'd decided to let it go tonight in case it was the last time that he was able to get drunk for a while. He absently wiped the foam from off his moustache. He had to shave off the beard that he'd worn for most of his adult life last spring so he could wear the gas mask when he went into DC. Allyson liked him clean-shaven, so he'd kept it shaved while they were together. He'd let it grow back out after her death, although he kept it neatly trimmed now versus the unruly mess that he'd allowed it to become before meeting the FBI agent.

What the hell was going to happen? The news out of New Jersey wasn't good and he was confident that the Army wouldn't be able to stop the horde if it made it past them into New York. If that happened, it was *adios* North America. His time serving his government had taught him to rapidly lay out the pros and cons of a situation and make snap decisions based on the evidence at hand. Everything told him that if New York fell, he needed to start moving and get out before others got the same idea and the roads became clogged with people trying to escape. The best way to do that would be to prep everything and be ready to go.

He picked up the notebook that he'd been writing notes in all night from beside him on the old, worn couch that he'd bought secondhand after he retired. He'd take food—there was a ton of prepackaged meals in the garage from when he worked at the hiking store—and water. Those weren't optional; without them you were toast. He'd likely end up as one of the scavenging maniacs that he warned the women at dinner about, and that wasn't in his nature. He was a legitimately bad person to meet in a dark alley if you were one of the bad guys, but he also had the unfortunate character flaw that made him want to help people. *Damn morals.*

He also planned to take weapons. A lot of them. Asher had his weapon of choice, an FN Herstal MK-17 Special Operations Forces Combat Assault Rifle (SCAR) with an attached sound suppressor for short and intermediate range engagements—he had two of the rifles in case one got damaged. He also had a Lapua Magnum .338 sniper rifle with 32Xs IR scope so he could reach out and touch someone, three Heckler & Koch HK45 pistols—one for his drop-leg holster, one for his camper and one for the glove box in the truck—several knives of various lengths and a tomahawk to take off limbs at extremely close range. He wanted to keep the different types of ammunition to a minimum so he wouldn't be sorting through boxes and boxes looking for the right thing if he needed to reload in a hurry. He also had more magazines than he knew what to do with, but if shit hit the fan, then he'd need them all.

Besides the food and weapons, everything else he planned to take was basically the same supplies that people would take on an extended hiking trip. He'd listed rope, twine, a sleeping bag, compass, several road atlases with close-up maps of the major cities, some cooking gear and spices, clothing, a camp shower, toiletries, solar charger for his cell phone and a separate backpack filled with a small amount of supplies in case he had to haul ass from his vehicle.

He needed to go to the store on the way home from picking up the camper and buy a shitload of dog food for Boomer. He didn't have nearly enough to last the month or so that he figured he could potentially be on the move for. About the only thing that he wanted, but made a conscious decision not to pack into the camper tomorrow, was beer. Asher decided that he wouldn't need the alcohol; it would be stupid and potentially deadly to drink too much and allow his senses to dull during a time like this. He planned to take the home beer-making kit that Allyson had given him in any case, both for sentimental and practical reasons. The jug would hold water initially and in the future, if things stabilized, he could brew some beer with all the supplies that he hadn't gotten a chance to use after that first brew last July.

He took a large gulp of his beer. The only time that he'd used the beer kit was the day that Allyson was killed. He'd been busy making beer and then he'd helped Rachel in her garden, so he didn't find out that she was dead until hours after it had happened. Reston had told him that she died instantly, but he doubted it. Unless it was a legit headshot, people often suffered for a while until they bled out or their heart stooped. Did she ask for him as she lay there dying?

Boomer's ears perked up and she lifted her head off of Asher's lap. A low growl escaped her throat as she stared at the front door. "What is it, girl?" he asked as his hand drifted over to the .45 on the end table. She whined in response.

The doorbell rang and Boomer started to bark. "What the hell?"

He stood up and crammed the pistol in the waistband behind his back, then pulled his shirt down over it. He sauntered drunkenly over to the door and pulled the side curtain away to reveal Rachel Robertson standing on his front porch. He looked down at Boomer and muttered, "Shit."

He unlocked the door and opened it. Rachel smiled hugely at him. "Hi, Asher!"

"Umm... Hello, Rachel. What's up?"

"Carly just dropped me off and I saw that your lights were still on. Can I come in?" she asked with a slight slur to her words.

He did a quick mental check of his home to ensure that everything was put away. Except for some generic photos of his SEAL team in front of concrete barriers and jungles, there wasn't any incriminating evidence inside on display. "Sure, come on in."

Asher stepped wide to allow her to come inside, then he closed the door and locked it behind her. By the time he turned around, she'd already made her way into the living room and stared at the pictures on the wall. "I didn't know you were in the Army," Rachel said as she pointed at the picture of his deceased friend Matthew Henderson and Asher in East Timor with a squad of Australian Commandos.

"Navy. When we went ashore, we wore the same type of uniforms as the Army guys."

"Hmm, I never knew that. Does the Navy go 'ashore' a lot?"

"Sometimes, to make repairs and things like that." He really had no clue what the regular fucking Navy did, but she was obviously drunk—as was he—and she would probably be easy to lie to.

"Wow, look at all these pictures of you with guns. And beards. I thought the Navy had to be clean-shaven?"

"Yeah, but we could grow it every once in a while... So, what do you need?" he asked, changing the topic.

She glanced at him and then dropped her eyes. "This is embarrassing. Don't think I'm stupid or something."

"Okay, I won't," he said flatly.

"It's just... Well, since Jim left me, I've been all alone over there and then tonight when you were telling us about the zombies... Asher, I'm scared. Like, really scared."

"Don't worry, Rachel. They're hundreds of miles from here and moving northward. Even if they came this way, we've got plenty of time to react."

"Can I sit?" she asked.

"Sure, of course. Here, let me move this," he replied and picked up his bug out list.

She sat on the couch and he fell onto the cushion beside her. "Oh, fuck..." he groaned.

"What's wrong?"

"Nothing. Hey, I'll be right back, gotta go to the restroom."

"Okay. I'll just watch the news," she jutted her chin toward the television that displayed the horrific scenes from the northeast.

"Alright, I'll be right back." He pushed off the couch and moved stiffly toward his bedroom.

When he got there, he pulled the pistol from his belt and slipped it into the bedside drawer. He'd forgotten that he had it in his waistband and sat down onto it hard. *Stupid*, he chided himself and rubbed the spot where the hammer had dug into his back when he sat down. Just for good measure, he decided to go to the bathroom and flush the toilet.

He returned to find Rachel reading his list. "Wow, you're really planning on doing this, huh?"

"Yeah, well I plan to stay alive. The way I see it, the only way to do that if this goes bad is to be prepared to go and then just go," he replied as he walked over and picked up his beer glass, draining it in one gulp. "I'm gonna get another beer. Do you want something? I have water, juice and beer, but I don't have any wine, sorry."

"Do you have any vodka?"

Asher considered lying to her and telling her that he didn't. *This is gonna go bad*, he told himself. *You've been drinking and you're lonely, she's been drinking and has lusted after you for almost two years...* "Yeah, I've got some Grey Goose."

She jumped to her feet and followed him into the kitchen. "That's the best kind," she said. "What kind of juice do you have?"

"Mmm, I think I have apple and maybe some orange juice."

"The orange juice wouldn't mix well with the wine I've had. I'll take the apple, please."

He grunted and opened the refrigerator. Inside were two more six-packs of his favorite IPA, the two bottles of juice, a couple dozen eggs and a leftover quiche that he'd baked. Everything else was empty. He pulled out the juice and another beer for himself. Then he selected a glass for Rachel from the cabinet, set it on the counter and walked to the pantry where he kept the liquor. The ice machine churned behind him as she got ice for her drink.

They sat down together on the couch and she sat cross-legged with her feet on the cushion. Boomer looked back and forth between them, likely wondering where she was supposed to sit, and settled for lying across Asher's feet. "Thank you for letting me come over to talk."

"No problem, it's what friends are for," he replied as he stared at the words scrolling along the bottom of the television.

"Hey! What time is it?" she asked in sudden alarm.

"Um, looks like 12:04. What's wrong?"

"Nothing. It's just... now that it's the 20th I'm officially divorced," she muttered.

He looked over at her. She was staring at the top of her glass. "Hey, I'm divorced. Twice. It's not so bad."

She looked up and smiled at him. "Thanks. I never knew you were divorced either. We've never really talked about personal stuff very often, y'know?"

"No, I guess we really haven't. It just never came up."

Rachel took a sip of her drink and set it on the coffee table. She shifted on the couch and leaned over into him. He lifted his arm and let her rest against his side. "Asher, I'm really scared. I know that I said that already, but it's the truth. There's a damned zombie outbreak. Zombies... I can't believe it."

He realized suddenly that he'd been absently stroking her blonde hair and stopped himself. "They've been in DC for years. I thought that we should have wiped them out while they were cooped up behind The Wall, but now they're loose and we have to deal with it."

They watched the news quietly for a few minutes until Rachel spoke in a quiet voice, "You know, Jim and I have been separated for more than a year. Every time you mentioned him in conversation, I always just lied and said he wasn't home or whatever."

"Oh wow, I'm sorry that I didn't ever notice, Rachel. I didn't... I was just busy with school and other things. I had no idea."

"We married after high school. People change so much over time. One day you just wake up and realize that if you'd waited a few years until you grew up, then you would have never been with that person. Strange, huh?"

"Yeah... Shit, sorry," he said when he caught himself running his fingers through her hair again. "I didn't mean to paw all over you. I was just being absentminded."

Rachel pressed herself into him more and slid her head down into his lap. "No, please, it feels good," she murmured sleepily. "It's nice to have a man touch me again."

He hesitantly placed a hand on her hip and let it rest there for a moment. Then a soft snore made him look down. Rachel had fallen asleep.

What the hell am I doing? he thought. She was a married woman. *Actually, she's a divorced woman,* his mind answered back. Was he ready for a relationship with this woman? He was still messed up in the head about Allyson's death. It had only been three months. And, even if they'd been separated for a year, Rachel just got divorced today. Of course, maybe neither of them was looking for a relationship. Maybe they both just needed something physical to help ease their pain.

The television beeped several times and he stared blurry-eyed at the reporter. "*The U.N. has declared all of North America to be quarantined. No flights or ships will be authorized to land on another continent if they left the United States or Canada within the past forty-eight hours. They will be forced to turn around or risk being fired upon*."

"Well shit," he muttered and shifted his hips forward a little bit so he could lay his head back against the couch's headrest. He lay back with a beautiful, vulnerable woman's head resting on his crotch, exactly where he would have wanted her on just about any other occasion. *Damn morals*, he thought as he closed his eyes to go to sleep.

TWO

21 September, 0348 hrs local
The Lincoln Tunnel, Manhattan Side
New York City, New York

"Keep it up, goddamn it!" Mike yelled into his helmet's microphone.

"*Sir, the barrels are gonna burn up. We've gotta let them cool down or else they'll be useless,*" Sergeant Gilstrap answered in frustration.

Mike knew the limitations of the tank's machine guns, but he'd been hoping to last more than ten minutes into the fight. Each round that went down the barrel of a weapon caused the metal to heat up. When you put a lot of rounds through it in rapid succession, then the heat quickly spreads. When you put a hell of a lot of ammo through a barrel, the metal can get so hot that it warps and loses the factory shape, which then turns the 24–pound barrel of the M2A1 .50 caliber machine gun into a heavy hunk of useless metal.

"Shit. You're right." He hated that he was going to have to retreat, but his crew had poured thousands of rounds down the length of the tunnel, decimating the creatures that swarmed toward New York and he needed to change the barrels or else they were out of the fight for good.

"Blue Three and Four, move up. We have to let our barrels cool," the Chaos Company commander ordered into his radio while Sergeant Gilstrap fretted with the replacement barrel for the M2. The large .50 caliber machine gun was mounted in the tanks' CROWS system. The CROWS, Common Remote-Operated Weapons Station, was a lethal weapons system that allowed the tank crew to fire the gun without exposing themselves to the zombies outside of the vehicle. It was joystick operated and the display monitor was mounted in front of Mike to use as the tank's commander. Each of the tanks in C/1-101 Cavalry had the CROWS installed and the captain knew that the system would be key in the fight ahead—as long as they could get the barrels changed.

Mike turned in his seat and looked through the periscope toward the rear of the tank. "Driver, back," he ordered. The massive 72-ton M1A2 Abrams began to move slowly backward as Specialist Greeley blindly followed the commander's instructions from the driver's hatch where he could only see toward the front.

Through the periscope, Mike saw the two tanks from his third platoon moving to either side of him as they came forward to fill the gap in the shallow line that his tank had created. His wingman, the company executive officer, was also pulling out of position so his tank could switch barrels too. The fight to save New York was fully underway.

They'd made the trip from Hoosick Falls easily enough. It had been a surreal experience as they traveled southwest in their Humvees and trucks, shadowing the semis carrying the tanks down the highway toward the impending fight. The lanes leaving the city were jammed with cars who'd become hopelessly stuck in their mad flight from the danger to the south, while the lanes that they were in remained closed to traffic by the state highway patrol. Mike's chest swelled with pride as men and women cheered them on when their convoy passed the snarled traffic jams. The military was America's only hope and the salvation of their country would start right here in New York.

Chaos Company had quickly unloaded their tanks and gotten into position yesterday morning before the creatures arrived. Their mission was to block access to the city through the Lincoln Tunnel while the other companies in the battalion performed the same task at the city's southernmost bridges and tunnels leading from New Jersey. Other National Guard units secured the Tappan Zee Bridge, the next closest bridge to the city from the west, and there were rings of men along the north of the city in case the zombies somehow tried to flank the defenders at the main southern bridges.

Mike had devised a rotating defensive strategy for his fourteen tanks to address the three tunnels that emerged from under the Hudson River. His plan involved a section of two tanks in overwatch and the other two-and-a-half platoons situated close to the tunnel's exit. Two tanks were placed at each exit, firing into the gaping maw of the tunnel. When those tanks needed to rotate so they could change their weapons' barrels or reload ammo, he'd call the second line of six tanks forward while the section in overwatch took care of any creatures that made it past them. The company Headquarters Platoon had the unenviable job of resupplying ammo to the tankers who were buttoned up tight in the safety of their metal behemoths. Further back, dismounted infantrymen had been set up to kill any zombies that made it past the tank company; they were the final line of defense.

Given the situation and the terrain that they'd been assigned, it was the best that Mike could come up with. Ideally, they would have had enough time to completely block two of the tunnels and then defend the one so there could potentially be an escape route in the future, but time was against them. Mike summed it up to his troopers in the age-old Army axiom: It is what it is. That meant, stop bitching about the situation and deal with the facts that were presented to you because you couldn't change reality.

By midday yesterday, the battalion's Alpha Company reported contact on Staten Island and the men of Chaos had listened intently to the battalion radio frequency as the reports filtered up to the headquarters. By nightfall, Delta Company had begun fighting at the Holland Tunnel and Alpha fought a retrograde operation to make it back to the Verrazano Bridge, which was held by the dismounted soldiers from the Headquarters Company. In less than six hours, they'd lost Staten Island.

Charlie Company's turn came soon after as the gunners began to discern the shifting, shuffling mass of zombies through their night vision sights. Mike had immediately ordered them to switch to infrared to determine if they were human or not. They weren't. The creatures moving toward them gave off no discernable body heat; they were as dead as any other inanimate object, except they were moving on their own accord.

Due to the way the tunnel sank below the river, they could only fire out to about two hundred meters before the angle of the tunnel became too great for the machine guns. That worked to the creature's advantage as they massed in the darkness and came forward in never-ending waves of the undead. Mike estimated that they killed close to a thousand of them in the first several minutes of fighting alone. Regardless of how many they killed, they kept coming and the machine guns began to fail from the heat of all those rounds passing through the barrels.

Mike unlatched the commander's hatch and heaved upwards against the door's weight. His 9-millimeter Beretta pistol led the way as he popped up from inside the tank to keep Sergeant Gilstrap safe while the gunner changed out the barrel of the Ma Deuce. The new quick-change barrel and fixed headspace and timing were a major improvement over the old model's screw-in barrel and quirky firing mechanism that he'd learned how to operate as a brand new lieutenant. Even with the improvements, the problem that remained—and couldn't be helped—that in order to change the barrel, the gunner had to leave the safety of the tank, exposing them to whatever was outside, be that infantrymen, chemicals or zombies.

Mike hadn't been able to hear much through the protective sound-muffling headset that he wore when he was down inside the vehicle, but now that he was exposed to the elements, he could hear the chugging of the machine guns at the tunnels. Each round exiting the barrel and racing toward another target seemed to thump against his chest, causing his heart to stutter and beat faster to keep up with the sound waves that assailed him. He longed for the wide, open fields and desert terrain where the Abrams was designed to operate, not this city defense where they couldn't maneuver or fire from long distances.

The machine guns from the two tanks to Chaos' rear began to chatter away. Mike jerked his eyes from the immediate area around his tank to the scene at the tunnel. One of the tanks on the far left had accidentally pivoted too hard when it backed up to change position with another behind it. When they pivoted, the tank ran into the one beside it, ripping the tracks off of both tanks, which blocked the replacement tank's ability to fire into the tunnel's exit. As the firepower had decreased significantly, the creatures took advantage of the situation and swarmed through.

"Shit! Get that barrel in, Gilstrap!" he shouted as his tank's loader popped up and started firing the 7.62-millimeter machine gun beside his hatch. Rounds from the Specialist Walker's weapon slammed into the zombies pressed against the disabled tanks. The small caliber wouldn't do much damage to the tanks or the crew inside, but it was devastating to the creatures caught in its withering fire.

The company radio frequency exploded in a series of questions as the men inside realized that their friends were shooting at them and Mike knew that he had to take charge of the situation before they panicked.

"Red One, this is Chaos Six. Stay buttoned up, we're just cleaning them off of you with the coax, over."

"Don't you fucking fire that Ma Deuce at us, sir!" the platoon leader answered back as Sergeant Gilstrap stopped working on the .50 cal and dropped back down into the safety of the tank to use the slaved machine gun.

There was a slight possibility that with enough hits from the .50 cal they could do some damage to the tank and possibly the men trapped inside, but the 7.62s wouldn't penetrate the armor. "We're not gonna do that, Ben," Mike answered. "Hang tight and we'll get you out."

"Roger. Can you see what the damage is?"

Mike's tank shuddered as the gunner slewed the turret toward the two tanks so he could fire the machine gun that was slaved to the barrel. The Abrams main battle tank bristles with weaponry. Aside from the 120-millimeter main gun, the commander has a .50 caliber machine gun—lovingly referred to as the Ma Deuce by those who've used it in combat—and there are two smaller 7.62-millimeter machine guns, one beside the loader's hatch that has to be fired manually and another that is mounted beside the main gun. Anywhere the main gun points, the second machine gun does as well, giving the gunner inside the vehicle the option to utilize the smaller caliber instead of the massive destructive power of the main gun.

"Yeah, your fucking driver knocked the treads off both your tank and Red Two's. You guys are disabled and we can't repair you in this environment."

"Shit, that's not good. Sir, what's the plan?" the platoon leader asked. Mike didn't even have the opportunity to respond before Red One yelled over the radio, *"Hey! Get back here, don't do it, Jones!"*

Fuck. Mike fumbled for his binoculars and saw the loader's hatch on the Red One tank pop open as one of the soldiers inside panicked and tried to escape. Too late to shout a warning, Specialist Walker had already unleashed a volley of fire from his machine gun. Mike watched in horror as the rounds slammed into Red One's loader, pitching him over backward across the top of the tank. Zombies swarmed the man and several wormed their way past Jones' body through the hatch inside.

It happened in a matter of seconds and Mike couldn't do anything about it, Red One's crew was gone. "Jesus!" he shouted and fumbled with the transmit switch on his radio. "Red One! Red One, this is Chaos Six! Ben, are you alright?"

"I can hear them back there, sir," a small, scared voice replied over the radio.

Mike thought hard for a moment to remember Red One's driver. The tank was designed so that the driver's compartment was separate from the main compartment and could barely be reached through a small opening that even a dog would have trouble making it through. Tankers usually kept a wooden dowel in the crew compartment that they could shove through the hole and tap the driver's helmet if the communication system became disconnected. It wasn't big enough for a normal man to make it through, but Mike had no clue about the abilities of the zombies; if that kid was still alive, he had to save him.

"Private Halloran, this is Captain Miranda," he answered calmly into the radio. "Take it easy and don't panic. The guys in the back are gone and those things can't get to you up there in the driver's compartment. We need to figure out how to get you out of there safely."

"O... Okay, sir," the young soldier replied.

"It's important that you stay as quiet as you can so they figure out that you're up there. Give me a minute to think."

Over the radio, the commander could hear the harsh *growling* of the creatures as they attacked the two men in the Abrams' crew compartment. He was pissed off at Jones, the loader who'd panicked and opened the hatch, killing all three men. Everyone was safe inside the tanks if they didn't open any of the access hatches.

Over the radio, Mike said, "Red Two, this is Chaos Six. Over."

"Red Two," the platoon sergeant answered back immediately.

"Look, here's the deal. Private Halloran is the only one left alive from Red One and we can't recover your tank with these creatures around."

"I'm sorry, sir, but we ain't gonna open these hatches and try to make a run for it. Over."

"Not what I'm saying, Red Two. We're going to abandon your tank, so put that bitch in reverse and pull back as far as you can with one track and the road wheels. Red Three will move up and take up your position to fire into the tunnel."

"With only one track, we'll be limited to a hard pivot behind Red One, but I can clear the position, sir."

"That's all I'm asking. You guys will have to sit tight. Then once we reestablish the initiative, we'll pull you guys out of there."

"Roger. Red Two moving now."

Mike peered through a set of binoculars as the tank's engines revved up and it began to back up. The track on the far side caught and propelled the massive vehicle while it grated along the front and then the side of Red One. The sprockets on the side with the missing track spun impotently, but the 1,500 horsepower turbine engine propelled the beast backward. As the tank got more traction, it began to turn since the remaining set of tracks only moved the one side of the vehicle and it ended up perpendicular, behind Red One.

"Red Two clear," the platoon sergeant reported. Immediately, Red Three's tank surged forward into the gap and began chugging away with their weapons to clear the tunnel.

Over his tank's internal intercom Mike said, "Alright, fellas. Let's clear those fuckers off Red One and then we'll move up and rescue Private Halloran."

The loader and gunner both raked the disabled tank with their machine guns, decimating the remaining creatures. "Driver, move forward. Get as close to Red One as you can, but don't hit them," Mike ordered.

His tank surged forward alongside of Red One. Bones were crushed while intestines and bodily fluids sprayed in every direction as the tracks split open the zombies' putrid, rotting bodies. "Private Halloran, this is Captain Miranda. My tank is sitting to the right side of you and my loader's hatch is open. Are you ready to exit the vehicle and come over here?"

"I... I can't do it, sir."

"Listen to me, Halloran. This is your one shot to survive. The area is clear right now, but you either come over here now or you're going to be left behind." Mike paused for a minute, waiting for the kid to answer. When he didn't respond Mike said, "Private Halloran, this is an order. Get your ass over here now!"

"Yeah, come on, man!" Specialist Walker yelled from the loaders hatch.

Something dark flashed beside Mike and out of his peripheral vision, he saw a shape fall down inside the crew compartment. "Fuck!" he screamed and dropped down inside to kill the creature.

"Hold on, sir! It's Halloran," his gunner yelled as the loader's hatch slammed shut.

"Holy shit. Halloran, you almost had a few more breathing holes!" Mike called over to the sobbing kid at Walker's feet. "You alright?"

"Yes, sir. Thanks for coming to get me."

"Well, we're not done yet." The commander turned in the turret to look behind them once more. "Driver, back!" he barked into the microphone.

The tank backed up in a straight line as Greely held the steering wheel steady. When they reached their previous position Mike shouted to Private Halloran, "Alright, here you go Halloran. We don't have room for you in here. The first sergeant's Humvee is about fifty meters directly behind us."

Over the gun's breach he saw Watkins reach down and grab a handful of Halloran's belt. The loader picked him up and virtually threw him out of the tank. Mike lifted his hatch and watched the driver scramble toward the Headquarters Platoon where the company's first sergeant sat with the extra ammunition.

Chaos Six checked his watch. It was almost 6 a.m., the sun would be up soon and they'd be able to see the bastards deeper into the tunnel system than they could now. Gilstrap slapped the top of the tank to get his attention. He'd begun to work on the Ma Deuce the moment that they stopped and now his thumbs up told Mike that they were ready to go, barrels changed and new belts of ammo loaded up into the guns.

"Driver, move up," Mike said and sank down inside the tank once more. He pulled the hatch shut and heard the other two hatches slam closed as well, letting him know that both Sergeant Gilstrap and Specialist Walker were inside the safety of the turret.

The tank clanked forward and he depressed the trigger on his joystick, firing the .50 cal down the tunnel. For the next fifteen minutes Mike and his crew rained metal into the horde that continued to press forward, heedless of their death. When his guns clicked empty, he simply ordered, "Driver, back."

As his command tank pulled backward, another maneuvered around him to take his place. He needed to piss badly, so he grabbed an empty Gatorade bottle and started to unzip his combat vehicle crewman's suit at the crotch. Before he could complete the action, the two tanks in overwatch began to fire.

"Shit. They're coming your way, Chaos Six! Stay buttoned up."

"Acknowledged," he replied and winced as the high-pitched pinging sound of machine gun rounds impacting all along the tank reverberated through the turret. No wonder Jones had freaked out.

"Steady, gentlemen," he whispered hoarsely into the internal tank frequency. Mike's nerves grated against one another with every snap and ricochet of the metal-on-metal barrage. He wanted to run away from the madness. It was insane to stay put and take the rounds; surely they'd hit something and the vehicle would explode.

That's what made Jones panic, look at what happened to Red One, he screamed to himself—it might have even been out loud, he no longer knew. "Steady!" he shouted into the radio, more of an effort to calm himself than the crew.

The rounds stopped as suddenly as they started. "*Dammit! Sir, this is Blue Two, they made it out of the tunnel and have already gotten into the company trains.*"

"What the hell?" He grabbed the periscope and watched in horror as thousands of zombies poured out of the far left tunnel where Red One and Red Two had collided. Red Three was sitting silent.

"Red Three! Red Three, this is Chaos Six. What happened?"

"*This... ee... Radio... own... ammo. Over.*"

"Shit. I think their radio's out," Mike muttered.

"*Sir,*" Sergeant Gilstrap's voice came over his headset. "*Sounded like they said they were out of ammo.*"

He thought back to his fight a few minutes ago. Had they been firing? He couldn't remember. *Shit.* Mike switched his transmit to the battalion frequency. "Wrangler Six, this is Chaos Six. Over."

A few seconds later, Lieutenant Colonel Espenshade's voice came over the radio, "*This is Wrangler Six, go ahead.*"

"Sir, they just got past us through the tunnel. Over."

"*Hell, Michael. You guys didn't even last four hours.*"

"I know what we didn't do, sir. What are your orders? Over."

Another pause as he assumed the battalion commander checked the map board in the Battalion Operations Center. "*Continue fighting where you are. Kill what you can. Over.*"

Mike blanched as he thought about the creatures that were already behind him. "Sir, are you saying to give up the city?"

"Bravo Company was overrun twenty minutes ago, Mike. Their hatches were open when they got hit. They didn't even survive first contact."

Bravo had been the farthest north of the battalion's companies, which meant the zombies were likely swarming into Manhattan now. "Holy shit. Why didn't you say anything? Over."

"Wouldn't have changed your mission. You've got to take out as many of those things as you can, Mike. We... The battalion headquarters got whacked too. They were dismounted and those things just swarmed over them. Alpha is holding the Verrazano alright, but... Those things are in the city behind us already. We're gonna have to abandon New York completely. I'm just waiting on word from the governor to reposition, maybe trap them in the city somehow."

It was Mike's turn to pause as he thought over the implications of losing the city. Finally, "This is Chaos Six, acknowledged. We'll stay buttoned up and kill what we can until we run out of ammo on the guns. Over."

"That's all I can ask of you, Chaos—hold on, there's a call from the governor that I have to take. I'll call you back."

Mike switched to the company frequency. "All Chaos elements, this is Chaos Six. Do not open your hatches to reload. Once you expend all of your ammo, that's it. Open those hatches and everyone on your tank is dead." He paused to decide what he would tell the company.

"Wrangler Six just told me that Bandit was wiped out and the zombies are already streaming into the city up north. Our orders are to kill what we can, then stand by for our rally point. Keep your hatches closed! Chaos Six out." He switched frequencies immediately so he wouldn't have to hear the questions and confusion of the men in the company.

He pressed in the numbers to the infantry commander's net on his radio keypad. "Marauder Six, this is Chaos Six."

A moment later the commander came back, *"Marauder Six."*

"Zombies coming your way. They got around us. We just got word that they're already in Manhattan behind us."

"Well, shit. What do we do then?"

"Recommend that you either move into hardened structures or the safety of your trucks."

"Not much of a help. Okay, I've got it. Thanks for passing along the message."

Mike acknowledged the man's comment and wished his men good luck, then switched back to the company frequency. Over the next twenty minutes he watched as one by one the company's tanks ran out of ammo that was loaded into their weapons. The zombies surged around them on their way deeper into the city; most didn't even pay attention to the giant metal boxes. "Chaos Nine, this is Six. How you holding up back there?" he asked over the radio.

The first sergeant answered immediately, "*We're holding our own. I'm glad the Guard upgraded us to eleven-fourteens last summer or else this would have been really uncomfortable.*"

The company had been issued new up-armored M1114 Humvees the previous June. The M1114 had integrated armor versus the older soft-skinned vehicles that the battalion used to maintain. The doors on their previous vehicles had been made of plastic sheeting stretched tight over a thin metal frame, whatever idiot had thought that a combat vehicle should be designed that way should have been fired. In the early years of the Iraq and Afghanistan wars, troops welded metal plates to the sides of their trucks in an effort to stop even the smallest of rifle calibers from wounding or killing the vehicles' occupants. But the older chassis weren't designed for that much weight; as a result, axles broke, vehicles tipped over during turns and sank deeply into mud. Enter the M1114, a drastically modified vehicle that was capable of performing under the stresses of combat. The only real issue that soldiers had with them was the diminished storage capacity in the hatchback area.

The lightly armored vehicles kept the members of Mike's company who weren't inside an Abrams tank alive. "Thank God for small miracles. Top, I think we're gonna have to reposition somewhere so we can reload our weapons."

"*I was waiting for you to give the order, sir. We should use our tanks to crush the ever-loving shit out of these things,*" the old tanker replied.

"Red Two, this is Chaos Six. How are you holding up? Over."

"*We're fine, sir. Sounds like we're just sitting tight like everyone else for now. Don't leave us behind when the company moves.*"

"Not a chance in hell, Red Two."

The commander switched back to the battalion command frequency and tried unsuccessfully to get anyone on the radio. "Shit," he muttered. Now was not the time to be taking a smoke break at the headquarters.

Mike almost ordered his tanks to begin moving around to crush the creatures, but his thoughts kept returning to how Red One and Two had collided and threw track and he decided against it. The driver's field of vision when he was buttoned up was only directly to the front, so he relied on the tank commander to tell him everything else. Once the hatch closed, it was like an eighty-year-old man with cataracts trying to tell his blind wife how to drive through rush hour traffic.

He tried for twenty minutes to raise anyone on the command frequency, but was only able to reach Demon Six, the commander of the battalion's Delta Company. They were holding their own at the Holland Tunnel for now. After another ten, he finally got sick of trying to reach the headquarters and switched the radio from the encrypted frequency-hopping mode that the military used to single channel, plain text; that meant that anyone with an FM radio could potentially hear what he said.

He began to scan through the channels and eventually picked up some chatter. Mike keyed his microphone in excitement, "This is Chaos Six of the New York National Guard. Is anyone out there? Over."

After a moment, a voice answered. *"This is Sergeant Barnes, New Jersey National Guard. Where are you at? Over."*

"My tank company is defending the Lincoln Tunnel leading into New York City from New Jersey. We lost communication with our battalion. Over."

There was a long pause and then Sergeant Barnes returned, *"Sir, are you with the 101st Cavalry? Over."*

"Yeah, roger."

"We got word that the battalion was wiped out. Satellite imagery shows the zombies streaming in at every bridge and tunnel into the city. We can see your tanks, but the creatures are all around you. Over."

No shit, he thought. "We're out of ammo for the machine guns. Can't reload without exposing ourselves to the zombies, so we're just sitting tight for right now. Over."

Another pause answered him and for a moment he thought that he'd lost the radio frequency. But then, *"Chaos Six, this is Colonel Shay. The president has federalized the National Guard all along the East Coast. You guys put up a good fight, but New York City and Long Island are lost. Do you have fuel to move? Over."*

"Yeah, we have full tanks... Why do you ask? Over."

"Look, son, you're not gonna like this, but you need to move out of the city. The zombies seem intent on taking New York for now, so we've been ordered to let them have it before we waste any more lives. The president is considering using the Air Force to blow the bridges and tunnels to trap as many of them as we can. We're setting up a rally point at Parsippany-Troy Hills in central New Jersey. Then we're going to set up a line of defense to keep them from moving further west."

"So we're just going to leave the people of New York to fend for themselves?"

"Not our call. Everyone has had plenty of time to obey the evacuation orders. If they're still in the city, that's on them. We're going to provide humanitarian supply drops to give any survivors a chance, but we have an entire nation to defend. Once we establish a defense to stop them from infecting the rest of the country, we'll go back in and clean them out."

Mike considered the colonel's words and then replied, "I just talked to the 101st Cavalry's commander forty minutes ago, sir. He said that they were holding the bridge from Staten Island and our Delta Company had the Holland Tunnel secured. Has something changed? Over," Mike asked.

"It's over. They bypassed the bridge and tunnel. Like Sergeant Barnes said, we have satellite imagery that shows the zombies made it into the city. Damn things started swimming across the river. If your commander is still alive, he isn't talking on the radio anymore."

Mike glanced over at Sergeant Gilstrap. The gunner listened intently to the conversation, but his eyes betrayed the feelings trapped inside. Chaos Six sighed and pushed the transmit button on the radio, "Yeah, roger. I'll relay the orders to our Delta Company down at the Holland Tunnel and give them the order to move also. Over."

"We'll gladly add your tanks to the mix, Chaos. I'm sorry that it's come to this."

"Me too, sir," Mike answered truthfully. He really was sorry to see the city fall. When they'd left Hoosick Falls two days ago, he'd honestly thought that they could hold out against the zombies at the tunnels and bridges. The battalion had some of the most modern equipment available in the world, how had they been overrun so quickly? It was just a bunch of brainless creatures that walked directly into the line of fire. How the hell had it come to this?

"Sir... Do we know how far they've advanced into the city? Over."

"Looks like the ones that are leaving the Lincoln Tunnel are meeting up with the ones from up north in midtown Manhattan. They've also begun to move east into the Bronx and Brooklyn in the south. There's nothing that we can do at this point to save New York."

"Roger, sir. We'll start moving as soon as we can."

"Sounds good, Chaos. I'll see you soon. Out."

Mike looked at his gunner once again. "Can you believe this shit?" he said. "We're giving up the city."

"It's fucked up, sir. Want me to call the company and relay your orders?"

Mike tapped the tips of his fingers hard against his knee. "Yeah, let's get the first sergeant up to secure the personnel in Red Two. Tell everyone else to be ready to move in ten minutes. I'll call Delta Company and Marauder to relay the rally point to them."

While he worked the radio he typed the location into his Blue Force Tracker computer system. It brought up a map and overlay a straight line from his current location to Parsippany-Troy Hills. He passed along the details to the tankers and infantrymen while he used the computer's stylus to drag the route to the most obvious roads. Once the route was charted, he could send that to everyone in the company and they could each navigate to the rally point individually if they got separated.

"Hey, sir," Sergeant Gilstrap interrupted his planning. "The first sergeant is moving now. He's going to back the FMTV up beside their tank and they're gonna get in the back. He'll reposition the truck and allow them to move from the back into one of the 1114s."

Mike thought for a moment. The FMTV—Family of Medium Tactical Vehicles—was a 5-ton cargo truck and the bed of the truck sat around four-feet off the ground, so it should be high enough to keep the men safe until they could make the switch to the Humvee.

"Good plan," Mike muttered. He'd known the first sergeant long enough to know that once the man came up with a plan, he would execute it and virtually nothing that the commander said would change his mind. The old tanker had always had a plethora of tricks up his sleeve in the past. As far as Mike could tell his plan was the best option available for the trapped crew. The commander chose to keep his mouth shut and leaned forward to his periscope so he could observe the rescue.

It went off without a hitch. The first sergeant popped up from the cab of the truck into the gunner's ring mount and killed the creatures on top of the tank with his rifle. Over the company radio frequency, he ordered the four men from the disabled vehicle to get into the back of the truck. All the hatches opened and the crew scrambled to the relative safety of the FMTV. Then, once they were secure, the truck pushed its way through the pressing horde toward the line of up-armored Humvees.

After the men from Red Two had transferred from the bed of the truck into the Humvees, the first sergeant called Mike on the radio. *"Chaos Six, this is Nine. We're ready to go when you give the word."*

"Good job, Top. Guidons, this is Chaos Six. Let me know when you're ready to go," Mike said into the radio. "Guidons" was the term used when he wanted all leadership elements within the company to pay attention to the radio; it was easier than calling them each individually.

Within minutes everyone had answered and Mike gave the order of march to the rally point that the colonel had given him. It would be Blue Platoon, followed by the Commander, then the two remaining tanks from Red Platoon, followed by the XO's tank and Headquarters Platoon in their trucks and Humvees, the trail element would be White Platoon.

It was about forty miles to Parsippany. The company's tanks had almost-full fuel tanks and could easily range the rally point. The big Abrams had a 490-gallon fuel tank with a range of 256 miles, which broke down to about a half mile per gallon. The engines could run on just about any kind of fuel in a pinch. They could accept normal unleaded gas, diesel and even high-octane jet fuel. All of those options had helped tankers in the past as they became separated from logistics supply lines so the company had the ability to keep going as long as they could find *any* type of fuel.

To get to Parsippany, they'd take the 495 through the tunnel, link up with New Jersey Route 3 to US 46 and then hit I-80, taking that all the way to where the colonel had told them to go. There were more direct routes, but the highways would allow for maximum maneuverability when the column was up to speed.

Out of the three tunnels, Mike chose to send the entire company through the center instead of dividing and meeting on the other side. It was about a mile and a half through the Lincoln Tunnel until they reached the New Jersey side. He was worried about vehicles down inside that they'd be forced to drive over because of the lack of space; not a big deal for the tanks and the recovery vehicles because they'd just crush them, but the Humvees and FMTVs could possibly have a hard time going over the scrapped metal. That's all he needed was for one of his vehicles to pop a tire or even potentially tip over due to the imbalance.

"Move out," Chaos Six ordered over the radio and watched as the first tank of Blue Platoon entered the tunnel. Zombies continued to pour out of the mouth of the opening and the vehicle crushed several as it began its descent into the tunnel. One by one the tanks disappeared until it was his turn to go and Specialist Greeley depressed the throttle to propel the metal monster forward.

It was slow going as the front of the tank dipped downwards while they descended. Luckily—or unluckily, depending on how you viewed it—the power in the tunnel was still on. The overhead lights allowed for a view of the mass of creatures slowly making their way toward the city. The tanks swam through a flowing river of former humanity. When one vehicle crushed the creatures and made its way past an area, the hole would close up immediately with more zombies, who would then be destroyed by the next tank.

The vehicle's desert tan paint quickly stained with the muddy brown color that resulted when blood mixed with feces, brain matter, intestines and the contents of whatever had been in the creature's stomachs when they died. Body parts were severed from their owners and pulverized under the 70-ton vehicles. The sheer amount of gore covering the vehicles was appalling.

While the smells from outside were kept at bay by the tank's air filtration system, before long the smell of vomit from *inside* his tank made Mike's own bile rise to his throat. The things outside didn't care that some of them were there one minute and gone the next. They didn't have friends or the responsibility of leadership like Mike did. How were humans supposed to fight against an unfeeling, uncaring enemy? Mike prayed that everyone in the company had taken his advice to get their families out of New York as he'd done, otherwise there would be a problem after they arrived at the rally point.

Mike chose to combat his own doubts by talking to the men of the company on the radio. He reminded them that they were the only hope for the rest of America and that the only way out of the tunnel was through it. If they stopped, their friends and fellow soldiers would be trapped and then they couldn't help the rest of the country against these things.

Finally, after an agonizingly long time, Chaos Six emerged from the tunnel into Weehawken, New Jersey. The city looked like the war zone that it had become. Thousands—maybe even millions—of the creatures marched steadily forward toward either the Lincoln Tunnel or further north toward other ways into the city. Mike longed to use the weapons of the war machine that he rode in, but to exit the vehicle to load the machine guns at this point would be suicide. Once they got farther away from the city, presumably there'd be fewer zombies. Mike would stop the column and order the company to load their weapons so they could kill while on the move.

He got a radio check from all elements to verify that no one had been lost in the tunnel and was relieved when everyone answered. Mike bid farewell to the city that he'd once called home before relocating to Hoosick Falls and directed his company toward the new defensive line. As they pushed their way through even more zombies, he wondered if he'd ever see New York again.

*****

21 September, 0752 hrs local
The Lincoln Tunnel, New Jersey Side
Weehawken, New Jersey

The Leader watched the humans leave. Much like the flying machines that they used in the home city, the men inside the giant vehicles were untouchable as long as they stayed inside. No matter, the Followers were now moving into the large city and their numbers would swell even greater.

The human resistance was weak and had crumbled quickly. The Leader was surprised at how easily they'd taken the city. The creature had expected to lose millions in the fight, but nowhere near that many had been destroyed. The Master would be pleased and surely order its Followers to attack the humans surrounding the home city. Once the home city was free, the remaining Chosen could follow the Leader's example and travel in the opposite direction along the coast.

Once all of the humans were gone, the Leader would then challenge the Master. It knew that it could beat the small Chosen in a physical battle, but the Master had a massive amount of power in its mind. The Leader planned to use the victory as a means of getting close to the Master when its guard was down and destroy it.

If the Leader had retained the ability to smile, it would have. Instead, the creature just allowed its hatred of the humans and the Master to grow.

*****

29 September, 0903 hrs local
Rocky Mountain Manor
Denver, Colorado

"Alright, tell me what we've got," President Wilson stated. "The goddamned network news keeps getting the information before I do and that pisses me off."

"Sir, we've completely lost Philadelphia, New York, Hartford, Providence and Boston. The creatures hit New York hard and continued north along the coast until just past Portsmouth, New Hampshire. Now it looks like they've turned around and are spreading southwest back into the more populated areas."

"Well fuck, Rob. Do you have any good news?"

The Secretary of Homeland Security picked nervously at his cuticles; the weather was turning colder and he got horrible hangnails every winter as his skin dried out. He looked up toward the president and replied, "Frankly, sir, no. These things continually wipe the floor with the police and citizens who stand up to them. There's just too many of them."

"I don't want to hear it, Rob," President Wilson said with a slice of his hand across the air between them. "I kept you on from the Holmes administration because you were the best fit for the job and we knew that there was a problem in DC. Don't flake out on me now. I need you to figure this out."

"Yes, sir," the Secretary answered. "We're at a loss on how to stop these things without requesting the military to bomb the hell out of the cities."

"Let me step in, sir," General Zollman said. "We have a plan to stop them utilizing a series of defensive lines to delay the creatures while we build an impenetrable fortification, in conjunction with the Canadians from the Hudson Bay to the Gulf of Mexico. We'll stop them east of the Appalachian Mountains and then counterattack to clean them out of the northeast."

"My God, didn't we learn our lesson with The Wall? Keeping those things contained is only inviting disaster in the future. Let alone the sheer magnitude of it all," Kelly Flannigan interjected.

President Wilson sat back and ran a hand over his face. "Let's hear him out, Kelly. So you're suggesting that we abandon the entire East Coast to these creatures, Gabe?"

"I'm gonna be honest with you, sir—"

"Good. Nobody else is ever truthful around me. Let me hear why you think this is a good idea, General. And how you think we could accomplish it."

The Chairman of the Joint Chiefs leaned forward to regain the distance that the president had put between them when he moved away from the table. "Sir, if we don't develop a defensive perimeter, then the zombies can overrun us—or simply bypass us—anywhere they choose.

"We need to delay them on the eastern side of the mountains, give our engineers, the Homeland guys—hell, even the state Department of Transportation—time to build the barricades. We'll start by blocking off the roads, use the terrain to our advantage, and keep them out of the rest of the country. The engineers that I've spoken with think that the big 40-foot shipping containers, stacked two high would be enough."

"That would be an astronomical number of shipping containers," the Secretary of Energy, an engineer by trade, muttered.

"It's 1,220 miles from Rochester, New York to Mobile, Alabama," the general replied. "The Canadians are already building their own version from the Great lakes to the Hudson. The math works out that we'd need 161,000 shipping containers for a single layer—which is what we should build first—and then double that for the second row.

"It's an insane cost and will take everyone working together, twenty-four hours a day. We made the mistake of letting them live inside The Wall and it came back to bite us in the ass. We're not going to do it that way this time. Once the new defensive barriers are completed we can go in and utilize specialized forces to wipe these things out. It will keep them from creating massive new armies when they overrun our defenses, killing our soldiers and civilians. We just need time to get the barrier constructed."

"And that's why you want me to use the National Guard and police as frontline troops to delay them," the president concluded.

"Yes, sir," the general conceded. "It's not any different than simply fighting them and falling back with each loss. We're just asking the lines to hold longer so we can construct the barriers and properly evacuate the civilians ahead of time."

Ryan Wilson let his breath out and then turned to the rest of his National Security Council and asked, "Okay, what do you guys think?"

Chip Bullis was the first to clear his throat, "Sir, I think it's the right thing to do. We get ahead of the outbreak, establish a viable response that will allow us to counterpunch and then ultimately defeat the enemy."

The man had been the CIA's top spook for Alfred Holmes' administration before being elevated to the Director of National Intelligence under President Wilson. "It also allows the people to see that we have a plan," Chip continued. "They will see the wisdom of avoiding as many losses as possible and take heart in the fact that we're going to kick the creatures' asses on our own terms once the proper conditions are set."

"I agree, Mr. President," Kelly said. As the Director of the Federal Bureau of Investigation, she wasn't technically part of the traditional National Security Council, but the president had valued her opinion for as long as he'd been in office and she'd been invaluable in securing the Charters of Freedom in the spring, which had been a major political boost for the man. "We're losing a lot of people with the piecemeal response that we've put together. We need to evacuate the population westward and establish an appropriate military response. If there aren't any civilians to the east of the mountains, we can utilize military fighter jets, helicopters, even limited non-nuclear bombing on massed groups of the creatures. It's a smart move."

The other standing members of the NSC agreed with the exception of the Secretary of Energy. "You execute this plan, Mr. President, and the entire eastern half of the United States will be a nuclear wasteland within a month."

"I'm sorry, John, what was that?" the president asked in alarm.

"I said that if we do this, then the East Coast will be unsafe for human habitation for a thousand years." John Wood consulted the open book on the table in front of him that contained his notes, "We have forty-seven nuclear power plants to the east of the Appalachian Mountains—possibly a few less depending on where you build the barriers; maybe even a few more in Tennessee and northern Alabama if we build the barrier that far west.

"We've been lucky so far because we have crews who were trapped and simply continued to operate the plants. If we could properly shut the reactors down and keep water pumping to the cooling rods long enough to avoid reactor melt down, then we may avoid an irreparable disaster. However, if those crews are compromised before they properly shut them down, then we'd have an ecological nightmare on our hands."

The president wiped his face with his hand again; it was becoming a nervous gesture with the man. "Okay, John, so you're saying that we haven't already begun the process of shutting these places down yet?"

Secretary Wood held up his hands. "They're private companies, sir. We can't direct them to shut down without a major incident."

"This is a pretty major fucking incident," General Zollman cut in. "We hadn't even thought about this yet... But it's your goddamned job to keep track of this."

"Don't talk to me that way, General. This may be a military response, but in case you've forgotten, I'm still the Secretary of Energy." The general accepted his rebuke with crossed arms and a smoldering stare.

"Alright," John continued and looked back to the president. "If you give me the order, I can get those reactors offline and safe within a week. Expect a lot of pushback from most Americans as we turn off sixty percent of their power. We'll experience brownouts all across the country, possibly complete blackouts in the Midwest."

"So my options are an unhappy voting base or a nuclear meltdown in the midst of a zombie apocalypse?" the president snorted. "I don't really see how this is even up for debate."

"I'm just letting you know that there will be repercussions to your actions, Mr. President. I agree that since the zombie horde has swelled to such great proportions there's no longer a real choice in the matter, but you need to know all the facts."

"I know, John. I appreciate it. Hell of a thing isn't it? Look at what happened to Alfred Holmes; he saved the nation six years ago, but he couldn't win his bid for reelection. The public is only concerned with what's good for them at the moment."

The Secretary of Energy stared blankly at him; this would be his decision. "Okay. Gabe, I need your troops to give John enough time to get those power plants shut down and their crews evacuated so we can bring them back online when we defeat the zombies. Start construction of the barrier now. I want both layers in the north complete as soon as possible since that's where the creatures currently are. Let's execute your plan to use the mountains as a natural barrier against the creatures and pray that we can evacuate our citizens and not simply abandon them."

THREE

04 October, 0719 hrs local
Asher Hawke's Residence
Rocky Mount, North Carolina

The sun streamed through the blinds in Asher's bedroom and hit his closed eyelids, waking him up. His shoulder ached and he realized that he couldn't move his hand. There was some type of strange pressure against him, holding him to the ground against his will. Instantly, his mind flashed to the idea that he'd been captured. Reality came quickly as the panic that had gripped his heart in an icy fist subsided. He'd been retired for a long time, what he thought was the ground was only his mattress and his arm was underneath his blonde-haired companion.

Asher shifted slightly and eased himself out from underneath Rachel's body. He staggered to the bathroom and closed the door for privacy. As he stood in front of the toilet, pins and needles exploded up and down his arm with the rush of feeling back into it. What was he doing? He needed to take advantage of the distance and get away from the East Coast instead of staying here with his neighbor.

The whole damn thing was complicated though. Once he'd learned that Rachel had been separated from her husband for so long—and was now divorced—he should have been able to give himself the green light to act on his carnal desires. But his loyalty to Allyson's memory held him back, so he and Rachel had just spent time getting to know each other. It was an accepted fact that the woman was going to sleep in his bed each night, but that was as far as either of them was willing to go at this point. They were using each other. His ruined soul benefited from the interaction with Rachel that stayed in the emotional realm instead of venturing to the sexual side, while she obviously enjoyed being able to sleep safely in his arms each night for the past few weeks. It was a little out of the ordinary, but it worked for the two of them.

Asher rinsed his hands in the sink and then reached for his toothbrush. He accidentally hit Rachel's overnight bag with his wrist, causing it to fall to the floor. He bent stiffly to pick it up and a three-pack of condoms fell to the bathroom floor. *Doesn't hurt to be prepared*, he thought and stuffed them back into the bag.

When he finished brushing his teeth, he went into the kitchen to turn the coffee pot on. He'd forgotten to set it the night before and *tsked* to himself that he was slipping. It was almost eight in the morning and he was just now waking up, another indication that his body had accepted the fact that he was retired and wasn't going to be getting any more calls to go save the world. Now he had to save himself—and Rachel if she wanted to come along.

With the coffee brewing, he walked to the back door to let Boomer out into the yard and then padded softly back to his bedroom where he slid across the sheets to the sleeping woman. Asher sat up on one elbow and watched her for a moment until her eyes fluttered. "What is it?" she asked sleepily.

"Nothing. Just making some coffee if you want any," he replied.

"Mmm, sounds good," she said and placed her hand on his side. She gripped tight, pulling her body across the short distance between them and snuggled her cheek against his chest. "I could just stay here all day though... It's nice."

He lay his head down and breathed deeply. The mild cucumber scent of her hair reminded him of Allyson. God, why couldn't he let himself move on? Rachel was a wonderful, interesting woman that he enjoyed spending time with; why did he have to compare everything about her to Allyson Harper?

Because this woman thinks I worked for an oil company for most of my adult life. He couldn't tell her what he'd really done. He couldn't tell her of the different shitholes he'd been to across the globe, answering Uncle Sam's call to do his bidding. Rachel was a gentle woman; she had probably never even purposefully killed anything bigger than a mosquito in her entire life. Asher was a hunter of men and had the scars to prove it—which he had to lie about when she inquired about their origins.

Why am I denying myself? Besides the whole "everything that she knows about my life before two years ago is a lie" thing, she's perfect for me.

Asher applied pressure to her lower back and massaged softly. Somehow she squirmed even closer to him and pressed the entire length of her body against him. Rachel shifted slightly and brought her face close to his. She looked directly into his eyes, searching for an indication of his intentions.

The sunlit room fell away as the former operative stared into her blue-gray eyes. In his periphery vision, he saw the corners of her eyes crease as she smiled at him. "What?" she asked.

"I didn't say anything," he murmured as her breath warmed his chin.

"Hmm," she replied and closed the few inches between them. They kissed deeply for several seconds and Asher's body responded to her touch. She pressed her fingers firmly into his back and rocked her hips into his.

Her hands found his face and she pulled back slightly. "I… Asher, what do you want from me?"

His mind reeled as if he'd been slapped. *What the hell?* "I don't want anything from you, RR. I just enjoy spending time with you."

She nodded and kissed him again before pulling back again. "You said that you made some coffee?"

"Uh, yeah," he replied.

Rachel ran the tips of her fingers over the hard ridges of his abdominal muscles, stopping just above the waistband to the sleep pants that he wore. Her fingers slipped underneath the elastic for a moment and then she pulled her hand away quickly. "Let's go get some coffee," she stated softly. "Do you have plans for the day or can I buy you breakfast?"

Asher couldn't believe it. She'd gotten him all hot and bothered and now she was disengaging? He really didn't understand women at all. But just as he wasn't quite ready for some type of emotional relationship, maybe she wasn't ready for something physical. He'd take it slow and see what developed.

"Breakfast, with you, sounds great."

Rachel's smile spread extremely wide and she pushed him gently to his back. Her leg swung across his body and she straddled his hips, leaning down close to his face and kissed him again. It was deeper and if possible, even more passionate than the one before it and she ground herself hard against him while he cupped her breast.

"Wow," she breathed. "We better get out of this bed before we both do something that we're not ready for yet."

His face must have betrayed his confusion because she answered, "I can tell that you're not ready for a relationship and I'm not ready to just hop into bed with anyone. Can we just keep this slow? It's been so nice connecting with you emotionally."

"Of course," he replied and self-consciously slid his hands out from under her nightshirt.

"Asher, I like you. I've always liked you and believe me, this is a dream come true for me, but I want to be sure that we both know what we're getting into, okay?"

"Rachel, it's no problem. You're right, I'm still hung up on Allyson, but we can move past that."

She rested her head alongside his neck and asked, "If she came back to you, would you take her?"

Shit, so this was it then. He had to tell her the truth. He wouldn't tell her about what he'd done or the operation that he'd participated in, so he wasn't violating his oath of secrecy. "There are some things that I need to tell you."

She slid off of him and sat up. She looked like she was ready to cry as she stared at her ankles. "You're not single, are you?"

Asher sat up quickly and placed a hand on her shoulder, then used his other hand to cup her chin and lift her face to him. "No, I'm absolutely single. It's just... There are some things about my past that I haven't been entirely honest about."

Her pupils narrowed as she focused on him, "What do you mean?"

"Do you want to go get the coffee and we can sit at the kitchen table?"

"No, I want to know what you mean when you say that you haven't been honest with me," she said as she crossed her arms across her chest, covering her erect nipples that poked through her thin nightshirt.

"Okay, first off, Allyson and I didn't break up. She was an FBI agent and was shot and killed last July."

"Holy shit! Are you serious?"

"Yeah, that's why I'm still hung up on her. I wasn't even able to be with her when she died."

"Asher, I'm sorry. I didn't know. Why didn't you tell me?"

He held up his hands, "It's alright. You had no way of knowing. Anyways, we met through my old job."

"In contract negotiations?" she asked.

He dropped his hands and placed them on her feet. "Rachel, I want to be honest with you, but you have to know that what I'm about to tell you, you can't ever tell anyone, okay?"

Her eyes narrowed once more and she slowly replied, "Okay."

"I didn't really negotiate contracts for an energy company. You know those pictures of me in the Navy?"

"Yeah?"

"I was a SEAL for fourteen years and then I worked for the government for an additional seventeen after that."

He read the look that crossed her face immediately and already knew what she was going to say. "I'm not some stupid bimbo at the bar, Asher. Do you really expect me to believe that you were a SEAL and some secret agent or something? Now I know that you're lying to me."

"I'm not, Rachel. I promise." He pointed toward the three raised scars near his clavicle. "AK-47 in Djibouti, not a frog spear as a kid." Next he pointed at the long vertical scar along his ribs and then at seven other smaller welts, "Shrapnel from when an Afghan kid blew himself up next to my best friend Matt Henderson—that's his picture on the television stand." Then he pointed to his thigh, "You haven't seen this one. I got hacked by a machete in East Timor—that one almost killed me. Between the blood loss and the infection from God knows what was on the blade, I was that close to dying." He held his thumb and forefinger close together in front of her nose.

She took a moment to put her thoughts together and said, "So, did you work for the FBI too?"

"No, I worked outside the country; the FBI is mostly concerned with domestic crimes. When I retired, I bought this place because it was still relatively close to all the government installations that I might need to visit for healthcare and such. I met Allyson last spring when she recruited me for a mission in Washington, DC."

"Wait," Rachel said as she unfolded her arms and placed her hands over Asher's. "Last spring, you went into DC, with the zombies?"

"Yeah, I was on the Constitution recovery team."

"Wow... Holy shit, either you're a *really* good liar or you're some kind of badass," she exclaimed, appraising his body anew.

"I've been extremely lucky and I'm very good with firearms." He grinned at her and continued, "I'm not a badass."

She smiled back at him. "And because you were in DC, that's how you know so much about the zombies..."

"Yes, ma'am. I think we might have stirred up the hornet's nest by going in there. We should have wiped them out when we had the chance and now we're getting our asses kicked by those things."

"Okay, I think that I could use that coffee now," Rachel stated and rolled sideways to get off the bed.

Asher followed her out of the room, letting Boomer inside before he went into the kitchen to get his cup of coffee. He was still pouring when Rachel walked up behind him and hugged him. She placed her head against his back and said softly, "So, when are we leaving?"

He snorted and turned around to face her. "You want to go with me?"

She looked up into his eyes and replied, "If you'll take me, I want to go with you. Your recommendations just got a lot more valid."

"So when I was just a contract negotiator, you didn't believe me?" he smirked.

"No! I..."

He bent down and brushed his lips lightly across hers. "It's okay, I'm just kidding. I've been thinking—mind if I finish getting my coffee and we can sit and talk?"

"Oh, yeah, of course," she answered and stepped back from him.

He finished making his coffee and they sat at the table. "We lost New York almost two weeks ago. I really wanted to leave the day that the city fell, but I stuck around. Then when blowing up the bridges didn't work, I hooked the trailer up to my truck. As of yesterday, the horde was coming back south from New England and ravaging Boston. I—What?" he asked, his eyebrows rising quizzically at Rachel's laugh.

She covered her mouth. "I'm sorry. I know it's not funny, but you actually said... You used the word 'ravaged' in a sentence!"

His scowl turned to an off-sided grin. "Yeah, I guess I did. Okay, the zombies killed millions of people up north."

Her smile faded as the reality hit her. "Oh shit, I'm sorry. That's... I'm not laughing at all those people's death, Asher. I promise."

Asher reached across the table, grasping her hand and used his thumb to stroke the ridges of her knuckles. "I know you weren't. It *is* kinda funny; I don't know where that word came from. Anyways, given how quickly they moved north and came back, if they came directly here, then we'd have about a week or so, but we don't know where they're going next. I don't want to get cut off here somehow."

"So, when are we leaving?" she asked again with a slight tremor in her voice.

"Hey, what is it?"

"I just... You didn't answer me when I asked if you wanted me to go with you. Can I go with you, or are you going alone?"

He was in a playful mood and considered saying something along the lines that he wouldn't be alone because he had Boomer, but decided that Rachel didn't know him well enough yet to get the humor so he didn't want to upset her further. "Rachel, I want you to come with me. You and I can make a great team... On one condition."

She looked up from his hand resting on hers, "What condition?"

"You've got to learn to shoot first."

*****

13 October, 0852 hrs local
Troy Meadows Wetlands
Parsippany-Troy Hills, New Jersey

"Sir, this is the most fucked up shit I've seen in a long time," the crusty old soldier confided in his commander.

"I know First Sergeant. I argued with Colonel Shay that this is not how tanks were designed to fight," Mike Miranda replied.

"It's the same as at the goddamned bridge. They've got us in a stationary defense, canalized so we can't maneuver and can't even effectively mass fires, unless they attack through the neighborhood there," he gestured in frustration toward the northeast.

It was true. The defensive line—if you could call it that—which the two remaining companies from the 101st Cavalry was situated along was the two interstates that fed into the city of Parsippany, New Jersey. The two roads formed a giant vee, funneling the creatures inwards. The problem was the terrain surrounding the roads. If the companies went forward, they would get mixed up in neighborhoods and behind them were marshy wetlands—absolute no-go territory for tanks—so they had to stick to the roads.

The twelve tanks operational from Mike's Chaos Company were situated along Interstate 280. The way they were set up, only one or two vehicles would be able to get shots in if the creatures moved directly down the road, which Mike suspected that they would. It was the path of least resistance, so the shambling horde would likely just flow up the road like they'd flowed into New York along the roads.

The city behind him was teeming with dismounted soldiers, but as far as he knew the 101st was the only armored force here. The rumor was that there were little pockets of resistance between Parsippany and Washington, DC where this whole mess started, which made sense considering how quickly they moved through. The East Coast had taken the brunt of the attack so far, but the plan was to stop the zombies' westward spread into the nation's heartland.

Mike had his doubts about this kind of fighting though. In his mind, they needed to go to places that afforded the humans the luxury of standoff distance. The standard infantryman's weapon, the M4 and the M16 carbine, had an effective range of about 500 meters, over 1,600 feet. They should set up long-range ambushes of the creatures, utilizing artillery and close air support to wipe these things out, not defending city-to-city, bad terrain-to-bad terrain.

Logically, he knew that the way they were doing it was the best way to ensure the evacuation of citizens, but the soldier in him abhorred the city fighting. At least the zombies couldn't shoot back, so that was something.

A group of four Apache helicopters flew overhead toward the east. "Yeah, Top," Mike answered using the familiar name for the company's senior enlisted soldier. "We need to keep moving farther west to get some maneuver area."

"You're goddamned right we do, sir. You saw the devastation that this one company of tanks did to those things in that tunnel. We must have crushed three or four thousand of them without ever firing a shot."

Mike shuddered at the memory of the blood and viscera that covered the Chaos tanks when they finally made it to the New Jersey National Guard's rally point. "Yeah, but for every one we killed, a hundred more took its place."

"Only in the beginning, there will come a point when there isn't a huge group of people for them to murder and increase their numbers. Then when they can't easily replace their losses, we'll be able to push them back."

The small satellite radio sitting on the front slope of the tank began to blare the emergency broadcast signal and several men from the company wandered over toward Mike's tank. The radio had long ago stopped that noisy nonsense because *everything* was an emergency, so this must have actually been something important to the men on the ground. He glanced at the Chaos officers and NCOs and smiled; best to put on a good face.

Once the series of beeps reached a crescendo, they stopped and a female's voice came out of the speakers. "*This is the Emergency Alert System. There have been confirmed reports of multiple commercial airliners shot down over both the Atlantic and the Pacific Oceans. Last night, seven airliners filled with US citizens were shot down by a combined European Union response and at least four planes bound for Australia and China have disappeared. No one has claimed responsibility for any actions against the Pacific flights.*

"*In a statement given by the President of the European Union, Viktor Blythe has stated that the planes were ordered to divert from the European continent before they were ultimately fired upon. From this point forward, planes or boats from the Americas will not be allowed to cross the 30th Meridian for fear of allowing the zombie virus to spread beyond the Western Hemisphere. This is a major departure from Mr. Blythe's previous declaration that the EU would assist the United States in any way possible. It would appear that we are truly alone in our fight against the zombies.*

"*In a joint statement this morning, the US and the Canadian governments have issued a general evacuation for the eastern sections of their respective nations. Every US citizen east of the Appalachian Mountains is hereby ordered to move westward to refugee processing centers in Birmingham, Nashville,*

Louisville, Cincinnati, Cleveland and Buffalo. If you live in the eastern part of Canada, you are ordered to move west of Ottawa to collection queues in Toronto, Barrie and Sudbury."

The woman's voice was replaced by a computer-generated male voice, "*This has been an announcement from the Emergency Alert System. Standby for a repeat of this message.*" The EAS tones sounded again and the men stared at each other in silence.

"Does that mean that we're ordered to evacuate also, sir?" someone asked from the small group surrounding Mike.

"No. We're here to delay these fuckers so our people can get away to those refugee centers," he answered.

Or maybe we are supposed to go, how the hell do I know? The New Jersey Guard colonel was less than open with information. He was a Military Police officer by trade and kept information close to his breast. To make matters worse, he didn't understand how to use any of the forces under his expanded command. Mike had gone to him several times with recommendations on improving their location, but after the first time he hadn't even been able to get in and see the man because his adjutant wouldn't allow it.

"Sir, where's the closest refugee center to Hoosick Falls?" Burtucci, one of the younger privates in the company, asked.

The commander thought for a moment and said, "I guess it would be Buffalo. Did your family evacuate before we left?"

"My dad didn't believe all of this was real, so he refused to leave. My mom wouldn't leave without him. Now that this is official, I'm hoping they left."

Mike decided that Burtucci's parents were dead. If they didn't leave before the horde swept north and took out most of New England, then they were likely part of the mass of zombies moving this way to attack. That was a sobering thought, *What if some of his soldiers were faced with their reanimated loved ones? Cross that bridge when we get there...*

"I'm sure they did. We'll see about getting a phone number or something for the Buffalo place," he glanced at the first sergeant.

"On it, sir," Top said with a curt nod.

"Alright, any more questions?" he asked the men circled around his tank.

The first sergeant waited for a few seconds. When no one ventured another question he shouted, "Okay, get back to your tracks and get ready. If the Jersey Guard's intel can be believed, those fuckers will be here within a few hours. That doesn't mean that some of them won't be early."

Mike sighed and pulled his cell phone from his pocket. He sent a quick text message to his wife in Hawaii. He'd hoped to be able to call her today, but they'd been in a constant run-and-gun since the battle at the Tunnel. He tapped out a quick message saying that he was alright and that they were going to stop the creatures in New Jersey before they killed any more people. He typed it as a reassurance for her; he hoped that it was true.

*****

14 October, 1328 hrs local
Troy Meadows Defensive Perimeter
Parsippany-Troy Hills, New Jersey

The sound of machine gun fire echoed across the marsh as the defensive line of tanks half a mile away fired their weapons. Shawn Ford stared across the open space in front of him toward the tree line which ran alongside the highway and hid his view. On the other side of the trees, so close that it seemed like he could almost reach out and touch them, was where the tankers fired their weapons at God only knew what.

In a daze, he looked down at the rifle in his hands. The weapon seemed impossibly heavy and foreign to him. Shawn wasn't a soldier. He'd spent his entire life about ten miles from this very spot, growing up in Newark. After high school, he began working full time in the family's Italian restaurant. He'd gotten married to his high school sweetheart and had a beautiful daughter less than two years afterwards. Now his wife was dead and probably getting shot at by the tanks over on the road while she marched forward as part of the ever-growing zombie horde.

He and his wife, Shana, had been trying to pack up the car to leave town when the creature stumbled around the corner of their row home directly into Shana, who held an armload of picture albums. Shawn didn't even have a chance to react before it had ripped her throat out and her arterial spray coated his face. It tasted salty. God help him, the only thing he could remember about that day was that his wife's blood was salty.

The fight or flight syndrome that people in television shows always talked about was real. It took hold of him and he ran. As the zombie devoured pieces of his lovely wife, Shawn jumped into the car where little Annie was already strapped into her car seat. The last memory he had of his wife was that thing cramming a long, stringy muscle or tendon into its mouth.

He drove west away from that nightmare. They didn't make it far before he was stopped at the Parsippany-Troy Hills defensive line. Even in his sickened, blubbering state, the guards had forced him to take off all of his clothes except for his underpants for an examination. Rightly so, the sheer amount of Shana's blood that soaked his clothing and hair made them overly cautious that he'd been bitten.

Now here he was; waiting in the cold to shoot a gun that he'd barely knew how to shoot. The Army had asked if he was willing to defend his country and when he answered that he would do it as long as his daughter was safe they'd given him a rifle and the name of a facility in Cleveland where they'd relocate Annie before the end of the day. Then a sergeant had also handed each recruit four thirty-round magazines and told them to sit on the edge of the field, aim for the zombies' heads and wait until they exhaled to squeeze the trigger. That was all the training he received.

They were the second line of defense behind the armored vehicles beyond the tree line. He assumed that there was another line somewhere behind him as well; otherwise if the zombies made it past the marsh, there'd be nothing to stop them from continuing toward the center of the country.

Shawn looked left and right at the men and women beside him. None of them instilled a lot of confidence in him. He figured that they thought the same thing about him. His companions were mostly city people who'd been lucky enough to escape the carnage of the horde when it moved through the first time. Each of them that he'd had the opportunity to talk to had basically the same story as him. They'd lost loved ones and their friends were dead. Each of them had somehow escaped death and now they were sitting in the cold to fight against those things in order to give others a chance at survival.

He *was* cold. The weather was getting positively chilly and the moist wetlands that the defenders sat near didn't help. "Hey, what is that?" someone to his right yelled.

A murmur went up and down the line as everyone squinted across the marsh at the solitary figure that emerged from the trees and begun to walk toward them. "Is that a soldier from the first line or is that a zombie?" Maria, the woman next to him, asked.

He adjusted his glasses and squinted into the early afternoon gloom. "I… I can't really tell," he admitted. "Wait, there's blood all over it."

A single rifle shot galvanized the line into action as hundreds of rifles followed suit. The creature stumbled backward and fell into the trees. "Cease fire, Goddammit!" the sergeant yelled through a bullhorn. "Everyone can't shoot at the same thing or else we'll run out of ammo. We need to communicate who's gonna fire or else—"

He stopped chastising the line when the same creature reappeared from the woods. It moved even more strangely than it had before. Shawn attributed that to all the gunshot wounds, but seeing the thing still upright after that scared the shit out of him.

"You!" the sergeant yelled.

Shawn turned his head slowly and saw the man pointing directly at him. "Me?"

"Yeah. I want you to aim for its head and shoot, just like I told you earlier."

"Uh, okay…" he muttered and turned back around to where the creature stumbled into an area containing muddy, ankle-deep water.

"Nobody else shoot!" the soldier shouted through his bullhorn. "I want you to see how quickly these things drop when you shoot them in the head."

Shawn felt hundreds of eyes watching him as he pulled the rifle tight against his shoulder. At the weapons issue point, there had been training aids that showed what the sight picture was supposed to look like when you looked down the rifle. He tried to remember it, but as he looked down the rifle, it became apparent what he was supposed to do. He lined the front sight post up into the middle of the vee and then centered it on the creature's head. He took a breath and then let it out like he'd been told. Then he pulled the trigger.

The weapon bucked against his shoulder and he jerked his head up to see if he hit the thing. Nope. He turned to look at the sergeant, "What did I do wrong?"

"You jerked the trigger," he said through the bullhorn. "Squeeze it gently. The weapon should surprise you when it goes off. Try it again."

Shawn nodded and reacquired his sight picture. He let his breath out and then gently squeezed his finger. The creature staggered as the round impacted it, but continued forward. "Good job! You shot low and hit it in the chest," the soldier said after he lowered his binoculars. "Adjust your aim a little to shoot higher. We didn't have time to zero the weapons, so you have to rely on Kentucky Windage to figure out where you need to aim."

Shawn gave him a questioning look and once more the soldier brought the bullhorn to his lips. "It means your weapon is shooting low, so you need to aim high in order to make the bullet go where you want it to. Shit," he pointed out across the field. "Figure it out quick, cause more of 'em just came through the woods."

The sergeant turned away from Shawn and yelled into the bullhorn, "Okay, this is it! We need to make a stand here and allow more time for the evacuation. Remember, aim for the head and gently squeeze the trigger, don't jerk it!"

Shawn focused on the zombie that he'd been firing at. It had sunk up to its knee in the marsh and struggled to pull it out. He lined up the shot and then adjusted his aim toward the empty air above the creature. The rifle jumped against the pocket of his shoulder and the zombie fell forward. "I hit it!" he shouted.

"Good job," Maria replied beside him.

He smiled over at her and then took aim across the field again. All along the line, the reports of rifles began to sound as the defenders tried to incorporate the quick lessons that the soldier had imparted to them.

More and more of the creatures emerged from the woods and the bullhorn sounded once more, "Okay, the marsh is slowing them down and they'll get caught up in the concertina wire! Save your ammo and let them get closer. The closer they are to us, the easier it will be to hit 'em."

Shawn pulled his cheek away from the rifle once again and watched the creatures bypass the one that he'd killed. They spread out across the boggy terrain like a mass of moving ants, jostling each other in their efforts to make it to the line of defenders. It was maddening watching them get closer to the line, but he understood the logic being the sergeant's order. In the distance, he could still hear the machine guns on the tanks chattering away. *If these are just the ones that got past the tanks, I wonder what they're seeing over there*, he thought.

His attention was quickly brought back to the situation in front of him. The creatures were about three or four hundred feet away—the distance from home plate to the fence on a baseball field. Shawn told himself that he'd wait until they were half that distance before he started shooting again. A few rifles cracked intermittently around him, but most of the shooters held their fire as well.

The shooting from the tanks died down and the big vehicles' engines whined as they began to move. "The tanks are abandoning us!" someone shouted.

"We're gonna die," Maria exclaimed and grabbed Shawn's jacket. "We need to leave!"

"Maria, calm down, we've got time to get away," he reasoned. "Our families are depending on us to stop these things. My daughter is back there and I'm gonna give her every chance to make it to safety."

Her lips thinned as she accepted his answer. "You're right. I'm sorry. I've just never been in a situation like this before."

"It's okay, none of us have. We'll figure it out and make it out of here alive."

She nodded and appraised his thin frame with a quick once-over. "I'm sticking with you when you leave. Don't forget about me."

"Deal," he replied and turned back toward the field. The damn things had already made it to his arbitrary line; he couldn't be sure, but it seemed like they were moving faster than they had a minute ago. He lined up a shot just above the head of a young blonde woman with half of her jaw missing and fired.

A large mass of the things quickly became tangled in the first couple of rows of coiled razor wire that had been stretched across the marsh from edge to edge. Anywhere that the creatures came close to the concertina wire, their clothing became entangled and skin ripped open. Eventually, the pressure from behind was too great on the ones in the front and they fell completely into the wire as their brethren trampled them underfoot in their efforts to reach the defenders.

The horde moved in that sort of jerky, forward movement across all three lines of wire as the humans fired into their midst. The next hour was a blur as people shot at every type of zombie imaginable. Shawn fought down the revulsion that grew in his stomach. Yesterday or the day before, these things were living, breathing people just like him. Now they were dying by the hundreds as more than five hundred civilians fired into their mass.

Then the screams began on the far left side of the line. The ground on that side was much more firm near the road, so the creatures hadn't been as hindered as they had been in the open field in front of Shawn. The defenders who hadn't already taken off were beginning to get overrun by the creatures as they made their way up the line. "Oh, shit! We have to go!" Maria screamed.

Shawn looked one final time at the crowd of zombies in front of them and then grabbed the extra magazines full of ammo lying on the ground. He crammed them into the pockets of his coat and struggled to stand holding the long rifle. All along the defensive line, men and women had left their weapons and ammunition as they fled. He shook his head, it would be impossible to replace those once the zombies overtook the area.

He glanced one more time at the mass of creatures and then followed behind Maria in headlong retreat.

*****

15 October, 2248 hrs local
The Wall
Near Annapolis, Maryland

The Followers swarmed over the walls and defeated the hated humans who'd kept them imprisoned in the home city for so long. After that, the Master of the Chosen ordered its forces to destroy the large human settlements along the water. Then the Master ordered them to spread out to attack everywhere at once.

It was a short fight. The stupid humans hadn't put up much of a fight outside the walls of the home city since they were trying to stop the Followers that the Leader commanded far away. The creature's brethren feasted on the bodies of the humans until they turned and then helped to carry on the attack.

The Master sent its forces outward without controlling them any longer. In the fight to escape the walls another of the Chosen died, so it decided that the best thing would be to overwhelm the humans with hundreds of attacks wherever the Followers struck instead of the large mass that they'd used to destroy the large cities. The last order that the master gave was to send some of the Followers into the water. The water would carry them away where they could continue the attack once it brought them back to the shore.

FOUR

16 October, 1312 hrs local
Asher Hawke's Residence
Rocky Mount, North Carolina

"Okay, I think that's enough," Asher told his student. "Go ahead and put the rifle on safe. You've got it."

"Yeah, those last three magazines felt really good," Rachel said with a smile over her shoulder at Asher. She hoped that they could go inside soon, she was frozen to the bone, but there wasn't a chance in hell that she was going to complain. She didn't want Asher to think that she was weak or would be a burden on him.

They'd spent a lot of time the past few days going over the basics of pistol and rifle marksmanship and they'd been out in the woods behind Asher and Rachel's house all morning putting rounds through the chambers of Asher's weapons, familiarizing her across a broad spectrum of calibers. She was confident that she had a good, working knowledge of all the weapons that Asher owned.

The next morning they planned to leave in his truck and head southwest down Interstate 95. Asher had suggested that they should try to link up with an old friend of his who lived in Florida, but he'd been unsuccessful contacting him, so they altered their plan accordingly. Once they hit Interstate 20 in South Carolina they would travel west and then figure out where they were going. He confided in her that he didn't like the uncertainty, but until they could find out more details about how the fight up north was going, it was the best that they could hope for.

"Ready to knock it off for the day?" he asked.

"Yeah, I'd love to go inside and get something to eat."

"Sure. I'll show you how to take the weapons apart and then you can clean 'em while I make a couple of sandwiches."

Rachel frowned. She hadn't wanted to spend the afternoon cleaning the weapons, but she understood the requirement to keep them clean, especially before they took off. "Yeah, okay. Maybe we can make a fire and cuddle up in front of it since it will be the last time we get to do that for a while."

Asher grinned, leaning down to give her a peck on the cheek and then jerked back quickly. "Holy shit. You're freezing!" he exclaimed.

"I'm okay," she lied.

"Come on. Let's go inside. I bet Boomer is going crazy anyways."

They walked back through the yard and the Boxer shot through the door the moment Asher opened it. She barely made it three feet off the porch before she squatted down to do her business. "Guess she *really* needed to go," Rachel commented while she watched the dog.

"She'll probably go back to the fence to figure out what we were doing back there for so long."

The retired operator set her up with a cleaning kit at the kitchen table and broke down the SCAR first. He cautioned her to clean only one weapon at a time so parts didn't get mixed up and flipped on the television news before heading into the kitchen.

Rachel sighed at the news. It was more of the same thing: America was fucked. The government instructed everyone in the northeast to move west, but turn back if they encountered any of the creatures. The television coverage had just been awful, nonstop blood and gore. It got to the point that she really didn't want to see anymore, but Asher was adamant that they keep it on, even if they didn't watch it.

Another series of beeps from the television drew her attention from the bolt that she scrubbed with a toothbrush. "What's new?" Asher asked as he drifted in with two plates.

"I don't know. They just had an alert, but it didn't say what for."

"Hmm, wait, what's that say along the bottom?"

She squinted to read the scrolling message. Her eyesight wasn't as weak as Asher's seemed to be, but it was hard to see the words from the dining room. "Huh, it says the president is going to have a news conference in a few minutes."

"Here, let me put that back together," Asher said as he reached for the parts she held. Rachel gratefully handed them over to him and went into the kitchen to wash the gunpowder off of her hands.

When she returned, the SCAR was completely assembled and sitting on the table, but Asher was standing behind the couch in the living room. "Hey, the press conference is getting ready to start," he stated when she wrapped her arms around his muscled waist.

"I guess you want to watch it, huh?"

He glanced over at her and nodded silently. "Okay, sit down," she said with a gentle push against his back toward the couch. "I'll get your sandwich."

Rachel picked up the plates and brought them both to where Asher sat on the couch. He accepted the meal with a quiet word of thanks. He was totally engrossed with the broadcast. She bit tentatively into the sandwich and glanced over at her... what? Her boyfriend? Her friend? Apocalypse survival partner? What the hell were they? Sure, they kissed—a lot, which was amazing—but that was about it. She wanted the relationship to move forward, she *needed* it to move forward physically or else she was going to go crazy, but she wasn't sure if they were mentally ready for the next step.

She'd already figured out that there was a lot of shit going on up in Asher's head. Rachel wasn't sure that she was prepared to delve into his mind if he opened up one night after they took the plunge and finally had sex. That left her with staying in the pseudo-friend zone until the time was right. But she also had reservations about waiting. What if they didn't get ahead of the zombies like Asher said they would and ended up getting killed?

Asher tapped her knee and asked, "Aren't you hungry?"

"What? Oh... yeah. I was just thinking," she admitted.

He gestured toward the TV. "Yeah this is some shit, isn't it? I think we have to leave tomorrow, any later and we risk getting trapped."

She peeled the crust off one of the pieces of bread to stall before she said, "Are we too late? Did we spend too much time here?"

"I don't think so. I mean, the infection map overlay shows very little southern movement from DC; it's all north and west. Plus, I think it's better that we got as prepared as possible before taking off. You can shoot now, so I'm much more confident that you can watch my back if we get into a scrap somewhere or need to scavenge for food."

"Okay," she replied. She had to trust him; she was so far out of her element that she didn't have any other choice.

The television interrupted their conversation with the announcement that the president was prepared to give his speech from Denver. Asher rested a possessive hand on her thigh and turned to watch what the man had to say.

"My fellow Americans, tonight I come before you to report on the disaster in the northeast part of our nation. It is with a heavy heart that I report that the entire East Coast, north of Washington, is firmly under the control of our enemies and the military force that we had stationed along The Wall has been defeated.

"These enemies are unthinking, uncaring and do not respond to any type of requests for peace. Those infected with the *A-Coll* virus truly are zombie-like creatures, no longer the men and women that they used to be. The Wall controlled the scourge for more than five years as we tried to develop a vaccine or a cure. But, the zombies have escaped and now we must stop them—this includes the recently infected. There is no cure after the initial infection takes hold. They must be killed in order to stop the spread of their disease.

"Our European partners have abandoned us to our fate, going so far as to shoot down planes and sink ships that approach their coast from the Americas. We assume that this trend will continue and the United States and Canada will remain alone to fight this threat. We can no longer expect help from our southern partners either.

"The President of Mexico called me this morning. They have mobilized every police officer and their considerable military to their northern borders. President Arnesto has assured me that if any zombie is foolish enough to wander that far south, they will break against the wall of Mexican forces. He has also offered safe haven for any American willing to stand shoulder-to-shoulder with the Mexicans and defend their border.

"But there is hope. Our military and several thousand courageous civilian militia volunteers have been able to stall the creatures at the twin cities of Parsippany-Troy Hills, New Jersey. Due to their combined efforts, we've been able to evacuate the countryside around the city and we expect to hold them to the east of the Appalachian Mountains until America can mount a counterattack to take back the Eastern Seaboard.

"We may have lost the cities of New York, Boston and Philadelphia; the birthplaces of our nation, our heritage. Yes, we may have lost hundreds of thousands of citizens to *A-Coll* because they had the initial benefit of surprise and terror, but we will win out in the end. We know what is required to defeat them now and once the creatures' advance is completely halted, we'll counterattack and destroy them once and for all!"

Several people in the room applauded and the president held up his hands to quiet them down. "I have ordered the full mobilization of every National Guard unit in the United States and if they aren't already in place along the defensive line, they are headed eastward as we speak. Additionally, this morning I signed the Presidential Order that waives all background check requirements to purchase a weapon. The goal is to arm the general population and allow them to defend themselves and their families against these creatures."

The president waited to continue as the reporters in the room shouted questions. In North Carolina, Asher looked at Rachel and said, "That's big news. On one hand, it may help everyone defend themselves, but on the other hand, it opens up the possibility for more deviant behavior and then the inevitable vigilante justice."

"What are you gonna do though?" she asked him.

"No, you're right. That's probably why the president authorized it; it's better to defeat the known enemy and then deal with the unknown in the future."

On the television, the president had finished his speech and opened it up for questions from the media present. He pointed off camera and said, "Yes, Kendra."

"Sir, what do you say about accusations that you riled up the zombies by going into the city last spring to retrieve the Constitution?"

"Kendra, that's just ridiculous. They'd obviously been biding their time until the conditions were right for them to escape unnoticed. The creatures didn't suddenly overwhelm a gate somewhere. They snuck out, under the cover of darkness and struck Philadelphia before we even knew that they'd gotten out."

"How did they escape then?" a male shouted from the crowd of reporters.

President Wilson searched the group for a moment and then said, "Oh, there you are, Christopher. The truth is that we don't know how they got out yet. The zombies don't show up on infrared and all satellite imagery of the city was negative for mass movement. We still had all of our forces on The Wall surrounding the region and none of the gates were breached. They didn't tunnel out or else the ground penetrating radar would have seen it, so they didn't go under The Wall. That only leaves the Potomac. If they were somehow able to breach the gates underwater, where we haven't discovered it yet, then that may be an explanation. We'll keep everyone informed as we learn the truth over the next few weeks. Next question?"

A hand shot into the view of the cameras, "Mr. President!"

"Jim," he pointed toward the upraised arm.

"How do you respond to the allegations that the federal government is holding out on the *A-Coll* vaccine?"

"I wish that was even remotely the case, Jim. The sad truth is that we only have about, what?" He looked off camera toward Dr. Jeremy Collins, the doctor who'd developed the antidote, who called out the answer. "Right. So, we've only got about two thousand vials of the antidote left.

"It's important to stress that it's not a vaccine—we're still working on that. We can't administer the antidote until *after* someone has been bitten. The antidote only works if it's administered immediately upon transmission of the virus. Once the virus really gets going in someone's system, there's no cure besides a bullet in the brain. We've kicked the production facility up into high gear, but it's an extremely slow process since it needs to be completely synthesized."

"Sir! Sir! Over here!"

"Yes, um... What's your question, Miss?"

"Julie Arnston, CNTV. You mentioned that our military stopped the zombies' advance in New Jersey... Is that just a strong point in a sea of zombies or is that a reference point in a line all the way from the north to the south?"

"Good question," Asher said to Rachel.

On the television, the president began, "Miss Arnston, I think you know the answer to that. We held the city against a concentrated mass of the creatures headed right for it. Next question."

The reporter jumped to her feet, "Mr. President, does that mean the zombie advance has been halted?"

The muscles in the president's jaw jumped up and down as he ground his teeth together. "No. They continue to advance to the north and south of the city. The point is that we *can* stop them. They're not the unstoppable horde that people think that they are. We can beat them, but we have to set the conditions to allow for separation. Once they get up close, they use mass to overwhelm defenders, but if we can engage them at a distance, then we can stop them.

"I want to be very clear, Miss Arnston. We have found a way to kill them, now we just need the time to set up a proper defense and then we can defeat them." He folded his notes and said, "No more questions." Then he stepped away from the podium and left the room.

Several journalists called after him as he strode confidently out of the briefing room. "Mr. President!" "Sir!" "What about the weapons policy?"

Asher flipped the television off and placed his empty plate on the coffee table. "Are you ready to leave? I think things may have just changed."

"What do you mean?" she asked in alarm.

"They're going to canalize the zombies into the passes through the Appalachians so they can engage on the back side at specific areas. You heard him; they don't have this figured out yet. They're trying to get it, but part of that involves keeping them from spreading out too much. If I was in charge of this operation, I'd begin by blocking all the roads somehow and forcing the group where I wanted them to go."

"How would they ever do that?" Rachel asked. "It's just too much area."

"I don't know, but I bet he's got people working on it. I don't want to get trapped on the wrong side of a barrier."

"So you're saying that we have to leave now?" she asked as she frowned slightly.

"It's probably best."

Rachel shifted her hips and pressed in close against him. "I was going to ask this tonight, but since we're going to leave before then… Make love to me, Asher."

"Um…"

She pulled her shirt up over her head and unclasped her bra, allowing her breasts to fall from their support. "I want us to be together here, in your home before we leave."

It didn't take him long to weigh his options.

*****

17 October, 0751 hrs local
Swamp Fox Campgrounds
Florence, South Carolina

Asher rubbed his eyes to remove the crusted discharge in the corners and then stretched his arms above his head. His hand bumped into the back of the dinner table cushions which made up the bed's headboard when the camper's dining area converted into a bed. The morning air was cold on his exposed arms, but his body was warm and comfortable with Rachel's naked body pressed tight against him.

After they'd gotten cleaned up and finished loading their last few possessions, they left his house a little after eight the night before. They traveled the five hours to the campground just south of the Interstate 95 and 20 changeover before they decided to stop for the night so they could make the decision whether to travel west from Florence or if they were going to go all the way south to Jacksonville and take the I-10 along the coast. The more he thought about it, the better the coastal route seemed to Asher. It would allow them to swing far to the south of the current threat, hopefully avoiding the large push westward that might happen along his previously planned route.

During the trip south, he called Allyson's parents in Charlottesville, Virginia and implored them to leave. Whitney Harper accepted his recommendation immediately, but her husband refused to leave their home. Asher countered with the president's plan to abandon the land east of the Appalachians, but Mr. Harper couldn't be swayed. They'd lived their entire adult lives in Charlottesville and their daughter was buried only a few miles from their home. Allyson's father ultimately convinced his wife that they were better off staying put where they knew their surroundings. Asher finally relented, but made Mrs. Harper promise to stock up on enough food to last the older couple through the winter.

The conversation irked him for the rest of the trip to Florence. The trip normally would have taken less than three hours to drive, but they were delayed outside of Fayetteville, as the road clogged with people trying to make their way onto the perceived safety of the Army installation at Fort Bragg. The Highway Patrol and military police were on site directing traffic to allow the people who were passing through to continue on their way while trying to sort out who was legitimately able to go onto the installation.

Once they'd cleared the traffic jam in the Fort Bragg area, it was open until they got to the interstate changeover where it seemed like everyone was crammed in tight. Rachel had found the Swamp Fox campgrounds on her phone's map application, so they continued the couple of miles down 95 until they arrived at the RV park. They rented a space and Asher expertly backed the camper into their space in case they needed to make a fast getaway.

"Hey, gorgeous," Rachel said as she covered her mouth to block the morning breath.

"Isn't that supposed to be my line?" he asked.

She nuzzled her nose against his neck and replied, "Nope. I said it first, so you can't use it now."

"Well, good morning beautiful. How about that?"

"Doesn't count, it's from a song," she teased.

"Huh? What song?"

"It's a country song," she replied. "Ooh, I've gotta pee, let me out!"

He obliged while she climbed over him and he admired her naked ass as she stepped lightly across the camper's cold linoleum floor. *God, she's got a nice butt*, he mused. *It's the perfect pear shape, reminds me of...* he shut the thought down. Allyson was gone; there was nothing to be gained by thinking about her sexually. She'd been an amazing person and he'd been lucky to be a part of her vibrant life, but she was gone. If he didn't let his memories of her go, then he'd never be able to connect with Rachel fully.

Asher groaned as he sat up. His back was stiff from the shitty mattress, they'd have to stop somewhere and buy a mattress topper. His muscles were still hard as nails, but he was feeling the years of abuse that he'd put his body through. He pushed himself off the bed and took the single step over to the kitchenette where the coffee pot sat.

He let out a yelp of surprise as Boomer's wet nose touched his own naked rear end. "Stop that!" he snapped at the dog before reaching down to scratch idly behind her ears.

By the time that he'd gotten the coffee brewing, Rachel had come back and pressed up close to him for warmth. She pulled the blanket off the bed and wrapped it around the both of them. "So, what's the plan?"

"I've been thinking about it," Asher answered. "If we stick to our original plan to travel west from here, we'll get into more traffic jams like last night since everyone from the East Coast is trying to get away. What do you think about continuing south to Florida and then heading west along the Gulf Coast?"

She thought for a moment and then said, "Do you think it would be safer to go that far south than it would be to try and get over the mountains as soon as possible?"

"I don't know. They're up in the northeast, but it's going to spread south quickly if those Army units hold in New Jersey and the zombies try to flow around them. We have the advantage of being able to go over sixty miles an hour while they walk, but if we get caught up in some kind of monster traffic jam on the 20, then we lose that advantage."

"What if there's the same kind of traffic jam in the south?"

"You're right. We just don't know what the situation is like."

She splayed her fingers wide and ran them through the hair on his chest. "Then I think the southern route might be better. If I was by myself, I'd go west at the first chance, so I bet a lot of people from the Mid-Atlantic are thinking the same thing."

He felt her shift behind him as she stood up on her toes and kissed his cheek from behind. The fact that she'd already brushed her teeth made him a little self-conscious, but it couldn't be helped right now. "So after we have some coffee and a quick breakfast, are you ready to go?"

Rachel nodded into his back, "Yeah. I'll get dressed and take Boomer outside if you want to cook something."

Asher turned around and pulled her into an embrace before disengaging and stepping back toward the restroom. "Sounds good. Eggs?"

"Yes, please. With some cheese," she answered from underneath a sweatshirt that she pulled over her head. By the time he came out of the bathroom, she was lacing up her shoes and then clipped Boomer's leash to the dog's collar.

"Come on, girl. Your turn," she muttered.

Asher watched her unlock the door and go outside. Dammit, I like that woman, he thought as he opened the cabinet to get a pan.

*****

18 October, 1317 hrs local
Highway 287 Defensive Line
Parsippany-Troy Hills, New Jersey

"Say again, Command?" Mike asked into his headset.

"I say again, you are ordered to reposition to Allentown, Pennsylvania," the voice replied over the radio.

"We're the only ground support that the dismounted defenders have!" the tank commander said incredulously.

"Understand, Chaos Six. The president has directed that we pull west of the mountains in order to maximize use of long-range weapons and give our bombers unrestricted targeting on the eastern side of the Appalachians. Once we halt their advance and remove the civilian population from their path, we will counterstrike on better, tank-friendly ground."

"What about the defenders? The civilians on the ground." He couldn't believe what they were asking him to do. They'd fought like the cornered animals that they were and kicked a lot of zombie ass over the last two weeks. The zombies had finally pulled back and stopped the constant westward push to make it around Mike's company and the ragtag mix of civilian and military men and women defending the ground behind the tanks.

"All efforts to evacuate are being made. As it stands, Parsippany is in danger of being bypassed. You put a major hurt on them, but the strategic fight isn't going to be won in New Jersey, Chaos Six. We need to preserve your tanks for the fight."

Mike Miranda slammed his hand into the side of the Abram's turret. "Dammit! They want us to relocate to Pennsylvania," he told his crew.

Sergeant Gilstrap leaned back and said, "What did they say about the guys outside, sir?"

"They're going to relocate them by truck and meet up with us at Allentown. Then we'll load up the tanks on low-boys and transport across the mountains."

"Are we abandoning the East Coast, sir?" Specialist Walker, the tank's loader, asked.

"Command said that we're going to trap them to the east of the mountains so we can go in and wipe them out," Mike said. "I don't like it, but it makes sense if we're trying to preserve the entire nation and not just a little town."

"God damn, I'm glad I'm armor, sir," Gilstrap said. "Those infantrymen are gonna be totally unsupported without us."

"I know it. God help me, I know it," the commander sighed.

He keyed the microphone on his headset again, "Alright Command, this is Chaos Six. Send me the grid to where we're going and I'll move my company."

"Sending it now. Good luck, see you soon."

He input the coordinates into his Blue Force Tracker and then made the call to the company first sergeant.

*****

18 October, 1328 hrs local
Lanidex Plaza
Parsippany-Troy Hills, New Jersey

The two observers watched the line of tanks drive south down Highway 287. "Hey, where are they going?" Maria asked.

"I don't know," Shawn admitted. "At the briefing last night, they said the armor was going to stay in place along the highway and support an offensive in a couple of days."

"Well, it looks like they're high-tailing it out of here," she muttered. "Great, what are we supposed to do?"

"I'll call the sergeant and see what he says."

"Fine. I'm gonna go pee." She walked over to the door that led down to the inside of the building where they were stationed. They'd been in the office building for the past two days after they were part of the successful repulsion of the zombie horde near the highway below them. Their sergeant had placed them at the top of this three-story building so they could look down on the highway below and report any movement by their enemy.

They'd also been able to observe the tanks lined up along the highway. They'd watched in awe as the tanks fired across the open area to the east of the road through the few skeletal trees and across the vacant parking lots. The big metal beasts had been the key to turning the tide and allowed the guys on the ground to counterattack and drive the creatures back the way they'd come.

It had been a learning experience for everyone involved. The main thing that the military learned was that the zombies were not mindless. According to the television documentary he'd seen on the initial outbreak, the zombies had acted differently then too. The ones in Indianapolis were more of the Hollywood shambling horde variety. But, the show alleged that the ones in DC had been semi-intelligent and conducted probing attacks against the defenders to try and escape.

These zombies reminded him of a hybrid of the two. They certainly seemed fine to wander aimlessly into oncoming fire and would stop at nothing to reach the humans, but they also stopped attacking and retreated the way they'd come. It was like they kept trying brute force and then when that didn't work; they'd stop and get sneaky. Shawn thought that it had been strange as he fired at the creatures with the hunting rifle he'd traded for the M4. Through the rifle's scope, he'd seen them shift all at once across the entire line; they simply turned and headed east. Those things were absolutely communicating somehow.

Maria caused him to jump when she reappeared and asked, "What'd you find out?"

"Huh? Oh, sorry. I haven't called yet."

"Give me that thing," she said with her hip cocked to the side and her hand out for the radio. "You may be able to shoot great, Shawn, but you suck as a commander."

"I never wanted to be in charge of anything, Maria. I just want to buy Annie enough time to make it to Cleveland and then I'm gonna take off myself."

"Yeah, well now we're stuck in the Army and like it or not, you're in charge because I won't do it. Now, give me the radio."

He handed the walkie talkie to her and she pushed the button on the side to transmit. "Sergeant Lumsey, this is Maria Bocanegra. Are you there?"

After a few moments, the sergeant's voice drifted from the tiny speaker, *"I'm here Maria. What are you seeing, over?"*

"The tanks are leaving. I thought the highway was gonna be the line that we held."

There was another long pause and then he returned on the radio, *"They're repositioning to our next defend site in Allentown, Pennsylvania. Headquarters is shipping everyone down there to give the Air Force a chance at them with their big bombs. We'll use Allentown as a staging site before we go over the mountains where we can trap them in the passes and make use of the terrain."*

"We're giving up everything east of the mountains?" Shawn asked.

Maria shook her head and then asked the question into the radio. *"For now,"* Sergeant Lumsey answered. *"Once we can get to a point where we're not running from defensive line to defensive line, then we're going to start counter-punching. The Army has been busy building a series of defenses on the western side of the mountains. They need a couple more weeks to get it finished, so we're moving down to Allentown while the zombies regroup."*

"Okay, so when do we get picked up," Maria asked.

"We have trucks already running back and forth. It's about 65 miles to the city, so each round trip is about three hours when you include fueling and unloading. The distance should give us about four days of prep time until the zombies reach Allentown, so we want to be ready for them."

Shawn grabbed the walkie talkie from Maria and angrily pressed the button. "When do Maria and I—and the rest of my team—get picked up? We're here at the edge of the city observing their movements and now you guys are leaving. Give us a pick up time."

Maria nodded her head. "See, that's why you're in charge."

He let out his breath with an audible sigh. After a few moments the radio crackled and then the sergeant said, *"Looks like you guys are going to be on the third trip. We need you in position there to keep observation on the zombies. Expect pick up around seventeen hundred."*

Shawn did the math in his head. Five o'clock was still three hours away. He didn't like the idea of being on the front line all by himself without the tanks guarding them. "You can't get us any earlier?"

"No. We need your group there to ensure that they don't sneak up on us while we're trying to pull back."

"Dammit," Shawn cursed to his partner. "I hate it, but it makes sense."

"What if they forget us?" Maria asked.

He shrugged. "What can we do?" Into the radio he said, "Okay. We'll expect you here at the Lanidex at five o'clock."

"Roger. We'll pick you up then. Stay safe and out of sight. Out."

The radio went dead and Shawn set it down on the low wall that ran along the top of the building that they occupied. He turned and rested his back against the wall and Maria sat beside him. They'd developed a friendship over the past few days of being stuck up on the roof alone together. The other two men in their team maintained the night watch and creeped out both of them, so they all avoided each other as best they could. It turned out that Shawn and Maria were both from Newark, but in reality, if this hadn't happened they would likely have never really talked to each other.

They ran in different social circles. She'd been Newark's first Hispanic female CEO of a computer company and he'd just been a part owner in his family's small Italian restaurant. Given Maria's former position it surprised Shawn that she deferred to him to be the leader of their small observation group. Maria said that it just made more sense because he was more forceful than she was by nature and gladly ceded the command to him.

"Should I go down and wake up Jon and Terry?" she asked, indicating the two National Guard privates assigned to the outpost with them.

"Maybe we should give them a heads up and let them know that we'll be leaving in three hours," he admitted. He thought about the way that those two watched Maria and asked, "Want me to go instead?"

"No, it's okay, I'll be alright," she replied, lifting her M4 rifle slightly higher to show him that she was armed. "I'll be right back."

Shawn watched her walk in a crouch to the doorway that led inside and then turned back around to the east. It was still his job—and the job of several other observation teams along Highway 287—to keep an eye on things until the town was completely abandoned to the creatures lurking somewhere out there.

The small, folding binoculars Shawn wore around his neck worked well enough to discern individual facial features out to about a half-mile and he could detect movement over a mile away with them. He scanned the area in front of him from left to right, but didn't see anything. It had been quiet for two days. His outpost had only seen five zombies since the big fight a few days before.

Of those five that they'd seen, he'd shot four of them in the head and Jon had shot the other one on the night shift. The other two watchers slept for about half of the day while Shawn and Maria were on guard and then they switched at night so Terry and Jon were on guard while the day shift slept in the office below. It worked well to keep them apart from each other.

The door creaked and he turned to see the three of them come slowly over to him so a zombie watching from the wood line wouldn't notice their movement. He nodded to the two newcomers and said, "I guess you heard the news."

"Yeah," Terry stated. He was a driver at FedEx when he wasn't participating in weekend drills for the Guard and his hulking frame showed that he spent a lot of time lifting heavy boxes. "So Maria gave us the rundown, but what's the plan?"

Shawn allowed the binoculars to rest at the end of their strap against his chest and turned completely around to face his group. "What do you mean? The plan is that we leave in three hours when they come to get us."

"No, man. I mean, how are we gonna do it?"

"Oh, *that* kind of plan," he replied and then thought for a second. "Okay, what about if we pack up our gear—you shouldn't have much—and then we'll consolidate it down by the front door. We'll observe from up here since we don't know if they'll come into the Plaza or if they'll just stay out on the highway. I'd be willing to be that they'll stay on the highway since they can get away quickly instead of getting trapped in the Plaza with all the small roads and buildings everywhere."

"So we don't know where they're going to pick us up at?" Jon glared over the top of his glasses.

"It didn't come up." Shawn responded. "They were busy trying to coordinate their withdrawal."

"And how do we know that they'll even come get us?" Jon continued. "I mean, we're way out here on the edge of everything; wouldn't it be easy to just abandon us too?"

"Yeah, it would," Maria cut in. "But think about it. They're not abandoning people, they're abandoning the location. We're gonna need every person that we can to fight these things later on. Just do your job."

"I don't take orders from a woman, Maria," Terry retorted. "Especially from some illegal Cuban bimbo. You better remember that or you'll regret it."

"What the hell, man?" Shawn said as he placed a restraining hand in front of Maria. "We're all in this together."

Jon cleared his throat and said, "The Army doesn't give a shit about four people out here in the hinterlands. Once the zombies realize that the tanks are gone, they're gonna come streaming in here, fast. We should get going while there's still a chance to leave."

"Yeah, but if they abandon us, we're just four more potential zombies that they'll have to fight later," Shawn reasoned. "They'll be here, guys. But in the meantime, we need to pack up our gear. Maria and I will stay up here while you guys make sure you have everything you need. Then, we'll need you to come up and change out with us so we can pack. Any questions?"

"I think they're gonna leave us, man," Terry reiterated with a glare at the Hispanic woman.

"We'll cross that bridge when we get there," Shawn said. "For now, let's plan that we're gonna get picked up and go pack our stuff."

He turned back, bringing the binoculars up to his eyes. It wasn't worth arguing with them. They were both so headstrong that they couldn't see beyond their own preconceived notions of what the military would do. Nothing moved out across the highway in the parking lots, but there were several buildings across the way that created a huge blind spot where anything could sneak up behind. Shawn didn't like the position, but it beat being down on the ground in the defensive line every day of the week.

"Good job putting those two back in line," Maria said beside him. "I don't get it. This is hard enough in the first place without people complaining about what needs to be done. It's the damned zombie apocalypse for Christ's sake!"

Shawn glanced over at her and frowned. "It's not the apocalypse, Maria. We can't think that. Otherwise, what would be the point of us fighting?"

She tapped a long, thin finger against her cheek and replied, "Maybe you're right." She thought for a second and then nodded hard. "You're right. This isn't the apocalypse; we're just fighting off an insurgency. These things are threatening our country, but we can stop them."

He grinned at her analogy, "Well, I wouldn't go that far, but I like the way you're thinking. Once we can get beyond the mountains and stop them from turning anyone else...."

She reached across and rubbed his shoulder. "I'm sorry about your wife, Shawn."

He suppressed the urge to cry; the time for crying was over. "Shana was a good woman. But I have to stop these things so Annie will have a future."

"Well, my future went down with my company and I don't have any family left that I know of, so I'll stick with you and fight as long as we need to."

"I appreciate it, Maria. I really do, but as soon as I can, I'm gonna go to Cleveland and get my daughter."

"Okay then. I'll stick with you until you leave and then find another unit to join up with."

Shawn stuck out his hand and said, "Deal."

Maria shook it, "Deal."

They sat in silence for several minutes until Maria said, "I'm gonna go check on those two. It shouldn't be taking them this long to pack up their backpacks."

"Good idea. I'll keep on watching."

The woman pulled herself up by the low wall and walked quickly back to the door. He picked up the binoculars again and looked through them. *What's the point?* he wondered. The zombies hadn't been around for a couple of days and he checked for them a few moments ago. They'd pulled back to lick their wounds and weren't coming back anytime soon.

Movement in his periphery vision around the edge of the binoculars' eyecups caught his attention and he pulled them away so he could see. "Son of a bitch," he muttered as he realized that it was the two men who'd went downstairs to pack their bags. They were taking off.

The door behind him opened and Maria burst out. She crouched next to him as he pointed toward the two deserters. "They took all of our stuff," she hissed.

"What?" he said in alarm.

"They took our stuff. Sleeping bags, food, water. It was starting to get dark, but I think they even took our backpacks."

He looked through the binoculars again, sure enough, Maria's purple backpack bounced off the back of one of the guys. "Can we shoot them?" she asked.

Shawn looked back at her. "No. We can't do that." He sighed and then slapped his fist against his thigh. "Dammit! Why wouldn't they just wait for the trucks?"

"You heard them. They think we're getting abandoned."

"Now they've deserted us. Classy guys," he replied and then had a thought. "Crap! We need to secure the door."

"Those assholes!" Maria exclaimed and stood back up.

Shawn briefly considered taking the radio with them, but decided against it in case someone tried to call while they were trying to sneak around. The radio would be a dead giveaway to their location. He set it down and followed Maria to the door that led to the building's stairwell. She had her M4 against her shoulder as they descended and Shawn wished that he had kept one of the military rifles instead of trading for the hunting rifle so he could shoot quickly in case something was in the building with them.

They reached the first floor landing and he peered through the small window in the door that opened into the cubicle farm. It seemed empty, but from where he stood, he couldn't be sure. "Alright," he whispered. "I'll go first, cover me. If anything bad happens, get back in the stairwell and up to the roof. Intel says that they can't climb stairs, so you should be safe."

"Got it."

He pressed the handle down and gently eased the door open while still staying in the relative safety of the stairwell. Nothing jumped out at him so he placed a tentative foot into the office space. Long shadows stretched across the floor as the sun angled in from the west. Cubicles and other pieces of office furniture created deep patches of darkness that could hide other survivors or zombies who'd made it through the doors that Terry and Jon undoubtedly left open.

Shawn doubted that there were any of the creatures in the building since he'd have seen them cross the highway, but he'd feel stupid if he was ripped to shreds because he didn't properly check the area. Maria stayed in the cover of the stairwell so she could shoot anything trying to sneak up on him.

He padded as silently as possible across the space toward the door. The shadows were so damn disorienting that he was certain they were full of creatures waiting to finish him. He risked a quick glance back at Maria and she gave him an encouraging nod to keep going. It was nerve-wracking but he finally got to the door and twisted the lock home.

He relaxed slightly, but knew that he still needed to clear the floor before they could feel safe. *Dammit! Why didn't the trucks just come directly here and pick the two of them up? If they'd done that, Jon and Terry probably wouldn't have deserted either.*

Shawn's nerves were shot by the time he'd walked around the entire lobby and office space, but they were safe. "Okay, let's go back to the third floor and see what they left us," he called softly to his partner.

When they got to the offices that they'd shared, everything that Maria had gathered over the past few days, including the precious few belongings that she'd salvaged from her home, was gone. "Those dickheads," she muttered.

Shawn grinned in the darkness despite his anger. He'd never heard the woman curse before. "They knew that most of the stuff in that bag was just personal stuff from my house in Newark," she continued. "I had photos of my parents in there, some cards and letters from my past, my jewelry box and a couple of changes of clothes. They didn't need any of that stuff; they just did it to be hurtful."

"You're right. If we see them at the Army camp in Allentown, we'll make sure to turn them in for theft and desertion," he stated.

"I'll stab one of them in front of the other one until he tells me where my things are," she promised. "What did they take of yours?"

Shawn was luckier than Maria had been since he'd put his pack inside a desk drawer. They'd taken his sleeping bag and the food that he had sitting on the desk, but they hadn't found the bag with his clothes and the family pictures of Shana and Annie. He breathed a sigh of relief because those pictures would be the only memory of his deceased wife that he'd be able to pass on to little Annie when she got older.

He shouldered his backpack and said, "Alright, let's get back up to the roof. We left the radio up there and they might have been trying to call."

"Yeah, okay. Lead the way, boss."

No one called the walkie talkie the remaining two hours that they watched together from the roof. They both checked their watches repeatedly as the five o'clock deadline drew near with no word from the Army if things were still on track. The thought of being forgotten was maddening and they had to convince themselves to give it time and let the evacuation continue.

Finally, Sergeant Lumsey called with only fifteen minutes to spare. "*Observation Team Four, this is Sergeant Lumsey.*"

Shawn picked up the radio and mashed the button down, "This is Shawn Ford."

"Alright, Shawn. The trucks are moving down the highway toward your location from north to south. They're picking up the first three teams and then they'll get you. You should be seeing them soon."

"Thank you!" Shawn almost shouted into the microphone. "Do we go down and like wait for them or what?"

"That's dependent on your cover and concealment to the highway. The creatures are still out there, so you need to stay safe while you're waiting for the truck."

Shawn popped his head up over the wall to assess how far they were from the highway. It was about one and a half football fields away, so it wasn't too far to jog with the little bit of gear that they had. He sat back down and lifted the radio to his mouth, "We're going to stay on the roof to observe. When we hear the trucks we'll run down to the road."

"Alright, I'll pass that info on to the drivers. See you soon."

The radio went silent and he unzipped the backpack. "Let's pack up everything so we can make a break for it as soon as the trucks come down."

"Good idea," Maria agreed as she grabbed the binoculars from around his neck and put them down inside the bag. Then she adjusted the strap on her rifle so it wouldn't bounce when she ran.

They only had to wait a few minutes until the sound of the big Army trucks' engines echoed through the plaza. Shawn put the backpack on and cinched the straps down tight. "Okay, that's them. You ready?" he asked his partner.

"Yeah, let's go," she replied. Once again, Shawn found himself following Maria's lead as she opened the door and took the steps downward.

FIVE

18 October, 1704 hrs local
Wedgewood Golf Course
Allentown, Pennsylvania

"Geez that was a long trip," Mike said as he stretched beside his Abrams tank.

"Yes, sir. But I got us here alright," Greeley said with a toothy grin.

They'd made the seventy-mile trip from their last defensive position in New Jersey to their location on the golf course in just over three hours. The time spent in the seat wasn't the problem, they were used to that; the distance wore on the men. Traveling in a tank—even with the vehicle's superb transmission and shock absorption—was not the same as taking a trip in a car. It was much more stressful because of the constant monitoring of the systems that was required.

The company commander counted to make sure that all twelve of his remaining tanks were present as well as the first sergeant and the headquarters contingent. They'd need to lager somewhere secure soon to perform maintenance on the tanks or else they wouldn't be much use to the Army. Frankly, Mike was surprised that none of the vehicles had gone down yet. The giant, hulking beasts were a wonder of modern military engineering, but as such, they needed constant attention and the operators had been hesitant about performing even the most basic preventative maintenance because it made them targets for the roaming zombies.

He hoped that the distance that they'd just added between the last known location of the creatures would give his men—and himself—some confidence that they had a couple of days of relative safety so they could do some work on the tracks. At the very least, they had to do the "After Operation" maintenance listed in the operator's manual and refill the fluids that one of the first sergeant's big trucks had been carrying with them since Hoosick Falls.

"Yeah, you got us here alright, Specialist Greeley. Good job seeing those signs too; otherwise we would have gone to the grid that we'd been given downtown."

On the way south along Interstate 78, there had been hastily-made road signs directing the tank company to go to the golf course. That suited Mike just fine since the open fairways gave them much more maneuverability and standoff distance if they had to fight. He'd called Command the moment that they arrived and learned that they'd be staying for no more than three days as they continued the westward retreat to the mountains.

He called the company's leadership together and gave the order for half of the crews to begin doing maintenance while the other half stood watch. It didn't take long for the golf course to look like any other field lager site as the men started their priorities of work and personal hygiene using wet wipes and washcloths.

Unfortunately, it also didn't take long for the locals to come out and begin pestering his men for protection against the creatures. It got so bad that Mike had to have the first sergeant set up a perimeter guard to keep the bystanders at bay. He didn't want to react to a situation quickly and accidently crush a civilian who was trying to stay close to the vehicles for defense.

He took the opportunity to call Trinity and the girls out in Honolulu. They'd been there since the morning after his father had called him to warn about the zombies in Philadelphia and he hadn't gotten very many chances to call her. He'd been skeptical of his old man's story, but as he'd listened to the older Miranda's experience, Mike had decided that it was better safe than sorry and sent his family away. A slight hitch in his chest made him pause as he thought about Marcus and Alice Miranda. They'd be long dead by now. He prayed that their zombies had already been killed so he wouldn't have to face them at some point in the future.

Mike had always been a realist. As such, he pushed aside the emotions. He couldn't do anything about his parents. He tapped the send button to complete the call to his free-spirited wife. They'd made for quite the pair;

he was a straight-edged military man while his spouse was more of a hippie than the neighborhood soccer mom.

The phone rang twice before Trinity picked up, *"Hello? Mike, is that you?"*

"Hey, baby. How are you?"

"Oh my God, I'm so glad that you're okay. The president said on the television that we lost New Jersey and that was the last place I—"

"We're okay. We repositioned to Allentown, Pennsylvania to rearm and refuel. Then we're going over the Appalachians into the prepared fortifications as a defensive line where we can use our tanks' weaponry to our advantage instead of sitting along a highway or tunnel." The ability to talk openly about their plans over the phone or radio was about the only advantage to fighting the undead instead of a human enemy.

"When can you come to Hawaii?"

Mike sighed. He didn't want to get into a fight with his wife on one of the rare occasions that he got to call her. "I can't come until we defeat the zombies. If my tank company hadn't been there, a lot more people would have died."

"You aren't a superhero, Michael. Somebody else can do this, you need to come to Hawaii and take care of your family. The girls need you... I need you. You've done enough, we need you here."

"Jesus, Trinity! I can't even fly there, okay. The Chinese or the Russians would most likely shoot down the plane. They're both trying to keep the virus trapped in America before it gets loose. I'm stuck here until we beat this thing."

She was quiet for a moment and he could tell that she struggled to hold back her tears. *"Do you want to talk to Brooke?"*

"Yeah, put her on," he said. Hearing from his three-year-old daughter would brighten his mood. It had started getting sour when the civilians came around and got worse as his wife refused to listen to reason. If men like him—a whole lot of men like him—didn't stand up and stop these things, then they'd lose the country, maybe even the entire planet.

"Hi, Daddy!" the little girl said into the phone.

"Hey, baby girl. Are you taking care of Meadow?"

He allowed himself to become lost in the conversation with his little girl for a few minutes of peace.

*****

18 October, 1709 hrs local
Lanidex Plaza
Parsippany-Troy Hills, New Jersey

Shawn and Maria reached the first floor and raced across the office space toward the door. The two remaining members of the observation team were ready to get picked. Their military point of contact had told them that the plan was to defend on the far side of the Appalachians where the creatures would be forced to go through the passes, canalizing them into easily manageable smaller groups instead of the large mass spread across a wide front. The humans would wipe out the zombies and then counterattack to take back the East Coast. After that, they'd spend months, maybe even years combing through the countryside in order to ensure that every one of them were gone.

Maria reached the door first and twisted the lock to open it. "Wait!" Shawn hissed from behind her.

"What?"

"We need to check to make sure that the way is clear."

"We were just up on the roof, Shawn. There's nothing out there. Let's go!"

He started to protest, but she was already pushing the door open. "Dammit!" he replied and rushed after his partner.

The night was getting darker as they raced around the corner of the building toward the highway. Shawn hoped that the trucks knew which building that they'd been in, otherwise it would increase their run by almost another hundred yards to come up parallel to the next building along the road.

Leaves crunched loudly under their feet as they ran across the small grassy area between the plaza and Highway 287. *Too much noise!* Shawn's mind screamed. They sounded like a herd of elephants and if there were any of the creatures around, they would zero in on the sound instantly.

It took them far longer to run the distance than Shawn thought it would as they finally burst out onto the pavement. The trucks' headlights shown weakly in the early evening light and he cursed as he realized they were still almost fifty yards away.

Shawn and Maria had expended almost all of their energy in the flat out sprint from the building and adding another run would likely put them over the edge of exhaustion. They started jogging slowly toward their salvation in the trucks when the eastern side of the road erupted in movement as thousands of zombies appeared from the far side of the road.

Shawn shouted out a warning and raised his hunting rifle to fire into the crowd of advancing zombies. The men in the trucks saw them as well and opened up with their machine guns. The creatures had timed their attack perfectly. Before the observation team could make it to safety, the undead completely ringed the trucks.

The men in the trucks fired wildly in every direction and rounds chewed up the ground around Shawn. "Maria, watch out!" he cried.

She didn't hesitate as she dove into the ditch in the direction that they'd come. Shawn paused for a moment to see if the trucks would make it out of the ambush, but it was too long. He was hit hard from the side and his rifle went tumbling down into the grass where Maria had fled. The dead hands of one of the zombies clasped onto his jacket sleeve and yanked him back the opposite direction toward its open mouth.

Shawn pulled his arm through the sleeve and turned out of the coat. He felt his backpack with their meager supplies and the pictures of Shana slip off as well. He chose to save the pack by dropping his rifle and grabbing it with both hands. Once he was free, he took off at a sprint after Maria.

The crashing of the leaves ahead told him where she'd likely gone and he yelled for her. The noise stopped and he pushed ahead blindly.

"Stay right there, Shawn," Maria said from the darkness.

"We've got to get back to the building!" he shouted.

"Were you bitten?"

He thought about her question and then felt his arm. It didn't feel damp from blood loss and there wasn't any pain. "No. It grabbed my jacket and I lost my gun."

There was a shifting in the leaves and then she said, "Okay, come on."

Shawn jogged forward and felt his way into the end of Maria's rifle. She had it leveled right at his stomach. "Are you sure that you didn't get bitten?"

"Yeah, I'm—" the crackling of dead leaves behind them near the highway propelled them into action. They forgot about checking Shawn for zombie bites and ran back toward the building that had been their home for the past several days.

He pulled up next to her, panting. "Can we make it back... To the office?"

Maria's arm shot out and said, "Its right here. Let's get inside!"

They felt their way around the building and it temporarily blocked out the sounds of their pursuers... It was getting darker by the moment and Shawn's hand slid over the rough block as they ran to help him stay close to the safety that the building provided.

The walkway ahead darkened with the shadows of the creatures as they emerged around the side of the building. Maria made it to the door and pulled on it in desperation. It didn't budge.

"Fuck!" she screamed in frustration. They'd gone to the wrong building.

*****

19 October, 1121 hrs local
Perdido Cove RV Resort
Pensacola, Florida

Asher checked his watch, it was almost noon and Rachel was still asleep somehow, even though he'd done all the driving. They'd driven more than eleven hours the previous day down the eastern coast of Georgia and then began heading west once they reached Jacksonville. When they finally made it to Pensacola, the girl had directed him to drive the ten miles from the interstate to the Perdido Key barrier island where they'd stayed in the RV park overnight. Asher had almost collapsed from the exhaustion of driving so far with the camper and had been grateful for the stop.

Last night, Rachel had petitioned him successfully to stay the entire day in Pensacola. He didn't want to admit it, but they needed a break from the constant planning and traveling. She was brand new to all of this and he wasn't anywhere near as young as he needed to be to keep up the sustained operations. She wanted to go sit down near the water and relax a little and he agreed that they were probably far enough south and west from the danger area out on the little island that they could afford to stay over for an extra night.

During the trip, he'd constantly monitored the announcements from the Emergency Broadcast System and everything seemed to be still north of Washington. There were some sketchy reports of the creatures being seen in Virginia, but the area was sparsely populated after the nuclear detonation, so it was hard to determine if those reports were accurate. The military units surrounding the city had been overrun and there was no one nearby to keep the zombies trapped behind The Wall, so it made sense that the creatures were likely in Virginia also.

Those reports were hard for Rachel to understand, but he'd been able to read between the lines. All it took was some patience and a significant force could be snuck behind the units around the city. The Army had likely been engaged to their front and then got rolled up from the side or the rear. He'd told Rachel about what he'd learned from his old buddy Hank Dawson about the creatures doing the same thing in the initial outbreak, taking out three or four of the refugee camps before they were stopped. The military had been able to make use of sonic pulse cannons to suppress the creatures and dispatch them before the outbreak spread beyond targeting the refugees.

He'd told her about his team in DC. They had the futuristic-looking sonic pulse devices with them when they infiltrated the city, but they'd never had a legitimate need to use them. Because of the four-hour recharge time, he'd made the decision to hold off on their use at the time, but hindsight being what it was, he could have used it successfully when they had to fight a defensive battle just to get into the National Archives.

Telling Rachel about the cannons had reminded him to try calling his friend Hank again. Since the retired Delta operator lived in Florida, Asher wanted to see if they could possibly stay the night before continuing their westward trip, but the man had been smart. The moment that he'd heard that the zombies were in Philadelphia, Hank Dawson flew his family to their timeshare in Honolulu 4,500 miles away.

Emory still had the survivor website and Hank had his retirement paycheck for income, so they didn't even need to get additional jobs to continue being able to make ends meet. To Hank—and to Asher—it made sense. He'd fought against an army of the Type Ones and lived to tell the tale. Asher was positive that there were some more of the originals left in the city, the Type Twos were just too stupid to act in a concentrated manner the way they had when they'd went after Allyson in the apartment building. Plus, the way they'd snuck out of DC into Pennsylvania convinced him that there was at least one of the creatures pulling the zombies' strings.

"Mmm... Good morning," Rachel murmured from the bed beside him, interrupting his thoughts.

He looked over. Her lithe, naked body was barely concealed underneath the blanket. "Morning," he answered. "Did you sleep alright?"

She stretched her arms above her head and the covers slipped down to expose one of her light pink nipples. "Mmm hmm," she said without covering back up, they were long past that awkward phase anyways.

Rachel sat up and glanced over at the curtained window. "What time is it?"

"Almost noon. You want some coffee?"

"Yes, please. I must have been exhausted. What time did we go to bed last night?"

He pushed himself up off the mattress so he could make her a cup of coffee. "Um, sometime around one or two."

"Last night was so nice... baby." Asher could tell that she had hesitated a little before she tried the nickname on for size.

He turned and handed her the half-full cup of coffee but held it out of reach until she gave him a kiss. After she'd accepted the cup he sat back down beside her and picked up his own mug from the floor where he'd placed it without worrying about Boomer getting into it—she hated coffee. "So we're at the beach, what do you want to do before we have to leave tomorrow?"

She took a long sip from her coffee and then said, "I want to go for a walk along the beach. It's too cold to go swimming but I bet it's just lovely near the water."

"Alright. Boomer will love it," he replied. "We'll have to give her a bath in the shower once we get back, though. We won't want that wet, smelly dog in the cab of the truck with us."

She nodded in agreement and then asked, "How long have you been awake?"

"A couple of hours." Asher held up the small handheld radio that he'd been listening to. "I've been checking for any more information."

She frowned and said, "Are we ever going to get past this? I mean, is it ever going to be normal again?"

"I hope so. We have to hope that the military and police will do their jobs and stop this."

She placed a hand lightly on his forearm and then tightened her grip like she didn't want to let him go. "Are you sure that you're okay going *away* from the fight instead of running toward it?"

He thought for a moment before he answered. He'd asked himself the same question a lot over the last couple of weeks. Maybe he was getting too old like he said all the time, or maybe Rachel had given him a reason to not go back. Subconsciously, there must be some truth to that since he hadn't rushed off to join some type of defense force or link back up with the military when the zombies first escaped into Philadelphia. He'd done his part and now that he was responsible for Rachel's safety, he had a valid excuse for not getting involved.

"I'm fine. I've done my part. I've fought these things before and we accomplished the mission they sent us to DC to do. It's time to let others step up and do their part." Then he looked sidelong at Rachel with a grin and said, "Besides, I have Boomer to look after."

She pulled him toward her by the arm and he had to hold his cup up to keep from spilling. "I'll give you something to look after, Mister!"

It took them a few hours to emerge from the camper. When they did, they walked hand-in-hand down to the water's edge while Boomer dug in the sand. They waved to several other couples and even a few kids were on the narrow strip of sand that the resort boasted.

The RV park was less than half full, but the presence of families on the beach was a welcome surprise to the couple. They'd been so caught up in escaping the menace in the north that they had forgotten that more than seventy percent of the country was still clear of the infected. Asher was convinced that with proper strategic, non-nuclear targeting, they could kill all of the creatures and end the threat.

Even with his mind constantly drifting back to the northeast, it was almost a perfect afternoon. The weather drifted up into the low 60s and they were comfortable in long sleeve shirts while they strolled across the beach. Asher bought them each a cup of Italian ice as a mid-afternoon snack and they walked out onto one of the small, empty boat piers that dotted a portion of the resort's grounds.

"This is perfect, Asher," Rachel said. "I wish that we could have started seeing each other before all of this... stuff."

He didn't want to ruin the moment, but he also wasn't going to agree with her assessment. If they'd begun a relationship before this, then he wouldn't have gotten to know Allyson and learned how to open up to a woman. Because of that relationship, he'd been able to connect with Rachel faster than he ever would have imagined possible. Even that had been unintentional as he'd been mildly irritated with her when she first started to be around him and he'd slipped into his old ways of wanting to be alone.

"Yeah, this has been a perfect day," he conceded. "Thank you for being here with me."

Rachel slipped her shoes off and sat down on the end of the pier to eat her ice cream while she stared out at the waters of the Gulf of Mexico. Her feet dangled over the edge, several inches from the surface of the water as it slowly surged back and forth. Asher set his treat on one of the support frames and bent to take off his shoes as well. Then he turned to loop Boomer's leash over a mooring anchor to keep her from running off while they were sitting with their backs to the shore.

Rachel screamed and fell into the water. Asher twisted around, lunging after her to try and grab her, but she sank below the waterline before he could reach her. He stared at the murky water for a second to see if she would pop back up, but when she didn't, he jumped off feet-first into the waves.

Asher went down to about ten feet before his toes touched the sandy bottom. He felt outward in all directions without coming into contact with anything but the pier's wooden pylon. He kicked over a few feet in the opposite direction, but still didn't find her. His oxygen soon began to give out, so he pushed himself toward the dim light above.

His head broke the surface of the water and he looked around, there wasn't anything visible. On the pier above, Boomer barked frantically at him to come back out of the water. He scissor-kicked his legs while he regained his breath and then inverted in the water to dive back down. He wasn't as cautious with entering the water this time since he knew how deep it was and went all the way to the bottom once again.

Asher alternated between searching under the water and shouting her name when his lungs forced him to go up for air. After ten minutes, he gave up; there was no way that she would have been able to survive underwater for longer than that. The best freedivers in the world could only hold their breath for ten or eleven minutes at a time; Rachel had screamed when she fell so she hadn't even had the opportunity to catch her breath. The former SEAL surmised that she got caught in some type of intermittent rip current below the surface and was pulled out to sea.

He reached up, grabbed the bottom of the pier and pulled himself from the water as he'd done hundreds of times back in the Navy. Boomer licked the salty water from his skin as he lay back on the wooden planks. He pulled the cell phone from his pocket to call 911, but it was soaked through and ruined. He dropped the useless hunk of plastic onto the deck and banged his hand against the pier in frustration.

Then he remembered Rachel's purse and sat up quickly. He dug through it until he found her phone and dialed the emergency services line. The operator said that she'd send a car immediately and within minutes he heard the wailing of sirens making their way toward the docks. He slipped his shoes back on and jogged out to the road to meet the officers.

They assured him that the department was already sending divers, but he could see in their eyes that they knew she was gone. It was likely the same look that was in his own as he talked to them. The two officers asked him the requisite questions to try and determine if foul play was involved, but they didn't seem too interested in going beyond the basic line of questioning.

Back on the pier, Boomer barked like crazy and jerked against the leash toward the shoreline. "What in the world?" Asher exclaimed. The dog had the leash in her mouth and tried frantically to chew her way through it.

"Looks like your dog is gonna hurt herself, Mr. Hawke," one of the patrolmen stated.

"Yeah, I'm gonna go out and get her before she falls off and drowns."

"Probably best," the other said.

He jogged out toward where Boomer struggled and she snarled at him. "Whoa, girl! Take it easy." The moment he lifted the leash off the mooring, she bolted toward the shore, pulling him off balance. It took a considerable amount of strength to keep her from dragging him and she choked herself on the collar trying to pull away from the end of the pier.

"Hey, what the hell is wrong with you, Boomer?" he muttered through clenched teeth.

She acted like she was trying to get away from something, so he looked over the edge into the water. A toothy-faced zombie grinned back at him.

*****

19 October, 1648 hrs local
The Castle, Smithsonian Institution Building
Washington, Dead City

The Master strode into the larger room connected to the place where it normally stayed during the day. The Followers on the walls reported that the Leader had returned to the home city and the Master knew that something important must have happened.

The Leader stood listlessly in the center of the room, staring blankly at the Master as it walked into the room. Despite its size, the Followers who were present turned their heads or looked at the floor in difference to its position.

You have come home, the Master's words projected into the Leader's mind.

Yes, I have news, it replied in similar fashion. *The large cities along the water belong to the Chosen. Our Followers move toward the remaining humans, but they run away and do not fight.*

Why is this?

We do not know, Master. Our forces have grown. There are so many of the Followers that I can no longer control all of them. Send another to help me.

It cannot be, Leader. Another of the Chosen was destroyed in the battle at the walls. There is only one other besides you. The other takes our Followers along the water the opposite way. As its mind spoke the words, the Master pointed southwards.

From deep in its memories of the time before the change, the Leader remembered the gesture to place its hand across its chest as if it could feel pain. *Now there are...* The creature struggled to remember the words and then, *There are three of the Chosen remaining.*

Yes, the Master replied. *The Master will stay in the home city. You will attack the humans. The Followers that you cannot control will kill what they find. This is acceptable.*

The Leader inclined its head in difference to the Master's wisdom. If it and the other Leader moved the Followers away from the water, they could continue to change more humans into the Followers and destroy the hated men who were far less superior to the Chosen.

SIX

19 October, 1721 hrs local
Perdido Cove RV Resort
Pensacola, Florida

The creature that looked up at him from the water wasn't really grinning; the skin around its mouth had simply rotted away to reveal the teeth beneath. It startled Asher so much that he fell backward, hard, onto his ass hitting the wood planking with an audible *thud*.

The thing hauled itself up the pier quickly, launching itself against the supine retiree. He brought his foot up just in time to catch it low in the abdomen and halting its momentum. The zombie was so waterlogged and rotten that his shoe pierced the putrid flesh, impaling the creature with his foot. It continued to reach for him with its outstretched arms, apparently unaware of the devastating injury to its midsection.

"Hey!" Asher shouted to the two police officers standing on the shore. "Help!"

The men looked at each other for a moment before acting. They'd heard the news and saw more footage than they cared to about the zombies up north, but they were almost a thousand miles from where the zombies were supposed to be and that way of thinking made them both hesitate. Both officers looked back and forth between the creature and the safety of their police cruiser.

Finally, the younger officer overcame his fear and started running toward Asher, who struggled for his life with the creature on the edge of the pier.

Asher heard the steps of the men running across the wooden planking, but he was helpless to do much more than keep his leg extended out in front of him so he could keep the creature as far away from him as possible. He had to keep his other foot planted on the pier to keep the thing from completely bowling him over. He was thankful that he'd kept himself in peak physical condition. If he'd taken the route that most of his former teammates had done upon retirement, then Asher figured that he'd likely be done for already.

He felt more than saw the police officers skid to a stop near his head. "Get off of him... Uh, sir."

"Just shoot it!" Asher said through gritted teeth as he struggled to keep his foot against the creature's spine. It had had redoubled its efforts now that there were multiple targets and it took every bit of Asher's strength to keep it at bay.

"I... I can't," the older cop said. "We have laws and—"

The sound of his partner's Glock 22 discharging into the creature's face interrupted his statement.

"Jesus Fucking Christ, Garrett! What the fuck?"

The fight left the zombie immediately and it slumped forward down onto its knees. Asher brought his opposite foot and pushed with everything he had. His foot—and shoe—pulled free and the creature tumbled into the Gulf with a loud splash.

"Holy shit! Holy shit! I just killed someone..." the kid muttered as he stared at the zombie floating face up in the water.

Asher stood up and clapped him on the back. "Thanks. I don't have anything on me that could have killed that thing without getting myself infected."

Garrett looked up from the body and focused on Asher's face. "What was that?"

"That was a Type Two zombie," Asher answered as he wiped gore from his shoeless foot onto the pier. "You need to get the governor's office on the phone and tell them that there are zombies down here... Immediately."

The older officer held up his hands, "Now wait a minute. Who the hell are you to tell us what to do? I ain't reporting anything until we've done our investigation."

"Don't be stupid, officer. That was a zombie. It came out of the water and attacked me. Just report it and let the people at the state capitol determine the response. The important thing is to get this out there. People need to know if these things are coming from the Gulf. You can bet your ass that they're coming from the Atlantic too. They're trying to flank the perimeter that the government is setting up."

The younger of the two had recovered enough to speak. "Come on, Mr. Hawke, all the reports that we've gotten said that they're up north, but to be on the lookout for strange behavior."

"My foot going into somebody who didn't care that it happened to him would be pretty strange behavior, don't you think?"

"Who are you?" Garrett asked.

"I'm former military," Asher said, which was *technically* true. "I fought against these things last year. That's a damned zombie in western-fucking-Florida—"

Asher stopped short and then looked down at the floating body. "Holy shit. I didn't even think of that, Rachel must have been attacked by that thing."

He replayed the incident in his mind as the officers asked questions that he ignored. She'd been sitting with her feet near the water and then suddenly screamed when he was bent over taking off his shoes—one of which was now missing in the creature's abdomen. That was why he couldn't find her, not a rip current below the surface of the water.

He sat heavily on the wooden pylon and rested his forearms on his knees. "I think I know what happened to Rachel," he muttered as he looked up at the police officers.

"What's that, Mr. Hawke?" Garrett asked.

"I think she must have been attacked by that thing."

"Then where's her body?"

"I don't know. Fuck. She trusted me to protect her from those things. Goddammit, I—"

"Mr. Hawke, calm down. Getting upset about things isn't going to help matters," the young police officer said.

Asher looked hard at the man for a moment and then let it go. "Are you going to call the state government about the zombies?"

"We'll ask our chief," Garrett replied.

"And I'll have to report the shooting. Damn! Hold on, I've gotta go call this in."

Things developed quickly then as more police officers began to show up and Garret was relegated to sitting with Asher. The officer took a liking to Boomer and she wouldn't leave him alone, regardless of how many times her owner tried to coax her away. The new police officers arriving on scene relieved the young officer of his weapon during the initial investigation but other than that, treated him like they normally would have.

Once they recovered the body from the water, it was plainly evident to all the officers who saw it that they weren't dealing with a person. Under their high-powered flashlights, they were able to see the severe damage that the creature had already sustained from its trip around the tip of Florida and into the Gulf of Mexico. There were zombies coming out of the water on the Gulf Coast.

The police chief called the state investigator's office immediately and Asher was glad to see the ball get rolling; he just hoped that it wasn't too late. If all the coastal towns could figure out a way to defend their shoreline against the invading force as they came out of the water, then they might be able to keep the underbelly of the nation safe from the scourge. The next thing that needed to be done was to alert the federal authorities of the situation so they could warn the island nations of the Caribbean and Central and South America.

The expanded investigation determined that with zero evidence to the contrary, the zombie must have killed Rachel. The police let Asher go back to his trailer and had Garrett take him in the police cruiser since he was missing a shoe that must have fallen out of the zombie into the water when they recovered the body. He had to drag Boomer away from the officer when it was time to go; she'd really taken a liking to him.

He cleaned up in his camper's shower, washing away the filth and gore that had dried to him during the lengthy police investigation. When he came out of the bathroom, Boomer stood in front of the door whining softly. "What is it, girl?"

She glanced at him and wagged her tail, but turned back toward the door and whined again. "You need to go outside?" he said with inflection and she wagged her tail once more.

"Okay, let me get dressed." Asher put on some clothes and shoes. The dog was acting strangely. She never just stood and stared at the door when she had to go out, she usually scratched at it or came to him and whined. The difference in her attitude was enough to make him grab his pistol and slide it into the oversized pocket of the hoodie that he'd put on to guard against the cold.

He unlocked the door and pushed it out into the night. Boomer almost knocked him over as she darted out the door and squatted less than two feet away. Asher stepped down out of the camper onto the gravel parking pad and walked out into the chilly night. He looked unconsciously toward the Gulf where the incident at the pier had happened.

Asher caught himself staring into the darkness and shook his head. *What am I doing? I need to start heading west.* The sound of a twig snapping behind him made him twirl and draw his weapon. After decades of training, he dropped immediately into a shooter's stance with his shoulders squared into the darkness. Nothing moved in the night and he slowly relaxed.

He stared into the darkness, cursing his older eyes for losing some of their sharpness. "Okay, let's go inside, Boomer," he told the dog and she turned to walk back into the camper.

She was halfway up the steps when she stopped and sniffed the wind, then a low growl came from deep in her throat. Twigs cracked under the feet of someone rushing from the darkness. Instinctively he slammed the trailer door behind the dog and before he could turn to face his attacker to fire his pistol, she was on him.

He'd seen a streak of blond hair before throwing his hands up and braced himself so he didn't lose his footing. Rachel bit hard into his forearm and he kicked out, connecting with her thigh. The chewing didn't lessen and he bashed the grip of his pistol into her shoulder blade. Rachel's clavicle collapsed with an audible snap and he brought the pistol down directly onto her shoulder joint, dislocating it. She finally pulled free and he felt a wetness flow down his arm.

Fuck! Asher kicked hard into her knee and the patella collapsed. He stepped backward and she toppled over onto her side. One of the characteristics that had freaked him out when he faced the creatures in Washington was how quiet they were when they weren't in a large group. Rachel's zombie was no different, regardless of what he'd done to her, she stoically continued to attack.

Even with a buckled knee, she struggled to stand. When she couldn't accomplish that, she began crawling toward him, pulling herself along with one hand across the gravel while her useless, dislocated arm dragged behind her. He took several steps back away from her to keep out of the reach of her crooked, grasping fingers.

Asher knew what he needed to do. As he continued to back away slowly, his mind raced. *She's not infected, she's just sick. I can take her to the hospital and they'll give her some medications and everything will be okay again. Why the fuck did we stop. I could have driven farther yesterday. I'm such a fucking scumbag for promising her that I'd take care of her.*

He knew that it was his responsibility to dispatch Rachel, but he had feelings for this woman. He'd just been intimate with her less than twelve hours before. Was God punishing him for all the things that he'd done in his lifetime? Over the course of his career in the Navy and at the CIA, he'd done a lot of unspeakable acts. He'd taken part in things that no one would ever hear him say, and now he was paying the price for it. First Allyson and now Rachel; they'd both paid the price for being too close to him.

He continued taking short steps back away from his former lover, leading her away from the camper while he thought. Asher made the decision to put the pistol back in his pocket; he didn't want to attract more of them if there were any around. It made him sick to his stomach to think that he was going to have to bash her brains in.

He risked a quick glance back toward his camper; it was still twenty feet away. He had a baseball bat just inside the door, but a little further inside was his tomahawk with a spike on the opposite side of the axe head.

After a quick nod to himself, he turned and jogged back toward the camper. The tomahawk would be the most humane thing without using his pistol, which wasn't registered in Florida. *It's strange the things that go through a person's mind once they know what they need to do,* he thought. *Who cared if his guns were registered at a time like this?* According to the Smithwick-Greenspan Gun Registration Act, anyone who discharged a non-registered gun in a state or territory not previously declared was subject to immediate arrest. Getting locked up was the last thing he needed when these fucking creatures were coming out of the water in Florida. He'd seen movies where inmates were left behind bars during the apocalypse. Starving to death with no way to kill himself wasn't high on Asher's bucket list.

When he opened the door, Boomer bolted through and put him off balance. "Boomer, no!" he yelled after the dog. She leaped across the short distance and landed near Rachel. The dog darted in to bite the creature's neck, but the teeth piercing her flesh didn't register like it would have on a human and Rachel grabbed the dog's front leg.

With a vicious twist, the zombie snapped Boomer's leg and pulled the helpless dog toward her mouth. Asher was too slow to react before Rachel's zombie sunk her teeth into the Boxer's throat. She jerked her head back and dark blood erupted into the night. He stopped short and surprised himself by letting out a soft sob.

"Goddammit, Boomer..." he muttered. There was nothing he could do for her now except avenge her. He went back to the camper and pulled the tomahawk from its nail near the door. Rachel had continued crawling toward him and was now less than five feet from where she'd first attacked him at the camper's door.

Asher stepped across the gravel and twisted the tomahawk in his grip. Her fingers brushed his boots as he slammed the spiked side of the tomahawk into the back of her head. Rachel's fingernails scratched a few more times against the leather on his shoes and then stopped moving completely.

He left the weapon impaled in her brain and staggered back to the camper. When he got inside, he ripped his shirt off and examined the wound in his arm. "Fuck. Goddammit!" he muttered and slipped sideways into the table.

His stomach started to twist and perspiration poured from his armpits. This was the start of the change. Rachel's saliva had gotten into his arm when she'd bitten him. He slumped down onto the bench seat and thought about the antidote that he had stashed away in his first aid kit.

"What's the point?" his words came out slurred as if he'd been drinking. He'd lost so much over the course of his life; two marriages, friends and teammates. Now in the course of six months he'd lost two women whom he could have spent the rest of his life with and even his dog was dead, killed by the fucking diseased creatures that he would soon become. The pistol slipped from his pocket and he cocked the trigger to ensure that it would only take three tiny pounds of pressure to fire the weapon.

He wasn't afraid to die. He'd faced death so many times that it no longer held any mystery for him. The gun found its way to the side of his head, a few inches behind and above his right eye. The .45 ACP round would crash through his skull and scramble his brain before he even had a moment to think about avenging Rachel and Boomer's murders.

What? He dropped the pistol to the table and rode the hammer forward. Asher was ashamed that he'd even considered committing suicide instead of seeking revenge against the zombies. Suddenly, everything lined up in his mind. He would go to Washington and find the Type One that controlled the zombies and kill it. Then the Army would be able to defeat the Type Twos that would blindly continue attacking into the face of their modern weaponry. His debt would be paid, and maybe the forgiveness that he thought of more and more often the older he became would be granted if he could destroy the leader and give his nation a chance at survival. But first, he had to stop the change that he felt coursing through his veins.

Asher tried to stand, but fell sideways out of the bench to the floor. "Ugh," he groaned and pushed himself along the linoleum toward the bathroom with his feet. Moving was so much harder than he'd expected it to be. The disease was taking hold of him quickly, but he continued pushing forward. *What was it that the FBI guys had said? Within one hour? Two?* He couldn't remember.

Finally, he made it to the bathroom where the first aid kit was under the counter. He willed his arm to work and brought it up over his head so he could open the cabinet. After a couple of tries, he got it open and pulled the kit from inside. It plopped heavily down on the floor in front of him. The zipper took several more tries to open and he dug through the kit until his fingers wrapped around a small glass vial.

The handwritten label swam into focus as he held it in front of his eyes, **"*A-Coll* antidote. Dosage: 20cc in vein, NOT artery for faster absorption. Must be administered within three hours of infection. Serum contains *C. tetani,* a bacterium which causes tetanus and lockjaw. Handle with care."**

He set the vial down on the floor and dug through the kit for a syringe. *Mother fuckers must be stronger than I am if they can last three hours,* he thought. He found the plastic tube and pulled that out of the box. With some deft maneuvering, he was able to pull the needle cap off and used his teeth to pull the plunger back and fill the tube with air before pushing the needle through the self-sealing rubber stopper on the antidote's vial.

He used his chin to inject the air into the vacuum-sealed glass vial and then pulled the plunger back out with his teeth. He held the needle upright while it was still in the vial and pressed the plunger back in to get the correct dosage. With any luck, he'd have another dose or two for future use. The toilet began to beckon as he wanted to crawl over and throw up, but he had to focus. *Which one was a vein, inside or outside?*

He thought back to his days in the Navy when he'd been the Team medic. It was a long time ago, but then it hit him. The Basilic vein was the large, visible vessel that could be seen on the inside of his elbow. The arteries were deeper in the arm. He hoped that he survived long enough to feel stupid.

The needle slid awkwardly into his arm and he cursed when he realized that the angle was too shallow; all he'd succeeded in doing was to skim the top of his vein and cut it open. He pulled the needle out and blood oozed out of the hole, adding to the mess on the floor. He had to go an inch higher along the path of the vein to get above the area he'd just injured and increased the syringe's angle. There was a slight resistance as the metal pierced the vein and then it slid in easily. When he was satisfied that the needle was where it needed to be, he injected the antidote.

*****

20 October, 1913 hrs local
Green Hill Plaza
Parsippany-Troy Hills, New Jersey

Maria nudged her sleeping partner. "Hey, wake up," she said. "It's getting dark outside, we should get ready to move."

Shawn rolled over on the hard tile floor and groaned. "Crap. This wasn't all just a bad dream?" he muttered.

She frowned and started to say something bitchy, but that wouldn't help their situation one bit. Instead, she smiled and replied, "Nope, we're living our own little shitty version of the apocalypse; right here in New Jersey. On the plus side, it was a beautiful day of zombie watching, guaranteed to keep even the angriest Cuban woman entertained. Wake up."

"Ugh. Are we gonna try to move like we'd planned this morning?"

"Yeah, I've been watching through the blinds for about twenty or thirty minutes since I woke up, but I haven't seen much movement outside except for some trash blowing across the street. They're all gone again."

Maria watched her fellow refugee walk to the deli's front window and carefully pry apart the blinds to look out into the vacant parking lot. When they'd gotten trapped outside of the wrong building two nights ago, they'd ran as fast as they could away from the horde sweeping through the Lanidex Plaza where they'd been assigned as observers by the Army for a few days.

They ran as fast as they could, dodging around the trees in the parking lots in an attempt to lose the zombies that pursued them. The creatures once again acted differently than they'd expected them to. The change was the third alteration to their behavior in as little as two weeks, so the pair was confused about their true nature or if their reactions to events were random.

When they first met the zombies in the bog, they'd attacked mindlessly, not caring about their injuries or death. But they'd also been cunning and could track down people who hid from them. Then, they acted as if they were concerned with losses and withdrew to find a way around the defenders in Parsippany—which is why they had to abandon the city or risk getting encircled. On the night that they fled from the horde, they'd acted like Shawn had always read about fictional zombie behavior. Once the humans had escaped the mob's line of sight, the creatures continued on in the last direction that they'd been heading without any inkling that their quarry had gotten away. It was very puzzling for the two of them.

They'd slipped the creatures and stumbled upon the little shopping center that they were in now just after nine o'clock that night, which when Maria thought about it, was simply pathetic. The shopping center was less than half of a mile from the plaza and it had taken them almost three hours of meandering and hiding to reach the strip mall.

Shawn had used Maria's rifle to break the lock on the door since he'd lost his when he had to take his jacket off because a zombie had grasped his arm. Once the lock was gone, they'd tumbled inside and hid out of sight from the shuffling group of zombies that pursued them. Within a few hours the creatures disappeared and they watched for movement outside well into the night until sleep had finally overtaken them in the early morning hours.

The sound of distant gunfire woke them up. A quick peek through the windows showed hundreds of zombies milling around the street in the pre-noon sun. Throughout the day, the creatures were thick in the surrounding area, but as the sun started to go down, they began to disappear. By midnight, they'd completely disappeared and the two of them watched most of the night without seeing any more. Then, this morning, the creatures had reappeared. Once more, they'd eventually gave in to their exhaustion, but not before they decided that the creatures must not be active at night and that their best bet for moving would be after darkness.

Maria walked back to the deli's restroom to relieve herself. It was disgusting in there, what with both of them doing their business for two days, but it beat shitting on the floor or going outside for the fresh air. She wrapped one of the green aprons that the employees had once worn around her mouth and nose and entered the room.

When she was complete, she wished for running water for the hundredth time—both to flush the toilet and to wash her hands—but the water had been out for several weeks. It stopped flowing shortly after the power grid completely failed. Of course, she had no way of knowing for sure, but she figured that the apocalypse was worse off for women since they had different requirements for staying clean.

Maria shook her head as she squirted hand sanitizer onto her hands and walked from the back of the store. She couldn't let herself go around calling this outbreak the "apocalypse" anymore. If she did so too many times, she'd end up believing it and losing hope. If she lost hope, then she'd probably end up getting killed in some stupid way.

"Hey, I've been thinking about what we could take with us from here," Shawn said when he saw her.

"Okay, what've you got?"

"Well, we can't take these, because they're too noisy," he said as he held up a handful of personal-sized chip bags before tossing them on the counter and opening one of the foil-lined containers. "But, we could take all the apples that haven't gone bad yet and we can take the hard salami in the back. I think everything else is either spoiled or too noisy, like the chips." He crammed a handful of the triangle-shaped cheesy snacks into his mouth.

"Well, we need to find a grocery store to hole up in tomorrow during the day," she replied. "I've got a shopping list of things that we need."

"Oh, yeah? Like what?" he asked.

"Like, well..." *Ah, the hell with it,* she thought. *He's gonna see the evidence in the bathroom anyways.* "I need tampons, Shawn. I started my period just now."

He held up his hands and answered, "Okay, never mind! I don't want to know the rest of your shopping list!"

"Well, we need to go. What if... What if those things can smell blood or something?"

Maria could see his face pale several shades in the dim interior of the deli. "I hadn't thought of that. Do you think they can?"

"How the hell should I know? Four weeks ago, I honestly didn't even believe that the zombies really existed in DC. We know for sure that they can see and hear. What if they've retained all of their senses?"

Shawn's face got the pensive look that it sometimes did when he really thought about a problem. After a few seconds, he said, "I don't think they can. Remember all those fights we were in on the east side of town?"

"Yeah, of course."

"Well, when people got injured, the zombies didn't swarm to them for the blood or something, they just kept on coming like they were only concerned with what they could see."

It was a thin hope at best, but it was something. "I hope so, otherwise we're done for. I've got a pretty heavy flow."

He threw the bag of chips on the counter. "Okay, that's it. I'm done."

"Don't be childish, Shawn. It happens to women; I can't do anything about it. We need to be serious about this."

"Yeah, sorry," he replied, properly rebuked.

"Okay, let's pack up then. I'm ready to try and make it back to our guys and then over the mountains."

They spent the next few minutes packing the food and bottles of water into a few bags. Shawn fit what he could into the backpack and then they made a makeshift knapsack from a few of the deli's aprons using the neck loops for shoulder straps for Maria. She made one more stop in the bathroom to change the toilet paper that she'd layered in her underwear and grabbed two more of the rolls to put into her sack.

Two knives from the deli completed their ensemble. As soon as he picked them up, Shawn told her that they'd need to find real knives with sheaths instead of these. She nodded noncommittally. If they happened upon a hunting store or something, then so be it, but she wasn't willing to alter their westbound course too much just to find some weapons. In fact, if the zombies continued to act in their current manner, then she'd just prefer to hide and avoid them entirely. However, that was one of the problems with these damn things; they didn't have any idea what was normal for them.

They peeked out the blinds a few more times to ensure things were safe. Once they confirmed that there wasn't anything outside the deli, they moved the table that they'd shoved in front of the door and Shawn led the way with his knife held out in front of him like it was a crucifix to ward off vampires. The thought made Maria grin in spite of their dire situation.

The early evening was already cold with a biting wind that found its way into all of the openings of Maria's clothing. It wasn't anything that she wasn't used to as a lifelong resident of New Jersey, but it still took her breath away after the warmth of the deli. They crept along the front of the building until they get to the corner and Shawn risked a quick glance down the side of the building toward the east. They were still alone so they ran across the road toward what looked like the beginning of a residential neighborhood.

They jogged down the middle of the street; it made more sense to keep in the center of the road to give them the most reaction time from either direction. Within a couple of blocks, they came to a T-intersection and they went left. Before long, the stress of being out in the open combined with the light physical exertion of jogging overcame the evening chill and Maria felt sweat dripping down the crease in her low back where her muscles came together and then sliding between her ass cheeks.

The road they were on curved in what Maria thought was almost due south direction and she wished that they had some sort of map. For all they knew, they could be on a loop that would feed them back westward out onto the road near the strip mall where they'd spent the past few days. Maria reached out and tapped her silent running partner when they reached an intersection. "Where are we?" she whispered.

Shawn nodded and pulled up his gait. He lifted the cheap flashlight that they'd procured from the deli and shined it on the street sign; they were at the corner of Lake Shore Drive and Berlin Road. "Okay, what does that mean?" Maria hissed.

"I know there was a lake in the southern part of town," Shawn replied. "I saw a map at the Army headquarters the day I volunteered to fight so they'd evacuate Annie. I wish we had a map or something now though."

"Do you know if this road curves back to the east, or can we keep following it until we get to a highway?"

"I don't know," he muttered. "What we need is a damned car! Do you think any of these houses have one in the garage?"

"Maybe?" she answered with a shrug.

He seemed to contemplate going to one of the houses and then reconsidered. "Where do the zombies go at night?"

"I don't know, man," she said quietly. "What are we doing?"

"As long as we don't end up going back the other way, we should keep going. We'll find a place to rest a few hours before the sun comes up since that's when they seem to be active. Maybe there will be a car that we can use."

Maria nodded and then realized that he couldn't see her in the darkness. Instead, she said, "Okay. Let's get going, then."

They started up their slow jog once more and after thirty minutes, they passed by a large firehouse on the right. Shawn stopped them. "We should go in there. I bet they'll have maps of the area."

"Good idea." She unslung the M4 rifle that she carried and followed behind Shawn. White letters on the front door indicated that they were at the Lake Parsippany Volunteer Fire Department. Her partner pulled gently on the doors and to their surprise, they weren't locked. The air didn't smell like any of the dead creatures were inside, but with the weather being so cold, they likely wouldn't rot as fast, which would help to keep the smell to a minimum.

Once the door closed behind her, Maria called out softly, "Anyone in here? We're survivors."

They waited a full minute before Shawn turned and twisted the lock home in the glass door behind them. They proceeded slowly into the firehouse, calling out that they were uninfected and asking if anyone was around. It would be stupid to get shot by a jumpy refugee taking shelter in a firehouse; it would be even more stupid to stumble into a nest of zombies with no way out. *They had to go somewhere in the night,* Maria reasoned, *but where?*

The building was vacant, so they secured the back doors as well and searched the dispatch room for a map. Just as they thought, there was a map of town on the wall. It turned out that they'd somehow gotten off of Lake Shore when the road continued straight and ended up on Halsey Road. The firehouse sat about a half-mile from Highway 202, which ran north and south on the far west side of town.

After another few minutes of searching, they found a folding tri-state map, which covered New Jersey, Pennsylvania and parts of New York. "Okay, we have a choice to make," Shawn stated once they'd looked at the map.

"Shoot," Maria replied.

"Okay, we know that the Army went southwest to Allentown and then they'll jump further west after that," he said as he jabbed his finger into the map near the Army's new defensive area.

"Yeah?" she prompted.

"Do we try to follow the Army or do we head due west down Interstate 80 on our own to get over the mountains as quickly as possible?"

Maria shifted her weight from one foot to the other. "You're in charge, Shawn. You make the decision."

"Don't give me that crap. We're a team, nobody's in charge. I think we should go due west. The zombies are following the Army and we know that the noise attracts them. We may be able to slip on by without the zombies knowing that we're there."

"Yeah, but the Army means safety."

"Does it? I mean, yeah we'd be safer if we were with them, but if we have to fight our way through a gigantic mob of zombies to get to them, what kind of safety are they providing? We would have already done all the hard work—*if* we even survived."

She hadn't thought of that. What good would it do them to travel all that way if they just got caught on the wrong side of the creatures? "Okay, you're right. So what does going due west get us?"

Maria tried to make out the pictures on the dispatcher's wall in the poor light of the flashlight while Shawn pored over the map. Smiling faces of young men in their heavy flame resistant jackets stared back at her. She idly wondered how many of them were still alive and how many of them were now part of the massive zombie horde that marched steadily westward.

"Alright, if we stay roughly on Interstate 80, we'll be about thirty miles north of Allentown. I'd be willing to bet that they'll be mostly massed near the sound of the guns—we're betting with our lives, really."

"Can we find a car?"

"That should be very high on our priority list. The map says we've only gone about two miles and I'm already exhausted."

Maria glanced at her watch. "It's just after midnight, should we keep going or stay here until tomorrow?"

"Dammit! I wanted to get out of town tonight, but it makes sense to stay here, since they're bound to have tons of supplies and we've already cleared the place. We can leave as soon as it's dark tomorrow night. We might even be able to find a couple of real backpacks if we search around."

They searched the firehouse together, neither of them wanted to be alone in the large, dark building. In the firefighters' quarters, they found a few changes of clothes that would fit them in a pinch, including a couple of sets of female clothes, and from under one of the beds they dragged out an old duffle bag that they could fill with food or the clothing that they'd pilfered.

The bathroom yielded the tampons and pads that Maria had desperately needed as well as some minor pain relievers and a fully stocked first aid kit. The little blue kit gave Shawn an idea to search the trucks for a backpack. They found a large bag topped full of medical gear that he dumped on the floor. He picked out the more basic medical supplies to take with them since neither of them knew how to use any of the specialized equipment and took the backpack so they could fill it with food.

The kitchen was a veritable cornucopia of foodstuffs. They jammed the bags full of canned goods, energy bars and unspoiled crackers. Maria even grabbed a can opener and a small saucepan that they could use to cook their canned food in if they found themselves out on the road somewhere. It was an unspoken admission that they may be on their own for a long time, far away from other people.

The last thing that they did was to go back to the garage where the fire trucks sat. They found some heavy-duty flashlights with good batteries, thick gloves and the firefighter jackets. The coat's thick material would be good to help keep them warm and act as a tough barrier for protection against the zombies' teeth.

"Do you think you could drive one of these things?" Maria asked as she slapped the side of the bright red fire engine.

"Uh, no way. They're standard transmission and I can't drive a stick."

Maria suppressed the joke that she wanted to make and said, "Damn. I was hoping that we could just take off in one of these. We'd be unstoppable."

"Probably not the low-key vehicle that we need."

"Yeah, okay. I'm tired and the sun is gonna be up soon. Are you ready for bed?" she asked.

He nodded and they trudged back through the firehouse and up the stairs to the sleep quarters. After they'd done their business and gotten cleaned up with a combination of bottled water and wet wipes, they chose beds that were next to each other, but as far away from the door as possible and settled in for a restless day's sleep.

SEVEN

22 October, 0847 hrs local
Wedgewood Golf Course
Allentown, Pennsylvania

Chaos Company began firing at the oncoming horde. The creatures walked into the line of fire with zero regard for self-preservation or tactics. Rounds from the tanks' machine guns tore into them and they died by the hundreds.

"Keep up the fire, boys! Remember to alternate between you and your wingman," Mike shouted into his microphone to keep the company firing. Less than thirty minutes prior, they'd gotten word from the scouts who were stationed on Highway 78 that the creatures were about a mile from where the tanks sat. In that time, the last few truckloads of civilians were evacuated away from Allentown to the next interim staging point outside of the state capital of Harrisburg.

The military's analysts had determined that the hordes from New York had joined with the creatures moving southwest from Maine and the remnants of those from between Philadelphia and the dead city of Baltimore to form a massive army of the undead. It made killing them *en masse* easier for the Air Force, but it also created a massive hammer that could smash through just about anything the defenders on the ground put together.

The intelligence weenies seemed to think that the large zombie army was following the US Army as it fought a delaying action, moving slowly westward toward the defenses being assembled in the passes and on the opposite side of the mountains. Besides spreading out, the zombies hadn't deviated from their course, choosing to follow the military and attacking them nonstop.

Mike's tanks were topped off with military-grade JP8 fuel and filled to overflowing with ammunition before the support elements departed as escorts for the civilian trucks. He thought about the ragtag train of civilian and military vehicles traveling to the next staging point. Allegedly, the state authorities had already begun the evacuation of Harrisburg before the first of the refugees from Allentown were set to arrive, but he didn't have any faith that the system worked as smoothly as they'd been briefed that it would. He'd seen too much "efficiency" during this war to believe that Harrisburg would be any less of a clusterfuck than the last two jumps had been.

Another thing that gave him pause was how long they could actually hold against the creatures. They'd been able to set a decent defensive perimeter in New Jersey during the month that the zombies had swarmed northward up the coast, but they'd only taken four days to move from Parsippany to Allentown and now the defenders were already preparing to move again once the transports were gone. Did they have time to delay the zombies long enough to set up a new perimeter?

Harrisburg was only about sixty miles away and if the Chaos Company tanks couldn't delay the creatures long enough, they could potentially be there in two days. They needed more time for the ground defenders to get into their trucks. Actually, what they needed was more tanks. One of the Blue Platoon's tanks went down for a cracked engine block yesterday so it would stay where it was with the crew using it as a defensive platform for as long as they could before they had to bug out.

That left him with eleven tanks to face millions of zombies as they marched westward from the East Coast. True, the Air Force had been pounding the shit out of them with conventional bombs, but the mass of zombies seemed unstoppable. Evidently, the president had learned the lesson from DC that nuclear weapons didn't work against them beyond the initial blast and had banned the military's use of nukes. The intent was to keep the land usable for the eventual re-habitation by humanity.

Mike watched his gunner decimate the creatures in front of him in the tank's monitor. Sergeant Gilstrap fired the coax at face level of the lead zombies and the rounds carried through, killing those behind them. "Sir, are you gonna get in on this fight?" his gunner asked.

"Shit, yeah. I was just thinking about our situation," the commander replied and grabbed the CROWS joystick to activate the large remotely-operated .50 caliber machine gun mounted on the top of the turret. He slewed the gun left to right to ensure that it was working properly and adjusted the crosshairs in the computer display to head height of the zombies several feet behind the leaders. That was the plan that they'd worked out, the smaller 7.62-millimeter machine guns would cut down the front ranks while the .50 cals took out the ones further back. The rounds from Mike's gun would easily carry through five or six of the creatures, effectively decimating the attack.

He feathered the trigger to fire short bursts and the Ma Deuce spit out rounds at 2,900 feet per second. Mike traversed the CROWS slowly back and forth across the crowd in front of his tank to maximize the effectiveness of the weapon. In his monitor, entire groups of the creatures collapsed in heaps, but the ones behind continued to press forward, climbing over their fallen comrades.

His headset crackled and the voice of the female radio operator from the headquarters filled his ears. "*Be advised, fast movers will be on site in less than one minute. Ensure that you are properly secured against thousand-pounders. Out.*"

Mike stopped firing the .50 cal and spoke up on the company frequency, "The Air Force is going to drop one thousand pound bombs in one minute. You should already be buttoned up, just double check that your hatches are fully locked."

He switched off his microphone and continued to fire into the horde. Mike couldn't do anything about the positioning of his men without potentially giving away their high ground on the golf course to the creatures. He just had to hope that the Air Force dropped toward the back of the mass of writhing bodies and not near the front. They were more than 1,500 meters away from the group, but if the pilots misjudged and dropped too early, even the M1A2 Abrams wouldn't be able to withstand a direct hit from that type of bomb; the overpressure alone would turn the men's internal organs into jelly.

Mike's eyes registered the explosions a half second before the sound wave hit and scrambled the tank's monitors. The vehicle rocked slightly as explosion after explosion slaughtered the zombies that they'd been firing at. After several seconds of almost constant explosions, the sound of the jets' afterburners kicking in reached his ears as they veered hard toward the north to hit the next group.

The Chaos tanks were far enough away from the impacts that he didn't hear any shrapnel hitting against the tank. But Mike knew that the troops on the line didn't have overhead cover; they only had layers of concertina wire stretched in front of them for protection. *Those poor, magnificent bastards.*

The optics on the CROWS compensated for the displacement and came back on line. Where there'd been a mass of zombies easily almost a mile across, there were now twisted, broken bodies as far as the camera's lens could see. Mike had no idea how many that meant had been killed, but it was easily in the tens of thousands in an instant.

Amazingly, things continued to move across the engagement area. Mike zoomed the camera in and scanned the ground where the bombs impacted. The creatures' bodies had been shredded by the explosions, but they continued to struggle toward the human defenders. If their brains remained intact, then broken bones and missing limbs didn't stop them in their unending quest.

He breathed a slight sigh of relief as he heard the faint, single-shot rifles of the infantrymen begin to fire. They were shooting the creatures that continued to move toward the defensive line, posing the greatest threat to the defenders. It was only a matter of time before the wire was breached or everyone ran out of ammo, and then they'd fall back and repeat the process again somewhere else.

For now, the men and women who defended their homeland could be proud that they put a major dent into the zombie population as they continued their slow, devastating advance westward.

*****

23 October, 0714 hrs local
A&P Food Store, New Jersey Route 10
Randolph, New Jersey

The creatures couldn't see very well in the darkness. Maria had figured that out the first night after they left the firehouse. They'd watched from the second floor living area to make sure the way was clear before making their move. They made the mistake of not searching their surroundings before they tried to leave the building and got into trouble. They went down the stairs, carrying their new bags full of pilfered gear and walked out the front door, directly into two zombies wandering near the street.

The creatures heard Maria's sharp intake of breath when she saw them and they instantly turned to come toward the noise. There were bushes lining the walkway that they ducked behind and the former executive was certain that the creatures would have seen them, but they didn't and continued walking toward the back of the firehouse toward where the noise had echoed.

They likely would have been able to stay hidden from the zombies indefinitely if Shawn hadn't had to shift his position because his thighs were tired from crouching like a catcher in a baseball game. The noise attracted the two zombies once again and they had to run or risk getting caught. They made it about ten feet before the sudden movement caught up with Shawn and he got light-headed and stumbled. Maria pushed him behind a large tree, but it was well in sight of the creatures pursuing them.

They didn't see the two humans and they shuffled past. The creatures even turned in a complete circle from twenty feet away and didn't see them lying on the ground. After a few seconds of casting about looking for a trail, they turned and headed in the direction that they were originally going.

"They didn't see us," Maria had said in awe. Then it made sense to them, looking back on it, how they'd been able to escape the mob when they'd accidentally gone to the wrong building in Parsippany. They'd been able to dodge in and out of the trees surrounding the office complex and lost their pursuers due to the poor eyesight and lack of critical thinking ability.

Since leaving the firehouse, they'd made their way slowly westward, but the relative peace of the nights like they'd had before was no longer available. Once the sun went down, the creatures now dotted the landscape in small groups, huddled together as the pair tried to slip past them. A few times, they'd had to throw old bottles or other trash in the opposite direction to clear the way of zombies when they chased after the noise. If it hadn't been so deadly serious, Maria would have laughed at the absurdity of it all.

They'd also had the misfortune to learn that the creatures could see very well in the daylight, though. They tried to see if they could travel in the daytime, but a harrowing chase had proven that only distance and sharp 90-degree turns would save them. The zombies weren't particularly fast, but they were relentless.

Their current planned hiding spot was a medium-sized grocery store along the New Jersey 10. They'd traveled all night long, each night for three nights and they were only about eight or nine miles from the firehouse in Parsippany. Besides the groups of zombies that they had to avoid, they spent a considerable amount of time each night searching for usable vehicles with keys. The problem with an organized evacuation was that the people took their possessions with them, apparently along with all the spare sets of keys for cars that were left behind and Shawn's jokes about Cubans knowing how to hotwire cars had gotten old quickly.

They circled the grocery warily; Shawn watched the surrounding area while Maria observed the store for movement or signs of break-ins which would indicate that they might not be the only ones there. They'd yet to find anyone else alive after they were abandoned by the Army when their pick-up team was killed, but there had to be hundreds—thousands—of people hiding in their homes and they were bound to meet up with others soon.

It didn't seem like anyone had been to the grocery store before them, so Shawn used a small pry bar that he'd liberated from the firefighters' tool chest to break into the back door. The snapping of the deadbolt sounded like someone had fired a shot in the early morning, causing Maria to jump. The noise echoed across the loading dock and off into the surrounding neighborhood.

"Shit!" Shawn hissed. "That was too loud!"

"Let's get inside," she replied with a worried look over her shoulder out toward the adjacent houses.

"Yeah, I think you're right." They slipped inside and used their heavy-duty flashlights—another find at the firehouse—to illuminate the produce receiving area.

"God, this place smells awful!" Maria gagged with her jacket over her nose.

"Let's clear this back area real quick and then secure the door to the outside," he answered. "Just be thankful that it's autumn and not summer."

The two of them walked rapidly around the stockroom together to make sure that they were alone and then returned to the door that Shawn had jimmied open.

"How do we secure it?" Maria asked, pointing to the broken handle.

Shawn shined his flashlight around for a minute until he found a large roll of packing tape. "I don't think we can lock it anymore. Maybe we should think about breaking a window or something next time." He paused and then picked up the roll. "Let's use the tape to keep it closed and then we can pile up some of these boxes in front of the door. That way, if the zombies get the door open, they won't be able to see us and think the place is empty."

"But they'll be in the way if we need to make a run for it," she reasoned.

"Yeah, but I don't know what else to do. It's better than nothing."

Maria acquiesced and they spent several minutes using the tape to hold the door closed and then another few minutes pulling the boxes of rotting produce from where it had sat for weeks. She threw up in her mouth and swallowed it twice before allowing herself to vomit onto the floor, but by the end of the ordeal, they'd successfully blocked the doorway against casual accidental opening and casual observation.

After they had the back area relatively secure, Shawn suggested that they clear the front of the store before they relaxed. They walked up and down every aisle searching for others, acknowledging that if there was someone else in the building, then they could easily have avoided the pair. When they got to the front of the store, they found an elaborate trap set up near the door.

"What the hell is that?" Maria asked.

"Uh... It looks like a booby trap or something."

The front door was unlocked. Stretched across the bottom was a thin piece of fishing line that ran to a pallet full of cans for weight. The fishing line was tied off to the end of a rope that ran through a pulley set into the pallet. The rope ran through the pulley, up to an eyelet set in the ceiling and then across to another eyelet directly above the doors. Suspended from the second eyelet was a huge rope net with what appeared to be a large grocery bag full of cans secured in the middle.

She pointed to the bag and said, "I bet those cans are to knock somebody out if they trip the wire."

Shawn looked around the store. "Whoever set this up probably knows that we're here," he whispered.

Maria was more inquisitive than her companion. "How is all of this operated?" she muttered.

She crouched near the fishing line and followed it in the opposite direction from the pallet. A razor blade was glued to the side of a carpet cleaning machine near the door. When the victim hit the trip wire, it would carry the fishing line into the razor and sever the line, causing the entire contraption to go into motion. The far end of the line attached to a brick suspended in the air.

"What the hell?" She searched a little further and saw that the brick was tied to the handle of an air horn, rigged to blow when the string was cut and the brick dropped. "Jesus, this is elaborate. Who could have done this?"

"More importantly, why?" Shawn asked. "We need to get out of here."

Maria glanced through the store's glass front. "I don't think we can. Look, some of the zombies are already starting to come out from wherever most of them go during the night."

A few of the creatures wandered across their line of sight at the edge of the parking lot. "Shit!" Shawn exclaimed. She moved quickly back to the front door and reached across the trip wire to twist the lock home.

"No sense allowing them an easy entry," she smirked.

"We gotta get out of here," he said and started toward the back of the store.

She jogged and caught up with him. "Hold on. Think about it. Whoever set that trap can't come out here in the daytime either—wherever they are. That air horn is to tell them that somebody's sprung their trap. They aren't expecting anyone to go through the back door. We might as well stay here; get some supplies and some rest, then try to leave before they come back."

Maria could tell that Shawn was considering ignoring her logic, but ultimately agreed that it made sense to stay put for now. They could stock up on non-perishable food and get some rest before they took off on the road again. She didn't like the prospect of staying where some shitheads had made a trap any more than he did, but it just made sense for them to do so. The air horn convinced her that they were likely close, but not close enough to be able to watch the store constantly.

Their first priority was to get the supplies together. They got a cart and went toward the aisles in the center of the store—which Maria usually avoided before the apocalypse. She used to hold the belief that the healthier food was on the perimeter of the store, whereas all the processed junk food was on the center shelves. Except for toiletries, she almost never went down the rows that held canned goods. Now, everything she used to eat was rotten and the processed stuff was all that survived a few weeks without power.

They quickly made their trip around the store and she said that she needed to get more tampons and some pads as well. "You can go down there, I'll stay here," Shawn said with his hands folded over his chest.

"Oh come on. We're supposed to stick together, remember?"

"You've already made me think about that nasty stuff, I don't want to have to go down there and pick it out with you too."

"Really? How old are you again?" she muttered and flicked her long, dark hair over her shoulder.

He stared back at her, indignant, so she let out a disgusted breath and walked toward the darkened interior of the store where they stocked the feminine hygiene products. She glanced over her shoulder at Shawn, but he wasn't visible. *What a childish jerk!* she thought. They were supposed to stick together, not get grossed out by human anatomy and something that she couldn't control.

When she got to the section containing tampons, she flicked her flashlight on and searched for what she needed. *The multi-pack is going to be my best bet*, she thought as she picked up the box with several different absorption capacities and placed it into her cart.

A row of smaller boxes caught her eye. *Oh, condoms... I wonder...* She glanced back where Shawn was supposed to be, but he still wasn't there. *Dammit, where is he?* The box of condoms went into her cart along with the tampons and she started walking back toward the front of the store where Shawn waited for her.

When she got to the end of the aisle, the shadows shifted and someone came out of the darkness. The last thing she saw was an upraised arm.

The arm came down and a rubber mallet connected with the side of her head. She dropped instantly and two forms stepped from the darkness into the gloom shining through the store's windows.

*****

23 October, 1202 hrs local
Asher Hawke's Residence
Rocky Mount, North Carolina

"Don't know why I left this," Kestrel said out loud to his empty home as he held up the sharksuit that he'd kept tucked away in the garage after he'd led the team to rescue Allyson and Steve Adams from Baltimore last summer. The suit consisted of thousands of tiny metal links similar to the chain mail that knights wore in the Middle Ages. The suits were designed to cover every inch of a diver's body when they went into shark-infested waters. It was also extremely effective at keeping zombie teeth from ripping into flesh like Rachel had done when she bit him in the arm.

Technically, he wasn't supposed to have kept the suit because of the radiation that it had been exposed to, but he'd placed it in a thick chest in the garage and covered it with old dental x-ray vests that he bought online years prior for a different assignment. He figured the radiation hazard was minimal since he'd worn the sharksuit under his radiation suit, anyways. Now he was glad that he'd kept it. It didn't matter to him if he survived, but he needed live long enough to complete his mission.

He'd been violently sick for two days after he'd injected the *A-Coll* antidote into his veins. He threw up all over the bathroom and even ended up shitting his pants in his delirium. Finally, he was well enough to stand and staggered to the window. Rachel's body still lay where he'd left it with the tomahawk sticking out of her head. Boomer was there as well. Nobody had come by to disturb the scene.

Asher worked his way outside and dragged the bodies into the camper. He laid them on the bed, covering them with a heavy blanket. The RV park was now mostly empty, but he was surprised that the dead hadn't been found. The police would have taken him to jail, regardless of how sick he'd been. It turned out that all coastal areas had been given a mandatory evacuation order and everyone left without so much as a backward glance.

He cleaned himself as best he could in the filthy bathroom and then made a sandwich in the kitchenette—he was ravenous. He'd become comfortable with death a long time ago, so it wasn't strange to him to have

Rachel's corpse laid out on the bed behind him. Besides, he was little more than a walking corpse himself.

The journey into Washington would be a one-way trip for Asher Hawke—the *Kestrel,* he corrected himself. Asher died with the zombie's bite. The Kestrel would make sure that this nightmare ended.

On the drive back to North Carolina, the abandoned countryside flew by. He saw evidence of rampant looting and rioting, including more than a few bodies lying unattended on the side of the road. Kestrel once again called his friend Hank Dawson to get as many details about the differences between the Type Ones and Twos as well as a refresher on their tactics. He needed to know everything about these things and Hank had spent months fighting the Type Ones during the original breakout.

"Hey, man. I need you to give me a rundown on the *Alexandria-Collins* Primaries again," he said when Hank answered the phone on the third ring. He knew that somewhere out in Denver, the DIA or NSA computers would begin recording the conversation since he'd said the name of the virus over the phone.

"*Well, hello to you too, Asher. What's this about?*"

"I'm going back to the city. I'm going to find the fucking Type One behind this and end it while we still can."

There was an obvious silence and then the soft click of a door shutting as Hank went outside or into a quiet room. "*What the fuck, man? What do you mean you're going back?*"

"She's dead, Hank. I couldn't protect her from a simple run-of-the-mill zombie. This has to stop and I'm gonna go get that fucker who's directing these things. Then the Army will be able to handle them."

"*What... I'm sorry for your loss.*" There was another moment of silence and Kestrel heard him reply to someone, "*Yeah, it's okay, babe. Old Army buddy....*"

A female voice said something that he couldn't understand and then Hank replied, "*No, I'm not going back. I... I just need a little bit, okay?*"

The woman said something else and then the door clicked closed once more. "*Sorry,*" Hank said into the phone. "*Emory's worried that someone is trying to convince me to go back into the fight again.*"

"Again?"

"Yeah, it's been almost nonstop since this began. Our old buddy Alistair Reston has called several times, asking me to come back and consult—at the operational level—not about the tactical level shit like you're asking."

"Alistair knows what he's doing. He's the right guy to coordinate and get the teams spun up on what to expect."

"I told him no. I mean, I packed up my family and ran like a little bitch away from the mainland... I hope you don't think less of me."

Kestrel grinned in spite of himself. Hank had gone into full civilian mode when he hung up the dog tags and started his family. "Nah, you did the right thing, Hank," he replied, trying to ease the guilt that was so obvious in his friend's voice. "You have a family to worry about. You did the right thing getting out of the Americas before they stopped the flights."

Kestrel paused to let that sink in and then continued, "Another thing that's happened over here in the southern part of the US is that the fucking zombies are coming out of the water. I was in Florida with Rachel when she went missing and I ended up fighting a zombie that came out of the water. Luckily the police were there and they shot it."

"Jesus, they're coming out of the water?"

He knew that if the weenies at NSA were listening in because of the keyword *"A-Coll,"* then they would pick up on that information right away. "Yeah. It was the Gulf side, so the thing had made it all the way around the tip of Florida. That's another reason why I have to take out the Type One. I don't think the thing making it that far was random—or isolated. I think they're being directed by that Primary in DC and it's trying to circumvent our defenses."

"My God. They could potentially make it all the way to South America."

"Well, they could make it anywhere in the world if you think about it. This has to end before it gets worse."

"That changes things," Hank said. He could tell from his friend's voice that he was thinking about one of those things washing up on the beach in Hawaii where his children played.

"It does, but not for you just yet, Hank. I'm going back to the city alone. I just need some intel."

"Listen, Asher. Are you sure about this? I mean, you've been there before. You know what it's like. You almost got yourself killed a few times the last time you went in."

"I already had to take an injection of the *A-Coll* antidote," he replied.

"What? You were bitten?"

"Yeah, Rachel attacked me. It was dark and I didn't know she was infected at first, but she bit me in the arm. I had to put her down."

"Shit, are you alright?"

"Yeah, it made me sick as fuck and I don't remember the last two days, but I'm slowly regaining my strength."

"Good, I'd hate to lose you, buddy."

Kestrel ignored the comment. "I'm headed back from Florida right now. I've got to stop at my house for some supplies. This is a one-way trip, Hank. I need a quick, down-and-dirty refresher of what you told me last spring when the team got your briefing at Quantico."

"Let's see," Hank said as a strange clicking noise filled Kestrel's ear. His friend had a habit of tapping his fingernails on a tooth when he was deep in thought. *"The Type Ones are the leaders. We thought we killed them all, but I'm convinced there are more of them—at least one of them. The attacks that the news has shown have been too targeted for a random mob of zombies." Tap, tap, tap.*

"If it was just the Type Twos, they'd wander around, maybe form a large group intent on reaching the same target and getting themselves all fouled up, but the footage shows these things staying together and moving as one. They attack across a large front instead of all funneling toward a sound... Nope, there's definitely a Type One keeping them focused."

"Do you think it's still in the city?"

"No telling, bro. We know the leaders can communicate, but we're not sure how. I saw one of those fuckers point at my team when we chased them down a tunnel and half of the zombies left in the room turned and delayed us."

"Okay," Kestrel sighed. "I'll go ahead with my plan to go into the city then. Any idea where one of those things might take up residence down there?"

"Well, that's the hundred thousand dollar question isn't it? There are so many theories out there, but I think that if it's still in the city and not out with the army in Pennsylvania, then it would be somewhere downtown."

"Downtown. Why do you think that?"

"We searched the periphery of that place thoroughly five years ago," Hank answered with a sigh. *"We spent hundreds of hours in the air as close*

as we could risk going near the areas of heavy radiation and we didn't see shit for a long time.

Hank warmed to the idea of determining where the creatures may have hidden and continued, "*There was always visual satellite imagery of a very large group of Type Twos staying downtown, even while there were massive firefights with the Army on the perimeter. Looking back on it, there was no reason for those things to stay downtown since we were making a shit-ton of noise during the fights; that should have drawn those things out to us.*"

It was Kestrel's turn to be contemplative. "Hmm," he answered. "Well, it couldn't hurt. I guess that's as good a place to start as any. Do you remember if they were more concentrated in certain places?"

"*I can't remember them being more or less concentrated anywhere. When you guys flew into the city, did you notice anything?*"

Kestrel thought back to the helicopter flight when they landed at the National Mall so they could go to the Archives. Nothing seemed necessarily out of the ordinary, although they did have to fight a running gun battle from the moment the team stepped off the birds. They had mobile sound buoys echoing throughout the city in an effort to draw them away, but it hadn't worked entirely.

He continued to think about it as he drove back from the south to his home. The creatures clustered around the National Mall had attacked the team immediately. Then they needed gunship support to dispatch a large group that came down Pennsylvania Avenue to investigate the noise of gunfire. There were definitely creatures being kept near the area for some reason; the more he thought about it, the more he became convinced that it was because they were guarding the Type One.

Once he completed his phone conversation with a rundown of the basic characteristics of the zombies, Kestrel made up his mind to start the search, building to building, in the downtown area. It was going to be a challenge unlike anything he'd ever faced before, though. Just to get to the city center would be at least a 25-mile walk from where he planned to go in at Gainesville, Virginia. Of course, he could go also get a boat and go up the Potomac River right to the downtown. The only problem with that plan was that the Navy was likely still patrolling the water, so if they intercepted him, it was game over.

No, the best bet for him to accomplish the mission was to go overland, right up Interstate 66 all the way downtown. It was harder—and probably more dangerous given the ground that he had to cover—but it made sense to avoid the feds; they'd try to stop him from entering the city.

He laid out the sharksuit on the garage floor before going back inside. Kestrel grabbed a quick meal of canned pork and beans and then went into the backyard where he planned to dig graves for Rachel and Boomer before he left.

It was easier to dig one wide grave instead of two, but he was still sweating freely in the crisp October afternoon by the time he'd finished digging the hole. The shadows had lengthened across his yard, indicating that night was approaching fast. He used bed sheets to lower the stiffened bodies into their final resting place and said a few words that no one would ever hear. The quick eulogy made him feel better about burying a second woman in less than six months.

"Rachel, I'm sorry that I couldn't protect you. You didn't deserve this; you came to me for help and you trusted me to keep you safe. I failed. I failed you and I failed our nation when I didn't finish the job the first time.

"I can't make up for the fact that you paid for my failure with your life, and if we meet again in the afterlife I don't expect your forgiveness. I'm going to kill that fuc— Sorry. I mean I'm going to kill that thing directing these attacks and give our country a chance to fight back. You were a great woman and I wish that we'd have gotten together under different circumstances."

He shoveled a few scoops of dirt over Rachel's body. It was just enough to put a thin layer of soil over the corpse and then he sat the shovel down. "Boomer, you were a good girl. You helped me through the toughest time in my life. I hadn't known that those types of emotions existed in me before Allyson and you were there to see me through the sorrow and pain. Oh, here you go, girl. I got you something."

He took her well-worn rubber chew toy from his pocket and gently dropped it down into the hole beside her. "Good girl," Kestrel cooed and began the slow process burying both of them.

Forty minutes later, he topped off their graves by inserting a wooden plank into the soft dirt of each. He'd used a permanent marker to write the details of who lay there and then used a clear spray paint to cover the boards to keep it from fading away in the weather. Maybe once they defeated the zombies, someone would find their graves and relocate them to an actual cemetery for a proper burial with a permanent headstone.

That someone wouldn't be the Kestrel; he was going to die on this mission. He'd survived the odds far too long and observed the death of his friends and relations far too many times. He'd be smart, take all the appropriate measures to ensure the success of his mission, but when it was over, so was he.

INTERLUDE

25 October, 0521 hrs local
Rocky Mountain Manor
Denver, Colorado

Thump, thump, thump. The pounding on the ornate wooden door sounded through the bedroom. "Mr. President! Mr. President, its Mark. Please wake up, sir."

"Oh for heaven's sake, Ryan; what does he want now?" Heather moaned.

The president briefly considered telling the White House Chief of Staff to go away. Of course, with the raging piss hard-on that he had, he also considered rolling over and having a go with his long-term girlfriend, Heather. She was usually willing to have sex whenever the president needed it, but later in the morning, not at... He looked at the bedside clock.

"Ugh," Ryan Wilson groaned. In a louder voice, he called, "Mark, it's five a.m.; what is it?"

"There's a Priority Alpha message, sir."

He rubbed his eyes with the palm of his hand. "What's Alpha mean again?"

Mark hesitated and then said, "Is Miss Wong with you, sir?"

"Just go find out what he needs, baby," Heather said with a gentle push to his back.

"Hold on, Mark. Let me go to the bathroom and I'll come out in the hallway."

President Wilson went to the bathroom and relieved himself, watching the stiffness leave his cock disappointedly. He put his robe over his pajamas and walked out where two Secret Service agents guarded the doorway to his bedroom and Mark Namath stood with a cell phone. "What's this all about, Mark?"

He held out the phone. "Sir, President Akulov is on the phone."

"The Russian?" he whispered.

Mark inclined his head, "Yes, sir."

Ryan mouthed the words, *What does he want?* Mark shook his head; he obviously didn't know. He sighed and took the offered phone.

After clearing his throat, he said, "Good morning, Vitaly! How are you?"

"Ah, Ryan! It must be early, I'm sorry to wake you, but I have urgent news."

He walked down the hall with the phone to his ear. "I'm sure it must be urgent for you to call at five a.m. so it's alright, my friend."

"Five a.m.! I'm so sorry; it is two in the afternoon here in Moscow. I would have called you later in the day if the information I have to tell you could wait. It can't."

Ryan stumbled down the stairs and Mark expertly caught his elbow to keep him from falling. He nodded his thanks to the man and mouthed the word *coffee* before answering the Russian president. "What information is that?"

"You have seen the news of the creatures from the District of Columbia coming ashore in Brazil, no?"

Ah, Ryan thought. *So that's what this is about.* "Yes, Vitaly. I've been given a briefing about the zombies reaching South America as well as a few of the island nations in the Caribbean. They're even starting to come up along the Gulf Coast and in Texas. Luckily, they're disoriented when they first come out of the water, so we've been able to dispatch them before they could cause any damage and begin another outbreak somewhere else besides in the northeast. I've ordered our National Guard to line the coast and we've informed our neighbors that they should do the same."

"Good, good! I'm glad that you are taking every precaution that you can, Ryan. It shows that you are the right man for the job."

"Well, thank you. That means a lot coming from such a powerful man as you, Vitaly."

"Taking appropriate precautions is what I want to discuss with you. There is no way of knowing how many creatures have escaped your nation and are now adrift in the ocean, is there?"

"No, of course not," the president answered as he sat down heavily behind his desk in the Manor. It wasn't the White House and the Oval Office, but they'd made a very nice headquarters for the federal government in Denver over the past few years.

"Then we can assume that there is the potential for these 'zombies' to wash up in Europe sometime in the future, no?"

Ryan accepted the cup of coffee that Mark brought him and then answered, "Yes, I guess there is a potential for that to happen if they were to somehow make it all the way across the Atlantic."

"Good. Your words steel my heart for what I have ordered my Army to do, then."

He paused with the cup raised halfway to his mouth and then slowly set it down. "What have you done, Vitaly?"

"I know that you have lost at least two full combat divisions of troops in the initial fighting, as well as many of your police officers and citizens to the zombie horde. I have ordered all four of my Vozdushno-desantnye voyska*—our airborne divisions—to begin loading aircraft. They will parachute into an area of your choosing to assist in the fight against these creatures. This is a full twenty-six thousand men. I will also authorize two motorized divisions to fly into an airport in the United States, another twenty-four thousand. Yes, my friend, I am giving you fifty thousand soldiers to assist you in eradicating this scourge."*

Ryan almost dropped the phone. He didn't know what he'd been expecting the man to tell him, but it certainly wasn't that he was going to send fifty thousand troops to American soil. "That's... Um, that's a great gesture from you. But I really can't accept it. We have a solid plan to funnel them into—"

"This is not an offer. Russia will either contribute soldiers to fight on the ground and thus prevent further spread of the creatures or we will bomb the United States to ensure that every zombie is destroyed."

"I don't... Are you declaring war on the United States?" Ryan asked incredulously. Mark, sitting across from the president listening to the one-sided conversation choked on his coffee and spilled what was in his cup across his shirt.

"No, Ryan," the Russian answered. *"I am offering assistance. I'm offering to put Russian lives at risk—toward a fight on your soil—in order to ensure that we annihilate the zombies before they destroy your country and then*

strike out against the rest of the globe. But I will do what I determine to be the best course of action for my nation if you do not accept my offer of ground forces."

"What about defending your own borders?"

"I have sent missives to the European and African nations outlining my intentions and I have recommended that they guard their coasts, much like you have done in your southern states. I have also mobilized all of the considerable Armed Forces of the Russian Federation—more than two million men in uniform. We will not allow this disease to spread into Russia."

"I don't know what to say."

"Say thank you, my friend. We are in this together, not as Russian and American, but as humans against these creatures. Together, we will be victorious!"

Ryan's mind reeled. It was true that they'd lost a large chunk of the Army that had been stationed around The Wall when the zombies broke out of the region, but he still had more than two million trained men and women already in uniform that he could put into the line, plus untold millions of militiamen. However, only about three hundred thousand of the military were infantrymen, the rest were logistics personnel, pilots and members of the Navy. The crack Russian forces would be a welcome addition to the defensive belt that the Chairman had established to the west of the Appalachians.

"Thank you for your offer of assistance, Vitaly. I guess we really have no other choice but to accept it at this point."

"That is correct."

"I'll let my Army know to expect you and tell our Air Force not to shoot down your planes."

"Thank you. Good luck, my friend. I will be in contact again soon. Enjoy your coffee."

The phone clicked dead and the president sat it down on his desk. "What's happening, Mr. President?" Mark asked.

"It looks like we're going to be hosting the Russian Army for a while," he replied.

EIGHT

26 October, 1344 hrs local
The Basement
Randolph, New Jersey

The constant sound of water dripping slowly nearby hammered into his brain and threatened to drive him insane. There was no telling how long that he'd listened to the dripping. He'd first noticed it the day that he was taken and beaten by the two men. They'd attacked him in the store while Maria—*Oh, poor Maria!*

The men attacked while he and Maria were separated. They dragged them away from the grocery store into a car, handcuffed together in the back seat. Maria was out cold, while he drifted in and out of consciousness from the blow to his head. The masked men had only driven a block or two when they went through an open garage door, which was promptly closed behind them.

Shawn didn't want to leave the relative safety of the vehicle because he knew that once they were in the kidnapper's place, the odds of escaping were much lower. The men punched and kicked him to get them out of the car and he finally relented, dragging Maria along with him. Then he had to carry her up the small set of garage stairs into a typical suburban home. Once they were inside, he was hit from behind again.

When he woke up, he was naked and handcuffed to the stair rails. Maria's muffled screams caused him to look over to where the men assaulted her. They'd used thick cord to lash her to a set of thick, wooden closet rods. She was laid out with her arms and legs spread wide. They took turns raping her for a long time, flipping the entire contraption over when they decided to go a different route on her tortured body. Blood streamed from every orifice of his friend's ruined body.

Shawn tried with all his strength to break the railing so he could go to her rescue, but he only succeeded in tearing the skin from his wrists where the handcuffs bit into them. The pain was excruciating, but it was nothing compared to what came next once the animals had temporarily satisfied themselves with Maria.

First, they used a mini baseball bat to beat him. It was one of those fan appreciation gifts that you got sometimes from a professional baseball game. The men laughed roughly as he pleaded for them to stop. By the time they were finished, his body was a mass of bruises and he could barely support his own weight. Then, one of the men, the blonde one he thought, came up with the idea to sodomize him with the bat. The other argued that he didn't want his little toy ruined. They used a full-sized baseball bat on him, cramming it into his body and laughing maniacally at his pain.

He passed out and woke up naked on the concrete floor of a dark room, still handcuffed, with his feet taped together. He didn't know where he was or how long he'd been there, but the dried, crusted blood on the back of his thighs made him think that he'd been there a while. Since then, the physical pain in his body had eased slightly when he lay perfectly motionless, but any type of movement was excruciating. He'd learned to roll to the corner so he could piss, but he hadn't had to deal with the terrifying prospect of taking a shit after what those animals had done to him.

The dripping of the water in the next room drove him crazy. He could only imagine what those two sadists did to Maria upstairs, but he was certain that she'd never walk again if they escaped from this house. Even with everything that he'd endured, he never thought about giving up; escaping was constantly on his mind.

He was certain that he could escape. His captors hadn't bothered check up on him since he'd woken up. Occasional thumps on the floor above him confirmed that he was in the basement of the house. He'd been too sore to try and slide his butt and legs through the handcuffs before, but he knew that having his hands in front would allow him to take the tape off of his feet. Then he'd find a way upstairs to rescue Maria.

Shawn rolled onto his back and brought his knees up to his chest. The pain in his body was excruciating and he felt the scabs in the creases of his asshole break open from the movement. Fresh blood poured down and pooled underneath him as his battered and broken ribs protested the pressure. He gritted his teeth to keep from crying out and slid his arms around his hips. The handcuffs scraped against his backside and tore away even more of the scabs, but he was able to work the cuffs up his thighs and finally, over his feet.

He lay on his back, panting at the exertion and a moment of doubt crept in. He wasn't sure that he had the strength that it would take to struggle up the stairs. Then, the thought of Maria trussed up and violated came back into his mind and he sat up. The blood began to flow more freely into his arms since the pressure of the handcuffs behind his back had restricted it.

The former restaurant owner grimaced as the pins and needles in his arms combined with the pressure of his bodyweight on his butt. He gently pulled the tape away as quietly as he could, unwrapping his feet and gaining feeling in those as well. The tape ripped away the hair around his ankles, but he was beyond the threshold limit of pain and barely noticed it.

Once his feet were free, he massaged the blood back into them for several minutes before attempting to stand. He'd never been a martial artist or even particularly athletic so he wasn't surprised when he couldn't stand without scooting back against the wall and pushing himself upwards. Even then, Shawn had to take a few more moments to walk around the room in an attempt to regain the feeling in his feet.

He had no way of knowing what time of day it was since he was in the basement and there weren't any windows in the room. If he went up the stairs and it was nighttime, then he may be able to kill the men in their sleep, but if it were daytime, the element of surprise would be the only advantage that he had. He couldn't afford to wait, though. He was already weak and getting weaker with each passing moment.

He turned and placed his bound hands against the wall and began walking forward, following the wall until he came to a corner and turned. He ran the length of the second wall and came to another corner. On the third wall, he came to what he was seeking, the doorknob. He tried to turn the knob, but it was locked. He let out a slight grunt of frustration and dropped his hands. But then his mind began to think logically and further process the situation.

The men upstairs were likely occupying it as a matter of convenience due to its proximity to their elaborate trap at the grocery store. The previous residents, hopefully safely away, probably wouldn't have put a lock on the *outside* of a door. He reached out, once again wrapping his hands around the locked handle. Then he traced the curve backward slightly and found the lock. A quick twist disengaged it and he cautiously opened the door.

The adjoining room wasn't quite as dark as the one he'd been locked in because a small sliver of light shown underneath the door at the top of the basement stairs. The miniscule amount of illumination allowed him to discern the outline of furniture and some haphazardly piled boxes. He guessed that his cell was some type of storage closet and they'd pulled everything out so they could put him in there. He rifled through the room, mostly by feel, to determine if there were any weapons that he could use.

His hands eventually closed around the handle of a hockey stick. It was a little long and bulky, especially for a handcuffed man, but it would have to do. Shawn crept up the stairs, praying that they didn't creak and give away his plan. What was his plan? He hadn't thought much beyond going upstairs and start hitting people.

He paused. *Should I be doing something different?* he wondered. Could he wait for them to come down to the basement and whack them when they came down? There were at least two potential problems with that. They would have light with them, possibly blinding him and there was no evidence that they'd ever came down to the basement once they'd initially deposited him down there.

Once again, Shawn's mind repeated the phrase that there was nothing that he could do about it. He'd just have to figure things out on the fly and adjust to the situation. He continued toward the top of the stairs and started to reach for the knob. Instead, he decided look through the crack along the bottom to see if anyone was outside. It would allow him to see some of the layout of the house and make it so he wasn't totally blind when he opened the door and all the light from the first floor came flooding in.

He lowered himself painfully to the stairs and peered through the tiny opening between the bottom of the door and that landing. Nothing moved, in front of him, but he could see the deeply tanned foot of someone lying on the floor. He had to assume that was Maria. He listened as well as watched, but couldn't hear anything, not even the woman's breathing. Finally, he'd decided his eyesight had adjusted enough that he wouldn't be blinded when he opened the door. *If* he could open the door.

This is it, he told himself. Now was the time. He turned the knob as quietly as he could and gently pushed open the door. The tiny squeak that the hinges made sounded like a banshee's screech in the stillness of the house. He charged through, the element of surprise lost, and prepared to begin swinging the hockey stick.

*****

26 October, 1401 hrs local
Intermediate Staging Point Harrisburg
Harrisburg, Pennsylvania

Specialist Greeley stared straight ahead at his buddy Walker as he drove the M1A2 Abrams backward off of the low boy's trailer. Walker wasn't looking at Greeley; he was watching Sergeant Gilstrap, who was several meters behind and to the side of the tank acting as the ground guide. The sergeant's arms were extended above his head so Specialist Walker could see him and follow his directions.

Between the two men on the ground, they passed the hand signals to the driver so he could unload the vehicle from the transport trailer. All the enlisted men were taught the skill during their initial armor training. The tank was too large to see over or to the rear, so a ground guide was needed behind the vehicle to pass the hand signals to the man up front, whom the driver could see by looking straight ahead.

They maneuvered Chaos Six off the truck and Mike Miranda watched as the massive vehicle lumbered into line with the remaining ten tanks from the company. One of the others—White Four, he thought—had an unnatural smoke bellowing from the engine and Mike hoped that they'd get at least a day of down time to perform maintenance on the sensitive vehicles. They were living on borrowed time with the tanks.

First Sergeant Jenkins walked up beside Mike and saluted. "Hey, sir. I just got back from talking to the sergeant major. You're not gonna believe this shit."

The commander turned to his senior noncommissioned officer. "What's up, Top?" he asked.

"So you know that we're going to defend this city for a while, right?"

"Yeah, they told us that over the radio. We'll use the river as a choke point, spread wire as thick as possible on the bridges, that sort of stuff."

"I still don't agree with the decision to not drop the bridges. Seems like we could have held New York—or at least Long Island—if we would have dropped the bridges."

"Command wants the bridges intact for when we counterattack."

The first sergeant grunted and then the gruff old veteran said, "Guess who we're linking up with here in Harrisburg."

"I don't know, one of the Army divisions? Maybe the First Infantry Division out of Fort Riley."

"I wish that was the case, boss. The Army is staying put west of the mountains in the defensive belt that's almost complete. We're linking up with the Russians."

Mike choked on the spit in his mouth when he sucked in a breath. "What?"

"Yeah, you heard me right, sir. We're linking up with the Russians. Apparently, they parachuted a whole shitload of troops in on this side of the mountains to help fight the delay while we finish the defensive fortifications."

"How the fuck are we supposed to work with the Russians? We don't speak the same language."

"I don't trust 'em to leave once we beat these things. That's what I'm worried about," First Sergeant Jenkins retorted. "I spent my first five years in the Army stationed in West Germany preparing to fight those fuckers when they came through the Fulda Gap. What are we doing letting them into our country?"

Mike thought about it for a moment. Besides the Chinese, Koreans and Vietnamese—all countries that we'd fought wars with in the past century—the Russians had the next largest army in the world. Sure, the Cold War had seen the two nations square off against each other as enemies, but it had never come to fighting. He sure as hell didn't agree with it, but the addition of professional military forces to the ragtag group of soldiers who were able to get to their units before the horde attacked and civilians who'd escaped getting killed had to be a good thing. Hadn't the US accepted British and Canadian help during the first zombie war?

"I don't know, Top. I think the Russians are risking a lot to put soldiers on the ground here in the US. I mean, this thing is isolated to the Americas right now, so what's their motivation to send troops over here and reduce their potential forces to fight this thing in their own country?"

"I think we're gonna have a fight on our hands on the back end of this thing, sir."

"I hope not, but we'll keep an eye out for them doing anything strange. Deal?"

"Well, if you tell me that we're cooperating with the Ruskies, then I guess I got no choice but to listen to you. Let's go liberate some vodka so we can make friends."

"I'll leave the scrounging up to you and the boys, First Sergeant. I'm gonna go over to the command post and see what the plan is."

"Good luck with that, sir. I don't know that they have any idea what the hell is happening any more than we do," the older man replied. "I'll break the news to the boys not to shoot the Russians the next time we move and then start kicking some ass to get this maintenance completed."

"Thanks, Top," Mike said and started walking toward the Tactical Operations Center, or the TOC as everyone called it. They typically jumped the TOC a couple of days ahead of the combat troops, got it set up and developed a plan for the defensive belt wherever they were.

One of the things that made Mike wonder about the zombies was that they seemed single-mindedly determined to attack the defenders instead of going around them. That showed some type of basic intelligence in them and gave credence to the claim that there was a super-zombie controlling the rest of them. That FBI guy told them about it before the fighting started in New York. He was so tired that he couldn't remember the details, but it was something about a holdover from the first war and they were supposed to be on the lookout for a zombie that acted and looked differently than the others. He hadn't seen anything but a lot of death and dismemberment.

Mike pulled aside the command post's tent flap and was immediately assaulted by the heated air escaping from inside the TOC. Even after a ten-minute walk in the afternoon sun, it took his eyes a moment to adjust to the bright florescent lighting suspended from the crossbeams overhead. Once he was able to see clearly, he walked across to the operations section.

"Hey, Mike," Lieutenant Colonel Grant, the 29th Infantry Division's operations officer, said when he saw him walking up.

"Afternoon, sir," he replied. Typically a division-level lieutenant colonel wouldn't be on a first name basis with a company commander, but as the only remaining tank company that the 29th had, Mike was allowed to come in and speak directly to the G-3 whenever he needed to.

The 29th was in charge of the newly-created Joint Task Force East Coast, which now ran all operations east of the Appalachian Mountains for several reasons. The 18th Airborne Corps out of Fort Bragg, North Carolina would have been a logical choice, but they'd been given operational control of the southeast with the 3rd Infantry Division out of Georgia to create a line extending from the coast to the mountains in an effort to keep the creatures from moving south and flowing around the mountain obstacles. The 82nd Airborne Division had been on duty at The Wall when the creatures broke out and had been virtually wiped out. The same could be said of the 10th Mountain Division from Fort Drum, New York. They'd responded to the attack on the city and besides a few stragglers who told tales of their losses, the only time anyone saw the 10th Mountain patch was on zombies in the engagement area.

The 29th had learned early in the fighting not to allow themselves to get trapped in a static defense—that's how the 10th had gotten overrun. They had tried to treat the zombie horde like a human enemy and stood to fight them, thinking that they'd give way to the significant firepower that the dismounted infantry division could bring to bear. The problem, obviously, was that the zombies were relentless; they didn't care if their numbers were decimated. The bastards just continued to press forward and now most of those soldiers from the 10th Mountain Division were dead.

Movable defenses and delaying tactics like the strands of barbed wire were the key to defeating an enemy that had no sense of self-preservation. Mike's tanks had helped to add an element of mobile firepower that the defenders east of the Appalachians sorely needed. As such, he'd gotten to know the division's operations officer well during their long battle westwards.

"What can I do for you, Mike?" Colonel Grant asked.

"Just trying to get a run down on our mission here, the length of stay and follow up on a rumor about Russians, sir."

"The Russian part is true. They jumped into our area of operations a couple of days ago. Hell, word barely reached us of their arrival before the first of the parachutes started appearing in the sky above the division headquarters. Most of 'em are preparing a series of elaborate defenses east of the city near Carlisle. We've told them to keep it focused on a defense in depth and develop long-range kill boxes so they have time to reposition once the zombies get closer, but you never know with the Russians.

"You know, when I first came in the Army, they were still teaching us about Russian doctrine and the tactics that they used weren't very different than those of the zombies. They would just throw lots of bodies at the problem until the enemy broke. Hell of a way to do business...."

The older man trailed off for a moment and then refocused on Mike. "As for staying here, I think we're gonna try for three or four days. I know your tanks need some serious maintenance downtime, so I think I can give you two days, but keep in mind that everything depends on the enemy. We drove a long ways from Allentown, so they should take a few days before they can make it this far, but we know that their methods—I can't justify calling what they do 'tactics'—we know that their methods change all the time. Intel isn't sure if that's them adapting or they just do random-assed stuff.

"You had three questions. What was the other thing you wanted to know?"

Mike ran through the short list in his head and then replied, "Our mission, sir. What are we doing?"

"That's right," he said and poked at the air like he was checking off a list. "Mike, your boys are gonna have pretty much the same mission as always, set up a defensive support by fire position for the dismounted troops, kill as many of the zombies as you can and then—"

A large, far away explosion rumbled through the thin plastic-coated canvas of the tent.

"That'd be another MOAB that the Air Force dropped on the horde outside of Allentown," the colonel said as he slapped his open hand on the operations map. "Let those fuckers recover from that!"

"We dropped a MOAB outside of the town?" Mike asked in disbelief. The GBU-43/B Massive Ordnance Air Blast Bomb, or the MOAB, was also known as the Mother of All Bombs due to its massive 21,000-pound weight and the devastating effects that it caused on the battlefield. The MOAB wasn't a nuclear weapon, but the extreme temperatures released by the thermobaric warhead destroyed everything within a mile of impact and the overpressure liquefied the internal organs of those unfortunate enough to be within a couple of miles of the point of impact, including the brain.

"Actually, we dropped three, two across the front of the zombie advance and that was the third one, right in the middle of the biggest horde. We have it running on a delayed loop up on KillTV if you want to watch it."

Mike had seen enough KillTV, the military nickname for the live drone video feed, to last a lifetime, but he was genuinely interested in this episode. Those creatures had ruined his nation, destroyed New York City and wiped out most of the population of the East Coast. "Sure, which screen?" he asked the operations officer when he looked over to the three display monitors, all playing different KillTV "shows."

"Middle one," he replied and glanced over. "Looks like this is pre-detonation, the B1 is lining up for the first drop."

Mike recognized the golf course that he'd fought so hard over. Sure enough, there was the disabled Blue Four tank with the cracked engine block. Tens of thousands of the zombies teamed across the open space, seemingly stalled in their attempt to find and kill their human enemies. The crosshairs centered directly on the Chaos Company tank and then they jumped upwards slightly before reacquiring the tank in the center.

"That would be the plane releasing that big mofo," Colonel Grant said from beside him. "God, I can't get enough of watching this video! You've been out there fighting them, so it's gotta be awesome for you to see us wipe out such a large group at one time."

Mike thought about Allentown, likely obliterated from the planet. Awesome wouldn't have been the word that he would have used to describe it. "Uh, huh," he replied noncommittally.

"You said that we've dropped three MOABs? Wonder why I didn't hear the first two?" Mike asked. Even though he talked to the colonel, his eyes never left the monitor as the bomb fell lower toward his company's vehicle.

"You were still in transit. We dropped the first two, thinking that we were kicking some ass. All it did was shake out the real horde of them that had been hiding from overhead observation. We didn't even realize there were that many of them in one place. You'll see it here in a few seconds."

The screen turned a brilliant white and the point of impact went pitch black as the ball of heat expanded outwards, effectively making the center of the detonation cooler than the surrounding area. The camera adjusted and the blacks and whites balanced out. The tank was gone, simply gone.

No, wait. There it is, Mike thought. It had been flipped on its side up against the foundation of the building near where the tank sat when it crapped out. The blast had enough force to lift a 72-ton vehicle up onto its side.

The screen reset and another bomb dropped from the B1 bomber. This one fell a little less than a mile away from the first into the mass of writhing creatures. They appeared to be twisted and broken, crawling onward with whatever muscles were still useable. Mike almost felt sorry for them as the next bomb came in and destroyed them.

"Here's the interesting part," the colonel stated as the camera panned back toward the east.

As far as the plane's camera could see, zombies poured from underneath the tree line, from buildings, out of whatever overhead cover that they had found, and fell upon one another, ripping and tearing themselves to shreds. It went on for almost a minute and then stopped. They regained control of themselves and started to return to their hiding places. But it was too late, they'd been seen by the Air Force and now the bombs would fall on them.

That was strange, he thought. *Why would they risk being seen like that? They sure do act like they know that we can see them from above.* Now *there* was a creepy thought. If they were hiding on purpose from the drone and satellite cameras above them, it indicated some type of higher brain function. It chilled him to the core to think about those things being able to think and act upon those thoughts.

"Okay, I haven't seen this part yet," the G-3 indicated toward the monitor, which was now showing another set of crosshairs on the area that had recently been occupied by the out-of-control zombies. The bomb disengaged from the B1 and fell, guided toward the target.

"This is the one that just went off, sir?" Mike asked.

"Yeah, we're watching the new feed that came from that last bomb. We didn't see it in real time because we were over there at my desk and then it went back to the earlier loop."

The area that had been targeted was roughly in the center of the large mass of creatures that had temporarily come out from the cover of trees and buildings. Once more the screen went white and then they watched the expanding fireball as it extended outward in all directions from the point of impact. Tens of thousands of zombies must have perished immediately in the blast.

They watched as the cameras zoomed out and nothing moved. They zoomed out further and almost a mile away, more of the creatures could be seen fighting each other. The text across the bottom of the screen stated that the bomber was "*Winchester MOAB, RTB*" which meant that they were out of ammo and returning to base.

The screen continued to show the zombies for a full minute before the plane banked away and the video refreshed to the original filmed section just before the first GBU-43/B drop. "So why are they fighting each other?" Mike finally asked after ensuring that it was the same video clip.

"Who knows for sure, but our intel folks have talked to higher about it already. Apparently, there's a non-lethal weapon that they used effectively in the first zombie war called a sonic pulse cannon that scrambled their brains long enough to allow beleaguered troops to break contact." The colonel held up his hands when he saw the look of anger flash across the company commander's face. "I know... I know, Mike. We've requested as much information about that capability as possible now that we know about it. Anyways, the folks out west of the mountains seem to think that the large shock waves temporarily scramble the brains of the zombies that aren't killed immediately. That's why they go nuts for a minute or two."

Mike accepted that as a good explanation, but he wasn't ready to give up on the sonic pulse cannon discovery just yet. "Sir, how many people have we lost in our delaying defense? If the cannon-thing could have stopped them from getting overrun... We've got to get our hands on these things."

"I hear ya, Mike. Not sure how good those things are though. The troops at The Wall had them and they were overrun anyways."

"Okay, sir, but any little bit helps, right?"

"Of course. That's why we've requested them. I just don't want to get your hopes up that this is the weapon that'll win the war. What's gonna win this war is the total annihilation of the zombie threat and that starts with good men and women behind a gun."

Mike nodded his head in agreement, but he wondered if those brain-scrambling weapons could be used to defeat the creatures somehow.

*****

26 October, 1442 hrs local
Western Edge of Allentown
Allentown, Pennsylvania

The Leader held the side of its head. It remembered from *before* that the thoughts originated from the head, but it couldn't understand why it had lost control of the Followers twice in a row during such a short span of time.

It had been coordinating the move to follow the hated humans, to destroy their army so the Chosen could rule the land without being destroyed by the weapons that the humans carried when a bright light obliterated thousands of the Followers in an instant.

The Leader had seen the light and saw Followers fall, then it was picking itself up off the ground and they were fighting one another. It couldn't make them stop until it was able to stand without falling over. Once it could stand on its own again, the creature regained control of its army and forced them back under cover, away from the eyes in the air.

The Master often warned the Chosen of the humans' ability to see them from the sky. The Leader doubted this at first, but now believed that it was true. Their enemies commanded the air like its forces never could, so it was up to them to overwhelm the men when they were on the ground and hide from the things in the sky. One day, the Leader would be able to destroy the final human and then it wouldn't need to hide the army any longer. It would return to the home city with its army and deal with the Master.

After the first bright light that ended the existence of thousands, another flashed not far from where the Leader stood. It was behind a building when the bright light occurred on the other side, away from its direct line of sight. When the Leader regained control of the Followers, it realized that a great multitude of them were no more. It was angry at first, but then decided against it.

Without so many to control, the Followers would be easier to direct now and the Leader could use them more effectively to destroy the troublesome humans once and for all.

*****

26 October, 1649 hrs local
Kidnapper's House
Randolph, New Jersey

Shawn charged out of the basement with the hockey stick raised above his head, prepared to swing it into the face of the raping bastards who'd kidnapped him and Maria. He stopped short and looked around; no one else was in the living room besides Maria. Her eyes were open wide at the sight of the naked, screaming man who'd just burst from the basement doorway holding a weapon.

He lowered the hockey stick and looked around for a moment before sliding across the hardwood to where Maria lay. Shawn knelt and pulled the gag from her mouth. "Where are they?" he questioned.

"Oh, Shawn! Oh my God, Shawn. I thought you were dead," she wailed.

"Are they here?" he demanded.

"No," Maria sobbed. "The air horn blew and they took off to see what they caught."

He shifted his position and began untying her legs. As he worked, he asked, "How long ago did they leave?"

"I don't know," she admitted. "I fell asleep until you came out of the door. Shawn, I'm sorry about... About what happened to you."

He didn't reply and continued to separate the knotted ropes. One side came free and he moved stiffly to the opposite side and untied that as well. Then he worked on the knots around her wrists. When her hands were freed, she threw her arms around him and sobbed, "I thought you were dead."

Shawn couldn't hug her back because of the handcuffs; instead he finally allowed himself to cry. "I'm sorry, Maria. We shouldn't have stuck around after we saw the trap. Oh, God, I'm so sorry."

She held him tightly to her as if she were trying to draw strength from him. "Can you walk?" he asked.

"I... I don't know." She broke away from him and glanced down at her crotch. "I'm pretty messed up down there."

"I'm sorry," he muttered again. He felt that the whole thing was his fault because he was the leader of their little group and had led them directly into the psychopaths' trap. As they embraced, he planned. He would take Maria to safety and then return to kill those two.

After a few minutes of holding each other, he finally broke away. "We need to get out of here. Let's see if you can walk."

Maria nodded and used the back of her hand to wipe away the snot that had bubbled out of her nose. As Shawn tried to help her stand, the garage door began to open and he froze. "Fuck, they're back! Hurry!"

She tried several times to stand, but she'd been strapped to the bar with her legs spread open and violated several times a day for three or four days; her body was too abused and she couldn't support her own weight. "I can't do it, Shawn. Get out of here. Leave me!"

"Like hell I will," he replied and pushed himself awkwardly to his feet. He picked up the stick and walked over to the door. "Lay down!" he hissed as the sound of the closing garage door filled the room. Briefly, his mind cleared of the murder that clouded his thoughts and he wondered how they had power to run the garage door opener. Everywhere that they'd been recently didn't have any electricity at all, how had the men managed to generate power?

The twisting of the cheap brass doorknob brought his attention squarely back to the here and now. The door swung open and the first of the men walked through. "Honey, I'm home," the blonde man said as he moved past Shawn, hidden behind the door.

He stepped away from the wall and swung with every ounce of hatred for the man who'd first suggested that they abuse him with the small baseball bat. The hockey stick impacted with the back of his head, right behind his ear and the splinters of wood flew across the room as the stick shattered and the man began to fall.

Shawn looked at the jagged end of the stick and then turned, thrusting it toward the open garage doorway into the throat of the second man who'd just rounded the corner. The sharp wooden spike pierced his neck and sliced open the carotid artery. Blood sprayed everywhere and the rapist fell to his knees clutching his fatal wound. As he fell, the stick was pulled from Shawn's hands and he stepped back toward the blonde man.

The kidnapper was beginning to stir and to push himself upward. Shawn searched for another weapon and his eyes rested on the blood-covered baseball bat leaning beside the garage door. He stepped quickly across the doorway and snatched up the bat. He raised it above his head and slammed the metal down onto the spine of the blonde man.

The rapist screamed and fell onto his stomach. Shawn brought the bat up again and smashed it downward onto his shoulder. The sound of breaking bones and the man's renewed screams rewarded his efforts.

"Hi, remember me?" Shawn said as he swung the bat into the blonde's ankle, shattering it. Then he broke the opposite hand from the shoulder that he'd hit.

"Shawn, stop it!" Maria shouted. "You're not like them. Don't torture the bastard. Just kill him and be done with it."

Her words stopped him and he glanced up at the woman. She was right. He *wasn't* like them; he'd *never* be like them. Part of that was the ability to control himself, though. He nodded his chin curtly toward Maria and raised the bat high above his head. He brought it down on the back of his skull with a sickening crunch. Then he did it again and again until there was nothing left of the man's head but mush. Then Shawn staggered toward the garage to ensure that the other man was dead.

The puddle of dark liquid that ran toward the garage door made Shawn think that he probably was, but he wasn't going to risk his or Maria's life on a whim. He jammed the end of the bat into the kidnapper's crotch as hard as he could. There was no reaction so he used the bat to push the ski mask up over the man's forehead.

Shawn stumbled backward and hit the wall, dropping the bat. The blank, lifeless eyes that stared at the ceiling belonged to Terry, the National Guard soldier who'd abandoned them in Parsippany. "Oh my God..." he muttered, unable to believe that the man who'd shared the observation post with him could have been capable of doing the things that he'd done.

"Shawn!" Maria called from the living room.

He closed down his mind and grabbed the baseball bat; he had a feeling that the bat would be his constant companion from here on out, both as a weapon and a reminder of what these people did to him. Shawn walked gracelessly up the steps, his legs felt rubbery as he sidestepped the bloody mass that likely used to be Jon, the other soldier from the outpost.

"What is it?" he asked, the bat elevated above his head so he could defend Maria.

"Are you okay?" she asked. She'd managed to sit up on her own and had her back resting against the side of the couch. "I heard a loud thump and then you dropped the bat. I thought... I thought..." she stopped and started crying again.

He continued across the room and slid down beside her. They'd faced their captors and survived.

*****

27 October, 0746 hrs local
The Wall
Near Centerville, Virginia

Kestrel stared up at the twelve-foot monstrosity in front of him. It cut across the interstate, ensuring that no one would be able to continue traveling forward, regardless of their purpose for being there. The Wall was a giant cinderblock structure, meant to trap the zombies safely inside and keep the nuclear devastation from spreading out toward the human population.

He'd been behind The Wall less than six months prior to today. At the time, he was already beginning to feel the desire to be what most considered a "normal" person, to settle down with a woman and maybe even have a family. Since then, he'd fallen in love with one woman and lost another that he genuinely cared for, both due either directly to the zombies or because of thugs who made a profit from their nefarious activities behind The Wall.

The part of him that wanted to settle down and raise a family was dead forever now that he'd lost Allyson, Rachel and Boomer. He no longer desired a future; he wanted revenge—and revenge in Kestrel's book meant that things ended up dead and forgotten to the annals of history. He was going to ensure that no one thought of the Type Ones again, except as an interesting footnote to the larger zombie war.

The operator looked around the base of The Wall for an entrance. He could expend a lot of energy and climb in over the top or he could find one of the many gates set into The Wall and enter through that. He knew from the pre-mission brief last spring that there were gates set at random points along the structure. They were usually close together, only a mile apart, but in some instances they were up to twenty miles apart. The government added the gates as a way to project combat power rapidly into the city if they needed to go inside. During the briefing, Alistair Reston had told them that if they were separated from their group, they were to make their way toward The Wall and walk along it until they found a gate.

Outside of each gate was a guard shack with keys, manned twenty-four hours a day with a guard who could let you out.

That was then. Now, the military force guarding the Dead City had been wiped out. Evidence of dead soldiers and dispatched zombies were everywhere along the highway coming in. He'd stared in disbelief at the dead. Most of the soldiers had head wounds, which meant that they'd turned after being bitten and attacked their comrades. Even though he didn't know them, they were his brothers in arms and it made him sad that they'd died uselessly because of the zombies. Kestrel had always thought that the president should have sent in specialized teams to wipe out the creatures while they were still trapped behind The Wall and those teams could have dispatched the zombies and even killed the Type Ones who'd orchestrated this disaster, potentially saving millions of lives. After the war, there'd likely be a political reckoning, although he wouldn't be around to see it.

Kestrel shifted his truck into first and eased his foot off the clutch. He turned north for no other reason than it was convenient and drove slowly along the cleared area beside The Wall looking for a gate to enter the region. The military had cleared large sections around the perimeter of buildings and vegetation to open up their fields of fire. In the end, they'd killed a ton of the creatures, but that didn't matter since none of them had survived the breakout.

The old Ford bounced along the killing grounds that the cleared area had become, often running over bodies and discarded weapons. From the positioning of most of the corpses, it looked like the soldiers had retreated southward and the creatures followed them killing indiscriminately. That likely meant that there was a gate somewhere nearby that he could use to get into the city.

About two miles after he'd left Interstate 66, Kestrel found the gate that he'd been looking for. He put the truck in park and examined the scene. The vacant stone archway was large enough that a full-sized military truck could pass through without a hassle and the metal gates lay on the ground, their hinges torn from the cinderblock. The zombies must have piled against them and the soldiers had foolishly relied on the strength of the steel. Kestrel had seen it before; regardless of the strength of the gates, with enough pressure—like thousands of zombies pushing against them—things that are welded or bolted together will eventually break. It was only a matter of time, and then they simply overwhelmed the small guard force.

If it had been a coordinated attack at every gate, with a Type One controlling the masses, then the units wouldn't have been able to respond and assist where the creatures broke through. It would have been a bloodbath. He could almost hear the screams of the young men as they were ripped limb from limb by the angry horde before they succumbed to *A-Coll* and joined in the rampage themselves.

He checked his surroundings and then hopped out of the truck when he was sure that he was alone. The metal links of the exposed sharksuit made tiny clinking noises until he slid an old BDU-type shirt over it and buttoned up. It was the uniform that he'd worn his last few years in the Navy and had even worn it on a few ops over the years. He'd felt a little nostalgic as he pulled it out of the closet and added it to his supplies. The pockets were great for holding all sorts of things and the camouflage would help him blend into the environment so the zombies, who had poor eyesight anyways, wouldn't be able to see him.

He wanted to see inside The Wall and thought about driving closer to his target for a once-over, but Kestrel wasn't able to get close enough for a clear view in his truck because there was an Army PLS truck stopped just a few feet beyond the opening. The PLS was a giant beast of a truck designed for hauling oversized equipment in the back. It looked like the defenders had tried to use it as a battering ram to block the entrance and failed. Whoever had been driving it went too far and allowed the creatures to pass behind the back end of the truck.

Kestrel walked up to the opening, his SCAR rifle at the ready. He'd decided to leave the Lapua Magnum .338 sniper rifle with the IR scope since he was likely going to be walking most of the way. Instead, he'd attached both a 20Xs scope and an ACOG combat optic to the SCAR that he could switch between for long- and medium-range targets. He also only had one of his three Heckler & Koch HK45 pistols. His original bug out plan to have two rifles—and the different types of ammunition—plus three pistols would have been too much weight to carry for days at a time now that he was going into the city looking for a fight instead of avoiding one.

He walked around the front of the PLS truck and was shocked at the number of bodies piled up under the tires and dangling from the bumper. The truck must have hit a large group of them as they were coming out of the gate and then finally stalled against the crush of the horde. They were the older creatures that he'd fought against last spring, he could tell by the sad state of their clothing. Years of sun, rain, wind and snow had taken their toll on the fabrics. Several of the creatures were still *alive* and swiped half-heartedly in his direction from underneath the massive tires, but they were too damaged to do anything to him. Still, he gave them a wide berth.

He started to continue by, but then decided against it. Kestrel didn't know how the zombies communicated, so he thought it best that he finish these ones off before they passed on the information about a human in the city. He pulled a giant 9-inch Bowie knife from his belt and jammed it through the soft eye sockets of seven zombies in various states of decay that were trapped underneath the truck. When he was done, he used the creatures' own tattered remnants of clothing to clean the gore from the blade before sheathing it once more.

The big Army truck's door squealed loudly as he opened it. If he could move the truck, then he'd be able to have a clear path down the street that the gate opened to. He climbed up and sat his rifle on the seat next to him. The truck used a push-to-start button to ignite the engine, but when he pressed it, nothing happened. He fiddled with a few gauges and knobs until he realized that the batteries were dead. *This thing isn't going anywhere,* he thought. *Oh well, it was worth a try... And now there are seven fewer zombies to worry about.*

He climbed down from the cab and checked the immediate area to ensure that there weren't any more of the creatures remaining before he walked back to his truck for the rest of the supplies. Once there, he sat his rifle on top of the truck cab and shrugged into a heavy coat, then pulled his backpack over the old uniform top. Inside the bag, he'd included more ammo than he could easily carry and enough rations for two weeks, water for a few days and salt tablets to help him retain the fluids instead of sweating them out.

He'd be able to pick up bottled water along the way, especially farther out from the nuke's epicenter. Like most nuclear weapons, the missile that the French had used contained low grade uranium, so it was likely that the radiation had dissipated enough that it wasn't really deadly anymore. That guy, Steve, was trapped in Baltimore for four or five months and he was fine, so Kestrel was certain that he'd be able to sustain himself long enough to get the job done.

The last thing that he put into place was his mask. It had a full face shield to allow the maximum range of view; it also had a gigantic scratch down the middle where a zombie had scraped its teeth against his mask in an effort to bite his face when he and the FBI agent Caleb Campbell had gone to rescue the downed helicopter's crew. That protective capability was his primary motivation for wearing the mask now, not because of the radiation.

He didn't bother with the radiation suit either. The Bureau had been overcautious when they made their team wear the gear. The man didn't plan to live beyond his encounter with the Type Ones anyways, so what was the point in restricting his movement if he didn't have to?

He checked inside the truck one last time to make sure that he had everything and then he left the keys in the ignition. If there were any survivors around, the truck would be a huge help to them in escaping the area. He pulled the SCAR off the roof of the truck and walked back toward the entrance.

It was now time for the payback to begin.

NINE

28 October, 1957 hrs local
The House Next Door
Randolph, New Jersey

They were battered and abused, barely able to stand, let alone walk, but Shawn and Maria couldn't bring themselves to stay in the house where Terry and Jon had molested them. After searching futilely for the handcuff keys in the cabinets and drawers for several minutes Shawn finally got the nerve to dig his hands into the pockets of his captors. The key was in the blonde man's front pocket and he'd had to rub his hands several times on the carpet to wipe off the cool urine that had soaked the deceased man's crotch into his pocket.

After he was free, Shawn had helped Maria up onto the couch and covered her with a blanket before going off to find their clothes. In the car, he found the biggest surprise of all: another woman, trussed up like they'd been a few days earlier. She'd screamed against the tape that covered her mouth at the sight of Shawn's naked form but he'd been able to convince her that he wasn't going to harm her. He showed her the raw, bloody rings around his wrist where he'd been handcuffed and told her that she was safe.

When he was certain that she wouldn't scream and attract zombies to the house, he took the tape off her mouth and then her feet before he helped her out of the back seat. The sight of Terry's blood-soaked corpse sent her over the edge and she screamed. He'd jumped toward her and covered her mouth, begging her to stop. The screams had brought Maria staggering out of the house into the garage where she appraised the newcomer shrewdly.

"Shut up!" she hissed. "You're going to attract the zombies and get us killed."

Maria, once an attractive, young Hispanic woman with beautiful, seductive hazel eyes, looked awful when she first met Katie. One of those eyes was swollen completely shut, there were bite marks and bruises all over her naked body and dried, crusted blood ran from her private areas in dark, almost black streaks in all directions.

Maria's appearance had been enough to make the woman stop and they'd explained to her what had happened. With Katie's help they found their clothes and the younger woman helped clean Maria up enough to get dressed. It was something that Shawn had been extremely grateful for, because even though it wouldn't have been sexual in nature, the woman would have likely suffered more mental anguish with him getting an up-close view of the damage.

Maria rested on the couch while Shawn and Katie searched the house for useful items. The electricity still intrigued him so he'd opened the window and could hear the chugging of a gas-powered generator far away. The two men must have run power lines to the house from a generator that they'd wisely set up quite a ways away. The true test of the power was the fact that there was hot water.

They decided immediately that they weren't going to stay in the kidnapper's house. It wasn't a matter of the dead bodies—they could have dumped those outside. The events of the past several days occurred next door, and *that* drove Shawn and Maria to insist on moving to a different house.

Katie had stayed with Maria while Shawn sneaked out the back door and across the yard to the house next door. He'd broken the back door's window and gone inside after unlocking it. The men hadn't even bothered to explore the homes around them; they had the supermarket and potential victims right across the street, so the house still contained the previous tenant's stuff.

Shawn decided that it would do and went back out the back door. In the yard, he noticed a thick red and black cable running from the house where the girls were off toward the sound of the generator. He'd followed the cable for half a block before seeing several zombies heading toward the source of the noise and he had to duck behind a shed to avoid being seen. Once the small group had passed, he trailed them toward the noise cautiously.

Another couple hundred feet further on he was able to see the generator with about twenty of the creatures clawing and biting it. There were another fifty or so dead zombies piled up near the curb where Jon and Terry must have been putting the bodies after they killed them when they needed to refuel the generator. He'd made his way back to the girls and told them about the generator and the zombies. There was no way to switch the power cable from one house to the other without turning off the generator first, so the house next door would remain without electricity.

Before the group switched houses though, they each took hot showers and felt clean for the first time in weeks. They also switched out their tattered travel clothes for the previous owners' clothing. The woman had been almost the same size as Katie and Maria both, but the man of the house had been huge. Shawn reluctantly put his old, dirty and travel-stained clothes back on before they relocated to the house next door, which actually contained better-fitting clothing for him.

They'd spent two nights in the house before leaving. Maria had developed a fear of being left alone, so Katie slept in the master bed with her while Shawn had to drag a mattress from one of the children's rooms and place it across the doorway on the floor. It was far from perfect, but it made Shawn feel better to keep the group together where he could see everyone.

This morning, Maria had announced that she was healed enough to continue their travel westward. They still believed that going west was the best thing that they could do since that was where the Army had gone and Shawn's daughter was in Cleveland beyond where the Army was setting up their defensive position. It left the unasked question of whether their younger companion would stay in Randolph or go west with them.

Katie asked if she could stay with the two of them, regardless of where they were going. She'd been on her own for more than a month when she decided to stay at her apartment when her boyfriend Chris left to go out on a supply run. That was the last time that she saw him and she'd been slowly traveling between convenience and grocery stores since then—which is how she'd been captured. She was trying to find some more substantive food than what she found in gas stations and risked going into the grocery store.

They traveled as a group to the kidnapper's house one more time for hot showers and a microwaved meal of canned food. They hated to leave the modern conveniences of electricity, but they knew that the generator would run out of fuel soon enough and none of them felt like taking on an entire group of zombies just to fill it up again.

When dusk neared, they packed their meager belongings into the Buick that the two men used and headed out into the cold night. On their way past the A&P Food Store, Shawn diverted and pulled up to the front doors. He hopped out of the car without an explanation and opened the grocery store's door. Then he stepped over the tripwire and went inside.

He reappeared less than a minute later with his old backpack slung over his shoulder. Once again, he stepped over the trap with an exaggerated step and then turned back toward the store. Using the folding knife that he'd taken off Terry's corpse, he cut the fishing line stretched across the threshold. The sack of cans came crashing down to the linoleum floor, echoing loudly in the early evening. Shawn jumped at the sound, but then the air horn began blaring as the brick swung free and depressed the trigger, causing even more of a ruckus than the net and cans had.

"What the hell did you do that for?" Katie asked from the back seat when he returned to the vehicle.

"You were hit by that trap," Shawn replied pointing toward the rapidly healing scab on her forehead as he shifted into drive and pulled away from the store toward the New Jersey 10. "I don't want someone else to get caught in that net the same way that you were. Only the next time, there won't be two rapists to clear out the zombies following the sound; they'd be dead meat."

The girl accepted his explanation and they made their way down the ramp onto the highway. With three-quarters of a tank of gas, Shawn felt much better about their odds of making it over the mountains than he had before when they were on foot. They'd faced evil incarnate and came out on top, gaining a useful companion in the deal.

Shawn's hand unconsciously went to the backpack that he'd retrieved from inside the store. The pictures of Annie and Shana were all that he really had left in this world that was his and he wasn't about to let them go. Now all he needed to do was get his little group across 150 miles of zombie-infested territory and then somehow make it to Cleveland. His little girl needed him and nothing would stand in his way of seeing her again.

*****

31 October, 1521 hrs local
Near Rosslyn Metro Station
Arlington, Virginia

Kestrel had decided early on to get off of Interstate 66. He only made it a few miles to Fairfax before he'd assessed that it would be quicker to simply travel east down Highway 50 to Arlington and then over the Potomac directly into the old capital city. Highway 50 fed directly downtown and ran along the northern edge of the National Mall.

When he'd initially conducted his map recon, he'd thought it would be faster to travel down 66 instead of the smaller highway, but the sheer number of cars that choked the interstate made him conclude that the straighter way would likely be faster. The missile hit at the height of rush hour six years ago. The administration announced the evacuation before it exploded, so the road was blocked by cars that got into accidents when they tried to turn around. Being a driver on those highways had stranded and ultimately killed a lot of people. He'd passed a lot of dried and desiccated corpses, trapped in their vehicles until the end of time—they were the lucky ones. People who'd gotten out of their cars were either burned alive by the superheated air or attacked by zombies as they stumbled hopelessly around the ruined city.

He'd fought and killed hundreds of the zombies, most of them alone and easily dispatched with his knife. There'd been two times that he'd been forced to use his precious ammunition and had to put down large groups of the creatures wandering aimlessly through the ruins.

He knew the damn things communicated somehow—which is why he killed every one of them that he encountered. What he didn't understand was *how* they did it; he couldn't hear anything when groups of them shifted directions like a school of fish. Thankfully, it was easy to anticipate their moves since they were concerned only with a headlong frontal attack. He could easily dodge the creatures and murder them at will. But the constant movement was beginning to take a toll on his body and he knew that if he didn't find something soon, then he'd need to take an extended rest in an apartment somewhere.

So far, he hadn't had to test the sharksuit's value and he planned to keep it that way. As he walked down the old, abandoned highway he looked forlornly to the right where the thousands of once-white headstones were now a dingy gray from the ash and fallout. He had friends buried in Arlington and their families would never be able to visit their graves again. Over a block away to his left was the Rosslyn Metro Station, the entrance beckoned him to explore and determine what was down there.

Kestrel grimaced when he thought about the extensive tunnel system under the city. It made perfect sense to use them as a place to hide from the satellites and helicopters that used to fly constantly over the region. He planned to check out the National Mall like Hank had suggested, then head down into the Metro tunnels to see what he could find. He didn't want to do it, but he knew that he needed to sweep them at least once.

Of course, he was a realist and knew that if a Type One wanted to, it could hide from one man indefinitely by simply staying a step ahead of him in the city. He admitted it to himself, but he was the fucking Kestrel; if there was a way to figure out the dilemma, then he'd be the one to do it. He chuckled to himself at the errant thought; he was the *only* one to do it. The rest of the military had its hands full trying to stay afloat against the army of undead created in the rapid fall of Philadelphia, New York, Boston and everything in between.

A noise from the Metro entrance made him drop to one knee and bring the SCAR up to his cheek. Another faint scraping told him that something was coming up the useless escalator stairs. He tried to remember from the times that he'd visited the city how long those stairs were, but it escaped him. He thought they were short, compared to some of the stairs—like the Medical Center escalators that went on for hundreds of feet.

The same scraping noise continued and he finally got tired of waiting. Kestrel heaved himself back to his feet, a slight groan escaping his lips that betrayed the age he felt weighing heavily on his joints from carrying the huge backpack full of gear. A quick shuffle over to the escalator entrance revealed a short set of steps that led to the entrance below.

A dismembered zombie lay at the bottom of the stairs, its one arm clawing uselessly at the step to pull itself up. Kestrel crept down the stairs slowly, eyes averted from the harmless creature at the base of the stairs, searching for more relevant targets. Nothing presented itself, so he examined the wretched creature.

It had been a woman once, long ago. Dried bloodstains trailed away to the depths of the subway where she must have dragged herself from years ago. There were several long, jagged rips in her skin that convinced him she'd been eaten by either dogs or rats. They'd pulled the meat and bones away from her legs, took her other arm, and left her with just the one to try and make her escape into the city.

Kestrel hadn't given any thoughts to the wildlife that lived within The Wall. He'd always assumed that the zombies killed everything, but that really didn't make any sense. Some things, like packs of wild dogs, would likely have been able to survive by learning to hunt the zombies. They probably wouldn't know the difference between a man and a zombie and he was thankful for the sharksuit once again.

The pathetic creature snapped its jaws at him, but couldn't get its torso to move closer and grasp onto any part of his body. Its eyes were sunken in and milky white, like a blind old lady and he wondered if it saw him or sensed him. At one time, he might have felt sorry for the thing, but he only felt contempt as he slid the knife from its sheath and he pushed the tip gently through the eye into her brain. A thin, watery substance oozed from the opening in the eye for a moment before the blackness began to cascade from inside of the thing's head.

Add another one to the long list of zombies that he'd put down on his journey. Most, like this one, were too crippled to be of much harm, but every one of them needed to be destroyed in order to eradicate the virus.

No one would ever know of the things that he'd done to help cleanse the city, but it still brought a smile to his face as he used the zombie's long brown hair to clean the sticky black ichor off his knife's blade.

*****

31 October, 1545 hrs local
US Route 22, Lehigh Valley Thruway
Allentown, Pennsylvania

Shawn pulled the Buick over to the shoulder and surveyed the scene stretching out below them. The entire city of Allentown was nothing but rubble. Most of the smoke had long ago blown away, but in a few places it still drifted lazily toward the sky where the fires had recently burned away the last of the flammable surfaces.

"Did we do that?" Katie asked.

"Yeah, we did that," Maria muttered from the back seat where she'd chosen to ride that day.

"So what do we do now?" the girl asked.

They'd known that the Army planned to go to the small city after Parsippany, but they had no clue where they'd gone after that. This morning, they'd decided to keep driving through the day, even though the zombies had been out because they thought that they'd be sleeping in the Army camp in Allentown before nightfall.

"I don't know," Shawn admitted. He really didn't know; he thought that they'd be safe and would be able to stop running every day. The two women looked to him to help keep them safe and it was wearing on him mentally. Maria was a shell of her former self and he didn't know if she'd be any good in a firefight or if she'd crumble. Katie had never used a weapon, not even a stick to defend herself from the zombies; she'd relied on staying hidden until Terry and Jon had captured her.

"I guess we should go down there and see if there are any survivors," Shawn stated as he grasped the shifter.

"Wait!" Maria cried. "Do you really think we bombed the camp? Don't you think it's more likely that they evacuated and then bombed the city after the army left? There's nobody left down there."

He took his hand off the knob and said, "Well, maybe. I guess that's probably what happened... Unless they were overrun and had to bomb the camp."

Katie grabbed his forearm, "Doesn't that mean there are zombies down there?"

"There are zombies everywhere," he replied, gesturing around their general location.

"Yeah, I mean, like a lot of them, not the two or three that we've hit with the car," the girl clarified.

"What else are we supposed to do?" Shawn sighed. "We know that the Army was going to set up camp near that town and we *don't* know much of anything else. There might be a clue about where they went or directions about where survivors are supposed to go."

"I know that I don't want to die," Katie stated. "It looks like everything down there is dead. Maybe we can just go around the town and keep heading west."

She had a point. They could avoid the town and just head west on their own, but the fact that he'd been hoping for the safety of the Army wouldn't stop nagging him. He turned in the seat to look back at his longtime partner. "Alright, Maria. You're the deciding vote. I want to go down and see if there's a clue as to where the Army went; Katie wants to go around. Whatever you say, we'll do."

"That's not how this was supposed to work, Shawn," Maria grumbled. "You're effectively putting this decision off on me. You should have reserved judgment until I'd given my recommendation and then made the group's decision." She smiled and then said softly, "You're a crappy leader."

He accepted her rebuke, "I didn't go to school to learn all this stuff. You have the leadership experience, that's why you should have been in charge."

"Look, I don't care what you two think about who's in charge," Katie muttered. "Just make a decision; there are zombies coming up the hill."

Shawn whipped his head around. Sure enough, a group of zombies from the city had noticed them. They were slowly ambling up the hill toward the car so they hadn't necessarily seen the humans, but they had noticed the vehicle.

"Okay, we're going down into the city," Shawn decided. The potential to get separated from the last remnants of humanity on this side of the mountain outweighed the odds of the city teeming with the undead.

Katie *harrumphed* loudly and clutched the large kitchen knife closely to her chest as Shawn shifted the car into drive. With any luck, he'd be able to get up enough speed to plow into the zombies and take them out.

*****

Oh my God! Katie screamed to herself. *These two are gonna get me killed!* She didn't know if putting her life in the hands of Maria and Shawn had been the right thing to do. She could have set herself up in that grocery store back in Randolph and been just fine to ride this thing out. There was food, water, even a bathroom.

But that would have meant staying alone at the store. She missed Craig, but he'd abandoned her and was probably dead; she didn't plan on ending up like him. If she was honest with herself, she was only a scared kid. She didn't know anything about survival, the fact that she'd gotten captured on her first trip that was farther than a couple of blocks from her apartment proved that with almost disastrous results.

No, until something better came along, she needed to stick with these two. She'd formed a tenuous bond with Maria in the week that they'd been together, even though the woman seemed to get annoyed with her quickly. Shawn was unsure of himself at times, but overall, he seemed okay. Besides, they had a car that worked and were steadily making their way toward the safe-zone so that was a point in their favor.

If they kept their current pace of about 30–40 miles an hour, they should make it over the mountains in a few days. Of course, that didn't account for the massive vehicle pile-ups that they'd ran into since they started traveling, which caused them to backtrack and change their route several times. Katie thought that was annoying; why couldn't people just drive like normal? Then everyone would have escaped and she wouldn't have had to see all the dead bodies and the gross zombies hanging around the scene.

The car accelerated down the hill and she accidentally let out a tiny shriek when they hit the first of the zombies that were coming up the hill. Shawn looked over at her like she was a baby and she stuck out her tongue at him. Hitting another human being—zombie or not—wasn't something that she'd ever get used to.

The movies always made it look so spectacular when a car hit a person. They would fly up and hit the windshield, then continue rolling over the vehicle to land in a heap on the pavement behind the car. In real life, that didn't happen. When the Buick hit one of them, their body got trapped against the grill and they'd claw at the hood until, inevitably, they would get a foot caught on the road or under a tire and physics took over, pulling them under the car. The car would bounce up into the air twice as first the front tire and then the rear ran over the poor creature and that was it; no dramatic battle by the passengers to dislodge the beast or a hand grasped onto the bumper to come back and get them through the rear window miles later. Just *bump, bump* and then it was gone—boring!

That's what happened with the first guy, and then again with another. Shawn ended up hitting and running over four zombies in that descent from the hilltop down into the ruined town. Almost immediately, he began to mutter things to himself and every few words Katie could make out things like "mistake" and "gone."

"What is it, Shawn." she asked.

He looked over at her, wide-eyed and gestured wildly around the car at the broken masonry and shattered glass that had once been storefronts, homes and peoples' livelihoods. Now everything was just a massive pile of junk. "It was a mistake to come down here. We're gonna get caught up in the rubble."

"Turn around then!" she squealed.

"We have to keep going," Maria moaned from the back seat. "We can't turn around now."

Katie twisted in her seat and asked, "Why, what's—" she never finished her question as her eyes focused out the back window where the older woman stared. The roadway behind them had filled with the dead who'd flowed out of the wreckage.

The creatures that pursued them were a truly wretched bunch. Broken bodies shambled along, missing limbs and necks wrenched at unnatural angles. The ones who couldn't stand used broken arms to pull themselves along, ragged body parts trailing behind them. Katie was certain that she even saw one of the creatures trying to roll down the hill, but it had veered sharply out of her line of sight into one of the rubble-strewn parking lots.

More of the creatures ambled out of hiding along the road as they drove. They were in some deep shit and the three of them knew it. Shawn pressed the gas pedal a little further and the gap widened.

The nose of the car edged around obstacles, scraping against large pieces of concrete as they attempted to continue their slow getaway through Allentown. The gap continued to widen between the things pursuing them and the back end of their vehicle and Katie allowed herself to hope that they would escape. She lifted herself up slightly to look at the dashboard, Shawn was driving a steady ten miles per hour and, more importantly, they had over a half of a tank of gas.

She turned to look back at the creatures; they were almost hidden from view behind the wreckage. Things were looking up. They'd make it through this hell and then go over the mountains to safety. Then, Katie's luck once again ran out as Shawn's curse exploded into the Buick's interior.

"What is it?" Maria asked and then muttered, "Oh."

Katie stared at Maria and the look on her face made her afraid to turn around. When the car slowed and then stopped completely, she finally turned to see what had happened.

Debris from the airport they'd passed blocked the roadway ahead and on the sides. They'd driven down the partially-cleared path as far as they could go and now they were trapped because the tail of a big airplane rested across the highway. There wasn't even enough room to turn the car around in the tight space that Shawn had driven into. The idiot had just kept blindly driving without thinking of alternate escape routes or any other way to go about traveling through the city besides the main road that they'd followed.

Katie realized that she'd made a very bad decision by joining Shawn and Maria. The deplorable state that they'd been in when she first met them should have convinced her of their bad luck. Now she was truly fucked.

Happy Halloween, Katie thought as she watched her death slowly come into view through the car's back window.

TEN

31 October, 1813 hrs local
Wreckage of the Washington Monument
Washington, Dead City

Kestrel had been here before. The zombies covered the National Mall like ants on a picnic basket, blocking his way to the buildings there. Why the president had continuously denied the clearance of the city was beyond him; those things were a scourge that needed to be eliminated. From his elevated hide position on the top of the hill he could see the skeletal remains of the very creatures that his team had killed on their last visit. It was one of the strongest feelings of *déjà vu* that he'd personally felt before and didn't like it. Nothing had changed since the last time he was here.

When he'd crossed the old Theodore Roosevelt Bridge toward Capitol Hill he'd caught a glimpse of movement in the shifting fog that seemed to be a constant presence in the city now that the wind was held at bay by The Wall and no longer blew across the region. To his experienced eye, that one small flicker of movement had meant so much more than it would have to others. He'd been on the Mall last spring when they assaulted the Archives; he knew that there was an unusual amount of activity there, which is why he'd decided to begin his search in earnest on the Mall.

He'd slipped silently up to the back side of the Lincoln Memorial and slid along the wall until he came around to the front and crept up the stairs. He needed to clear the area between the memorial and the pillars of the World War Two memorial on the east end of the Reflecting Pool before he could move to the Mall. There had been about thirty of the creatures—

one full magazine—that he dispatched and then continued on to his next objective, the Washington Monument. In hindsight, those were likely just spillover from the massive group that stumbled around on the Mall before him now.

He'd chosen the Washington Monument as his next location because it was elevated above the Mall where the creatures were heavily concentrated. The elevation would provide him with an excellent observation point to determine which building they were protecting. Once he learned all that he could from them—and as long as he could stay hidden—it would be a time consuming task to kill all the creatures before he moved forward, but doing so would allow him greater freedom to maneuver so he could do what he needed.

He crept cautiously along the broken length of the Washington Monument's remains. Kestrel trailed one hand along the massive obelisk's side as he walked to help keep him in line with where he wanted to go and for the experience of touching the monument itself. The moment he reached the top of the monument's small hill, he knew that he was in business. The National Mall was covered with hundreds, if not thousands, of zombies. He knew without a doubt that they were guarding something in the area.

Kestrel had planned ahead for the large number of creatures and packed 2,000 rounds of ammunition for his dual-scoped MK-17 SCAR in his backpack—over 73 pounds of 7.62-millimeter ammo. At first, he'd questioned bringing so much ammo and his back had *really* questioned the decision over the last four days as he had to hump it around with him. His mind told him to dump at least half of the ammo since he'd only seen one or two of the creatures at a time, most too crippled to be a threat and easily dispatched with his knife. But he'd held on, pushing those thoughts of weakness to the back of his mind. Seeing the target-rich environment in front of him, he was grateful that he hadn't pussed out and he planned to make use of all the ammunition.

The nuclear explosion toppled the Washington Monument all those years ago and it was broken into several useless parts behind him. The base of the obelisk up to about fifteen feet high looked to be relatively intact, while the rest of the structure stretched away toward the west where the blast's overpressure had pushed it. Kestrel used a small hooligan tool to open the doorway inset on the side of the Monument. Then he secured the door and climbed the remaining stairs to the highest point remaining where the staircase ran along the eastern side of the wreckage. He sighed involuntarily when he set the ridiculously heavy backpack full of ammunition on the stairs beside him. *Oh yeah,* he thought as he checked his fields of observation and fire on each side. *This will do perfectly.*

He worked the drawstrings on his backpack quietly and laughed to himself about the absurdity of the military uniforms these days that used Velcro fasteners in place of buttons and simple tie strings. In this situation, the opening of the fabric would have echoed across the open area and drawn the zombies directly to him, leaving him stranded inside the obelisk.

He peeked inside the bag at the small cardboard boxes of ammunition. To save on weight, he had the ten magazines on his chest rig and another five in the backpack, but the rest of the cartridges were in their factory-sealed cardboard boxes. He'd have to reload his magazines by hand since the speed loader strapped to the inside pocket would make too much noise. It would be tedious work, but he had time. If he played this right, he'd have all the time in the world.

The operator eased the rifle up onto the granite wall carefully; it wouldn't do to accidentally knock off a large chunk and bring the entire group over to him. The fog couldn't be helped, it was an element of the environment he'd have to deal with.

His sense of revulsion at the creatures rose as he observed them through the long-range scope on his SCAR. He'd been up close and killed a lot of them, but he hadn't actually watched the way that they reacted to stimuli and seemed to ebb and flow as a group. The more he watched them, the more he believed that they communicated in some way because there was a pattern to their movements. It felt like he was observing at an ant colony working to bring food back to the hive.

The operator wondered which building along the Mall that they had been protecting. Large museums lined the entire length. The only places that he felt that he could rule out were the National Archives and the National Museum of Art since they'd visited those places extensively last spring. The crowd surged back and forth in one mass near the fourth and fifth patch of dirt that had once been the lush, green grass of the Mall. There were hundreds of zombies spread out along the length of the open area by themselves, but they were likely just the ones that couldn't get near the main group.

After watching the crowd for over an hour, he was confident that the Type One controlling these things was in one of two buildings. There was the red brick building that jutted out close to the Mall on the south side that looked like an honest-to-goodness castle and there was the large National Museum of Natural History directly across from that one on the north side. The creatures were incredibly thick in front of those two buildings, so he was confident that it had to be one of them. He'd been to the museum before during his counter-observation training for the Agency, but he didn't have any clue what the red building had been when the city was still alive.

He'd seen all that he needed to and decided that it was time to make his move. He lined up his first shot, far into the middle of the pack away from his own position on the hill. He'd decided to begin there in case the creatures figured out that something was wrong, hopefully they wouldn't head toward his position and instead go to where their fellow zombies had died.

He'd also determined that the best course of action would be to kill the healthiest-looking ones first. Those would be able to move quickly if they identified his location. A large male ambled across his scope. Its clothes had long since rotted away, which meant that it had been out there, on guard in the elements for a long time. *Yeah, you'll do nicely, Big Guy*, he told himself.

Breathe, exhale, pause, squeeze and observe. A thick stream of blackish crap erupted from its head and flew into the evening air. The big zombie dropped like a sack of shit. Kestrel waited for a reaction from the creatures around the one he'd shot, but none of them seemed to notice. A couple of them even tripped over the body until they communicated to one another to avoid it and then the crowd parted ways around the corpse while still moving at their normal pace. His spine tingled at the pure insect-like nature of the creatures. Insects felt no remorse and had no sense of self-preservation; their only goal was to further the hive's lifespan.

He lined up another shot and took his time killing creatures one at a time at various points within the mass. He went with headshots to make every round count and changed out magazines as needed. Kestrel rapidly went through all five mags in his backpack, plus the one that had been in the weapon when he started, 180 rounds total. Every shot had been a kill. It had taken less than fifteen minutes and he'd barely made a dent in the crowd. It had gone quickly, but this would take a lot longer than he'd anticipated and he would have given his left nut for a gunship. That wasn't coming, he was alone. The only thing he could do was to clear the zombies himself, so he sat down and began the tedious work of manually reloading the magazines as quietly as possible.

The ten full magazines in his chest rack remained untouched. Those were for run and gun firefights, like if his position became compromised and he had to go quickly, possibly even leaving behind the heavy backpack full of ammo. It was a lesson he'd learned early on as a SEAL in East Timor fighting with the Aussies against Muslim terrorists. Always leave yourself with readily accessible ammunition and reload your mags when possible; you never knew when you'd need them.

Finally, nine empty cardboard boxes lay scattered on the ground, each empty of its twenty 7.62-millimeter rounds to fill the six thirty-round magazines. Kestrel stood and placed the rifle on the crumbling wall once again and began selecting targets at random from the crowd. *Time to cull the herd.*

*****

31 October, 1824 hrs local
Lehigh Valley International Airport
Allentown, Pennsylvania

They were trapped. The creatures had followed them into the wreckage, effectively removing any escape route back down the highway and now the way forward was blocked off by, of all things, a big jumbo jet on its side. "Well what are we going to do now, genius?" Katie snarled.

"I don't know. I'm... I'm thinking!" he stammered.

"You better think a little faster, because we're about to have company," Maria stated from the back seat, much more calm than the younger woman.

"We could abandon the car and make a run for it," Shawn suggested.

"No, I'm not walking anymore if I don't have to," Katie said. "We could turn around and ram them, right?"

"There's not enough room to get up enough speed. We'd just end up getting trapped along the road and then the creatures would trap us when we stop," Maria said.

"Our only option is to get out of the car," Shawn agreed. "We can find another one before too long."

"How'd that work out for you last time you went looking for cars?"

"Katie, you're not helping. Why are you being like this?" Shawn asked. He did *not* need her attitude right now. He wasn't happy about being the group's de facto leader and their insistence that he be the one to make the final decisions about their fate. It seemed like everything was a life and death decision; he just wanted to make a simple choice for once—something mundane like most of his decisions in life had been before the apocalypse.

The teenager's face softened and then she replied, "You're right, Shawn. I'm sorry. I'm stressed out that I might die in a few minutes."

He glanced into the rearview mirror at the slowly advancing mass of undead behind the Buick. They were certainly rambling slower than the ones that he'd seen before, especially those back in Parsippany. Once again, it seemed to Shawn that the creatures had changed how they operated. It was certainly strange, but he didn't have time to think about why they kept changing their tactics.

What he did have to think about was what they were going to do. It was an easy decision, there really weren't any choices left except to abandon the car. "Okay, we're gonna grab our gear and go. There's no way that we can make it past them in the car and if we get stuck in here, then we're done for."

Katie grumbled, but the other two passengers opening their doors got her moving in the right direction. Shawn wondered briefly what they were going to take. They hadn't accumulated a lot of random things, but they had a decent supply of food and borrowed clothing. He hated to lose any of it, but they didn't have enough backpacks to get everything. Plus, they'd gotten lax about re-packing their supplies into their packs and now they didn't have the time to stuff everything into them.

Stupid, Shawn thought. He needed to get his shit together and be a leader. They couldn't afford to make mistakes. No more shortcuts. This new world meant that they had to be prepared to flee at any moment. If something happened to one of them, it would be his fault. These two women looked to him to help keep them alive, they were his responsibility and it was time he started acting like their leader.

"Let's go. Stuff what food you can into your backpacks and don't forget your weapons," he ordered as he opened the trunk. It was a disaster, they'd put food in the back without boxes or bags of any kind and it had flown everywhere when they weaved around the rubble in the city. They were going to lose most of it.

He crammed a few cans of soup into his pack and checked the creatures. *Had they sped up?* He didn't know, but they were definitely closer than where he thought they should be. A few more cans went into his bag and then a noise made him stop and look skyward.

The sound of far off helicopters made him stop. If there were helicopters, then maybe the city hadn't been abandoned! He wondered if they could get up on top of some of the wreckage and make a fire that the pilots could see. *One thing at a time, Buddy*. He eyed the zombies again; he was sure that some of them had seen the car now. They'd altered their course and now headed directly for them instead of following the crowd. It was time to go.

"Okay, that's it. They've seen us. We're leaving," he said. He wanted to shoot into the group of them with Jon's rifle, but he knew that would only alert all of them that they were there, not to mention everything within earshot of them as well."

"But what about all of our stuff?" Katie pleaded.

"We'll get more. It won't do you any good if you're dead. We're going that way," he said as he gestured toward the wreckage of several taller buildings with the infamous baseball bat.

*****

31 October, 1835 hrs local
En Route to Target Location
Allentown, Pennsylvania

The beating of the rotor blades pounded into Kevin's chest. He loved the feeling of soaring above the ground, flying across the devastation below at over 125 miles per hour. Since the zombie war started, he'd put in tons of hours flying in the Guard's helicopters, which was something that the young sergeant wouldn't have been able to do if there hadn't been a war.

As infantryman in the Indiana National Guard's 76th Infantry Brigade Combat Team, the Night Hawks, he'd deployed to Afghanistan, but all of his movements had been by ground in the giant MRAP vehicles; none of their missions had been in helicopters. It took a zombie outbreak to get him and his squad up in the air. It was exhilarating and terrifying at the same time.

The young noncommissioned officer had been running search and rescue missions for weeks now as part of the brigade's forward deployed element. His battalion had been attached to the newly-designated Joint Task Force East Coast that was commanded up by the New Jersey Army National Guard's 29th Infantry Division. Their missions ran almost nonstop as the command found new groups of survivors that the rescue teams had to go out and secure.

Kevin secretly wondered what good it would do to rescue all of these people. What they should have been doing was focusing on wiping out the zombies, not flitting around, risking soldiers' lives to rescue a couple of people at a time. Sure, it was the right thing to do for the individuals, but was it the right thing to do for the country? His squad could kill hundreds of the creatures from the safety of the air instead of inserting behind the lines and potentially getting themselves killed while they were on the ground.

That wasn't his mission. All he wanted to do was kill zombies, but he'd do his duty and follow his orders.

The headset that he wore over the top of his helmet crackled and then he heard the co-pilot's voice, *"Hey, Sergeant Lamar, we're one minute out from the insertion point."*

"Thank you, sir. We're ready to go," he responded into the headset's integrated microphone.

"Roger. We'll find a nice, calm place to put you down this time."

He winced at the pilot's statement. Yesterday they'd put down in Quakertown, Pennsylvania to search for survivors, where they'd been inserted onto the football field and the zombies came out of the woodwork for a meal. Thankfully, they were the kind that just wandered around wherever their feet took them and attacked only what they could see; those were mostly harmless on an individual basis and were easily killed without much effort. Not like the ones that continued to attack the bulk of the Army. That kind was different somehow, like a swarm of angry ants. There were rumors among the troops that all of the zombies were the same until they got together and then they got smarter collectively.

Kevin didn't know about that, but he'd watched groups of the creatures work together to find ways *around* obstacles when he was on the defensive line the first few days of the war when his unit was sent east. Since then, the governor had imposed restrictions on the way his troops could be used and front line fodder wasn't one of them. He laughed to himself, *Thank goodness for the Russians.* They loved being in the line and challenging their manhood against the creatures. They'd lost so many soldiers to stupid individual acts of bravado, but he was glad that they were on the humans' side instead of fighting against them.

He glanced out of the door as the back of the helicopter dipped slightly in preparation for landing. It looked like they were coming down onto the roof of the mall—which had sustained significant damage, but the satellite imagery made it appear to be stable enough for the troops to walk across. He would make the call on the ground about whether or not to leave the safety of the roof after he assessed the local situation.

The door gunner on the opposite side let off a quick burst and the pilot came back on the radio, *"Okay, Smitty tagged a few off to the south of our position. We're going to begin hover... Now. You're cleared to exit the bird."*

The infantryman took the headphones off and turned toward his squad. Using a combination of hand gestures and screaming above the helicopter's big engines, Kevin ordered his soldiers to dismount the bird. Once he was sure everyone knew what he wanted, he rotated the locking mechanism on his own safety harness, swung his legs out over the side of the helicopter and then jumped the two feet down to the roof of the mall.

It only took a few seconds for everyone to get onto the roof and then the Blackhawk was lifting skyward. The pilots would fly to a location about a mile from the Lehigh Valley Mall and then the door gunners would open up, making a lot of noise and hopefully drawing away any of the creatures that had begun movement toward the drop off location. They'd used the technique successfully on every mission that Kevin's team had run so far and it worked brilliantly.

"Got visual on the target vehicle, Sergeant."

Kevin walked quickly to where Specialist Vaccaro pointed out toward the highway. He squinted, but at that distance he couldn't see well enough to discern what she pointed to. "Are you sure?"

"Positive, Sergeant," she replied with a curt nod of her chin. "My parents had a 1991 Buick LaSabre. I'd recognize that outline anywhere."

He opened a small aftermarket pouch strapped to his ballistic vest and pulled out the miniature folding binoculars inside. After scanning the area that she indicated for a second, he saw the target, a dark gray early '90s model Buick. *Damn, that girl's got some good eyes.*

It looked like they'd traveled down the main highway until they came to the choke point where there was too much debris to turn around and a freaking airplane fuselage blocked the way forward. Zombies surrounded the car, but they weren't actively trying to get inside, which meant that the passengers had already fled or were doing a *really* good job at hiding inside the vehicle. If the creatures knew that they were inside, they'd be attacking the car.

"The roof is secure, Sergeant," another of his soldiers called over to him. The rehearsals were paying off, they knew that immediately upon setting down, they had to ensure that the roof was free from any potential threats and that access to the area was secure.

"Alright, guys," Kevin addressed his squad. As he spoke, he pointed out beyond the mall parking lot to US Route 22. "We know that there was a Buick traveling west down that highway right there and now it's sitting on the other side of the river, abandoned. Even though we're too late to intercept the occupants while they're still in the car, our mission hasn't changed. We'll move out from here, find any survivors and kill any zombies that we see. Questions?"

"Wouldn't it be smarter to hold up here overnight and then go out in the morning?" Private Majors asked.

He grinned as Specialist Vaccaro slapped the private on the back of the helmet and answered, "Nope. We know that the Buick was moving at least an hour ago when we were scrambled for this mission. Sometime during our flight, those people had to abandon their car which means that they're on foot in Indian Territory and don't know their way around. We know that they're close, if we wait until the morning, they could be miles from here if they went in the opposite direction."

"Majors is just afraid of the dark, Sarge," Private Folsom said.

"That's because there really *are* monsters in the dark," Vaccaro answered darkly. "We've got this, Sergeant. Let's go rescue those people."

"Alright. Set up the beacon lights on the wall and let's go do this. We leave in five minutes."

*****

31 October, 1849 hrs local
Lehigh Valley International Airport
Allentown, Pennsylvania

They'd been running for more than ten minutes, but the girl knew that they hadn't gone nearly far enough to be safe. When she glanced back at the airplane wreckage, it was still clearly visible, even if the zombies weren't. It drove her crazy that despite her injuries from less than a week ago, Maria seemed like she was a machine, running smoothly and not out of breath or overly tired.

Before all of this went down, Katie hadn't thought that she was out of shape. She went to the gym once or twice a week and walked a long ways across campus every day back at school, so she thought that she'd easily be suited for a life on the road when her boyfriend suggested that they leave the safety of their apartment near the County College of Morris back in Randolph. One day, he'd left for a supply run and never returned.

The need for food and water had driven her farther from the apartment and that's how she ended up with these two. They were alright, but she felt like the third wheel and was shocked to find out that they'd only known each other for about two weeks. They seemed to work very well together and she could easily see them dating, although Shawn's wife had been killed only a month ago.

Katie thought it was strange how much more time there seemed to be in each day when you were bored out of your mind. Not having television or the internet made each day drag by and they seemed almost twice as long as a normal day. Then, add to that the three days of being cooped up in the car, driving at twenty miles an hour and she was ready to go insane. She'd been both frightened of the prospect of leaving the car and exhilarated for a change in the scenery.

But now, she was flagging. Her side hurt and she wished that she'd skipped the KFC in favor of the treadmill more often. Her companions weren't all crazy in shape or anything, but she could tell by the way that they moved that each of them went to the gym regularly. No one foresaw this crazy scenario happening, but if they did, would people have changed their lifestyles or would it be a struggle no matter what?

Of course, she'd never know; for now, she had to take a break. "Hey guys!" Katie called softly. "I... I hafta take a break. I can't keep up."

Shawn slowed down to a walk while Maria continued running for another twenty feet. Finally, she stopped and turned toward the girl. She had her hands on her hips and one side cocked out like she was pissed off to have to wait for anyone else.

"What's wrong, Katie?" Shawn asked with concern. The bastard wasn't breathing hard either.

"I just need to walk for a minute. I'm all light-headed."

He glanced up at Maria as they walked to where she'd stopped. "She took that knock on the head from those cans," Shawn stated. "I don't want to stress her body too much. We put enough distance between us and the zombies for right now. Let's slow down, conserve our energy and think about finding a place to bed down for the night."

"Shawn, are you kidding me?" Maria asked, now folding her arms defensively across her chest. "*Our* bodies are pretty fucking stressed, but we're finding the strength to go on. These things are the most active during the day, we should keep moving at night while we have the chance."

The group's leader looked back and forth between the two women. Katie could tell that he wanted to keep going—Maria obviously did—but she really was tired and didn't know how much longer she'd be able to go at the pace that Maria set. Her life had been laid back before the end came. She wasn't used to all of this stress and physical activity.

"I can keep walking, Shawn," she admitted. "I just can't do the non-stop running that you two can."

Shawn reached out and put a comforting hand on her shoulder. "We can't keep going forever either, Katie. We've just seen what these things can do up close and that fear is what's motivating us to keep going. Come on, let's keep walking west, we'll eventually find a car or a sign that will tell us where the military went."

She looked around at the devastation in the pale moonlight and stated, “I don’t think we’re gonna find anything in this town, Shawn. They destroyed it.”

He was silent as they walked down the road, making their way around, over and sometimes under the scattered wreckage. Thankfully, they hadn’t found any bodies but Katie figured it was only a matter of time; you couldn’t have this level of damage and not have dead people.

Suddenly, Shawn let out a soft cheer and pointed off in the distance. “Look at that! That’s a sign if I’ve ever seen one!”

Katie followed his outstretched arm and saw a bright light shining into the sky. With zero electricity, even a flashlight would have stood out in the night, but the light that had unexpectedly appeared could be seen for miles and miles. Then, another light came on a small distance away from the first, followed rapidly by a third and fourth, all shining radiantly into the sky.

“Holy shit!” she muttered.

Maria stopped short and placed a warning hand across Shawn’s chest. “What if it’s a trap?” she asked.

Shawn pressed her hand down and pulled her into an embrace. Katie could hear him mumbling something into her ear and see Maria’s head nodding, but what passed between the two of them was a mystery to her.

Finally, Shawn broke away and said, “Okay, we’ve got to take that as a sign that *somebody* wants us to see. Since we don’t know who it is, we’ll have to be careful and approach it with caution. I don’t want us to get captured by some weird-assed gang of thugs so we’ll use the wreckage to sneak along and once we get close enough to see what it is, we’ll make the determination if they’re friendly or not. Deal?”

The girl noticed that Maria’s fingers were tightly intertwined with Shawn’s, but didn’t say anything about it. “Yeah, of course,” she replied. “We’ll be quiet, sneak up and make sure it’s the Army and not some cult or something and then decide what to do once we get there.”

“Okay, let’s get moving again,” Shawn stated. “Remember, now that we know that we’re not alone, we need to be on the lookout for traps and stuff like that.”

“And zombies,” Katie quipped.

*****

31 October 1751 local
Crockett County Courthouse
Ozona, Texas

"Alright... Alright, dammit! Enough already! Everybody quiet down. What's going on, Calvin?"

"The Mexicans are roaming all over the desert by my house, that's what!"

"Okay, so what?" Crockett County's Commissioner replied with a sigh toward the two men who blocked the doorway of his office. Even from behind his desk, he could smell the whiskey oozing out of their mouths and the pores of their skin. He hoped this didn't take too long, he had plans tonight. "We're only seventy miles from Mexico; the Mexicans are out in the desert all the time."

It was true. Ozona was only about seventy miles, as the crow flies, from Del Rio, which was right across the border from the Mexican state of Coahuila de Zaragoza. Just to the west of the border town, only another fifty or so miles, the United States' Big Bend National Park boasted the most rugged and vacant land in all of Texas; it was a major point of entry for both drugs and illegal immigrants. Grayson had seen hundreds of Mexicans making their way illegally across his land since he and Jamie settled in Texas more than six years ago after they'd evacuated from Indianapolis, so it wasn't a big deal to him anymore.

It was after five on Halloween and he'd planned to take his kids, Jessica and Gregory, trick-or-treating this year. He wasn't sure what was making all of his constituents so upset, but he'd made a commitment to his kids that he wouldn't miss the holiday again this year. He'd just call Andre over at the local Border Patrol office—like they were supposed to do—and have him go investigate. Even Sheriff Cochran would have been a better alternative for Calvin and Nathan than the county commissioner, but the two drunks knew better than to go inviting the law into their lives.

"A few illegals ain't the problem, Mr. Donnelly," Calvin Espinoza said. "What I mean is there's a whole Mexican army driving around my ranch!"

"Calvin, is this like the time you swore that we were being taken over by aliens disguised as armadillos and jack rabbits?"

"You know that I took that back. I was just mistaken by all the crazy lights out there in the sky," the old drunk muttered with downcast eyes.

"Hell, Calvin. Just last week you and Nathan were in here telling me that the Russians were invading, now it's the Mexicans?"

Grayson sighed again as Nathan raised his hand like he was in court or school. Finally, he said, "What is it, Nathan?"

"Well, Your Honor, I—"

"Please, how many times do I have to tell you two to just call me Grayson or Mr. Donnelly?"

"Uh, okay, Mr. Donnelly. In Calvin's defense, we heard about the Russians on the internet radio show and the reports keep coming that they're up there in the Virginias fighting against the zombies."

The mention of zombies changed Grayson's mood. He couldn't believe that the nation was once again facing a major outbreak of *zombies*. He'd fought against the damned things and helped to contain them in Indianapolis before they'd been wiped out there. He'd even gone to Quantico last spring as a Type Two "expert" to brief the FBI team that was responsible for recovering some of the United States' most prized possessions—which also apparently kicked the hornet's nest.

Grayson tried to not to think about those dark days in Indianapolis often. Yes, he'd met his wife, Jamie, and made lifelong friends in Curtis and Julie Long, and Sam and Gretchen Johnson from Three Pillars and Bill Downs and his daughter Carrie from Pecan Valley, but when they got together, they almost never mentioned their time in the quarantined city. The thought of the quarantine then made him think about Major General Ian Clarke and the British Prince of Wales' Division that had ringed the city while the Americans fought on multiple fronts against the zombies in DC, the militias in the Midwest and the gangs in the cities. It was a perfect storm of discontent and terrorism that almost brought the nation to the brink of anarchy and he wasn't sure if America would survive this war.

"Okay, I don't know about the Russians being on American soil helping to fight the zombies; we've accepted help from other nations before, but an army of Mexicans running around the desert? That's a little hard to swallow, guys."

"I knew you wouldn't believe us, so I took pictures of them. There's a whole mess of 'em and they look like they're headed toward Ozona!"

Humor him for a little bit; you've got time until the trick-or-treating starts. "Well how many people are in this army of yours, Calvin?"

The older man dug into his pocket and pulled out his cell phone. "Here, take a look. It ain't a whole mess of illegals; it's the actual Mexican Army. They've invaded!"

Grayson sighed and glanced at the clock on his desk once again before accepting the phone. "Just swipe the screen from right to left to go back and forth between pictures," Calvin directed.

He looked down at the smart phone's small screen. The old man had taken pictures from what looked like his back porch. They were grainy and hard to see when he tried to zoom in on subjects that were far away, but there were definitely a lot of pick-up trucks, SUVs and even several non-US wheeled military vehicles out across the flats near the old man's house.

He swiped the phone from the right and grimaced at the picture of Nathan peeing on a toad in Calvin's yard and laughing like an idiot. "Really?" Grayson asked and held up the phone for Calvin to see.

Calvin grinned despite himself and replied. "You went the wrong way, but that's when we noticed the Mexicans. Go the other way on the camera roll."

He did as asked and tried to forget the image. He went past the first photo that he'd seen and then went into ones that he hadn't seen yet. They certainly looked like an invading army. Some of the pictures were better than others and he could see a lot of men and wheeled vehicles driving across the open scrub desert behind Calvin's house. Grayson looked up from the phone and asked, "Where'd you take these photos, Calvin?"

"Right off of my back porch! And I looked it up on the internet, those big army vehicles are infantry carriers. They hold six or eight soldiers per vehicle, plus all those men walking. I'm telling you, they're invading!"

Grayson was concerned that the two men had actually found an army of Mexicans invading the United States. "How long ago did you take these pictures?"

Calvin looked over to his best friend and drinking partner before answering. "What? Maybe five minutes before we left and then a twenty-minute drive into town."

"That's 'bout right," Nathan slurred.

"Alright thanks, fellas. You two did a great job coming in here and telling me about this. I've got to call the sheriff and then the governor's office," Grayson answered. *So much for getting any trick-or-treating in with the kids,* he thought as he picked up the phone to dial Joe Cochran's number.

ELEVEN

31 October, 1903 hrs local
Lehigh Valley Mall Parking Lot
Allentown, Pennsylvania

"Hey, Sergeant, I've got movement," Specialist Vaccaro stated in the strange, detached voice that she always seemed to use when she watched the KillTV for information during a mission.

Kevin edged up next to her to look at the small tablet computer that she held. The tablet showed a direct video feed from one of the drones flying above. The Army had been given dynamic retasking authority over the entire unmanned aerial vehicle network to support the ground movement of troops as they fought against the creatures on the ground. It drove the Air Force crazy to give up control of their birds to the ground-pounders.

"Are those our civilians?" the sergeant asked as he pointed to the small, ruggedized screen. It was amazing that they had a potential visual on their objective so he could readjust their planned route before they'd found their way out of the mall's parking lot. In addition to the overturned cars and general wreckage in the area from the MOABs that the Air Force had dropped almost a week ago, the squad had already encountered several zombies that were attracted to their beacon lights and had to be dispatched quietly. That took time that the civilians running for their lives didn't have, so Kevin used every advantage that he could to get to them as quickly as possible.

"Hold on, let me switch to infrared. If they're human, they'll show up bright and rosy, if they're zombies, they'll disappear...."

"And if they're recently deceased, we might be walking right up to our death," Private Majors muttered from a few feet away.

"Dammit, there has to be a better way," Kevin muttered. The fact that the creatures didn't show up on IR was a huge advantage, but the team's mission was to go rescue people trapped behind the main zombie offensive line. Often, the Army had no clue where those civilians were located until they started moving around to look for food, shelter or weapons and then the satellites or drones caught them and a rescue team was scrambled. Unfortunately, when people started moving around, they tended to get dead. Several times, his team had deployed to a target location and found the people that they'd been sent to rescue had already turned. The problem with infrared was that the human body would retain heat for several hours and they'd went forward expecting an easy extraction, only to end up besieged by the newly-transformed zombies.

"We could always yell out 'Marco' and if they answer back 'Polo' then we're good to go," Vaccaro answered sarcastically.

"And if they moan back, I'll answer them with Karen here," Private Folsom quipped as he patted the 40-millimeter grenade launcher mounted underneath his M4 rifle.

"Or, we could just let them come to the lights," Majors said hopefully.

"I swear to God, Majors, if you don't quit being such a pussy, I'll cram this rifle up your ass and squeeze off a few rounds," Folsom replied quietly while still managing to convey his message.

"Alright, all of you; knock it off," Kevin ordered. "While you three stupid fucks are making jokes and threatening each other, we could get ambushed. Practice good noise discipline, or I *will* get my revenge once we get back to base. You get me?"

He looked back and forth between the privates as they each nodded and then glanced over to his real problem child. She wore a wide, toothy grin. "What's your problem, Vaccaro?"

"Oh, I've just never seen you so fired up before, Sergeant. Maybe there's hope for you yet."

Kevin was in a strange place. He outranked Specialist Lisa Vaccaro in the Indiana National Guard, but in the civilian world, she was his boss. They both worked for a pharmaceutical sales company in Evansville and by a twist of fate, they were also in the same platoon in the Guard. Before the zombie war, they'd been in different squads and it wasn't a big deal, but the attrition from their time in the defensive line had taken over half of the company out of action and this squad had been cobbled together from the remnants of everyone else left alive.

Vaccaro turned out to be a great soldier with an even better sense of humor about the situation, but there was always that lingering doubt in the back of Kevin's mind that she was evaluating everything he did—both as a noncommissioned officer in the Guard as well as his potential in their civilian job. It was just another aspect of the National Guard that he'd have to work around. The unit had tried to do the right thing initially, but attrition had forced the situation, now he just had to grin and bear it while still doing the best that he could as a soldier and leader.

He chuckled uncomfortably and said, "Okay. Let's get focused on what we're doing, people. We need to find out if those are our civilian targets or if they're zeds, and then we need to act accordingly; either we rescue their stupid asses or we murder 'em."

Kevin cross-referenced where they were with the heat signatures on the tablet and decided that they should stay with the plan he'd came up with on the roof of the mall. "The satellite imagery has confirmed what I thought; they're traveling down Route 22, more or less. We're going to continue on our preplanned route to the checkpoint, call it in and then wait for them to come across the river to us. Questions?"

When there were none—and thankfully, no more attempts at witty banter—he said, "Alright, let's move out."

The four of them continued forward, sliding around overturned cars and stepping as lightly across the shattered glass as possible.

*****

31 October, 2013 hrs local
Lehigh Valley Thruway
Allentown, Pennsylvania

Maria was exhausted. They'd been doing a mixture of running and walking when Katie couldn't keep up for an hour and a half now. That girl was really starting to get on the older woman's nerves; she was a complainer. Maria wasn't in the best shape of her life either, especially after what happened at the house in Randolph, but there wasn't a chance in hell that she'd say anything to the others about being so tired.

Bocanegra's don't quit, we face our problems and deal with them to the best of our abilities. You'll either sink or swim, but you will never quit. That's what her father always told her. She'd faced adversity her entire life and surviving the zombie outbreak was just one more stumbling block in a long line of hardship. Her parents came over from Cuba in 1981 as part of the so-called "Mariel Boatlifts." She was born in Florida while her parents waited processing through the large refugee camps that the American government had established for the immigrants while they weeded out the criminals and mentally insane that Castro had sent over as part of the exodus from his country.

Her father spoke very little English when he first arrived in America, but he'd been able to find work at the docks and eventually made friends with the owner of the company over the years. When the opportunity to move to New York and oversee the operations of a new expansion came up, Papa was the owner's designee to shepherd the shipping company's rising reputation.

Life in New York City had been hard for Maria since it always seemed like she was the new kid. Her father continued to promote within the company and they moved to a nicer area of the city, again causing her to be the new kid, but even worse, she was now a Hispanic kid in a white school and felt totally alone. Her father had told her that there were two options in life: She could either sink or she could swim. It was that simple, downhome message that resonated with the thirteen-year-old girl and she decided to swim.

She dove headfirst into her studies and joined honors clubs, even playing a few sports here and there. By the time everything was said and done, Maria had graduated as the salutatorian for her high school class and gotten a major scholarship for college. Her father became ill with cancer during her first year and she immediately flew back to New York to be with him. Even as he lay dying in the hospital bed, he reiterated the one mantra that had sustained his lifestyle and became her way of life. *Bocanegra's don't quit. We either sink or swim, but we don't quit.*

He died after a very short time in the hospital. Maria's mother told her that he'd been sick a long time and had hidden it from his daughter and coworkers. He didn't want them to think of him as weak or feeble and had worked up until the very end. He never quit—and neither would she.

Maria held up once again while Shawn coddled Katie. "Let's go! We have to be less than four blocks from those lights," she whispered when they caught up to her.

Katie smiled at her and replied, "I'm trying, Maria. I really am. I'm just not used to all of this physical activity."

She snorted softly and then, "Okay, keep trying your best. We're almost there. Once we're safe with the Army, then you can rest."

Maria could clearly see the girl nod in the light of the full moon. *Fine, maybe I should cut her some slack. If she's trying her hardest, then that's all I can ask of her.*

They walked slowly for another couple hundred feet and then the roadway ended in a massive fifty-foot drop off. "Holy shit!" Maria exclaimed loudly in surprise. She regained her composure and in a quieter voice she said, "If the moon hadn't been so full, then we might have just walked right off into the..." She paused as the sound of rushing water far below confirmed her thoughts before continuing, "Into the river."

Shawn walked up beside her and peered into the darkness. "I guess the bridge is out, huh?"

Maria thought about how they'd be able to get across in the darkness. She could see small segments of the bridge protruding from the water's black surface, but not enough to allow them to cross safely without swimming most of the way. Plus, she had no idea how strong the river's current would be. They could get separated and swept away if it was moving fast.

"Hey guys," Katie's small voice penetrated the darkness. "Come over here and see."

They walked several feet off to the side where Katie stood. When they got there, she pointed at a bent and twisted sign that let them know that they were looking at the Lehigh River, but there wasn't any other information. "See what, Katie?" Maria asked.

"The bridge sign. It says that this is the Lehigh River."

"So?"

"I think the river is pretty slow this far south," Katie said. "It starts up in the mountains, but we're so far away from there, that we should be okay crossing it."

"And how do you know that?" Maria probed.

"It's just something I remember reading somewhere. I don't know, maybe it was on a piece of garbage along the highway. With the bridge out and the river valley between those lights and us, we need to cross. I can't swim very well, but if it's slow and shallow, I'll be okay."

Maria couldn't argue with her logic, so they went back to the edge to determine the best route down the embankment to the river below. After a few seconds of examining the remains of the bridge's jagged concrete and rebar foundation, they decided that trying to make their way down along the old road's path would be nearly suicidal so they walked around to where the trees once lined the sides of the road and the steep hillside leading to the river bank. It was tough work climbing over all of the downed trees and debris, but they eventually made it to the bottom.

"The river isn't as wide as it looked from up there," Shawn remarked. "It looks like it's about the same distance from home plate to second base. That's only, what, 120 feet?"

"Something like that," Maria replied as she stared at the water rushing by. "But the river looks like it's moving pretty fast to me."

"Maybe if we walk up and down the bank for a little ways, we'll find a place that doesn't look so deep," Shawn suggested.

Maria sighed. This wasn't supposed to be so hard. Why was the bridge out? Even more confusing, why was the entire town bombed to smithereens? She could maybe understand it if they'd been walking across corpses all day long, but there'd been less than fifty that she saw and a whole lot of zombies that seemed intact enough to kill them; hardly worth the devastation that the Army or Air Force or whomever had done to the place. She'd seen firsthand how accurate shooting of small, individual weapons did the job that grenades and artillery couldn't do. All that stuff did was make crawling zombies instead of walking zombies.

Behind them, higher up on the slope, a twig snapped. The resulting noise echoed across the silent night like a gunshot.

"What was that?" Katie asked.

"Someone's up there," Shawn answered truthfully.

"Or something," Maria amended.

"Okay, I don't think we have time to find a shallow crossing spot," the group's leader said. "We need to go across now!"

"You think so, Shawn?" Maria asked sarcastically.

"Guys, maybe I was wrong about the water. It looks really deep... and fast," Katie amended.

Several loud thuds and more twigs breaking indicated that a large group was now coming toward them. Their heads whipped back along the path that they'd used to get down to the river and as one, they peered into the darkness. At that distance, the moonlight allowed them to see several man-sized forms stumbling and falling down the slope. "I think they found us," Shawn said.

Maria didn't wait to see what his suggestion would be. She knew that he would try to find some alternate way around the situation because of Katie—a way that would likely get them killed if they waited around too long. He was smart, but not good at snap decisions, so sometimes she had to take matters into her own hands. She started wading out into the water.

"Hey, where are you going?" Shawn asked.

"Across. I suggest you do the same. Put the river between us and them and make it to those lights."

"Can they swim?" Katie asked with a hint of panic in her voice.

Maria continued to splash out into the water. "I don't know. But I know that *I* can and that I'm faster than those things."

Shawn harrumphed behind her and then his feet flapped into the water too. "Come on, Katie. Let's go!"

"I can't. The water is too fast!"

Maria stopped then and turned around. She was about one third of the way across and the water was up to her mid-thigh. If she were closer, she would have slapped the girl across the cheek to knock some sense into her. "Katie! Get your ass out here or you are going to be zombie food," she screamed at the girl in an effort to galvanize her into action.

It worked. Katie stepped off into the water, protesting about the cold, but at least she was moving. Maria turned and continued to make her way across. She made it to about the halfway point when she stepped off a ledge into the middle of the river channel and sank into water deeper than her head.

Cold water filled her nostrils as the river churned above her, twisting and turning her body as the water rushed by. She began kicking her feet and used her arms to pull herself upward. Her head broke the surface to the sounds of Shawn's shouts. She swam *away* from his voice since he'd been behind her and soon, her shoes began to scrape against the muddy bottom.

A few more feet of swimming and then she tried to stand. The water was once more just above her navel and the woman stood up. "Shawn, the deep part is only about ten or fifteen feet across," she called.

"Are you okay?"

"Yeah," she replied but then realized that he was easily fifty feet upriver from her. The fact that she'd been swept that far downstream in the short distance meant that the water was extremely fast. "The current is really strong though, be careful!"

"Okay. I'm about where you were when you disappeared," he answered. Maria hoped that all the yelling they were doing wasn't just attracting the zombies on this side of the river, but at least they would be separated from the ones that she knew were pursuing them on the other side.

Katie's small form continued out to where Shawn stood and the older woman could tell that they were talking, but couldn't make out what they were saying. "Shawn, behind you!" she shouted.

A group of twenty zombies had emerged from the wreckage behind him and begun stumbling toward the river. Katie shrieked and clutched Shawn in a death grip. Maria could see Shawn shaking the girl and decided that she was going into shock. *It's up to me.*

She unslung the M4 that she'd carried the entire way since Parsippany, New Jersey and hadn't fired it since they fled that day that their rescue truck was overrun. She'd been afraid that the loud report would just draw more of the creatures to their location, so they'd relied on stealth and quiet to stay safe. The time for sneaking around was gone, her two companions were in danger and exposed in the middle of the river.

Maria used the pistol grip to pull the stock of the rifle firmly into the pocket of her shoulder like Sergeant Lumsey had taught her in New Jersey. The current tugged at her body, threatening to unbalance her, so she knew that firing close to Shawn would be out of the question, but she would sure as hell shoot at those things farther away. She wished for something to rest her front hand on so she could have a steadier shot, but there was nothing available. Everything that the noncommissioned officer had drilled into them came crashing back to her. She widened her stance to steady her upper body and went through the motions to control her breathing.

She peered through the small combat scope mounted on the weapon's rail system and the first zombie appeared. It was less than two hundred feet away and the scope's red dot bisected its head. Maria squeezed the trigger and the rifle bucked slightly against her shoulder. She'd known what to expect and she was able to reacquire the sight picture almost immediately because she'd had the rifle tight against her body.

The one she'd shot was down, floating in the shallows on its back where it had pitched from the force of the round. She mentally congratulated herself and moved to the next target. Another hit. The third round impacted on the rocks behind her intended target as she missed. She did a quick mental check of shooting fundamentals and decided that she must have jerked the trigger too hard since the round went wide to the right.

Katie's screech caused her to break the cheek-to-stock weld that had been drilled into her. The girl ran *toward* the zombies and Shawn called after her. He started to follow, but Maria yelled, "Shawn, leave her! There's nothing you can do!"

His indecision was almost palpable. She could see that he wanted to go after the girl, but to do so was akin to suicide. Finally, he turned and dove into the river to begin swimming toward her. Maria grinned in spite of the situation. *He's smarter than I am. I bumbled into the river and got disoriented; now he's in control of the direction he's going.*

She refocused on Katie splashing back toward the shallows. What was she doing? She shot another of the creatures before Katie got too close for her to shoot any more of them. The girl had turned parallel to the riverbank and sloshed through the thigh-deep water as the zombies fell into line, trailing behind her. She was going to make it! The water slowed the creatures and she was gaining separation on them with each step.

Then something odd happened. The zombie closest to the girl fell to the side and began to float slowly downstream away from the group. Then another creature fell. Before long, the girl was running on the rocky shoreline with none of the zombies left to follow her. She disappeared behind the jagged stump of what must have been a massive tree before the bombs knocked it over and Maria couldn't see her any longer.

Maria brought her rifle up and used the scope to look at the corpse of the first zombie where it floated idly in the shallows because the river hadn't pulled it into the main channel. There was a hole in the side of its head leaking a thick black fluid. She checked a few more of the bodies; all of them had the same injury—a single bullet hole in the head.

She turned quickly to the slope behind her that led out of the river valley and back toward the lights that they'd been trying to make. There was a sniper up there somewhere with a silenced rifle—*a damned good one at that.*

Shawn's splashing brought her attention back toward the river. The sniper's actions were out of her control; they were exposed down in the valley and if he wanted them dead, then they would be. "Over here!" she called softly to Shawn as he made his way across the channel.

He climbed out of the deep and turned to the far bank. "Where's Katie?" he asked.

"She got away into the wood line."

Shawn ran his hand over his forehead and up into his hair to wick the water away. "She refused to swim. She was okay with wading, but I don't think she knew how to swim. When she saw you disappear under the water, she just shut down and refused to go any further. The zombies were less threatening to her than the water."

"Well, she got away because of somebody up there," Maria said as she pointed across her body toward the ridgeline above them.

"Yeah, let's hope the man upstairs keeps her safe," he replied, misunderstanding her.

"No, not because of God," Maria muttered. "There's a sniper up there, killed like eight of the dammed things while you were swimming across."

He turned quickly to peer up into the darkness. "Are they on our side?"

"I don't know. They definitely aren't on the side of the zombies and they haven't shot us yet, so we should go up there and see who they are."

A bright flash of fire above them indicated where someone was. The light was followed by a hollow thumping noise that drifted down and then the far bank exploded in a loud detonation.

Maria turned to see smoke on the bank and several more zombies making their way across the rocky expanse. Then another explosion sent several bodies flying. Whoever was above them also had some serious firepower besides the sniper rifle. The sounds of the detonations echoed down the river valley for several seconds before silence once again descended across the city.

She hoped Katie would be alright, but at the same time, she was furious at the girl. Why had she agreed to cross the river if she was so terrified of the water? Why hadn't she just told them; they could have found another way around the river if she'd only opened up and told them about her fears. Now she was stuck on the eastern shore with a lot of zombies coming in. Maria wanted to feel bad for the girl, to mourn her loss, but for some reason she couldn't make herself do so.

Shawn tapped her on the shoulder and she turned back toward the opposite side of the river where a man in an Army uniform had emerged from hiding up along the top of the bluff. He waved at them to come up. Shawn grasped Maria's hands and they interlocked their fingers before they walked out of the water to face whoever was up there. Once they emerged from the water together, they continued to hold hands, relying on each other for support.

*****

31 October, 2139 hrs local
Rocky Mountain Manor
Denver, Colorado

"You've got to be fucking kidding me!" Ryan Wilson declared as he leaned back on the sofa. Recently, he'd taken to sitting directly on the couch with the smaller inner circle of his National Security Council. It made the setting more intimate and he felt that it facilitated more open communication than with him sitting behind his desk or at the head of a table.

"I wish I was, sir," Rob Griffith answered. "Our Texas offices received word from Ozona, a small Texas town about a hundred miles from the border."

"Wait. Ozona, Texas?" Kelly Flannigan asked incredulously.

"Yeah, why?" the Homeland Security Secretary enquired.

"I'll be damned. The Crockett County Commissioner was a consultant for us when we went into Washington to recover the Declaration of Independence last spring."

President Wilson was mildly interested about this aside, so he let it go for the moment. "What in the world would the commissioner of some backwater county in Texas possibly have to offer the FBI about zombies?" General Zollman asked.

"His name is Grayson Donnelly," Kelly answered. "He was one of the only survivors from Indianapolis. Grayson led the defense of a small community within the quarantine zone for more than half a year. They became really good at striking out against the zombies there and creating a safe zone around their base."

"So he was brought in as a zombie expert for your men?" the president completed the piece of the equation.

"Yes, sir. He's a valuable resource to have."

"Good, I'm glad that we have decent people on the scene," Ryan said before turning back to business. "How the hell did we miss this invasion, Chip?"

"Well, I guess the Mexicans were counting on all of our resources being locked up with the fight in the east—and they are. We weren't watching anywhere else."

"As the director of our national intelligence agencies, I expect you to focus on *all* of the threats to the nation, Chip. The military can focus on the zombies. Now we have an invading army from Mexico of all places. What do we know?"

"We retasked satellites immediately to fly over," Director Bullis replied. The president liked that the man didn't make excuses or even give some bullshit apology; there wasn't any time for that crap. A quarter of the nation was under siege and now there was an incursion into the underbelly, far from the fighting. He needed answers.

"Our read from agents in Mexico is that President Arnesto is not behind this like we thought when we saw the initial photographs. The Mexican government remains committed to assisting the United States with the zombie problem."

"Okay, great. Arnesto will keep the Mexican border safe from zombies *entering* his country, what the hell is he doing to stop his damned army from crossing *into* the States?"

"Sir, the invading force belongs to the Herrera Cartel, which already runs a semi-autonomous region in the northern Mexican desert. They've made a claim to Texas land that originally belonged to Mexico centuries ago when the Texans carved out their own country from the Mexicans," Chip stated. "Ernesto Herrera, the head of the cartel, has riled the northern

Mexican citizens up with nationalistic goals. We think that he plans to try and take a small chunk of desert to see how we react. If we just turn a blind eye because we're too weak to stop the cartel, then he'll establish a kingdom for himself in between Mexico and the US."

"Oh, he'll find that we're far from weak," the president fumed. "We're certainly not going to allow some drug lord to set up some damned extra-judicial stronghold. How is this even happening? Does the rest of the world think that we're that weak? That we'll just let criminals and thugs take our land and we won't do anything about it?"

The DNI shrugged and replied, "It's hard to tell, sir. Our assets report that some of our enemies perceive that yes, we are weakening daily. This is the second zombie war in six years, we've had massive civil unrest and the economy is in an extreme recession. In addition, we're spread extremely thin with troops—"

"I've talked to the Texas National Guard's Adjutant General," the Chairman of the Joint Chiefs interrupted. "The Texans have already sent most of their National Guard forces to assist with the effort in the northeast and the governor mobilized the Texas State Guard to assist with keeping order in the cities and patrol the shoreline for zombies coming up from the Gulf. He's already moving the State Guard troops from both El Paso and San Antonio toward the town."

"Wait, aren't the state militias unarmed?" Kelly Flannigan interjected.

The president threw up his hands. "I won't tell if you won't, Kelly. We're gonna have to suspend some of the laws that protect our citizens in order to protect the country. We already have tens of thousands of men and women in the northeast fighting under the direction of the Army; they're little more than a militia anyways."

The Director of the FBI nodded silently, properly rebuked. "We need to get some actual military forces out there to assist those militiamen," the president continued. "What do we have that's close?"

"Ozona is right in the middle of Fort Bliss and Fort Hood, but most of those troops are up on the Appalachian Defensive Line. The only soldiers left at both of those installations are the ones guarding the wire," the general admitted. "However, we do have a lot of recruits at bases in San Antonio, only a few hours away."

"What kind of recruits?"

"The Air Force basic training is there and the Army has Fort Sam Houston, which is where our medical personnel train."

"So you're saying that they're active duty troops who know how to follow orders and shoot a rifle?" the president clarified.

"Yes, sir. But they're still very young with hardly any officers or noncommissioned officers there to assist them since they're at training bases," General Zollman answered.

"They've received a lot more training than the civilians that we have facing the zombies up north, right?"

"Well… Yes, sir. But the zombies are an unthinking, uncaring mass of flesh; this is an invading human army down there in south Texas."

"We don't have the time for that type of distinction. Those kids are going to have to do the job until we can get full Army units down there," Ryan decided. "Are there any more forces—anywhere—that we can pull for this?"

"In all honesty, I'll have to see what we have, sir," the chairman admitted. "We've already pulled all of our forces worldwide; the only things left in our forward deployed locations are perimeter security and skeleton crews to ensure that the facilities remain habitable for our eventual return."

"Immediately after this meeting, send what we can to that town. Put—what was your guy's name, Kelly?"

"Uh, you mean Grayson Donnelly, sir?"

"Yeah, him. Put your commander on the ground in contact with Mr. Donnelly since it's his town and he has experience in guerilla warfare. Plus, he's the guy who reported it when our own intelligence agencies missed this outright attack on American soil, so that's another feather in his cap."

Ryan glanced at Chip Bullis, prepared to shut his protest down; the man wisely didn't say anything to the contrary. "We've done an amazing job with keeping this country afloat so far, folks. I am not going to stand by and let some Mexican drug cartel fucker attempt to take a part of our country.

"Mark, get me President Arnesto on the phone," the president told his Chief of Staff. "I have a few things to say to that bastard—chief among them is to ask why he can't control his own problems and keep them on his side of the border."

"Yes, sir!" Mark Namath replied enthusiastically. Ryan knew that regardless of the outcome of the zombie war, he'd be criticized throughout history as the guy who let it happen. That may be true to some extent since he didn't wipe those things out when they were trapped behind The Wall, but he sure as hell wouldn't be known as the president who allowed an invading army to take land away from the United States.

TWELVE

01 November, 0256 hrs local
Lehigh Valley Mall
Allentown, Pennsylvania

"Well, you two are some lucky sons a bitches," Folsom remarked while he lovingly stroked his grenade launcher. He'd been the one who shot the grenades across the river to try and give Katie a fighting chance of survival amongst the dead on the far bank.

"Thank you, Mr. Folsom," Maria replied after reading his uniform's nametape above his right pectoral muscle. "I'm sure your marksmanship allowed our friend to get away."

"You're gosh-danged right it did!" he replied. "I blew those mother fuckers to kingdom-come, didn't I?"

"Yeah, great job, Private Folsom," Sergeant Lamar answered. "You made sure that those pathetic creatures wouldn't make it across the river."

The young man affected a look of genuine hurt and the sergeant amended his earlier statement so he would understand, "Dude, without your fire support, that girl would have been done for. Good job."

It was enough for the infantryman and he sported a big grin at his squad leader's compliment. "Thank you, sergeant!"

"So, who is the sniper with an absolutely amazing aim?" the woman, Maria, asked looking from person to person among the four-man squad that had been waiting for her and Shawn at the top of the river valley's walls.

"That would be Specialist Vaccaro," the noncommissioned officer answered. "She's one hell of a shot with her M14."

"Thanks, Sergeant Lamar," the girl answered. "I missed with two of my shots, though. I spent eleven rounds to kill nine of the enemy; that's just not acceptable in my book."

"I think you did an outstanding job, Miss Vaccaro," Maria remarked. "You saved Katie's life and gave her a shot at survival; the rest is up to her."

There was an uncomfortable silence as the soldier quietly accepted the praise that she wasn't used to receiving for her actions in the military. The Army prided itself on remaining relatively quiet and not seeking individual recognition, so for the woman to tell Lisa that she'd done a good job was a new experience. The specialist liked hearing that she'd performed up to the standard and saved yet another life in this fucked up zombie war.

"Thank you, ma'am," Lisa replied. "The National Guard gave me the absolute best training available as a squad-designated marksman and I'm glad that I was able to use my training to help out your friend."

"That brings up my comment about the girl who took off back toward the eastern bank of the Lehigh River," Sergeant Lamar stated. "After Folsom fucked—I mean, after Private Folsom shot those zombies with the grenade, we have no idea where your travel partner took off to. Our satellites weren't directly overhead and the power is obviously out in Pennsylvania, so we have no idea of where she went after we lost visual of her. I believe that she continued back along the eastern riverbank, but there's simply no way to be certain."

"Thank you," the older woman responded. "We'd only known her for a few days. Apparently, she couldn't swim and decided that facing the zombies was better than swimming across the river."

"I wish she would've held out just a few minutes," the sergeant muttered with a depressed frown etched across his features. "We have rope with us; we could have rescued her."

The sadness in Lamar's voice made Vaccaro frown also. She'd been working up the nerve for weeks to let him know that she liked him. Then they got put together in the same squad and screwed everything up. Lisa thought the world of Kevin Lamar, but they were professional soldiers and there was no way she'd act on those feelings now that they had a formal working relationship established. Maybe once the war was over and they went back to Indiana she'd be able to transfer squads and then see about a relationship with him. For now, he was her NCO and she was the squad's designated marksman; that was it.

"We could try to go across the river and establish another set of beacons," Vaccaro suggested. "That might get her to come in."

Her squad leader smiled forlornly at her. "We could, but it's too dangerous. Those grenade blasts stirred up the creatures on the east bank and brought 'em running. Going over there now would be nearly suicidal; we'd have to wait until they disperse."

"So all the shooting just brought more of them toward Katie?" Shawn asked.

"I'm afraid so, sir," the sergeant acknowledged. "We got her some initial room to run, but if she didn't take it and just hunkered down somewhere, then she's probably already gone."

Vaccaro watched as Maria slid closer to Shawn unconsciously for support. He slid a hand around her waist, friendly, but not *too* familiar or possessive. They'd been through a lot together, but she didn't think that they were dating. She glanced at Sergeant Lamar again. Did he even like her? Even more to the point, did he know that she liked him? If he did, he sure didn't let on.

"Look, your friend survived behind the line for more than a month. That means she's stronger than you think and she'll be okay," Vaccaro said in an effort to ease their pain.

"We'll let our battalion headquarters know that she got separated during the rescue and to be on the lookout for her," Sergeant Lamar continued where she left off. "If they see evidence of her—or any other survivors—we'll scramble a rescue crew just like we did for you. When she pops up, we'll get her."

Maria nodded her head. Lisa could tell that she was sad, but she also got the vibe that it was more for the situation, not necessarily for the girl who'd ran off. She'd always had good intuition, even as a kid, and for some reason she felt like there was bad blood between the two of them. Maybe the girl tried to move in on Shawn and Maria didn't like it. Whatever the issue was, it didn't bother her that Katie wasn't around anymore.

"I hear the helicopter," Majors said. Vaccaro hoped that guy straightened up; she genuinely liked him, but even her good nature was starting to wear thin of the guy's constant jitteriness.

"Took 'em long enough," Sergeant Lamar deadpanned.

"You know those flyboys gotta have their crew rest, Sarge!" Folsom replied with the old slang for the word that persisted in the National Guard.

Soon, the blinking lights of the single helicopter could be seen speeding across the sky toward their position on the roof of the mall. Once, not too long before, a single helicopter mission would have been unheard of, but the standard operating procedure of the Joint Task Force East Coast was to use resources as sparingly as possible, which allowed for multiple missions like theirs to occur simultaneously by dedicating one bird to one squad. Besides, it wasn't like the zombies had any type of rocket launcher to take out the helicopter.

The squad's noncommissioned officer in charge gave instructions to the pilots to land the helicopter on the roof; the area was secure and they hadn't seen any of the creatures on this side of the river yet. The two refugees that they'd been sent to find bent almost double at the waist and covered their eyes against the incredible rotor wash that had now become just another part of Lisa's daily job. It was almost comical to watch the two of them run hunched over behind Kevin as he strode upright toward the helicopter. The spinning rotors were so far above everyone's head that there was no way they'd ever be in danger of getting hit as long as the blades were functioning normally.

Vaccaro used the side of the helicopter to pull herself up into the passenger area and she shuffled sideways to sit across from Maria, who was trying to cram a pair of foam earplugs that the crew chief had given her into her ears. Once those were in place, she leaned across and showed the older woman how to buckle her shoulder and lap harnesses before securing her own.

Within seconds, Kevin gave the thumbs up and the helicopter leapt skyward. Once again, Lisa wondered at the relationship between their precious cargo as they cried and held onto one another. It was a touching moment as their tears glistened in the helicopter's red interior lighting and she was proud that she'd been able to help them.

She glanced at her squad leader and he flashed a huge smile at her along with a thumbs up. She wondered if he knew how much she wanted him to hold onto her the way those two held each other. One day she hoped to have the opportunity to find out.

*****

01 November, 0658 hrs local
Lehigh Valley International Airport
Allentown, Pennsylvania

"Oh my God, ohmy God, ohmygod..." Katie whispered to herself repeatedly until the words became blurred and indistinct. She had her ass pressed up against the side of some type of burned-out vehicle on the runway while she rested her upper body on her knees and gasped for air.

So far, she'd been able to keep ahead of the latest crowd that had flushed her out of her hiding spot near the old airport fence line, but she wasn't sure how much longer she would be able to continue and avoid the pursuit. She knew that stopping for longer than it took to catch her breath meant instant, painful death. The same thing had likely happened to Chris, her boyfriend. He'd likely run until he became exhausted and had to stop, then they got him.

Of course, this was that bitch Maria's fault. Katie would have had plenty of energy to keep going right now if the woman hadn't forced her to run for hours the day before and used up all of her energy. In between gasps for air, the beginning of a hysterical fit was forming. Every third or fourth breath was replaced by a sob; it would only be a moment before she fully broke down if she continued to allow herself to think about the situation.

What else was she supposed to think about though? Shawn and Maria abandoned her. She told that asshole that she couldn't swim and he insisted that she try to cross the river anyways. She knew that the water meant certain death, if she could get away from the zombies on the riverbank, then she had the same chance of surviving that the three of them had traveling cross country the past few days. He refused to come with her and just abandoned her to her own fate.

Those two deserved each other. Once she got back to the world, made it out of Pennsylvania and into the refugee area, she'd make sure that everyone knew how those two had left her to die. They'd be tried as criminals in court and she'd be vindicated in her decision not to cross the river. The thought of survival and the prosecution of the two who'd condemned her to death gave her renewed strength and the panic that had threatened to overwhelm her subsided. She *would* stay alive and she would make sure that those two paid for what they did to her here in this crappy shell of a town.

But first she had to survive.

Katie could hear them shuffling forward, searching. It was the same each time she stopped and hid; they'd be in hot pursuit after her, but once she disappeared from their line of sight, they didn't know where she'd went and would search about for her. They'd found her each time and last time it had been very close; they'd almost surrounded her. If that happened, she knew that she was a goner.

What she really needed was someplace to hide inside. Unfortunately, the military had seen fit to destroy every building that she'd come across. The devastation was nearly complete; there wasn't a single building left standing that had all four walls and a door that she could lock to protect her from those things. They were really dumb, but they were persistent.

That's why she was on the runway now. The terminal looked to be intact, inviting her to the safety of the building. Her chest had finally stopped heaving, so it was time to go before they caught up to her again. The terminal was only about half a mile away, she should be able to make it in less than ten minutes and then secure the doors against the dead. There would be plenty of food at the restaurants for one person, she could ride this thing out at the airport, maybe even put up a sign on the roof so the military would know that she was in there and could get rescued. The more she thought about it, the better the idea of staying in one place for as long as possible sounded.

She flexed her butt muscles to help push off the vehicle's wreckage and started her slow jog/walk combo that she'd been forced to use since those two traitors had drained all of her energy. The runway leading to the terminal was littered with the wreckage of planes, emergency vehicles, pieces of the fence line that had once surrounded the entire place and chunks of concrete from God only knew where. If they ever wanted to make this airport useable for airplanes again it would take a Herculean effort to clear away the damage that the Army had caused.

The slow shuffling sound of the feet behind her increased as the zombies saw her emerge from behind the truck. Their near silence was unnerving. If they'd have moaned like they did in the movies, that would have been better than the silent pursuit, only betrayed by the sound of their feet on the pavement or when they ran into something that made noise. At least then, she could focus her energies on wishing that they'd shut up.

She turned to see how far behind the group was and stumbled. She caught herself with her hands before her face hit the ground and pushed herself back upright with considerable effort. Katie brought her hands up close to her face to examine where the concrete had scraped up both of her palms and thin streams of blood were already beginning to peak out of the abrasions.

She squeezed her hands painfully to stop the bleeding and cursed Maria and Shawn once again as she gently dabbed the blood against her pant legs. They hadn't let her sleep yesterday and she was exhausted because they left her on this side of the river. She'd been running all night. *Yeah, once I'm rescued from the terminal, I'll expose those two frauds who masqueraded as helpful people. They used me as bait to get away*. She'd make sure that they got what was coming to them.

The anger allowed her to continue forward. When she'd fallen, the creatures had been less than a hundred feet behind her and they were much closer now. She'd have to step it up a little to add distance between her and the main part of the group. The first zombie was less than two car-lengths away and it was time for her to get going.

Katie forced her abused body to begin moving once more and gradually increased her speed until she was jogging tiredly toward the terminal. The rough, heavy slapping of her feet on the runway sounded impossibly loud in comparison to the scrape and shuffle of the zombies behind her. The irregular sound of her footfalls would bring more of them her way, but she knew it would be alright once she got inside the terminal. It was just a little farther, and then she'd be safe. There'd be plenty of food to replenish her depleted energy stores.

Katie finally made it to the building as the sun peeked over the eastern horizon and she staggered to a ragged halt in front of a metal door marked "**EMPLOYEES ONLY**" in big, bold letters. She assumed that the door led into the baggage area as an easy way for baggage handlers and airport workers to move between the building and the areas where the planes parked. She decided to give the door a try, hoping to be lucky enough that it would be unlocked. Once she got inside, she'd be safe and could rest. The door handle twisted easily in her hand and she pulled the door toward her. Thankfully, the employees hadn't locked the place up tight when they'd abandoned it. She stepped inside and gagged. The baggage area smelled like rotten meat.

"What the?" she muttered before using her jacket to cover her mouth. All the food in the powerless refrigerators must have spoiled and now the place just reeked like nasty week-old carryout. It would take a little getting used to, but at least she was safe. Plus, hopefully the smell wasn't bad up in the passenger waiting area where there was more open space for it to dissipate, she reasoned with herself. Banging on the door that she'd just came through reminded the girl to lock the doors and then she groped her way blindly in the dark toward the light of the staircase leading to the upper level.

Scraping noises in the darkness reminded her of the sounds that the zombies outside made as they walked. *Stop that,* she chided herself. Her mind was obviously playing tricks on her. She was safe inside the terminal. The doors had been closed so there was no way one of those things was in here with her.

Regardless of her logic, she increased her pace toward the stairwell. She'd feel much better up in the light. Her shin slammed into something hard and metal causing her to shout out in pain. She trailed her hand downward to make out the seat of one of the heavy bench chairs that was in the baggage claim waiting area. There was also a huge lump already forming on her shin where she'd hit the damn thing.

Several more shuffling sounds came from the darkness and she began to get worried that maybe she *wasn't* alone in here. Heedless of the tripping hazards, she started to run toward the beckoning light. She ran headlong into something soft and fell hard onto her rear end. The smell of rotten meat was overpowering now and she had to use her hand to wipe away some type of nasty, wet substance from the side of her face. It stung the open abrasions on her hand and made her whimper in pain once more.

The shuffling noises intensified and then something rubbed roughly against her back. She caught her breath and held as still as possible. A zombie had just walked right into her and then careened off to go wherever its feet took it. *Ohmygod, ohmygod, ohmygod!*

Katie stayed as still as she could manage, but it was maddening to think that one of those things was in here with her in the darkness. How had it gotten in the building? Finally, the sound of the feet faded as the creature made its way toward the banging of its brethren on the employee door. She jumped to her feet and started to run. She'd get up the stairs and then find someplace to hide; those assholes had said something about the zombies not being able to climb stairs. She'd be safe in the terminal above.

The girl's movement was all that the zombies in the baggage waiting area needed to hone in on their prey. They began to close in on her from all sides, attempting to surround her before she made it to the escalator. Katie screamed in panic at the sudden cacophony of noise that the creatures made as they rushed toward her, bumping into benches and overturning trashcans in their haste to reach her.

She sprinted blindly toward the safety of the stairs. If she could only make the stairs, then she'd be alright. As she neared the opening, the complete blackness gave way to the gloom of the early morning's light streaming down through the opening in the ceiling where the escalators once ran twenty-four hours a day. She could barely discern the distinctly human shapes of the creatures as they emerged from the darkness and zeroed in on her.

One of them reached out from beside her, its hands materializing from the shadows to clutch at her arm. Another shriek from the frightened girl and she juked to the side like she was a running back on the football field. The hands that almost grasped her fell back into dim obscurity while others reached out for her.

Katie twisted and turned to avoid the creatures and the scattered detritus of the baggage claim area. She ran like a woman possessed, her life depended on it. The zombies were too slow to stop her and she remained a half step ahead of each of them as they individually attempted to grab her. Fleetingly, Katie's mind thanked God that the things were too stupid to work together and often thwarted each other's attempts to reach her by knocking one another away in their haste.

She burst into the illuminated stairwell and took the stairs two at a time until she was several feet above the outstretched arms of the horde below. Katie sat heavily on an escalator step and sucked in ragged gasps of air. She'd made it! Even though Maria had tried to kill her by wearing her out, she'd dug deep inside, found the strength to surge ahead of the zombies, and reached the safety of the stairs.

They reached for her from below and their arms slapped against the glass sides of the escalator walls beside her. Bloody and smeared handprints quickly obscured her view to the sides and she looked to the base of the stairs where several of the creatures had fallen and couldn't coordinate their movements enough to pull themselves up over the steps to reach her.

Katie sighed loudly. She couldn't stay in the airport. She'd thought that the airport would be her refuge, but with the creatures infesting the area below, she couldn't stay here. After she caught her breath and got some food, she'd exit at the street level and begin making her way to someplace else. Her mind caught on the thought that the zombies that had been following her from the river were now stuck outside on the runway level and that there was a building between her and the group. She was going to get a fresh start on her escape—except for being dog-tired from all the running.

She didn't hear the creatures shuffling to the glass railing above her on the terminal level as she stared at the shifting mass below her. She wondered how the zombies had gotten in the airport and if everywhere that she tried to hide would have the same problem. Something made the hair on the back of her neck stand up a split second before she heard the noises above her. The girl twisted her head around just in time to see several creatures fall down the escalator toward her.

Her screams of panic and then pain fell dully on their ears as their rotting fingers tore her to shreds. They ripped muscle from bone, plucked out her eyes and ripped away the soft tissue of her ears, nose and lips. One of her arms was wrenched from its shoulder socket and twisted violently back and forth. The ragged bones inside cut through muscle and tendon until her arm tore completely away from her torso. The creatures' anger at being trapped was so great that when they were done, there was little that remained recognizable about young Katie's body.

*****

01 November, 0923 hrs local
Wreckage of the Washington Monument
Washington, Dead City

Kestrel examined his handiwork. Over the course of the night and again in the early morning he'd killed over a thousand zombies. He'd blasted through more than 1,500 rounds and each of those correlated directly to a dead creature lying on the National Mall. He'd gotten so tired of just shooting them in the head that he'd fallen asleep overnight and then woke up to begin the killing again in the morning.

As he thought about all the zombies that lay dead before him, he knew that they were guarding something in one of the buildings. He'd faced little to no resistance during most of the trip into the city from The Wall. Once he got here, the things had been so thick on the Mall that he couldn't even see the far side down by the base of Capitol Hill. Now he could see statues on the fountain clearly when the fog cooperated.

While he stood at the remaining side of the Washington Monument and watched the few lingering creatures weave their way in and around their dead companions, he wondered if the Type One knew that its army had been decimated. Did it maintain that level of contact with them or had it given them a task and forgotten about them? Last spring, the FBI had used sound buoys to draw most of the creatures away from the National Mall so they could land their helicopters for the move over to the Archives. It didn't seem to notice back then that the creatures had left their posts, so he thought that the Type One was used to complete and utter obedience so it didn't require constant check-ups of the Type Twos. Or maybe it was too busy managing the fight to kick humanity's ass.

Thinking of the mission to secure the Declaration of Independence, the US Constitution and the Bill of Rights made him think of Allyson. The thoughts came unbidden. He didn't want to think about her, it was just too painful and distracting. He adjusted his body position to sit down along the inside wall underneath the observation window to rest his back while he thought about her. He'd tried to move on from Allyson's memory by being with Rachel, but the truth was that there simply was no comparison. Rachel had been an amazing woman in her own rights and possibly one of the nicest people that he'd ever met, but he'd never fully given himself over to her like she had to him—because of his feelings for Allyson.

Kestrel knew that he was hung up irrationally on the dead woman. That's why he'd readily accepted the opportunity to take the one-way trip into the city to search for the Type One. His mind had clutched at any excuse to remain relevant after he'd lost the second woman in his life who really meant anything to him. He was comfortable facing his own death, he just wanted it to be on his own terms, like Allyson's death had been when she'd died during an operation, doing what she loved. He didn't want his death to be like Rachel's, who'd died just because she wanted to dangle her feet off the pier into the ocean and had been at the wrong place at the right time.

He didn't want that, he wanted to go out fighting. In retrospect, that was likely why he'd been successful as an operator. He'd never backed down from a challenge and after his mandatory retirement, he continued to challenge his body every day. He was a fighter. Coming into the city to kill the Type One was a fight, he wasn't quitting on life. He was taking the lifelong desire to fight into the harshest environment imaginable. This was to be the challenge that he'd sought his entire life.

His resolve hardened once again and he pushed the thoughts of Allyson and Rachel from his mind. Thinking about them—and the man he had started to become while he was with them—wouldn't be helpful to his mission. He had one final operation to go on to save his nation. No one else in the president's administration or in the military seemed to understand that you had to go after the head of the threat; simply cutting off the arms and legs wouldn't stop the zombies. He smirked, *that* statement could be taken both literally and figuratively.

He'd been a counterterrorism expert for his entire adult life; he knew how these things worked. In the most basic sense, the zombie threat could be dealt with in the same way that the Agency dealt with terrorist networks. Killing the lackeys and foot soldiers—in this case, the zombie horde that had swept across the entire northeast—was important to protect the population. However, if you wanted to eliminate the problem, you had to find out who the leaders of the terrorist organization were and put them out of action.

That was what he was going to do today. He was going to cut off the head of the zombie hierarchy. Once that was gone, it would be up to the Army to destroy the zombie horde rampaging across the United States. They'd be able to do that once he'd eliminated the Type One.

Kestrel picked up another cardboard box and tore it open to begin reloading all of his magazines. It was something that he'd done more times than he wanted to count as he examined the thick carpet of brown paper littering the stairwell. After this reload it would be different, though. The time for sniping from a distance was over; now it was time for the wetwork. It was time to take the fight inside.

*****

01 November, 1014 hrs local
MacDonald Family Farm
Emporia, Virginia

Nicholas MacDonald changed his mind. He used to think that he hated all the people that constantly streamed through his tiny hometown at the crossroads of Interstate 95 and US Route 58. The endless north-south grind of the interstate combined with all the motorcycle traffic and on the state road to create the perfect storm of travelers taking up every pump at the gas stations and every seat at the restaurants in town. The two roads dumped their visitors into his town year-round and he'd been fed up with it.

Now, however, Nick's hometown looked almost deserted—hell, it *was* deserted and the idea that everyone was gone frightened him more than he cared to admit. None of the restaurants were open because of the evacuation and the one gas station that remained open charged ten bucks a gallon for gas to take advantage of the people trying to escape the approaching zombie horde that had swept through Richmond a couple of days before and were moving southward toward Emporia.

He'd decided to stay. He wasn't quite complete with his fall harvest yet and that equated to a lot of money sitting on the ground at his farm. During the warm months, he grew corn and soybeans, but he also had a large patch of land—35 acres—devoted to crops that he planted in July and August for a late fall harvest to keep the income flowing later into the year. Right now he had turnips, kale and broccoli that were just about ready to harvest and he'd be damned if he was going to lose that profit. They'd be able to withstand a light frost, but if he dithered around and waited too long, a killing frost would ruin his crop and set him back quite a bit.

So Nick had stayed while his neighbors left. He'd even agreed to feed and water his neighbor Jim's small herd of beef cattle since he'd taken off with his family for the alleged safety of the Appalachian Defensive Line. Nick shook his head as he surveyed the emptiness of Emporia and thought about all those people who must be there at the defenses. He'd seen lots of movies about diseases and quarantines so he could imagine the mass hysteria as people lined up at the gates—or whatever the government had set up—to get into the safe zone west of the mountains. The sheer number of people in such a small area drew the zombies toward them, which was more dangerous than staying put in Emporia.

He'd come into town to get some gas for the farm so he could finish his chores. Both the tractor and the flatbed needed fuel, but seeing the outright price gouging that the corporate gas station charged had made him see red. He'd talked to the manager—the only employee left at the store—about it, but the man hadn't budged. The manager was some corporate jerk-off from out of town, not a real local. He'd told Nick that if he were going to risk his life to provide gasoline to the residents of Emporia, then he'd make sure that he got paid well for doing it.

That turned Nick's anger into thoughtful reflection; he was a businessman too, after all. He didn't continue his father's farm out of altruistic ideals or some type of environmentalist statement; there'd been money to be made in the organic farming business and he'd grown up helping his father before he passed, so he knew where to start and how to turn a profit. The fact that all of the big city folks who ate his organic produce and sent cards and letters to the farming association about how appreciative they were of their farming methods was just an added perk.

Nick ended up purchasing the fuel at double the normal rate and then went over to the Cracker Barrel for breakfast. That had been closed, so next he tried Shoney's, then McDonalds, Burger King and even Taco Bell. Everything in Emporia was locked up tight. Finally, he returned to the gas station and paid way too much for two of those crappy egg and sausage sandwiches that were under the heater for several hours. He should have known better because his stomach hurt and he still had a full day of work ahead of him.

He winced as he took a sip of the garbage that the gas station passed off as coffee and put the cup back in his cup holder as he drove slowly down the abandoned road toward Jim's place. He'd gotten the chores done on his farm before he came into town this morning, but Jim's herd still needed to be fed, watered and some hay put out so they could munch on that during the day and remain active. It wasn't hard work over at Jim's place, but it sure as heck was time consuming.

Nick considered gunning the engine and speeding down the main strip of town. He'd grown up here and had always wanted to race down Atlantic Street. Because of the interstate and highway intersections though, the police had always been too numerous for him to waste his hard-earned money on a speeding ticket. Now it seemed like even the cops had left Emporia. It was just Nick and the open road.

Sure, it was reckless and wasteful of the fuel that he'd just put in the truck. Yes, he was a grown man and should have outgrown those types of youthful urges. But, the idea brought a smile to his face, something that didn't happen often these days since Janie left him and took the kids to her mother's last year. No one else was around; what harm would there be if he drove like a maniac?

The fact that there wasn't anyone around to get hurt by his actions clinched it for him and he pressed the accelerator to the floor. The old truck shot straight down the road toward the eastern end of town at over 65 miles per hour. Everything sped by faster than he would have thought imaginable before this happened and he laughed out loud at the stupid joy that something so simple brought to his heart. He took the slight angle at the church and then buried the pedal for the long three-quarter mile straight stretch. The old farm truck hit 90 and began to shake in the back end, so he eased off the gas and eventually slowed enough to take the hard southward turn toward Jim's farm.

Nick was still smiling broadly when he pulled into Jim's driveway. The fact that he'd driven 90 miles per hour in the middle of town was exhilarating to the lifelong resident of Emporia. That kind of high would last all day long while he did the chores on both of the farms. He whistled happily to himself while he went about the business of feeding the cattle and let the repetitive nature of the tasks carry his mind away from the worries of Janie and the zombie outbreak up in the northern part of the country.

He was almost done at Jim's farm when movement near the edge of the fence line a few hundred feet away caught his eye. Something was different about the flash of movement that Nick had seen in his periphery. It wasn't a cow or deer, he'd grown up with those his whole life and he no longer noticed their movements. He stared at the spot where his brain had registered the movement, but nothing else showed up.

Nick wasn't a big believer in the whole extra sensory perception thing, but the hairs on the back of his neck were sticking straight up and *something* wasn't right about the situation. Then he realized that something else was wrong. The woods, normally so alive and vibrant with animal sounds, were quiet. He'd been so busy working and then searching for the source of the movement that he'd seen that he didn't realize that the birds and even the incessant barking of the squirrels had stopped.

"Forget this nonsense," Nick muttered and set down the bag of grain that rested on his shoulder. The cows could go a day without the final little bit of grain and without their hay, Jim would understand.

He walked quickly back to the grain room and threw the latch to make sure that the door would stay shut. Jim would understand him not feeding the herd, but if a few of them got into that grain room, they'd eat themselves to death. Nick had seen cattle do that before; it wasn't a pretty sight. The cow's sides had bloated up to over twice their original size as the enzymes in the animal's stomach digested the grain and produced gas that couldn't be released fast enough. They'd called the vet and she used tubes, inserted through muscle in the beast's sides, to try and vent the gas from each of the animal's four stomachs. In the end, after two days of cleaning nasty day-glow green ooze that constantly plugged the tubes in order to keep them clear to vent the foul-smelling gases, the beast had died anyways. The meat had been poisoned by the gasses and wasn't safe for human consumption, so they had to haul the carcass off for the coyotes to eat. No sir, even if he was scared of something in the woods, Nick wasn't going to let that happen to any of Jim's cows on his watch.

It only took a couple of minutes to secure the feed room and get most of the farming implements put back where the dumb animals wouldn't hurt themselves trying to get into the barn. When he was done, the sense of things being out of place remained and he made a beeline for his truck. He didn't even bother to take off his boots, which were covered in cow manure, before he'd thrown the truck into gear and tore down Jim's long driveway.

Nick slammed on the brakes. A shuffling mass of humanity blocked the exit onto the state road. Bloody, dejected and clothed in all manners of dress, they looked like refugees from a movie to Nick. They were moving around Jim's fence and then onto the street, headed toward town. "What in the world?" he said out loud.

Several of the people noticed him and turned down the driveway away from the main group, which continued its slow walk toward town. Nick was unsure of what to do. Something about them wasn't right. They walked funny, like they were... "Oh shit!" he cursed, which was something that he rarely did.

He knew that what he was seeing were the zombies that he'd thought were so far away, up near Richmond and further north in Pennsylvania. These creatures had somehow made it all the way to Emporia without the authorities learning about it. *Or maybe the police knew, but they'd been killed before they had the opportunity to tell anyone*, his mind rationalized. Whatever the reason, he was in a world of danger.

The Ford protested his efforts to shift it into reverse and the grinding of the truck's gears caused more of the zombies to take notice of him and break off from the horde to follow the sounds down the driveway. Finally, the truck went into gear and he sped backward down the gravel road toward Jim's farm.

About halfway down, he eased up on the gas pedal and took in his surroundings. The fence that ran next to Jim's driveway stopped more of the creatures as they drifted from the woods up toward the noise of his truck. He'd helped his neighbor replace the fence last fall, so he knew that it should hold for a little while, but the things were pushing hard against it, heedless of the five strands of barbed wire tearing into their skin.

Then, he saw it. His manure-covered boot slipped completely off the accelerator and the truck drifted to a halt. One of the creatures seemed to stare right at him. It looked different than the others. Its skin was the color of wheat ready for the harvest and had the weathered look of old leather. Nick felt his bladder release and a warm sensation filled his crotch and then under his rear end as the urine seeped along the vinyl seat. He swore to God that the thing smiled at him.

You will die.

"What?" He whipped his head wildly from side to side in a panic to figure out who'd talked to him. He slid his foot back onto the gas pedal and pressed it down. If he could make it to Jim's house, he would be alright.

The truck accelerated slowly back down the driveway and he struggled to keep it under control at speed. Then, through the back window he saw the fence give out as the hooks that held the wire to the T-posts stretched from the pressure of all those zombies and the barbed wire fell away. Creatures tumbled into the roadway behind him and he hit several of them. The truck's big back bumper plowed them underneath until the truck's rear axle became high-centered on the bodies and its tires lost contact with the ground.

He shifted the truck into low gear and tried to move forward and then back into reverse to get off the pile of bodies. Nothing worked, he was stuck. Hands began to beat against the side of the vehicle and he knew that his chance at escape was gone. There was no way that he'd be able to make a run for it through the growing crowd.

Stupid human. Like all the others.

The voice sounded loud in his head once again and he realized that it wasn't coming from someone speaking to him, they were *inside* his head.

"What do you want?" he whimpered.

Death.

The crowd of bodies parted in front of the truck. The creature that he'd noticed earlier walked toward him. It didn't have the odd hitch in its step that so many of the others seemed to display and the thing oozed confidence as it stared at him through the windshield.

"Go away!" he shouted.

Your time has ended.

The truck began to rock even harder as the creatures pressed in close began to beat and claw at the sides in earnest. The back end slid several inches as the creatures on the passenger side hit the vehicle harder than those on the left. Nick felt the truck slide off the pile of bodies and one of the tires touched the ground.

"Go to hell!" he cried and pressed the gas pedal to the floor.

The engine roared and the rear tires spun on the bloody gore that had spilled from the first creatures that he'd hit, but they wouldn't catch. The slippery mess was too much for the old, bald tires to grab any traction and the creatures pressed close didn't allow for any type of momentum to begin.

The engine continued to roar as the creature in front of him slammed both hands down on the hood of the truck. *Enough! You are beaten, human. Join the Followers.*

Nick took his foot off the gas and bent down to reach under the seat where he'd stashed his pistol. His fingers curled around the heavy rubberized grip that the sheriff had warned him several times about keeping in his vehicle. Sheriff Newman could kiss his hind end for all he cared. If he was going to meet God today, it would be on his terms.

Slowly and deliberately, he brought out the Smith & Wesson Model 460 that he used to hunt deer. The double action handgun's 10.5-inch barrel, massive .460 Magnum cartridge and the 10Xs scope that rested on top made the pistol the perfect handgun for hunting. He'd eschewed the rifle in favor of the pistol almost a decade prior when he read a magazine article about the skill and challenge associated with handgun hunting. Now, he was thankful that the weapon was also maneuverable in the small space of the truck cab.

There were only five rounds in the pistol. The rest of his ammo was at home in the closet, so he'd have to make each one count. He briefly considered taking his own life, but that was a sin and a guaranteed one-way ticket to Hell, which wasn't an option. *What am I gonna do?* he wondered.

Take him, the creature's voice exploded in his head.

It was time. He cocked the hammer back and raised it to the windshield. At this distance, the zombie's face filled the scope and Nick swore that he saw a flicker of recognition in the thing's eyes as he squeezed of a round. Years of hunting for food with the pistol had taught him how to bring the weapon up and fire accurately at his target, every time. Today was no different.

The blast from the hand cannon cracked all of the windows of his truck and made his ears explode in pain. But he didn't flinch or drop his view from the creature as the round shattered the windshield and went through the forehead of the zombie. The creature flew backward and he knew that if a bullet to the brain killed those things like the internet said that it did, then it was gone. He'd hit it slightly off-center above one of its eyes, that was a kill shot every time.

He used a finger to dig into his ear in an effort to clear out the ringing before re-cocking the pistol. The zombies all around him seemed to be going crazy. They beat senselessly on the sides of the truck, no longer focused on getting him specifically; instead they seemed to lash out at everything in their grasp. He didn't know how long that would last, but the fact that they were disoriented and not trying to kill him was the opportunity that he needed. He wasn't going to overlook the Lord's gift.

The sliding glass in the back window was just barely wide enough for Nick to fit through, but he made it into the bed of the pickup and leapt from the back onto the ground. He didn't bother to look as he sprinted the final eighth of a mile to Jim's farmhouse. He fumbled with the woodpile on the back porch until he found the correct piece of firewood that had a house key taped to the bottom.

The key fit perfectly into the lock and he burst into the house. He slid the deadbolt home and leaned heavily against the door as the creatures began to pound on the opposite side. With a sigh of relief, he eased the hammer down on his pistol and pulled the old flip phone from his pocket. He didn't think anyone knew that these things were this far south yet. The news had said they were up near Richmond, so it was time to change that.

He had a friend from high school who was in the Virginia National Guard. He'd know who to tell in order to pass the message along. He scrolled through the address book on his phone until he found Rich's number.

Nick finally got through to his friend, who assured him that the Army would intercept the creatures in southern Virginia now that they knew where they'd disappeared to. Rich's confidence bolstered his own once he was complete with the conversation and he risked a quick peek out the window.

There were at least fifty zombies in the area surrounding his hideout, most of them seemed to be stumbling around or waiting, while there were several still pounding relentlessly on the truck. That made him sure that the ones who hadn't seen him were just waiting for something to emerge or to go back to the main group so he reached out slowly and twisted the rod to close the blinds. If they hunted by sight, he didn't want them to see him moving in the house.

Several hours later, the beating at the front door abruptly ceased and he could hear the cattle in the barn going crazy. He wondered what was going on, so he climbed the stairs to the bedrooms. He felt a little guilty invading Jim and Connie's bedroom, but he reasoned that it was okay since he was just going to look out the window and not touch any of their private things.

The cows had come back to the barn expecting their evening feeding and were attacked by the zombies instead. As before, it looked like the barbed wire fence around the barnyard had proven to be little protection against the press of the zombies and even though several were hopelessly entangled in the wire, the rest were attempting to attack the animals.

Jim's herd proved to be the creature's undoing as the cattle moved in a group from one end of the field to the next and Nick watched in fascination. Two of the older cows had been set upon by the group near the fence and torn apart, but the rest of the herd ran away. The zombies moved in a ragged group toward the cattle who cowered against the fence until the danger was too great and then they surged forward into the zombies to go to another section of the field.

Nick watched the stampeding cattle decimate the zombies again and again until there were only three or four of them upright. Even without the fence near the barn, the cows never left the field and the small group of zombies continued to chase them while the original creatures that had been trampled clawed at the dirt with broken limbs and crawled pathetically after the cattle.

After it became apparent that the zombies wouldn't stop pursuing the cattle and that the herd wouldn't leave the field, Nick sighed and tramped back down the stairs to the back porch. A quick peek out of the side windows told him that there weren't any of the creatures close by so he unlocked the door and eased out onto the porch.

He picked up Jim's axe and walked slowly toward the field. The zombies would chase those animals until the end of time if he didn't put a stop to it and he told Jim that he'd take care of the herd while he and his family were gone. Besides, Nick couldn't stand animal cruelty and he was going to make those things pay for spooking the cattle so badly.

THIRTEEN

01 November, 1048 hrs local
The Castle, Smithsonian Institution Building
Washington, Dead City

The Master contemplated what this meant. It felt the Chosen in the south die; that only left two of the original Chosen to continue the fight against the humans. The Followers would continue the attack, but without the Chosen to direct them it would be reckless and not massed. That type of all-out attack would leave them vulnerable to defeat—one small group at a time.

The creature wondered what had happened to the Chosen. How had it died? The plan called for the Chosen to move its Followers from city to city in secret, reappearing at new locations as a surprise to destroy the population and wreak havoc among the defenders. It was not to expose itself to danger. It was the Master's own plan, which was different than the slow, steady march that the Leader in the north used after it had achieved the first surprise attack.

The Master didn't know how far the second attack had advanced in the south. The last time it had communicated with the Chosen, they were still very close to the home city. The plan called for a two-pronged attack on the humans, not one major attack in the north and a million insect bites in the south. The Followers would quickly lose their cohesion and begin to separate, attacking whatever they happened across.

It briefly considered leaving the city and going to the Followers in the south to lead them to victory, but it discarded the idea. The army needed a strong central base in the home city to allow it to advance upon the humans. It also considered recalling the Leader and its army to defend the city. The Followers in the south hadn't visited nearly the damage on the humans as the northern army had; the way lay clear for the humans to bypass the disjointed Followers and come into the walls.

Within the walls of the home city, the humans would find a considerable presence of Followers. The Chosen were perfect in mind and body, but the humans possessed technology that they could not use. It was the only drawback to the war that the humans had started by entering the home city.

Still, the armies of the Chosen were strong and the Master relied on the physical strength of the Followers, not their intellect. It sent a quick thought to the Followers defending the city to be extra vigilant for the humans attacking and felt a sudden emptiness that it hadn't noticed before.

Followers far away acknowledged in their own way, but the ones outside of the Master's home did not respond. The Master sent another thought to them to change their pattern to a more widespread distribution on the open area between the buildings, but it was met with general silence again. A few of the Followers replied, but not the overwhelming mental blanket that the Master had expected.

The Master wondered if it had somehow lost control of the Followers outside. Had its mind drifted so far at the loss of the Chosen and their dwindling number that the Master had forgotten to hold its Followers accountable? It tried to reestablish its mental control of the Followers in the city and was met with a vacant area of the defense near the building.

A loud crash down below where its Followers stayed brought the Master's attention to the situation at hand. The humans were attacking! It concentrated for a moment and called all of the Followers in the home city to its location before it turned to the three Followers that remained with it always. It had chosen the three because they still possessed the mental capacity to climb the stairs from the first floor to the second; they would be the Master's final line of defense if the Followers below weren't enough to stop the humans.

It tried to reach the Leader in the north to tell it what was happening, but the creature was too far away. The Master of the Chosen was in danger of being eliminated and the others wouldn't even know.

*****

01 November, 1451 hrs local
Texas Defense Zone
Ozona, Texas

What am I supposed to do with these people? Grayson thought. He'd received a personal phone call from the president, which was ironic since it wasn't his first call from a Commander in Chief. He'd talked to President Holmes a couple of times while he was quarantined in Indianapolis. The new guy, Ryan Wilson, seemed likeable enough, even though Grayson hadn't voted for him.

The president asked him to use the town of Ozona as a base for the military operation against the Mexicans out in the desert. From what he could gather, the force that the Army planned to send was a bunch of privates just out of basic training and their Drill Sergeants. He'd spent twelve long, grueling years in the Army and knew the dangers of using brand new soldiers to perform missions, but the president said that the regular military was fully committed fighting the zombies so it was all that could be spared.

President Wilson also let the details drop that it wasn't the regular Mexican Army. Turns out, one of the Mexican drug lords, Ernesto Herrera, was trying to expand his semi-autonomous state from northern Mexico into the United States. That bit of news was both relieving and worrying for Grayson. Since it wasn't the entire Mexican Army attacking, there was the possibility of stopping the incursion flat. However, since it was a drug cartel, the level of violence could be expected to increase dramatically. The Herrera Cartel tended to be savage and not leave many survivors in their wake.

Grayson had also talked to the Governor of Texas about using the National Guard yesterday. He'd been told that an infantry company from the 36th was all they could spare since everyone else was busy killing zombies that washed up on the shoreline. The shoreline defense was extremely labor-intensive because of the length of the Texas coastline; they had to cover every square inch of property or else risk an outbreak behind the Appalachian Line. He did promise that elements of the Texas State Guard, which was a pseudo-military organization, designed to backfill the National Guard when they were mobilized and away. Beggars can't be choosers.

As soon as he informed the governor about the invading force, Grayson had begun to make the phone calls to pull in the ranchers and homeowners outside of the city limits. Most thought he was trying to pull some type of Halloween prank on them, but eventually, he'd been able to convince people to move their families into the relative safety of town. He also authorized the citizens to carry firearms, state weapons permits be damned.

The cartel soldiers hadn't attacked the town yet, but Grayson was sure that Ozona was their target. The next closest town was Sonora, thirty-five miles away, and they'd need a place to get food and refill their water supplies. From a drug distribution standpoint, Ozona was also a good place to be since it was on Interstate 10, right in the middle between San Antonio and El Paso. Anything produced or refined in Ozona could be sent to a major city within hours.

The biggest problem in the commissioner's mind was how to secure the town. American towns weren't designed to become fortresses. Most towns, this one included, had multiple roads in and out with a lot of space between buildings. To make matters worse, Grayson's city was in the middle of the Texas scrub desert, so there were no natural obstacles to use to their advantage. He might be able to block the roads so the cartel's vehicles couldn't use them, but they'd likely just drive around any obstacles outside of town and it would be impossible to stop the dismounted men with fencing and barriers alone.

He'd decided that blocking the roads was just a waste of resources that he didn't have, so while he was calling the homeowners, he had the sheriff begin placing defenders around the town. While the terrain around the town allowed the cartel to attack from any direction, Grayson was sure that if they attacked, the invading force would come from the most direct route in the south. Calvin Espinoza's farm was about fourteen miles outside of town near Pandale Road, which was the only road that went through the hills to the south of town leading all the way to the Mexican border.

Then, this morning, the first of the soldiers from Fort Sam Houston had arrived by, of all things, yellow school buses. They were young and had weapons with only a minimal amount of gear. Fort Sam was primarily a training base for the medical community, so they didn't have all of the high-tech gadgetry that the rest of the Army used. The Drill Sergeants got their soldiers off the bus and into a formation, but it was immediately apparent to Grayson that they were looking for some type of direction.

He'd spent the morning going over the town maps with the noncommissioned officers and the few officers that the military sent along with the trainees. The soldiers knew the basics of military tactics and were qualified on their weapons, so Grayson was confident that they'd be able to defend the town until a regular Army unit arrived.

Grayson thought about his children, Jessica and little Gregory, and wondered if he should send Jamie out of town, maybe over to San Antonio. They didn't need to get involved with this mess. But then again, he had no idea if the roads leading to the city were safe. The government—both state and federal—had failed to notice a large paramilitary force moving across the desert and it had taken the town drunks to raise the alarm. Would his family be safe or should they stay in Ozona where he could keep an eye on them?

The phone on his desk rang and he picked it up before the second ring. "Donnelly."

"We got a situation, Mr. Donnelly."

"Hey, I was just wondering when you'd call," Grayson answered. Sheriff Cochran's report was due to him at 2:30 and it was almost 3 p.m. "What's going on?"

"Sorry about missing the call, we got into a skirmish with the cartel folks out near the cemetery. John Castillo got shot in the head during the fight. He's dead, Grayson."

The pit of Grayson's stomach dropped out. John was his best friend. They got together every Saturday with their families at the Ozona Country Club. The girls played tennis or swam with the kids while John and Grayson played two rounds on the club's 9-hole golf course. He'd just spoke to John that morning and they'd joked about the Mexican "army" that threatened the town.

"Shit," he muttered while his mind raced through what needed to be done for Christy and the kids. First and foremost, though, he needed to ensure that the town was safe. He compartmentalized his personal feelings and addressed the matter at hand.

"What's the status of the town's perimeter?" The bastards had come directly up Route 163 from the south like he thought they would.

"We repulsed 'em. Pretty sure that we got a few of them too," the sheriff replied.

"How large of a force did they come up the road with?"

He could hear Joe relay his question to someone and then he returned, "They had six trucks full of men. When they got to the roadblock, they dismounted and tried to go around it. That's when we opened up on 'em."

"Wait. Did you say that *we* opened up on them?" Grayson asked.

"Yessir. We defended our town against those invaders and sent a few of them to hell. Those Army kids may not look like much, but they can shoot!"

Grayson hung his head and rested his elbows on the desk. He hadn't thought about the implications of the defenders initiating the fight. Would some armchair quarterback flay them alive in court after this was over? He'd always imagined the scenario where the enemy would attack and they would be the ones to open fire, then the townspeople and soldiers would be forced to defend themselves—which was acceptable under Texas law. Of course, given the county's history, he shouldn't have been surprised. Crockett County was named after David Crockett, who died in the battle of the Alamo. Just looking around Ozona at the street names indicated the aggressive nature of the town: Santa Anna Street, Man O' War Boulevard, Bold Ruler Street—there was even a road called War Admiral Street.

He decided that the only thing that he could do would be to defend their actions in court if it ever came to that. The enemy action had been aggressive in nature by attempting to bypass obstacles and the townspeople had reacted accordingly. "Okay, good job," Grayson responded to the sheriff's enthusiastic endorsement of the recruits that they'd been sent. "Make sure everyone is prepared for another attack, maybe from a different direction this time."

"Already way ahead of you. You ain't the only one with military experience. I'm a Marine and served in Desert Storm, remember?"

"Yeah, I know you're doing a great job out there, Joe. I just want us to be prepared for those bastards," he replied. Then he changed subjects to the one that weighed heavy on his heart, "Has anyone notified Christy Castillo about John's death?"

"Not yet. I was gonna head over there to notify her after I made another round to make sure that everyone knew about the scrape that we got into with the cartel. That'll motivate 'em to keep a better watch on their areas."

"Good idea. I need you to focus on the town's defense, Joe. I'll go out to the Castillo's and notify Christy and the kids."

"Well, I sure don't envy you, Grayson. Thank you for doin' that for me."

"Yeah… Alright, I'm gonna head over there before she learns about it through the rumor mill first."

"Yup. I'll call you at six."

"Call my cell. I might still be at John's house," Grayson recommended.

They hung up and he called Jamie. It would be better if both of them went over to break the news to Christy.

*****

01 November, 1539 hrs local
The Castle, Smithsonian Institution Building
Washington, Dead City

Kestrel sat down on a small pile of rubble near the large hall's edge. He took a ragged breath and finally looked at his surroundings. He wasn't really into architecture, but the place must have been a beautiful building at one time. The light brown walls extended upwards to the cathedral-style arches that stretched impossibly high into the room above, their surface curving gently inwards until they connected in the center. All along the roofline, triangle-shaped openings allowed the autumn day's light to filter in from above. The glass was mostly broken now, letting in years of dirt and rain that collected into pools of filth on the marble floors. At the end of the massive hallway, three large rectangular windows with arches along the top and a large circular window combined with smaller half-round windows set into one wall to let in even more light.

He hadn't gotten a chance to see much of the building, though, because the moment Kestrel opened the heavy wooden doors he was attacked by zombies. He ended up in this part of the building out of sheer dumb luck. Looking back on it, what he should have done was lured the creatures outside so he could go back to his sniper hide, but Kestrel hadn't expected there to be so many of them inside and had allowed himself to get cut off from the doorway back to the National Mall. He'd fought with the large Bowie knife and his suppressed HK45 pistol, constantly needing to move from one position to the next because the creatures would flank him and not allow him enough room to do anything else from that location.

Kestrel flexed his hand several times to loosen the stiffness that had crept into his fingers from gripping the knife for hours as he stabbed, slashed and parried the outstretched arms of the zombies that had been in the building. He rubbed his aching, overworked thighs. All the crouching and standing at the ruins of the Washington Monument where he'd killed thousands of zombies with his scoped rifle was beginning to take its toll on his old body.

Until he'd gone inside the building, he'd just felt tired, now he felt *old*. Kestrel didn't want to think about how he'd feel after he dealt with whatever was in residence in this building and then headed into the Metro tunnels. *I'm too old for this shit*, he muttered while he continued probing his body to determine if there were any broken bones. Some of the zombies had been ferocious, much stronger than their counterparts, which may explain why they were in the building protecting the Type One instead of the rotters that he'd dispatched outside.

He stopped at his left side where he already knew that several of the ribs where broken. One of the big ones had tackled him and both of them landed across a metal rack—actually Kestrel had landed on the rack, the zombie landed on top of *him*. Besides his ribs and stiff, aching joints, the only other real area of concern was his right forearm.

In the next room over, a zombie had pinned his arm against its body while trying to claw his face away. Another creature had crashed in and bit down hard onto his arm. The sharksuit kept the thing's teeth from penetrating his skin, but the zombie ground its teeth back and forth, jerking like a wild dog pulling meat from a carcass. He'd eventually been able to get his left hand across to jam the empty pistol's silencer through the eye socket and into the brain of the creature that had his arm trapped. Then he'd been able to transfer the knife from his right hand to his left and stabbed the fucker that used his arm as a chew toy.

Several of the links from the sharksuit had embedded into his skin and ripped across as the creature twisted its head. Kestrel was concerned about the zombie's saliva that had probably made its way into the wound. He had to finish this mission and it had been twelve or thirteen days since he'd taken the antidote, was that too far between doses to be effective? Or was it too *close* together to be used safely?

He knew that the *A-Coll* antidote contained a healthy dose of the bacteria that caused lockjaw and tetanus—it said so right on the bottle. Also, multiple warning labels stated that if you took it before you were bitten, you could develop those illnesses. That's the last thing he needed when he didn't know if there was only one of the Type Ones in DC or if there were more of them—although, he was almost out of ammo. He'd have to break into a police station and get into their supply locker, but that wasn't a big deal.

Back to the matter at hand, he reminded his errant thoughts. Should he take another dose of the *A-Coll* antidote or let it ride? Once he started displaying the signs of infection, it was too late and the medicine wouldn't do any good. How long had it been since he'd been gnawed on? Probably close to twenty minutes, he guessed. That was about the limit of where he needed to make a decision whether to take the antidote.

He stared off across the hall at the piles of dead zombies. It was times like this when he really wished that he smoked. He'd seen it time and again with the men and women that he served with in combat. If he were a smoker, a simple cigarette would give him something to do to mellow out his thoughts and relax him. But he wasn't, and the three things that he'd found to help him to relax were all dead.

"Well, shit." Kestrel's voice echoed eerily around the open space. Surprisingly, the bodies of the dead and the broken windows, open to the outside, did little to reduce the reverberation of the sound. He made his decision and rummaged inside the huge backpack until he found the first aid kit. He couldn't risk getting sick and dying before he finished exploring this place and killed whatever those things had been protecting. If he ended up contracting tetanus or lockjaw because he hadn't needed to take the antidote, then so be it, this was a one-way trip anyways.

Kestrel stood roughly and carried everything to a supply closet before going inside. Then he secured the door the best he could using a length of rope, one end tied to a metal shelving unit and the other around the doorknob. He didn't know if he'd have the same reaction that he'd had the first time he took the *A-Coll* antidote—he'd been out for days with that dose. Once he was satisfied that the closet was as secure as he could make it, he pulled the battered uniform top off and then opened the sharksuit so he could pull his arm out of it.

He went through the ritual of filling the syringe with the correct amount of the antidote and then positioned the needle above the vein in the crook of his arm. It tore a tiny hole and blood trickled freely as he fished the needle around inside his arm to ensure that he made it into the vein. He smirked when he finally felt the gentle pressure as the metal found its way home. *You'd think that as many times over the years that I've given myself an IV that I'd be better at this,* he mused.

Once the 20cc's of antidote was injected, he broke down the needle and hastily put everything in his pack before shrugging back into the sharksuit. If he passed out, he wanted to ensure that he was fully protected in as secure of a location as possible. The bite that he'd sustained from Rachel had been a nasty gash which allowed the *A-Coll* virus to enter his bloodstream rapidly. This injury was just a few minor scratches with zombie drool smeared across them, so the onset of the virus' effects in his system should, in theory, be slower. But it would be just as deadly in the endgame.

He closed his eyes to rest for just a moment. He was so tired and frankly, too old for this type of non-stop movement and lack of sleep. Only a few more days and he'd complete the mission...

*****

Kestrel awoke with a jerk that caused the chain links on the sharksuit to tinkle like a wind chime. He'd been dreaming about Allyson's death again and his mind's insistence that she'd gone on the mission because he'd told her not to. But that was the past; there was nothing he could do about it. Besides, he didn't even know if it was true. The aches and pains in his body caused his mind to focus quickly on the present. He was still alive and still inside the broom closet. The antidote had worked as advertised.

He checked his watch. He'd been asleep for about thirty-five minutes and didn't feel any worse for wear, so he must have taken the antidote soon enough to not become infected—or the bacteria was slowly spreading through his body and he wouldn't be able to open his mouth in a couple of days. At least that would give him time to kill the Type One before he became ill in the darkness of the tunnels under the city.

He stood up and shouldered his backpack. The operator had decided that when he went to check the upper levels he'd leave it at the base of the stairs so he wouldn't get tangled up with it in a confined space. He'd personally seen the zombies in Baltimore pile themselves up on top of each other to reach higher levels, so he knew that there was a way for the creatures to go up to different floors. The Type Ones, however, were drastically different; they *could* still climb stairs.

During his discussions with Hank Dawson, Kestrel learned that in their first engagement with all of the Type Ones at the Pentagon, the creatures had clearly negotiated the stairs somehow and went to the upper levels so they could throw things at the combined Army Delta and Naval DEVGRU teams. Hank had also said that when they fought the final large group of them at the National Harbor, several of the creatures had somehow scaled the building and watched them from the rafters of the destroyed convention center.

Hank also told him that they used weapons like clubs and developed rudimentary tactics other than a frontal attack to get to the operators. That was only after about a week in their new forms, Kestrel wondered how much the remaining Type Ones had changed and evolved over the course of six years. That was a lot of time to become better at just about everything.

What am I doing? he thought suddenly. *I should leave. The Chosen are too dangerous; they'll kill me if I don't go back to where I came from.*

It was a thought that came unbidden and was totally out of character for the retired operator. He'd never doubted his abilities before and had faced some major trials and tribulations over the years. "What the fuck is wrong with you, old man?" he asked himself as he began untying the rope from the doorknob.

I'm scared. The Chosen are too powerful for me to defeat. I'll never leave the home city alive.

Kestrel squeezed his eyes shut and used the palm of his hand to hit himself in the side of the head. "What the hell is a 'Chosen'?" he asked out loud once again. "Man, I must be losing it; I'm already talking to myself."

He coiled the rope and stuffed it in the cargo pocket of his pants. He briefly wondered why he'd put the rope in his pocket instead of in the backpack; he'd never carried a rope in his pocket before. His subconscious must have determined that if he left the pack at the stairs, maybe he'd need it. It was another difference to his standard operating procedure.

Something was going on upstairs in his head. Was that a side effect of the antidote that he'd slept through the last time?

When he opened the door, he was surprised by how many more creatures had wandered in the building. There were easily another fifty of them. "Shoulda locked the front door," he muttered as he brought up his SCAR and started clearing the room methodically.

They're just going to keep coming. I'm almost out of... bullets. I need to run away before more of them arrive!

Kestrel knew that something was wrong. He'd *never* thought about retreating before today. In fact, he'd decided that this would be a one-way trip since everything important had already been taken away from him. *What's a 'Chosen' and why did I think of this place as the 'home city'?* Sure he'd spent a lot of time in the DC area because that's where the Agency's headquarters were, but he never would have considered DC his home before those random thoughts a few moments before. The fact that he had to search for the word 'bullet' was a dead giveaway to the man who'd spent thirty-one years of his life intimately involved with guns and ammunition.

"Who the fuck do you think you're dealing with asshole?" he shouted into the building. His voice echoed for a full second before dying away. "*I. Am. The. Kestrel!*" he said through gritted teeth. "Get out of my head!"

You are nothing, human.

"So, you are in my head then," he answered with a smirk as he swapped magazines and walked rapidly toward the first set of stairs that he saw. From the outside, the building appeared to have four towers—one on each corner—and then two more in the front where he'd entered. He had no clue how many of those actually had floors and how many were just decorative, though.

Yes, I am inside your head. I can make you kill yourself with a simple thought. Leave the home city now.

"I don't think so," Kestrel replied. He began climbing the stairs until he came to a landing in front of a large wooden door. While he'd been asleep, it had become too dark to see properly so he turned on the infrared light mounted to his rifle and flipped down the night vision goggles over his eyes. The civilian version of the device that he owned wasn't nearly as good as the four-tubed panoramic night vision device that he'd gotten used to using in the Agency because it only illuminated what was directly in front of him instead of the wider angle of view, but it was still a drastic improvement over the naked eye.

He kicked the door open and rushed into the room, clearing the space quickly and then he went back to the stairs. As he was descending, he said, "If you could have made me harm myself or control me, then you would have stopped me long before I cleared out your personal bodyguard. I think that you're just hiding somewhere, scared of *me.* You know that the day of your death has come."

Stupid human. The Master of the Chosen is not scared.

Kestrel moved to another set of stairs and remembered to drop his backpack this time. He'd gotten flustered before and deviated from his plan. "What are the Chosen anyways?"

It is the Master and the brethren. We are so much more than you humans will ever be.

Kestrel cleared his mind and said, "The Chosen are a dying breed. Once I kill you, everything is over for your army."

The Followers will destroy all of you. They are spread from the great water to the mountains.

"Your Followers aren't doing so well." Another room cleared, he continued up the stairs to the third level. He didn't like talking, it was distracting to him as he tried to search, but he needed to keep this thing talking so he could trick it into giving him the information that he needed.

We are as numerous as the stars.

"And getting your ass kicked every step of the way. The Followers don't have any leadership and are getting killed by the thousands in each fight."

You lie! The Leader reports that they continue to advance and create more Followers every day.

"Your 'Leader'? Is that some type of subordinate?"

The Leader is Chosen, yes.

The third level was clear, so he made his way down the stairs.

"Well, the Leader is lying to you. He's not doing as well as he says he is." Kestrel stopped on the stairwell and concentrated on clearing his mind of any thoughts. "Your Army is almost totally destroyed up north. Do you have another Chosen to take his place?"

The Leader and the Master are the last of the Chosen.

Kestrel grinned like he'd just stolen money from the offering plate. "Just the two of you, huh? What happens when you die?"

The Master will not die. You will die, human!

A scraping sound below him on the stairs made Kestrel stare down the rifle's combat optic. Within seconds, a large zombie appeared around the turn in the staircase. It *climbed* down the stairs awkwardly toward him. He laughed out loud and dropped the SCAR on its sling down to his side. He drew his knife and waited as the lumbering giant focused on lifting its leg and then setting the foot down on the next step.

When it was three steps away from him, Kestrel reversed the grip on the knife and stepped down two steps. He plunged the full nine inches of metal through the top of the creature's skull into its brain. The zombie started to fall backward and its weight pulled Kestrel forward. He lost his balance and fell down on top of it before rolling several more steps, coming to rest on the hallway's floor.

"Ugh, fuck. That sucked."

Your body fails you.

"Damn. I was hoping that was you back there on the stairs."

Foolish human. You cannot kill the Master.

He heaved himself to his feet and stumbled up the stairs to retrieve the knife. "Then come on out and let's test your theory."

The Master does not take orders. Leave the home city, now!

"I've got some unfinished business first," Kestrel replied. "So, where is the Leader?"

With the Followers.

"Up north or here?"

I don't understand what 'north' is. Kestrel grinned to himself once again, the Master was clearly becoming flustered and beginning to become desperate.

He began walking toward one of the corners of the building and then stopped. The Master had obviously sent a special zombie after him, one that retained enough muscle memory to know how to climb stairs, even if it was a pathetic approximation of human abilities. It had gotten to him quickly—in zombie terms—so it hadn't come from the corner towers.

His eyes drifted toward the back of the building. He could see a wide set of steps leading upwards. *That* was where the Master stayed.

The operator wiped the gore from his knife's blade on his pants leg and sheathed it. Then he reached down and grasped the pistol grip of the

SCAR, pulling it up into the crook of his shoulder and limped toward the back stairwell.

"I'm coming for you, you bastard."

The Master is ready for you.

****

01 November, 1613 hrs local
Intermediate Staging Point Harrisburg
Harrisburg, Pennsylvania

"So, you're heading to Cleveland tonight, then?" Sergeant Lamar asked Shawn.

"Yeah. My little Annie was evacuated from Jersey to Cleveland."

"I wish you'd change your mind. We need good men like you to fight against the zombies."

Shawn shook his head. "I'm sorry, Kevin. I just can't do it anymore. More times than I care to remember Maria and I almost died. I don't want Annie to be an orphan."

The sergeant nodded understandingly. "I get it, man. You've been through a lot. We'd love to keep you, but it's time for you to see to your little girl. What about Maria, do you know what she's planning to do?"

"We're not a couple or anything," Shawn replied. He didn't notice Kevin's eyebrows shoot up in warning. "I mean, it would be great if she wanted to come along with me, but I can't speak for her—"

Shawn was startled as a hand grasped his arm and turned him around. Before he knew what was happening, a pair of full lips descended on his. He was dimly aware of Maria's dark olive complexion and the smell of freshly scrubbed skin before he lost himself in her kiss.

When they separated, he stared intently into her hazel eyes. "I'm coming with you, Shawn," Maria stated. "There's nothing you can say or do to stop me."

"Uh... Um..."

"Wow, I think that's the first time that I've seen you speechless since we rescued your ass this morning, Mr. Ford!" Lisa Vaccaro said from behind Maria. She'd obviously walked up with the woman and wore a clean uniform compared to the one that she'd worn earlier when they were on the mission.

"Please, it's Shawn," he replied with a grin. "It's cliché to say this, but Mr. Ford was my father."

"Okay, Shawn," Lisa said with a duck of her head. "Our phones are crap, but Maria and I have already exchanged email addresses so we can keep in touch. I hope that you guys make it to Cleveland."

"Thanks. I bought a car from one of the townspeople who are fleecing refugees, so hopefully we'll make it there in a few days. If everyone wasn't running westward over the mountains, the trip would normally only take six or seven hours, but now? I don't know. I'm going to shoot northwest for a ways to try and get some distance from the zombie horde since it seems to be following the Army toward the west."

Maria slid her arm through his and took a half step closer to him. "We'll make it, don't worry," she said.

Kevin smiled and glanced at Lisa. Her eyes betrayed the longing she felt for him. "It's a good plan," the sergeant said as he questioned his soldier's look silently.

"Oh, wow. Are you two seeing each other?" Shawn asked ignorantly with a big grin on his face.

"What? No! I'm... Um, I'm her squad leader. That's against the regulations."

He felt a slight tug on his shoulder and Maria squeezed his arm closer. "He doesn't know, Shawn," she said.

"Know what?" Kevin asked.

"Yeah, what are you talking about?" Shawn questioned.

Maria rolled her free hand. "You should tell him, Lisa!"

The specialist looked back and forth between them and Sergeant Lamar for a moment and then said, "Okay. I was going to tell you tonight anyways, sergeant. I—Maria made a request for me...."

"Oh for heaven's sake, girl," Maria exclaimed and pulled her arm from Shawn's grasp. "As a rescued refugee, we're authorized to make requests for supplies and stuff from the Army. Well, I asked that Lisa be transferred to a different company so the two of you wouldn't be in the same command!"

"You what?" Kevin thundered. "Specialist Vaccaro is the best soldier that I have! She's the glue that holds those men together. That was absolutely not your call."

Maria looked hurt for a second and then set her jaw. "You're getting another qualified soldier of the same rank for her. I did it for you, idiot."

"What do you mean that you did it for me?" he asked incredulously.

"I, uh... Sergeant Lamar, Maria and I were talking and I told her about the National Guard's policy about soldiers in the same organization dating, so she took matters into her own hands."

"Dating?"

"You're a blockhead, sergeant. I like you," Lisa stated.

"Did you forget that I'm an NCO? I can't date a junior enlisted soldier."

"Yeah, about that," Maria said.

"Oh, for the love of God! What else did you do," Kevin asked.

"Well... Part of the reintegration for the refugees is to identify anyone who went above and beyond to assist you in your rescue. I told the officer about Lisa's skills with the rifle and how she single-handedly saved Katie's life. Then he asked me a few more questions...."

"And?" Kevin's inquiry sounded more like a demand than a question.

"He told the commander—a lieutenant colonel is a commander, right? He told the colonel and Lisa is getting promoted to sergeant!"

Kevin looked over to the specialist. "Yeah, it's true," she answered softly.

"The battalion commander is giving me a battlefield promotion to E-5," Lisa continued and then looked up at Kevin. "That means we'll both be NCOs *and* we won't be in the same command once the transfer goes through."

"I... Well, that changes things, but... You like me?" he asked. Shawn pretended not to notice Kevin's bright red ears and cheeks.

Lisa nodded as she bit her lower lip. "So kiss, you two!" Maria said excitedly.

"We're in uniform. We can't," Lisa said. "But I'd love to see about later tonight."

Kevin looked confused and embarrassed all at the same time. *Women, man. Nobody understands them,* Shawn thought and wrapped his arms around Maria.

*****

01 November, 1621 hrs local
The Castle, Smithsonian Institution Building
Washington, Dead City

The hallway echoed loudly as he plodded slowly up the stairs and his feet pounded against every step with a solid *thud*. The Master knew that he was there anyways. Why try to hide from it? There was only one way out of this situation; he had to face that thing upstairs and kill it.

Kestrel had stopped bothering to taunt the damn thing. While he'd limped across the Great Hall he'd sent a text message to Hank telling him that there were only two Type Ones left, he was on his way to kill the one in the city and not to ask any questions about how he knew. He'd also told Hank to call Alistair Reston and let him know that the last remaining Type One was controlling the zombie army in the north. Reston would know how to pass the information along to the Army so they could begin searching for it and end this war.

Kestrel flexed his fingers one at a time around the pistol grip of his MK-17 SCAR. The rifle felt perfectly balanced in his hands, almost as if it was a part of him. He'd fired thousands of rounds from the rifle over the years, but never as many in as short a period as he'd done in the past two days. That experience had made him even more appreciative of the weapon's fine manufacturing.

He took a ragged breath and the broken ribs all along his left side seemed to float on their own. The creature had hit him hard. ***Probably broke the bones completely away from my sternum.*** He wasn't just tired now; his body was starting to fail him. He'd taken it to the limit over the past week and the hand-to-hand combat had simply pushed him over the edge.

He glanced down at the next step that he planned to place his foot on and a shadow jumped from around the curve above. The creature landed on top of him and he crumpled into a ball before tumbling several steps with it locked onto him. The zombie brought both hands down onto the either side of his head and slammed it backward onto the stairs. He didn't have enough time to react before it slammed his head backward into the marble again.

Kestrel's vision started to go dark at the edges and he flexed the muscles in his neck against the pressure. The zombie stopped trying to bash his brains in and bent down. He heard the creature's teeth grind hard against the sharksuit on his forehead before he felt it.

His rifle was trapped, so he had to rely on the HK45 once again. The pistol had been a lifesaver on so many close-combat situations—including today—that he couldn't imagine any other secondary weapon. The Bowie knife was a very close third place. He placed the barrel of the weapon against the side of the zombie's head.

"So long mother fucker," he grunted and squeezed the trigger. Black gore and chunks of brain matter flew against the bricks of the Smithsonian's stairwell.

He shoved the body off of himself and sat up gingerly. Blood ran down his neck and between his shoulder blades, the fucker had done a number on him before he'd been able to kill it.

"You weren't so tough after all, you stupid fuck," he shouted at the dead zombie. "So much for the Chosen."

Why do you celebrate? The Master awaits.

"Fuck! How many of these dipshits do you have?"

We are like the stars.

"Well, shit. Hold on, I'm coming."

He had to use the railing to pull himself upwards. He'd thought that his body was failing before that attack, but now he was sure of it. In addition to the flowing wetness from his parietal lobe, his neck had hit the stairs when the zombie landed on him. He pushed against the back of it; there was something spongy bulging out near where his spine crossed the line of his shoulders. That couldn't be good.

Kestrel's head lolled from side to side as he used the railing to pull himself up each step. He felt like dog shit in a fire pit. He was falling apart and the only thing keeping him together was the sharksuit. The operator wondered what else was in store for him once he reached the Type One's lair.

He finally reached the top of the stairs and came to a landing with another of the heavy wooden doors. Kestrel sighed and prepared himself for another fight. He was tired of this shit. When he'd ensured that his weapon was ready to go and that the knife was within easy reach, he kicked the door hard. It slammed backward and impacted against something softer than the wall.

That meant that the creature was hiding behind the door, probably planning to jump him when he went inside. He rushed through the gaping doorway and pivoted hard to his right. His broken ribs protested the sudden movement, but he didn't pay any attention to them. This was almost over.

The door began to swing closed once again and he fired two rounds into the head of the zombie that had fallen hard against the wall when the door hit it. The thing crumpled immediately. He wondered what the hell it had been thinking hiding behind the door.

And then all thoughts ceased when the tip of a sword emerged from his stomach.

The Master knew you would find the Follower. I am smarter than you.

Kestrel coughed and blood dribbled down his chin. "Oh, fuck," he muttered as his gloved hand slapped at the blade. He turned to see the Master, the creature that had just killed him.

He tried to laugh, but the blade impaling him wouldn't allow it. The zombie standing before him used to be a woman, only about five foot two. Her parchment-like skin had begun to peel slightly away from her mouth, revealing just a tiny bit of her jawbone, giving him the impression that she was frowning. His mind grasped at the notion that the Chosen really did look different than the other zombies, Hank had been right.

"I just got whacked by a chick," the operator mumbled with a bloody grin. Both of his miserable excuses for a marriage and the two women who'd recently shared his bed all coalesced into the creature before him. He'd always had problems with women; his entire life had been one failed relationship after another and now, the final moments of his life would be spent with another woman who'd just stabbed him through the back, severing the bottom of his lung and slicing his intestines open inside his abdomen.

The Master reached for him and he was too weak to stop her from tearing the NVGs and gas mask from his face. *You are beaten. You will now become a Follower.*

She opened her mouth and he watched in a daze as her teeth closed in on his face. From somewhere deep inside, he felt a rage grow. He was not going to die without completing his mission. He still had all of his weapons and he was a goddamned SEAL. SEALs don't quit.

"Fuck you, bitch," he said and head-butted her across the nose. The force of the blow was enough to send her staggering back a few paces, allowing him the room to bring the rifle up.

Burning gases blew out of the end of the silencer, bathing the room in white light.

The Type One—the Master—that he'd came to Washington to kill, fell backward with a neat little hole just above the bridge of her nose. The back of her head would be a disgusting mess as the 7.62-millimeter round exited the skull at more than 2,300 feet per second.

Kestrel grinned drunkenly and reached behind his back. It took him a few tries, but he finally grasped the handle of the sword and pulled it out. The rusted metal cut him even more as he pulled it awkwardly to the side and once it slid free, he felt a large amount of blood and other fluids spill down his ass.

Pulling the blade from his body sent him over his pain threshold and he collapsed on top of the Master's body.

"Dammit, I left my Band-Aids downstairs," he choked with a laugh. *Even in death, I can't take anything serious. No wonder I....*

The darkness took him and he passed into the light.

*****

01 November, 1729 hrs local
Boger Concrete Building
Jonestown, Pennsylvania

The Leader felt the passing of the Master. It knew that it was now the last of the Chosen. It was now the most powerful of all the creatures in existence. Nothing would stop it from achieving victory now that it had become the Master.

The Followers advanced further every day and destroyed more of the humans that stood against them than they could afford to lose. Before long, the Followers would finally smash the humans into the ground and live in peace.

The *Master* sent a call to the Followers in the area to attend to it. They must learn that it was the new Master, that it would lead them to victory and the end to the human occupation of their lands.

Within minutes, a massive crowd had swelled around the buildings where the Master stood. The Followers needed to be able to see their new Master. With considerable effort, it climbed to the top of a pile of broken concrete rubble and looked upon the mass of its Followers, reveling in their adoration and desire to carry out its every order.

The large crowd of zombies attracted the attention of several intel analysts in Offutt Air Force Base, Nebraska. They were part of the United States Strategic Command, charged with watching the zombie army's advance from satellites high above the earth. They zoomed the lenses of several high-resolution cameras mounted in the satellites and saw the creature climbing up the mound of broken concrete while the others stood watching, more swelling the crowd every moment. This event was something new and unexpected after weeks of catching only fleeting glimpses of the horde except when they were too close to the human defenders to hit them with large-scale attacks. It was an opportunity.

Several rapid phone calls occurred and all Air Force jets in the vicinity were redirected immediately from their previous bombing missions to the small town outside of Fort Indiantown Gap, Pennsylvania. Planes lined up like they were sitting in traffic and pounded the site to dust. The zombie that had distinguished itself from all the others by climbing high above them took a laser-guided GBU-16 Paveway II 1000-pound bomb directly through the top of its head to begin the airstrike.

In the end, eight jets dropped a total of thirty-three 500-pound bombs and six 1,000-pounders in and around the strange gathering of zombies. The analysts compared the size of the gathering to a college football stadium and conservative estimates said that eighty thousand creatures had been incinerated or so badly broken that they'd never move from the area again. Other analysts placed the loss at much higher; pointing out that by the time the planes got there, the zombies had been so tightly packed in a half-mile circle around the creature that satellite imagery couldn't determine individual targets.

It was a major victory for the humans who'd been forced to hunt and destroy small pockets of zombies, all the while knowing that there were millions more hidden from view above. The sense that they'd passed a pivotal moment in the war was palpable at the command center in Offutt. This was the opportunity that they'd been waiting for.

Not long after the airstrike was over, one of the analysts noticed a massive movement along the highway. The creatures that weren't killed in the strike headed directly toward the defending army that was only a few miles away. The analysts' celebration stopped and they began passing the information to their Air Force brothers and sisters.

The zombies were done hiding; they were out in the open, prime targets for the jets and bombers flying above.

FOURTEEN

07 November, 1202 hrs local
Appalachian Defensive Line
Somerset, Pennsylvania

Mike surveyed the sea of humanity in awe. It was insane how many people and cars attempted to flow through the gates for processing into the holding area before being allowed to continue on to safety in the west. The fighting was heavy up in the mountains—terrain that was impossible for tanks to be utilized effectively—so the decision had been made to move Chaos Company all the way to the defensive belt instead of trying to use them in the mountain passes. The company had relocated to the Appalachian Defensive Line the previous night and set up their tanks on the *eastern* side of the walls with several other battalions of tanks. They were just a cog in the wheel of Big Army now.

Even with all of the floodlights and vehicle headlights the night before, he hadn't appreciated the sheer scale of the defenses that had been erected over the course of the last month and a half. They'd used whatever material they could find to build the new wall, but the primary components were the large forty-foot shipping crates, stacked two high, stretching as far as Mike could see. The engineers had welded massive bars of steel across each container to help keep them from being pushed apart and allowing the line to fail.

They'd also included a lot of cage-like turnstiles that each had to be triggered manually to turn. He'd seen the same simple technology used at high-security military installations worldwide and thought it was a good way to allow refugees through the defenses while still maintaining the proper measure of security. The Army could allow people to move through into the secondary line of security behind the line made out of the shipping containers.

Beyond the first line, he'd been told that there was a holding area comprised of several layers of fencing where every person moving through was physically checked for bite marks. It wouldn't do any good to blockade the eastern third of the country if somebody got sick on the other side of the defenses. There were mobile guard towers erected both inside the holding area and ringing it as well. Behind the first holding area was a third, heavily guarded layer of fencing and likely, there were more beyond that one, the government wasn't taking any chances.

Mike had never seen anything like the defensive line before. It made him proud to think of the sheer level of ingenuity and cooperation that it had taken to design and build the structure in such a short time. He briefly wondered how far north and south that these defenses went, but it only made sense that it stretched from the Gulf all the way to the Great Lakes and that the Canadians had done something similar on their side of the border.

Chaos Company was on the far right of what had been described to him as a defensive bubble. All along the Appalachian Mountains, defensive belts had been built. They'd blocked and canalized the roads through the mountains down to a relative few major routes that each fed into the massive "bubbles" where they now sat. Each of the bubbles spread out around large open areas to allow the maximum use of weaponry at the farthest distance. The other areas were simply blocked, forcing the refugees—and eventually the zombie horde—into kill boxes.

The number of people made it impossible for the soldiers in defensive positions to move in order to get their supplies, so everything was delivered via drone to the company area. The medium four-engine drones flew nonstop over the area, climbing and descending in vertical flight patterns to drop off cases of food and water as well as ammunition when needed. It was another example of American ingenuity and he was positive that they'd win this fight because of simple innovations like that.

On the engagement side of the defensive barriers were the soldiers like Mike and his men. The tanks, each a miniature fortress of its own, were positioned to provide firepower at the maximum distance possible. Dismounted soldiers patrolled the mountains, intent on finding and fixing the enemy at the greatest distance possible from the line. The Russians had eagerly volunteered to be the force that fought in the mountains. They were inserted by the hundreds of helicopters—military and civilian—flying all over the place.

As far as Mike knew, the main force of zombies was still far to the east. The last definitive contact that they'd had with the creatures was in Newville, Pennsylvania. He'd been there, fighting the creatures yesterday morning to protect the last major evacuation of the civilians before the Army jumped again.

The fighting for the last week had been frantic and non-stop. The brief lulls in battle and nighttime reprieves from the zombie attacks had ceased. They came on relentlessly and were killed in even greater numbers than any of the engagements during October, but they had the numbers to continue to press forward and overwhelm the defenders.

Rumors spread like wildfire that the special zombies who'd controlled the masses had been killed in a covert raid on Washington. They all started with the general statement, "So-and-so works in the headquarters and he overheard some bigwig saying as much." Now that the control was gone, the zombies just attacked whatever they saw instead of the careful moves that the horde had made before.

Real, solid intelligence, however, indicated that the southern group of zombies had been stopped cold. They'd been moving virtually unmolested through Virginia, but a combined pounding by the Air Force and Army units from North Carolina and Georgia smashed them to smithereens. Now the Army was combing through the state to kill the stragglers using large speakers to call them out of the woods.

Mike used binoculars to scan the crowd for signs of infection. *Unless there was an obvious outbreak or panic, it was useless to watch the crowd from this distance,* he thought. The tank's guns would kill hundreds of people if they tried to fire them into the crowd, so his main job was to simply observe and report while his men glassed the crowds through their scoped weapons.

Nothing seemed out of the ordinary with the crowd, so Mike took a few moments to relax and call his family. Trinity and the girls were still doing well in Hawaii, but they were ready to come home. Home, what did that even mean anymore? It would be a long time before the East Coast would be habitable again. Even after they destroyed the zombie horde, months—if not years—would be needed to seek out and destroy all the zombies. It would take even longer to collect the millions of bodies and burn them to avoid the rampant spread of disease.

Mike didn't know what the future held, but he knew that it would be full of challenges and the zombie scourge would remain a threat wherever people happened upon the creatures across the vast expanse of the east. Plus, there was the threat of the creatures that had floated out into the Atlantic; those things could end up anywhere in the world given enough time and they'd probably be dealing with small, localized outbreaks from time to time for decades.

The more he thought about it, the better moving to Hawaii full-time sounded. He was done with the Army; the past month had been too bloody, too taxing on his spirit. The family had plenty of money from his days working on the New York Stock Exchange and his skills transferred to just about anywhere. *Yeah, flowered shirt and shorts year round and zombies thousands of miles away*, he mused. *Hold on Mirandas, daddy's got a little bit more work to do, and then I'm coming home.*

*****

08 November, 0921 hrs local
Texas Defense Zone
Ozona, Texas

"So that's it, then?" Grayson asked skeptically.

"Looks like it," Joe Cochran answered with a smile. "Those helicopters that the Army sent turned this thing around right quick."

Grayson allowed himself to join the sheriff in a smile. After almost a week of constant skirmishing with the Herrera Cartel, the Army had finally been able to send three Apache helicopters from Fort Bliss in El Paso to support the operation against the drug lord's men. They'd been down for maintenance issues and hadn't been able to make the trip to the east with the rest of their battalion. Now that they were finally able to fly, they'd been sent to Ozona.

The helicopters provided close air support and hit the cartel's forces with pinpoint accuracy that couldn't be achieved with fighter aircraft. The jets' show of force hadn't done much to dissuade the Mexicans, but the bullets from the Apache's 30-millimeter chain gun firing into their positions this morning had ended things quickly.

"Yessir, those cartel boys took off back toward the south and the helicopters cut 'em down even as they ran. I guess that pansy president decided that he doesn't want to have to fight them again in the future."

Grayson thought about it for a moment. The men, even if they were retreating, were still an invading army on American soil who'd killed thirty-four citizens—that Grayson knew of. He would have done the same thing in the president's place. "Good riddance. Have we been able to leave our defenses yet?"

"Yeah. We took over a hundred prisoners and seized a bunch of vehicles, though most of them are too busted up from the fighting to be of much good besides scrap metal."

The commissioner glanced at the clock. "It's awful early, but I think this calls for a celebration, Joe."

Grayson turned to the small refrigerator in his office and produced a bottle of Texas white port wine. "Care for a glass of Texas' finest?"

"You bet your rear end I do!" the sheriff replied leaning forward expectantly in his chair.

Grayson opened the bottle in silence and poured three fingers of the pale liquid into glasses. He handed one to Joe and raised his own glass. "Here's to the defenders of Ozona!"

"To the defenders," the sheriff answered and tapped his glass lightly on Grayson's. He took a sip and leaned back in satisfaction. "I love the brandy flavor of this stuff. Makes it a lot better than regular wine."

"It's my favorite too," Grayson confirmed. "So we've cleared the local area of the cartel, how far out into the desert have we sent our men?"

"Not far. The Apaches didn't show up until this morning and they've only made a few passes around town. I want to be sure that they haven't set some sort of trap for us before we send out the troops."

Grayson nodded in agreement. He and Sheriff Joe had met the pilots at the football field at five-thirty to describe the cartel's positions surrounding the town. It hadn't taken them long to begin identifying targets, primarily because the Mexicans started shooting their rifles at the helicopters, which was a dead giveaway to where they were and never a good idea.

"I heard the gunships lighting up the attackers, but I didn't think it would end so quickly."

"Typical criminal thugs," the sheriff snorted. "They thrive on terrorizing and threatening an unarmed population. Then when they face some resistance, they high-tail it out of the area."

The phone rang unexpectedly and Grayson picked it up. "Donnelly."

"*Grayson Donnelly?*" the voice on the other end of the line asked.

"Yeah, who's this?"

"*Please hold for the president.*"

"Uh, okay..." He looked up at Joe, "It's the president."

"Well, put it on speaker, son!"

Grayson pressed the speaker button and set the phone down on his desk. After a moment, the president's distinctive voice drifted from the speaker, "*Is this Grayson?*"

He cleared his throat and said, "Yes, sir. I'm here with Sheriff Joe Cochran who's been leading the defense of the town."

"*Well good morning, gentlemen. I just got the good news.*"

"I just got the word myself, sir. Seems like good news travels fast."

"*I've got my ways,*" the president chuckled. "*Congratulations on the victory.*"

"Thank you, sir," Grayson answered. "It was the sheriff and his men along with the soldiers that you were able to spare that helped keep us from getting overrun until the helicopters were able to show up."

"*Sorry about that, Grayson. I wanted to send more troops sooner, but those damned zombies have proven to be a big problem out east.*"

Grayson swallowed hard. He knew the military sense that it made to face the greater danger first, but it had been his friends and townsfolk who'd suffered because of the decision. Even if he didn't like it, he knew that it was the same decision that he would have made if he were in the president's place. "We lost a lot of good people, sir."

"*I understand that, and I'm truly sorry. Please accept my sincere apology for the timing of everything. Make no mistake, those men and women who died are heroes. I've already asked my staff to begin preparing the appropriate documentation so everyone will know how much they contributed to the defense of our nation.*"

"Thank you, sir," he replied.

"*Listen, I'm proud of you—and of you Sheriff Cochran—you deserve to feel that pride as well. Both of you embody the American spirit.*"

Grayson didn't really know how to respond, so once again he said, "Thank you, sir."

"Alright, I've got some other matters to attend to. The tide seems to be turning in the east and Crockett County will forever stand in the minds of our future generations as the place where ordinary citizens stood against an invading army and came out on top without the help of the most powerful army on the planet. Once again, great job, gentlemen. Goodbye."

The phone went dead and Grayson lifted the receiver and placed it back on the base to turn off the speaker. "Well, that was unexpected," he said with a quick sip from his glass.

"Unexpected, but classy," the sheriff replied.

"Sheriff Joe, are you coming around to our president's side of things?"

"Not a chance," the older man replied. "He's an idiot. Maybe he's a classy idiot, but he's still an idiot."

Grayson smiled. He was glad to see that the past few weeks hadn't changed the sheriff's attitude or outlook on the world. The commissioner knew that the people of Ozona and Crockett County would eventually recover from their experiences and be stronger because of them. They'd stood up to an invading army and saved the nation from a blindsided attack to its underbelly. They were the true heroes.

*****

10 November, 1329 hrs local
Cleveland Public Auditorium
Cleveland, Ohio

Shawn weaved the old station wagon through the congested downtown traffic toward the auditorium where the refugee reception center on the outside of the city told him that Annie was housed. His hands were sweaty on the steering wheel as he thought about facing his daughter and answering her inevitable questions about Shana and he readjusted the rearview mirror to ensure that the backpack with the Ford Family photos was safe in the back seat for what must have been the hundredth time.

The trip from Pennsylvania had been a much longer journey than he or Maria had ever expected. They'd tried to make their way far enough north to get above where the zombies drove everything in front of them like he'd told Kevin and Lisa, but the roads became hopelessly blocked by residents who'd created barriers to protect themselves and their communities. They lost precious hours of travel bumbling along from blocked road to blocked road and had finally been forced to go back to Interstate 81 near Harrisburg. As they neared the city once again, they could feel the ground rattling from the massive fight that took place on the eastern side of the city. After wasting an entire day, they were able to get on Interstate 76 and then onto the 70 for the journey westward through the mountains.

The trip took almost six days of waiting just to make it *through* the Appalachian Defensive Line because of the crush of bodies trying to flee the zombie menace and all the soldiers everywhere, constantly checking and re-checking to make sure that nobody who made it through the security areas was bitten or trying to smuggle any zombie war trophies. He'd been scared to death as he stared down the impossibly large gun barrels that the tanks would get spooked about something in the crowd and fire into everyone.

Thankfully, that hadn't happened while they were there. Once they made it through the gates into the holding area, things went faster for them, but all the inspections took forever and it took another two days to unfuck themselves on the western side of the defensive line so they could drive the rest of the way.

Shawn had maxed out his credit card paying for gas along the way, but the needle hovered just above empty and the low fuel light had been on for the last twenty minutes. Now that he was here in Cleveland, though, nothing would stop him from getting to his daughter today.

"There it is," Maria said as she pointed to the auditorium.

He nodded and followed the signs to park the car, which died as he turned into the parking lot. "Outta gas."

"It's okay, babe. We'll figure it out once you get Annie," Maria assured him.

He nodded and leaned across, kissing her excitedly. Their relationship had blossomed during the long hours of boredom during the journey and he was eager to introduce Maria to Annie.

He put the car in neutral and they both pushed from their side of the vehicle. It was a maneuver that they'd become quite adept at during the days in the queue through the defensive line. It made more sense to just push the damn thing than waste the gas starting it. They let it drift the last few feet into a parking spot and Shawn put it back into gear and took the keys out of the ignition.

They jogged across the street holding hands and went through security to the ticket sales window where the children's records were held. He stepped up to the counter and told the woman that he was here to pick up his daughter.

"What's her name?"

"Annie Ford, from New Jersey."

She scanned a printout and then made a checkmark next to Annie's name. "Okay, fill these out," the worker said as she handed him a stack of papers on a clipboard.

"Are you serious? I've come all this way to get my child. I'm not filling out paperwork before I see her."

"Look, Mr. Ford, do you see my two heavily-armed guards over there," she pointed to the soldiers that had patted him and Maria down when they entered. "You aren't going to get your daughter out of this facility until I determine that you are who you say you are. Part of that process is matching up the forms that you filled out when you entrusted the care of your child to the United States Government."

Her face softened and she said, "Look, I understand that you want to see your child. I assure you that she's okay. Let's just do this to cover both of our asses."

"It's okay, Shawn. We've waited weeks and been through... a lot," Maria tried to calm him. "Let's just fill out this paperwork. The sooner we complete it, the sooner we'll see Annie."

He nodded in frustration at the government's efficiency and accepted the clipboard. Ten minutes later, the worker led the two of them through a set of locked doors into the auditorium. Cots and blankets littered the floor while children of all ages lounged in the seats surrounding the main floor.

As they walked down the side aisle, Shawn scanned the faces to find that of his daughter, but didn't see her. Finally, they'd made their way across the sleeping area to a small side room. The worker opened the door into a modified classroom where a teacher was going over elementary math.

"Excuse me, Miss Henderschott. I've got a parent here to pick up one of the children."

The teacher stopped and looked up. Before she could ask which parent was there, Annie jumped up and ran to her father. "Daddy!" she screamed and ran to him.

Shawn knelt and hugged his daughter like he was never going to let her go again.

*****

23 November, 1001 hrs local
Carroll Park
West Philadelphia, Pennsylvania

The banging on the front door resumed again. The creatures had stopped trying to get in weeks ago and the old man hadn't heard them in a long time. Now it seemed like they were back.

"What is it, dear?" his wife asked.

"I don't know, Alice. I thought we were past the zombies trying to get in the house. We haven't made any noise or anything, I don't know why they're back."

The banging began to be more rhythmic than anything that the creatures had ever done and a metallic voice said, "If anyone is still alive in Carroll Park, this is the United States Army. We're here to rescue you!"

"What did he say?" Marcus Miranda asked his wife.

"He said it was the Army!" Alice said. "Do you think it's Mike?"

"Oh, don't be a fool, woman. Our son is dead. It's a miracle that we made it this long." Marcus got down on both knees next to his bed and began to pray in thanks to God for their salvation. He'd reestablished his long-ignored relationship with the Lord during their captivity in the Philadelphia row home. Only Alice's obsession with canned food and their slow metabolism had kept them from starving to death over the long weeks, but they were almost out of food and Marcus had been contemplating how to get more food without exposing himself to the creatures outside.

"Okay," he said when he was done with his prayer. "Let's go downstairs."

It took them a little while to make it down the stairs, malnutrition was starting to settle in and take its toll on their old bodies. The knocking had stopped by the time they made it to the front door and Marcus could see a shadow retreating down the sidewalk.

He opened the door and shouted, "Wait! We're here!"

The soldier turned around and Marcus was shocked to see a much younger version of himself staring back. "Dad! Mom!" Mike Miranda shouted as he ran toward them.

"Oh my God, son. You're alive!" Marcus exclaimed and hugged his child.

"The same could be said about you, old man!" Mike said with a smile as he pounded his father on the back. "I saw the broken window and I feared the worst. I just couldn't bring myself to go inside."

"We're safe now, son," Alice answered and threw her arms around Mike's waist.

It was a miracle that all three of them survived and Marcus offered another silent prayer of thanks.

*****

28 November, 1104 hrs local
KYXR Television Studio
Denver, Colorado

The lighting in the studio was dimmed slightly to allow for the proper setting befitting the President of the United States of America. The black velvet curtains that they'd hung behind both chairs had been meticulously cleaned and then arranged to maximize the different layers of light and shadow. A potted plant was strategically placed where it would be in the shot just over the president's left shoulder to help break up the lines and add a dash of color. Everything about the interview setting was perfect.

Abigail Munroe had waited over a year for this exclusive interview with the president. They'd scheduled the interview more than six months ago and she was glad that he was able to keep to his calendar, even with the war out east. Abigail had been a staunch supporter of his during the election and had the honor of hosting the debate between then-Senator Wilson and President Holmes. Since then, her opinion of President Wilson had steadily declined as he made poor economic decisions followed by possibly starting a second zombie war when he invaded Washington to steal some old American relics.

She'd taken her initial set of questions and thrown the second half of them out the window. She wanted to take advantage of being the first reporter to conduct a one-on-one interview with the president after the end of major military actions in the east. The questions that she'd decided to ask would likely piss the man off, but it was her place as a journalist to ask the tough questions and not fawn all over the man like some type of sycophantic fool. If her interview went well, she could easily see her small Denver political correspondent position shifting to one of the major networks.

A Secret Service agent came through the doorway and stood just inside as the president walked in behind him. Mark Namath, the White House Chief of Staff, walked in after the president, followed by the president's personal secretary Sarah Pendergraff and several more musclebound guys wearing suits and earpieces. The damn agents had been all over the studio for a week asking questions and scanning everything with little handheld wands. Abigail had even caught one of them going through her office trash one day. She was ready for them to just leave everyone alone and get out of her life.

"Good morning, Mr. President," she said with a forced smile and an outstretched hand.

"Morning, Miss Munroe. I'm all ready to go and skimmed through your read-ahead questions. Did you have any last-minute adds that you want to let me know about so I can give myself a few minutes to prepare?"

"Oh, we'll stick mostly to the script, but I do have a few unscripted questions that may come to me if we have time," she replied. It wasn't a *total* lie; they would have a few unscripted questions.

"That's fine then," the president answered. "Sarah, how long do we have?"

His assistant checked her watch and replied, "We have to leave here in thirty-five minutes in order to make it to the American Cancer Society luncheon, Mr. President."

"Alright, that gives us about thirty minutes then, Miss Munroe. Which chair do you want me to sit in?"

Abigail indicated the chair where they'd planned to have President Wilson sit and said, "Please sit here and we'll begin when you're ready."

The president sat and adjusted his suitcoat before saying, "Alright, I'm ready now."

She nodded to the producer who ordered both cameras to begin recording, one angled to record Abigail from the front and the other positioned so the president was centered in the shot. "We're ready, Abby."

It was the morning now, but she knew that this would end up as prime time footage, so she looked directly into her camera and began, "Good evening. I'm Abigail Munroe with KYXR Denver News and tonight I have the opportunity to interview a very special guest. Good evening and a belated Happy Thanksgiving to you, Mr. President. It's nice to have you with us tonight."

The president had played the game long enough that he knew not to look into the camera, instead he looked at Abigail and said, "Good evening, Miss Munroe. Thank you for having me."

"First, I want to tell you how much of an honor it is to have you in the KYXR studio. I know our viewers are excited to hear what you have to say about matters which affect everyone, not just those of us who live in Denver."

"The pleasure is all mine," he replied with what appeared to be a genuine smile. Abigail almost hated to do what she planned to do, but it was her career and if she didn't take some risks, she'd be stuck at the local level for the rest of her life.

The first twenty minutes of the interview went exactly on script. She asked him the pre-arranged questions about the economy, job creation in the coming year and the new natural gas and oil pipeline agreement between the US and Canada. The president seemed to be absolutely at ease and in his element discussing the topics. *He should be, I fed him the questions already,* Abigail thought.

Then, it came time to go off script and begin asking the hard questions. The questions that everyone wanted to know the answers to, but either hadn't had the opportunity to ask or were too chickenshit to do so. "Thank you, Mr. President. Now, I'd like to switch gears away from the future and discuss matters that are happening today. Will that be alright?"

The quick flash of fire across the surface of the president's eyes were the only indicator that he wasn't happy that the next question wasn't about the bill to legalize marijuana use nationally. "Of course, Miss Munroe. What would you like to know?"

This is it, dive in. "Sir, we've seen estimates and flat-out guesses about the zombie war's death toll from every federal agency and the national news networks; how many people do we truly believe have died since the first reported attack in Philadelphia on the sixteenth of September?"

The president seemed to relax a little as if he knew that question would likely come up in an interview and had been prepared by his people on how to answer it. "As you know, the figures have been all over the place. We've only recently begun the clearing efforts after the last of the gigantic zombie hordes was wiped out near Bedford, Pennsylvania. However, our Department of Homeland Security puts the estimate at a conservative sixty-five million Americans who perished in the war."

"Sixty-five million? What about the United Nations' claim of more than a hundred million dead?"

"I'd love to see where they got their figures from," he retorted. "Look, there were about a hundred and five million people living in the northeast and the areas in Virginia and Florida where secondary outbreaks occurred. We put a stop to the ones in Virginia and Florida very quickly, but the northeast was a total loss before we even knew what was happening. That being said, the population in our own refugee centers and the numbers of people who processed through the Appalachian Defensive Line would make the UN's hundred million claim invalid.

"Like I said, Miss Munroe, it's still very early in the cleanup process and we know that there are still pockets of these creatures out there that our soldiers and police officers find every day. It will be a long time—if ever—before the final numbers of those who perished are known."

"Thank you. My next question is about our international foreign relations; specifically those with Russia and Mexico. We had a large group of guerilla fighters from the Herrera Cartel invade our nation without their government stopping them and we seemingly wasted the lives of more than 50,000 Russian soldiers who'd deployed to assist the United States in our fight against the zombies. How are we going to recover from an international slap in the face by Mexico and explain the deaths of their loved ones to the Russian people?"

"Firstly, those soldiers didn't die in vain as you're suggesting. They died valiantly defending the citizens of the United States," the president answered with a slightly elevated voice. "Their Russian commanders continually volunteered for the toughest assignments, missions that they knew were extremely dangerous, and saved countless American lives in the process, so don't you dare say that the lives of those men were wasted."

Abigail realized that he'd paused for her response and attempted to compose herself. She hadn't expected such a vehement response from the man across from her. "I uh... Of course, Mr. President, I stand corrected. The Russians played a key role in the salvation of our country."

He nodded his head and continued, "Thank you. I just wanted your viewers to know that those men died bravely and for a cause much larger than themselves. I want to thank my good friend, President Akulov, for sending Russia's sons and daughters to aid the United States in our hour of need. I also want to offer my condolences to the Russian people for their grievous loss. Your American friends and partners will forever be in your debt.

"As to the Herrera Cartel, I've talked with President Arnesto at great length about the incident. We lost thirty-four brave Americans fighting against those people and the Mexican government is deeply saddened at our loss. However, this isn't a Mexican problem or an American problem, it's a societal problem. Until we can stem the continued rise of the drug culture in our two nations, these types of incidents will persist. Mr. Arnesto and I plan to meet in the coming weeks to outline a new anti-drug task force with the charter of seeking out and arresting criminals like Ernesto Herrera."

Okay, he's stuck to the party line so far, she thought. "Thank you for your candid answer. Next, I'd like to address the accusations that the zombie war started because you kicked a hornet's nest when you ordered troops to infiltrate Washington this spring to recover the Constitution."

"I think we've talked about how absurd that accusation is on several *national* news broadcasts, Miss Munroe. I'd prefer if we discussed a different topic."

"Mr. President, how do you explain that for six, almost seven years, the zombies seemed content to stay behind The Wall and leave us alone? It wasn't until we started sending troops in that they struck out against us. That seems to me like pretty solid evidence that they would have stayed put without attacking."

"We've gone through this before and I'm sticking to what every analyst in my administration believes. The creatures needed a way out of the region. The Wall was too heavily guarded to allow them a chance to break free. The zombies found a way out when the Marchione Family damaged the river gates sending divers through to rob banks. They escaped through the river gates underwater at the first opportunity that they had. It just so happens that the robberies and the recovery effort overlapped."

Well, shit. He didn't take the bait on that either; he's good. Time to go for it. "Okay, I know that our time is running short, Mr. President, so I have one final question for you."

He smiled like he'd swallowed a live worm, "Alright, Miss Munroe. What else would you like to know?"

"The KYXR Denver News team has learned that several House and Senate members from your own party have sided with Democrats to call for your impeachment from office on the grounds that you acted treasonously against the United States by starting the Second Zombie War. How do you respond to those allegations?"

The president glanced off camera to where his Chief of Staff sat on the edge of his chair. Abigail looked over in time to see Mark Namath shaking his head. *They don't know!*

"Honestly, Miss Munroe, this is the first that I've heard of impeachment proceedings against me. Where are you getting your information?"

"You know that I can't reveal my sources, Mr. President. But know this; the movement is going to happen on the floor of the House within the next couple of days."

"Treason?" the president asked, letting his voice betray his disappointment.

"Yes, sir. They feel that your actions..." Abigail referred to her notes and read them verbatim, "'Assisted a rebellious supernatural army to seriously detriment the power of our sovereign nation, leading to a near-total collapse of our society.' How do you respond to those allegations?"

"I think that it's absolutely false and is nothing more than political posturing in an effort to pin the blame on somebody for what happened. I did not assist the zombie forces in any way. There was—"

"What about hiding the fact that there were sentient zombies controlling the others? If that information had been more widely known, there might have been a concentrated attack on those types of creatures. Instead, we ended up with anywhere from sixty-five to one hundred million dead."

Abigail took a deep breath. She couldn't believe that she just cut off the President of the United States! He'd stopped to listen to what she had to say.

"That information wouldn't have helped the common soldier or the people fleeing from the zombies. If anything, it would have only increased the panic. I chose to keep it on a need-to-know basis in order to protect the people, not to conspire against them.

"All of my actions have been taken to preserve this great nation, a nation that I love dearly. I know that the American people will see through my opponents' misdirection and understand that their government did everything that we could to keep this nation together while it was unraveling around us."

The producer got Abigail's attention and gave her the signal that there was only thirty seconds left. She nodded in understanding. "Alright, I believe our time is up, Mr. President. Thank you so much for this opportunity and for your answers to all of my questions."

"The pleasure is mine, Miss Munroe. Thank you for having me."

"And thank you for watching, Denver. Goodnight."

The studio lights faded to nearly black. The moment the red lights on the top of the cameras flashed to green the president stood up. "What the hell kind of bullshit was that?" he shouted.

"It was an interview. The people of Denver need to know your stance on matters. I think you did—"

"Frankly, I don't care what you think, Miss Munroe. We're through here."

The president stormed out between the two Secret Service agents and Mark Namath stepped over to her. "You know, that was pretty low, young lady. You may think that ambushing the president is the kind of quote-unquote journalism that will get you promoted, but it won't. It will do the opposite because you'll be blackballed; nobody will do an interview with you. I hope you're proud of yourself."

Abigail didn't have an opportunity to respond before he had already left the room. She whipped her hair back behind her neck and mumbled, "I *am* proud of myself, Mr. Namath. Damn proud."

EPILOGUE

01 December, 1019 hrs local
The Castle, Smithsonian Institution Building
Washington, Dead City

The heavily armored operative plodded up the back staircase. He couldn't believe what he was seeing. Thousands, literally *thousands*, of bodies littered the National Mall in front of the Smithsonian Castle and the interior was filled with them as well. Given the powder burns and injuries on the bodies inside the building, most seemed to have been shot at extremely close range or even...stabbed?

The fact that one man had done this was simply insane. Nothing like it would ever be seen again and he was grateful for the camera that he wore to chronicle the exploits of the man that he believed to be somewhere inside this building. Hank Dawson had come to find his friend and bring him home.

It had taken quite a bit of work by both Hank and Alistair Reston to convince Director Kelly Flannigan to schedule a meeting with General Zollman. The Chairman of the Joint Chiefs had taken even more convincing to allow a retired Army Delta operator to enter the military quarantine zone behind The Wall. He'd finally relented because nobody knew what the fuck had happened those last few days of the war and he needed answers.

It hadn't taken Hank long to call in some favors and he got a Black Hawk ride into the city where his friend had texted him from. The messages had been direct, simple to understand and meant as a one-way conversation; that was the Kestrel's way.

He made it up the stairs and saw the body of the female Type One. It had a neat bullet hole right in the center of the eyebrows where a perfectionist like Kestrel would have placed it. Then he took in the whole scene. Dried, smeared blood covered the floor and there was his friend. The man looked as if he'd simply gone to sleep. Next to him was an old, rusted Roman gladius, soiled with dried blood as well.

His experienced eye worked out what happened quickly. Kestrel was distracted by the zombie behind the door and the Type One used the sword to kill him. It had likely observed the Type Twos' inability to penetrate the chainmail armor that he wore and used the sword to up the ante. It worked, but not before the Kestrel had sent it to hell.

Hank pressed the button on his chest, "This is Dawson. I found him. We're up the back set of stairs on the second floor."

Three men, wearing the same chainmail that he wore, came in and assisted him with the body. The government had already secured the plot next to Allyson Harper's grave and once everything was set, he'd be buried beside her in Charlottesville, Virginia.

Before they picked Kestrel's remains up off the floor, Hank placed his open palm on the forehead of one of his oldest friends from the Special Operations community. "Good job, Asher Hawke. You were one hell of man. I'll make sure that everyone knows your story and you will never be forgotten."

ABOUT THE AUTHOR

A veteran of the wars in Iraq and Afghanistan, Brian Parker was born and raised as an Army brat. He moved all over the country as a child before his father retired from the service and they settled in a small Missouri town where the family purchased a farm. It was on the farm that he learned the rewards of a hard day's work and enjoyed the escapism that books could provide.

He's currently an Active Duty Army soldier who enjoys spending time with his family in Texas, hiking, obstacle course racing, writing and Texas Longhorns football. His wife is also an Active Duty soldier and the pairing brings its own unique set of circumstances that keep both of them on their toes. He's an unashamed Star Wars fan, but prefers to disregard the entire Episode I and II debacle.

Brian has authored several books across multiple genres, including post-apocalyptic fiction, zombie horror, paranormal thrillers and children's fiction. His next project is *Easytown,* a sci-fi noir detective series set in New Orleans fifty years in the future.

FOLLOW BRIAN ON SOCIAL MEDIA

Facebook: www.facebook.com/BrianParkerAuthor

Twitter: www.twitter.com/BParker_Author

Web: www.BrianParkerAuthor.com

THE JOURNAL SERIES
by Deborah D. Moore

After a major crisis rocks the nation, all supply lines are shut down. In the remote Upper Peninsula of Michigan, the small town of Moose Creek and its residents are devastated when they lose power in the middle of a brutal winter, and must struggle alone with one calamity after another.

The Journal series takes the reader head first into the fury that only Mother Nature can dish out. Book Five coming soon!

PERMUTED
PRESS